A

Head Over Heels

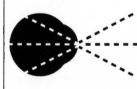

Head Over Heels

Susan Andersen

WHEELER
PUBLISHING

Published in 2002 by arrangement with
Avon Books, an imprint of HarperCollins Publishers, Inc.

Wheeler Large Print Book Series.

The text of this Large Print edition is unabridged.
Other aspects of the book may vary from the original edition.

Set in 16 pt. Plantin by Al Chase.

Printed in the United States on permanent paper.

Library of Congress Cataloging-in-Publication Data

Andersen, Susan, 1950–
    Head over heels / Susan Andersen.
        p. cm.
    ISBN 1-58724-271-0 (lg. print : hc : alk. paper)
    1. Large type books.   2. Family owned business enterprises —
Fiction.   3. Washington (State) — Fiction.   4. Restaurateurs —
Fiction.   5. Restaurants — Fiction.   I. Title.
PS3551.N34555 H43 2002
813'.54—dc21   2002020342

*For the best little brainstormer
in the continental United States
(and quite possibly the known universe).*

*Dedicated, with love,
to Caroline Cross,*

*for talking me down the clifts of insanity
on a near-daily basis,
for digging me out of more pits
than I care to think about,
and for much-valued friendship.*

*And in memory of Auntie Jean,
who is sorely missed.*

— Susie

Childhood is what we spend the rest of our lives trying to get past.

ANONYMOUS

1

The wail of country music and the bar's smoky, beery smell hit Veronica Davis like a smack upside the head the moment she pushed through the Baker Street Honky Tonk's door. It immediately took her back, bombarding her with a raft of memories.

None of them wonderful.

Stopping just inside the doorway, she drew a couple of deep, carefully controlled breaths and watched a thin haze of smoke drift by on the current she'd created. It wafted and eddied, taking on the multicolored hues of the neon liquor signs that passed for decor in the dimly lit bar. Votive candles, in what she'd swear were the same smoke-smudged glass containers that had been there twelve years ago, flickered in the center of each table.

There was a momentary lull while the jukebox switched to a new song. Voices rose and fell, balls clacked at the pool table in the corner, and glasses clinked as a waitress gathered empties from a table and stacked them on a tray. A flash of panic threatened to stop the breath in Veronica's lungs, and she forcibly reminded herself that this was merely a brief visit to introduce herself to the new bartender/manager Marissa had hired, and to get a quick overview of how the bar was doing. She hadn't worked here for years and didn't intend to ever again, so there was no earthly reason to feel as if she should turn tail and run.

As the waitress balanced the tray of empties in one hand and leaned across the table to wipe up a spill, Veronica remembered only too well how perpetually sticky the tables seemed to remain, no matter how often you washed them. She remembered, too, as a raucous group of men at another table made lewd remarks about the way the waitress filled out her jeans, the constant nerve-wearing commentary.

Oh, God. Considering the circumstances that had brought her back to Fossil, she hadn't thought her stomach could possibly feel more chewed up than it already did. But she'd been wrong. For while she'd never forgotten what it was like to dodge the free and easy hands of drunken men, it had been a long time since she'd had to deal with it, and its gut-churning immediacy had long ago faded.

But it all came rushing back as she watched one of the men take advantage of the waitress's occupied hands to grab her bottom. An old, familiar taste of impotent fury flooded Veronica's mouth as he grinned at his friends and gave the rounded cheek beneath his palm a squeeze. Incensed, she started forward.

She stopped dead, however, when the waitress's loaded tray dropped to the tabletop with a horrendous crash. It caught the side of the candle holder, which skittered across the table but luckily stopped before it toppled over the edge.

"That does it!" The cocktail waitress's furious voice rang clear in the sudden cessation of conversation, and reaching back, she raked crimson inch-long fingernails across the man's hand, then whirled to face him as his hand jerked back.

The drunk yelped in outrage and surged to his feet, sending his chair clattering across the floor. "You *bitch!*" Droplets of blood began to form in the raw scratches across his hand and he stared at them incredulously. Then, making a fist, he drew it back as if to strike her.

A strangled protest slipping up her throat, Veronica tried to get to the woman's side. But before she could push past the patrons who'd climbed to their feet for a better view of the ruckus, a deep male voice roared out.

"Knock it off!"

Like everyone else, she stopped dead, arrested by the sheer authority that had an entire bar freezing in its tracks.

Then she saw the person responsible for it and simply stared.

Whoa, Nellie. This must be Cooper Blackstock, the new bartender Marissa had hired to manage the bar.

He was big and dangerous-looking, with those narrowed, assessing eyes and stubborn jaw, that

9

hard-as-granite body, and those cheekbones sharp enough to slice. And that *hair*. She couldn't seem to stop staring at it as he came out from behind the bar, for it was like nothing she'd seen on the career men she dated.

Good gravy, did he *dye* it? The adult men in this small eastern Washington town would never dream of doing anything so feminine, but that *had* to be dyed. Short and punk-rocker spiky, it was a pale, Nordic blond that looked nearly white against a face surprisingly tanned for January. Yet the bold slash of his eyebrows and the spiked fringe of his lashes were blacker than the devil's soul, his skin was olive-toned, and his eyes were an impenetrable bittersweet chocolate brown.

Fossil was a conservative town, and the Tonk's clientele could be merciless with someone as different as this guy was, so he *had* to have taken a rash over his exotic appearance. But if the go-to-hell look in his eyes was any indication, he was utterly unheeding of anyone's opinion but his own. He strode through the crowd with an aggressive, this-is-who-I-am-and-you-can-just-kiss-my-ass-if-you-don't-like-it attitude, and people who hadn't budged when Veronica was trying to go to the waitress's aid parted like the Red Sea before Moses at Blackstock's approach.

The drunk thrust his hand out for inspection the moment the bartender arrived at the table. "Look what she did to me," he complained. His mates' mocking comments about a woman beating him up fanned the already roaring blaze of his ire, and he puffed up like a bantam rooster. "I oughtta sue her butt!"

"You ought to keep your hands *off* her butt and count yourself lucky she doesn't sue *you* for sexual harassment." Cooper picked up the chair and set it down at the table with a thump. He gave the patron a hard stare. "You owe her an apology."

"The hell you say! Lookit this — she drew blood!"

"Damn right I did," the waitress agreed. "I'm sick to death of these idiots thinking my tits and ass are public property. So, you know what, buddy?" She shouldered past the bartender to get in the face of her harasser. "I don't *want* your stinking apology. Feel free to stick it where the sun don't shine!"

Then, whipping off the white apron around her hips, she turned back to Cooper and slapped the garment against his stomach with enough force to double over a softer man. "I quit! You don't pay me enough for this shit."

"Rosetta, wait; don't do this to me." His big fist crushed the apron as he watched her stalk behind the bar, bend out of sight for an instant, then pop back up with her purse in her hand. "*C'mon.* We can work this out —"

"No. We can't. I've had it up to my eyeballs with these jerks. I'm gonna go get me a job where I don't have to deal with men who find their per-

11

sonalities in the bottom of a bottle."

Silently empathetic, Veronica stepped out of the way as the waitress brushed past her and headed for the door. Watching it swing shut behind the woman, she experienced the first little spurt of cheer she'd felt since arriving home from Scotland to be greeted with the news of her sister Crystal's death. Good for Rosetta. Veronica had lost count of the number of times she'd longed to quit exactly like that. But she'd been stuck, because this was Daddy's bar, and he'd been an old-school chauvinist who'd refused to hear of it. And her love for him had neatly caged her in.

She almost turned around and walked out now. The bartender was going to be short-handed, and probably tied up tighter than a submissive at a bondage festival just trying to see to it that everyone got served quickly. It was unlikely he'd have a free moment, let alone the time to give her a rundown on the bar's status.

And yet . . .

If she left now, she might never come back. Unlike Crystal, who'd always reveled in the ongoing party that was the Tonk, Veronica couldn't remember a time when she hadn't disliked the place. If it had been left up to her, she never would have stepped foot in the joint again.

But Crystal was no longer here, and Veronica had a responsibility to fulfill, so it was time to behave like an adult and get on with it. Mentally girding her loins, she walked up to the bar.

She waited as the crush of customers who'd brought their empties up to be refilled began to thin. Then, as the bartender built a drink for the last one in line and made change, Veronica squared her shoulders.

He looked up as she stepped forward, and gave her a comprehensive once-over. "You're new around here," he said in a low voice. "I'd remember that skin if I'd seen it before." His gaze seemed to track every inch of it before his eyes rose to meet hers. "What can I get you?"

Veronica blinked. Wow. She was surprised the men of Fossil didn't keep their women under lock and key around this guy, for even she could feel the sexuality that poured off of him in waves, and he wasn't at all her type. "Are you Mr. Blackstock?"

"Yeah, but call me Coop," he invited and flashed her a smile that was surprisingly charming for someone with such watchful eyes. "I'm always tempted to look around for my dad whenever I hear anyone call me mister, and he's been gone a long, long time." Then he became all business. "Since you know my name," he said, "I assume you're here for the job."

"No!" She stepped back, her hands flying up as if they could push the very idea away. *Oh, no, no, no* — she'd sworn when she graduated from college that she would never serve another drink as long as she lived. It was a vow she'd kept, too, and she intended to *keep* on keeping it right up until the day they planted her body in the cold, hard ground.

Seeing those dark brows of his lift toward his blond hairline, she forced her shoulders to lose their defensive hunch and her hands to drop back to her sides. *Oh, smooth, Davis. You might wanna try keeping the idiot quotient to a bare minimum here.* "I'm sorry, I should have introduced myself." Head held high, giving her fine wool blazer a surreptitious tug to remind herself she'd come a long way from the Tonk, she stepped back up to the bar. "I'm Veronica Davis. I just stopped by to see how the place is doing."

He stilled. At least she thought he did, but the moment came and went so quickly she was left wondering if perhaps she'd simply imagined it, for in the next instant he seemed perfectly relaxed, his smile every bit as charming as it had been a second ago. She blew out a weary sigh. It had been a very long day and exhaustion was clearly making her see things that weren't there.

"You want to know how it's doing?" Coop demanded coolly. "Well, I'll tell you, lady, right this minute not so hot. But things are looking up now that I've got you in my sights. Here." He tossed her something and reflexively she reached up to snatch it out of the air before it hit her in the face. "Put that on," he instructed. "And get to work. We're shorthanded."

She looked down at the white chef's apron in her fist, then dropped it as if it were a cockroach, her head snapping up to stare at him in horror. "I'm not serving drinks!"

"Listen, Princess, I've got one waitress who called in sick and another who just quit. You want the Tonk to close down and lose a night's receipts, that's up to you. But don't expect me to knock myself out if you're too high-toned to sully those lily-white hands schlepping a few drinks."

She glared at him, but he merely shrugged a big shoulder and reached for the pitcher that a customer at the end of the bar held out for a refill. He set it in the sink and grabbed a clean one, tilting it beneath a spigot. Veronica watched the play of muscles in his forearms below the shoved-up sleeves of a buttercream-colored sweater as he regulated the flow of beer down the side of the pitcher; she scowled at the rawboned knobs of his wrists and the sheer size of his big-knuckled hands.

Who *was* this guy, with his farmer's body and his warrior's eyes, to tell her what to do? What gave him the right to threaten her with the bar's closure? Technically, she was the owner here, and that made her his boss. If anybody should be giving orders, it was she.

But she was just too worn out and emotional to get into it. Particularly with someone who looked the type to relish a good fight, and the more down and dirty, the better. Not to mention he might simply quit like Rosetta — and wouldn't *that* just be the icing on her cake.

Still, it didn't keep her from resenting his attitude. He didn't know her. He didn't have the first idea how hard she'd worked to get away from this place, so how dare he look at her as if she were too snooty to do an honest day's work?

If she was smart, she'd just walk away right now, the way she should have done earlier, and to *hell* with the bar. Let it fall down around everyone's ears; she really didn't give a rat's rear end.

Except . . . the Tonk was her niece Lizzy's inheritance, now that Crystal was gone.

Gone. Pain slashed through Veronica. Her sister had been found murdered last month, and Lizzy's father, Eddie Chapman, had been charged with the crime. And just to make things *really* special, mere hours after the judge at the preliminary hearing had determined there was probable cause for a trial, Eddie had skipped town.

Leaving his daughter a virtual orphan.

Except for her. Veronica straightened her shoulders. Lizzy still had her. And she owed it to her niece to keep the Tonk going until a buyer could be found. Given the situation and the twisted convolutions of the legal system, God only knew if the child would ever realize anything from Eddie's holdings. So Veronica was determined to scrape together every red cent she could in order to secure Lizzy's future.

She bent down and swiped up the apron. Straightening, she removed her blazer and carefully folded it, then tied the apron around her hips and reached for a tray. She met the dark-eyed gaze of the bartender, who'd paused midpour to level a get-a-move-on look at her. *Nazi bastard.*

But aloud she merely said, "Here," and passed him her jacket and purse. "Where do you want me to start?"

She was run ragged by the time the bar closed down for the night. Exhausted, she pulled off her apron, dropped it in the basket beneath the bar, and collected her belongings. She didn't even have the strength to shoot Coop a dirty look, and if you asked her, the man had missed his calling as an SS officer. Without a word, she turned and dragged herself to the door.

"Night, Princess."

She flipped him a succinct one-handed gesture over her shoulder, and his low laugh followed her out the door.

The house she'd grown up in was just across the street, a fact she'd deplored when she was a kid, but was grateful for at the moment. She fished the key out of her purse and let herself in.

She nearly tripped over the suitcases she'd dumped in the hall earlier tonight. She'd gotten into town too late to pick up Lizzy, so she'd dropped off her luggage and headed across the street to the bar. Her thought had been simply to get the duty call out of the way so she wouldn't have to obsess over it. Then she'd planned to come back, unpack, and fall into bed to get a good night's rest for tomorrow.

So much for best-laid plans. Veronica stumbled into the living room and turned on a lamp. Then she blinked several times, thinking her eyes must be deceiving her.

Surely it was merely being blinded by the sudden light after the dark hallway that made everything seem so brassy. But when she narrowed her eyes to take a good hard look, nothing dimmed. "Oh, my God."

The room was all done up in red flocked wallpaper and gold fabrics, and every item that wasn't nailed down appeared to have been gilded to within an inch of its life. She'd never seen such an accumulation of ticky-tackies in one place in her life.

"Damn, Crystal," she whispered. "Why not just raise Lizzy in a whorehouse? It would probably be more subdued." She stared in amazement at the table lamp she'd switched on: It was painted with overblown roses, trimmed in gold leaf, and dripping with crystal teardrops that clinked and chimed where the brush of her hand had set them in motion. Picking up a crimson velvet pillow that had *Reno, The Biggest Little City in the World* embroidered in metallic gold thread, she fingered its fat tassels while trying to find just one furnishing that was a neutral color or unembellished by curlicues, gold, or fringe. But every item her gaze lit upon seemed more garish than the one before, and she was appalled right down to the bottom of her artistic, restoration specialist's soul. When the heck had Crystal accumulated all this? The house hadn't been crammed with this stuff the last time she'd visited.

Veronica suddenly found herself completely and uncontrollably furious.

"If this isn't just typical, Crystal! You never did have a lick of taste. And you sure as hell never had common sense. You just had to keep working all your stupid angles, didn't you? God, I can't believe you're such a bimbo!" Ambushed by her use of the present tense, she shook her head furiously. "Were, I mean. I can't believe you *w-were* such a dumb, reckless . . ."

Grief sucker-punched her out of the blue, and clutching the pillow to her stomach, she collapsed onto the tufted brocade couch beneath a huge black velvet painting of a bullfighter. Folding at the waist, she sobbed into her knees, tears flowing in an unstoppable stream that soaked spreading circles on her khakis.

Oh, God, oh, God. She couldn't believe her sister was dead. And not just dead, which was hard enough to accept, but *murdered*. That was something that happened in movies, in books — not to people one knew.

It was no secret that Crystal hadn't been the nicest woman in town, and they'd fought like a couple of cats more often than not. But she'd been her *sister*, and precious memories etched Veronica's mind of moments when Crystal had been sweet, or big-sister protective, or so downright funny it could make you nearly wet your

19

pants laughing. She hadn't deserved to die like that, to have her life choked out of her beneath the unrelenting hands of an enraged man.

A noise out on the back porch brought Veronica's head up. Sniffling, she sat up and wiped the tears from her cheeks with her palms, swiped the edge of her index fingers beneath her eyes. She had a view straight through the kitchen archway to the back door, but there was nothing to see. She shrugged. It was probably one of Mrs. Martelucchi's cats.

Then a man's shadow crossed the door's shade-drawn window, and Veronica's heart kicked hard against the wall of her chest, before starting to pound. The back door knob jiggled and she shot to her feet, the cushion in her lap tumbling to the floor. She looked around for something to use as a weapon and snatched up a gaudy, gold-toned replica of an Erte statuette. Heart lodged so firmly in her throat she could barely breathe, she wrapped both hands around the statuette's base and instinctively assumed the batter's stance she'd learned playing sandlot ball behind Murphy's Feed and Seed. The kitchen door creaked open.

Muscular shoulders and spiky blond hair, backlit by the porch light, sparked a synapse of recognition in her overloaded brain a millisecond before a deep, ironic voice drawled, "Tossing the joint for valuables, Princess?"

She nearly tossed the statuette at his *head* for scaring several years off her life. Trying to get her galloping heart back down to a normal rhythm, she forced herself to carefully lower it to her side. She refused to relinquish it entirely, however. "What do you want, Blackstock? And where do you get off, just waltzing into Crystal's house like you own the joint?"

His voice was full of amusement when he said, "In a way, I do — at least a portion of it. I live upstairs."

Veronica sucked in a shocked breath. "*Excuse me?*"

He closed the door and crossed the kitchen, stopping in the archway. Hands stuffed in his jeans pockets, he propped his shoulder against the doorjamb and gave her a crooked little half smile that inexplicably sent sparks of awareness shivering down her spine. "I said, I live here. Ms. Travits rented me the attic apartment when she hired me to run the bar."

Marissa did that? *Dear God, Mare, what were you thinking?*

Then guilt suffused her. She owed Marissa everything for holding things together when no one had known where Veronica was, or how to reach her to tell her about Crystal. Marissa had gone above and beyond the ties of an old friendship to take care of matters she never should've been called upon to handle.

But renting space to this big bruiser in the house where Veronica and Lizzy had to live was not one of her smarter moves, and Veronica didn't intend to live with it. Taking a step toward

Coop, she tilted back her head to meet his gaze and said firmly, "I suggest you get a good night's sleep, then, because tomorrow you can just go look for someplace else to rent."

He had the temerity to laugh. "Forget it, sugar — I signed a lease. If you have a problem with the arrangements, *you* move."

"Don't be absurd. Lizzy's been through enough — she's going to need the continuity of at least living in her own home."

Something flashed across his face, and his voice was contemptuous when he said, "Like I'm supposed to believe you're full of concern for your niece?"

He might as well have slapped her, and Veronica's head snapped back. "*Excuse* me?"

"Nothing." His face expressionless, he shrugged. "Never mind."

"The hell I'll never mind! What was that supposed to mean?"

"It meant you were right in one part of your little directive, sweetpea — I do need a good night's sleep."

And, leaving her to fume in outraged frustration, he pushed away from the doorjamb, turned on his heel, and took the back stairs two at a time to the top floor.

2

James Cooper Blackstock awoke the following morning the way he always did: from deep sleep to immediate, alert consciousness between one moment and the next. Rolling onto his back, he frowned up at the ceiling at the discovery that the first thing on his mind was identical to the one he'd gone to bed with last night.

Veronica Davis. Damn. She had no business being on his mind at all, so what was *that* all about?

Tossing back the covers, Coop climbed to his feet, then stretched until his joints popped. He scratched his stomach, gave his morning erection a couple of absentminded strokes, and headed for the bathroom. Okay, it was probably just because her looks didn't even come *close* to what he'd expected. He'd anticipated a woman just like her late sister. Although he'd never met Crystal, he'd heard plenty these last couple weeks about her flamboyance and overt sexuality. Who would've thought little Miz Veronica would turn out to look more like Snow White instead, with that sleek black hair, those smoky green eyes, and that skin?

Man, that white, white, strokable skin.

Coop picked up his toothbrush and scowled. Wasting such baby softness on a Davis was a crying shame. Because Veronica might attire herself in khakis, white T-shirts, and little ballerina flats; she might even give a decent impression of a princess forced into servitude just because he'd made her serve a few drinks. But in all the ways that mattered, she was exactly like her sister Crystal. She was just another Davis woman without an ounce of concern for anyone but herself.

Coop brushed his teeth and slapped on some deodorant. Then he spread foamy shaving cream on his face and reached for his razor. He may not have ever met Crystal, but he knew her just the same. Watching his mother had educated him on the ways of women looking to become upwardly mobile, and from everything he'd ever heard, Crystal probably could've taught *her* a thing or two. It wasn't simply a matter of old prejudices rising up to color his view, though. He knew the type of woman Crystal was from letters and telephone conversations with his half-brother Eddie, who, despite having grown up the only heir of the wealthiest man in Fossil, was probably the sweetest guy on earth.

And one whose belief in the goodness of everyone had landed him in a world of hurt.

Coop rarely believed in the goodness of anyone, and Crystal in particular didn't deserve that kind of faith. When she was twenty-eight she'd seduced his twenty-year-old half-brother. He suspected she'd deliberately gotten pregnant so Eddie would have to marry her, only to have Eddie's father nip that plan in the bud. Still, she'd gotten around it by using Lizzy, whom his brother loved more than life itself, as a bargaining chip. And if that didn't pretty much say it all, Coop'd eat his Marine-issue combat boots.

Crystal had been a user, a woman who'd made a habit of playing all the angles and looking out for number one. Hell, she'd been a homicide waiting to happen. But Cooper also knew that Eddie hadn't killed her, and he'd come to Fossil to prove it.

Being able to rent these rooms in the Davis house had been an unexpected bonus. He'd had the entire place to himself for almost two weeks, and had gone through every room with a fine-toothed comb, looking for evidence to clear his brother's name. But the only proof he'd found so far was that Crystal had been self-absorbed and narcissistic. Her clothing stuffed every closet to overflowing, and he'd come across photograph after garishly framed photograph of her, with her blond-streaked brown hair all teased up, her makeup layered on, jeans tighter than a coat of spray paint, and her tops unbuttoned to the legal limit.

He'd found exactly one photograph of Lizzy. Coop paused with the razor poised above his Adam's apple and took a couple breaths before he ended up slicing off something he might need in the future. But, shit fuck hell. His brother had been throwing every resource at his disposal into trying to gain custody of his daughter, and the fact that he'd been charged with her mother's murder instead just went to show there was damn little justice in the world.

Hearing a noise down in the kitchen, Coop rinsed the remaining shaving cream off his face, pulled on a pair of jeans, and jerked a sweater on over his head. Veronica wasn't a damn bit better, and although he'd stopped letting women get to him the day he'd walked out of his mother's house more than seventeen years ago, last night little Miss Ronnie had all but made steam blow out of his ears.

Chump that he was, he'd felt almost guilty when he'd come in and found he'd driven her so hard over at the Tonk that she had tears drying on her cheeks. But then she'd had the nerve to invoke Lizzy's name as an excuse to make him vacate the house, and both guilt and sympathy had gone up in smoke. If she'd been so freaking concerned about her niece, she would've hauled her ass back to Fossil a month ago.

Pushing aside the thought that he was a fine one to talk, he left the bathroom. Hell, it wasn't as if he'd *intended* to keep his identity as Eddie's brother a secret when he'd come to Fossil. But when he'd learned Lizzy wasn't staying in her own home because her Aunt Veronica had better things to do than come home to take care of her, he'd made a trip up to the Bluff to introduce himself to the woman who *was* looking after her. Before he could do much more than state his name, however, Marissa Travits had mistaken him for an applicant for the vacant position at the honky tonk. And it had occurred to him that the Tonk would be an ideal place to gather information to clear Eddie's name.

And *that,* in the long run, would serve Lizzy much better than an uncle she wouldn't even remember, since she'd only seen him once or twice when she was a baby. Especially an uncle who didn't know diddly about little girls.

He loped down the back stairs but stopped dead at the base of the staircase. Veronica sat sprawled in a chair at the kitchen table, her upper body draped across the tabletop. Her hair was mussed and her chin was propped on her fist while she stared blearily at the gurgling coffeemaker.

He'd seen any number of sheer, slinky little nighties while going through Crystal's dresser drawers, but Veronica's attire bore no relationship to any of them. Instead, she wore turquoise thermal pajamas and a pair of wool socks. She apparently didn't share her sister's penchant for flaunting her sexuality.

So it pissed him off that he got half hard anyway, seeing her in what amounted to a set of colorful long johns.

He scraped a chair back from the table and dropped down on it. "I'll expect you at the Tonk by eight tonight."

"Expect all you want." Her moss-green eyes had been drifting closed, but she pried one open and peered at him. "If you're lucky, you might even see me there."

"Might, hell. We were shorthanded *before* Rosetta quit — now it's critical. We need a lot more help than we've currently got, and until someone answers the ads I've got out, Princess, that means you."

Both her eyes were open now and if their expression was anything to go by, she wasn't pleased with him. That was just fine with him, because he wasn't exactly delighted with her, either.

Then her eyes narrowed until they were little more than glints of green glaring out at him between dark lashes. "Listen, stud-biscuit —"

He jerked upright in his chair, his hand whipping out to shackle her wrist to the table. "What did you call me?"

"Oh, I'm sorry — don't you like nicknames? Gee, and I just adore being called princess-honey-sugarpea."

"*Sweet*pea," he corrected. He felt the corner of his mouth twitch up. "Sugarpea's a good one, though; I'll have to remember that." He tested the texture of her forearm with his fingertips. It was every bit as soft-skinned as it looked, and he immediately quit doing that, sliding his fingers out from beneath her loose pajama sleeve. Knowing she expected a display of temper, he raised a brow at her instead and gave her his best good ol' boy smile. "Okay, then, stud-biscuit it is. Actually, that's a handle I can wrap my mind around — given how well it fits and all."

"Wonderful," she said in disgust and jerked her hand out from under his. She pushed to her feet as the coffeemaker burbled into silence, and went over to pour herself a cup. "Maybe I oughtta just call you Mr. Humble instead."

Coop found himself enjoying this exchange a little too much, and he rose to his feet as well. "You can call me anything that tickles your fancy," he said, staring down at her. "Just have your butt at the Tonk by eight."

Then he turned and left the room before sleepy green eyes and a challenging attitude could make him believe he was dealing with a different kind of woman than he knew to be the case.

An hour later Veronica stood in the bedroom, her nose wrinkling in distaste at the odor wafting off her blazer. She'd washed the strong scent of cigarette smoke off her skin and out of her hair, but her good jacket still reeked of it, and she tossed it aside to be dry-cleaned. She might have to work at the Tonk until a new waitress could be found, but she'd be damned if she'd bring this smell home to Lizzy every night. What kind of example would that set? She finished dressing, then went in search of the phone book.

An hour later, she left the house on Baker Street and headed for Marissa's. It had been a dozen years since she'd lived in this sleepy little town, but it never seemed to change much between her visits home. Oh, some of the apple orchards on either end of town had given way to new housing developments, additional fast-food joints had popped up along the main drag, and a new Big K had been built just off I-82. But Fossil was still pretty much a one-horse town. And its flatlands and surrounding hills still sported the same depressing mud-brown and dusty beige hues of winter.

Birch trees stretched denuded branches toward a crystal-blue sky, though, and cast their foreshortened shadows along the streets and sidewalks. Winter sunlight poured through the windshield of her car as she drove across town, a welcome break from the largely overcast skies of Seattle, where she lived now.

And where she would continue to live with Lizzy just as soon as she found a buyer for the Tonk and the house.

Minutes later, she drove into a circular driveway behind a large timber-and-river-rock house and cut the engine. Then she simply sat for a moment, staring at the back of the lavish home. The Bluff, as this area overlooking the town and the river beyond was called, was the rich folks' part of town, and Veronica could never quite get over the fact that her oldest friend lived here now, and had for some time. Marissa had certainly come a long way from her Baker Street house, which was jammed so close to Veronica's they used to utilize the low fence dividing the properties as a stepping stone from one back porch to the other.

She smiled. The low stone fence that marked the boundary of Marissa's property from her nearest neighbor's was a far cry from their rickety wooden version, and it was a safe bet that nobody used it the way she and Marissa had used theirs. A woman could kill herself trying to hop porches between these homes.

Oh, God. *Kill*. The word wiped the smile from her face. Berating herself for her appalling lack of sensitivity to her sister's death, Veronica reached for the door handle. How could she already forget about it so easily? She'd only learned of it two days ago.

The kitchen door banged open as she climbed from the car, and Marissa flew across the brick patio to the driveway, waving her arms in the air and screaming with joy. Veronica's mood skyrocketed, and the two women met in the middle of the yard, exclaiming and hugging each other tightly.

Once upon a time, their friends had called them Mutt and Jeff, because Marissa was a couple inches shy of six feet tall and built along generous lines, while Veronica was a fine-boned not quite five-five. They didn't fit any better now than they once had, yet Veronica felt as if she'd come home when she was hauled into her oldest friend's warm, cushiony embrace.

Eventually Marissa stepped back and gripped Veronica's shoulders in her long, impeccably manicured hands to hold her at arm's length while she inspected her from head to foot.

"You cut off all your hair," she said, touching Veronica's sleek bob. "How very chic — I like it. Did you have it done in Europe?"

"Yes, in Edinburgh." Then the guilt she'd been living with since getting back from Scotland rose up to swamp her. "Rissa, I'm so sorry I didn't think to leave a number where I could be reached. I can't believe Crystal's funeral had been over and done for nearly a month before you finally tracked me down." She laughed, but it was a short-lived sound, lacking humor. "God, when I think how full of myself I was! That castle restoration was my big break, and I thought I was pretty hot stuff to have gotten it all done on time and on budget. I feel so guilty knowing that while I was busy congratulating myself over the future clients this project would bring me, Crystal was already dead and buried."

Marissa gave her a shake. "Well, stop it."

"You're right, you're right." Veronica took a deep breath, blew it out, and stepped back, straightening her spine. "This isn't about me."

"Of course it's about you — your sister was murdered!"

That stabbed straight to the core, but Veronica shook her head. "No, it's about Lizzy losing her mama, having her daddy accused of the killing, and her aunt missing in action when she needed her most. How's she doing? It was so hard to tell during those two brief telephone conversations."

"Oh, Ronnie, she breaks my heart." Marissa took Veronica's hand and led her into the house. They crossed the gleaming slate floor of a kitchen whose granite countertops were cluttered with family flotsam, and whose state-of-the-art fridge bristled with children's art. "She acts as if nothing's happened, but it has to be eating her up inside. Not only has she had to deal with the loss of both her parents, but you know what this town can be like — everyone and his brother knows every last detail of *why* Eddie and Crystal are gone and is busy talking about it."

They settled on the great room's overstuffed couch, their knees tucked up and bodies angled to face each other. "None of this has driven her further into her shell, though, which is pretty darn remarkable, considering her shyness." Marissa smoothed the tail of her fat, sandy brown braid through first one fist, then the other. "My kids tell me some of her classmates have given her a hard time at school, but luckily she's got a decent network of friends. God knows Dessa's a fierce little supporter. And Riley came home with a bloody nose the other day for defending her from one of his fellow third-graders."

"You've got great kids, Marissa."

Dimples punched deep in her friend's cheeks. "Yeah, who knew? Just when I think military school sounds like a good plan for the two of them, they turn around and do something that makes me so proud I could bust." She shrugged.

"I suspect it's a conspiracy to see how fast they can drive me to gibbering insanity, but what's a woman to do?"

Veronica snorted. "Like you'd change a thing about either of them, even if you could. You've done a great job of raising them. It had to be tough with Denny's death."

"Yeah, it's been tough at times, but it's been five years and life goes on — especially when you have kids." Marissa shrugged. "You just do what you have to do."

"Well, what you've done is stellar. And to take on my problems, too . . ." She reached out and touched Marissa's shoulder. "I owe you so much. For taking care of Lizzy and for keeping the Tonk going."

"Oh, pooh." Then Marissa fanned herself with her hand. "Speaking of the Tonk, though, isn't that Cooper a *honey?* And he's such a sweet-heart!"

"A sweetheart?" That wasn't exactly the first description to pop into Veronica's mind.

"Yes, indeed. He's so charming and easy to work with, and he doesn't drink up all the profits like the first guy I hired."

Charming? With everyone except her, maybe. And please, easy to work with? "You think he's a *sweetheart?*"

Marissa laughed. "Okay, I'll admit he doesn't look like your basic sweetie pie —"

"I'll say. He reminds me of one of those vampires that're so popular on television these days.

And not the new-age sensitive ones who're always trying to reform their wicked ways, either. He's more like the badass archvillain one that pillages his way through the populace."

"Nah, too tan," Marissa disagreed. "I wouldn't mind being pillaged by him, though." Then she laughed and leaned forward to give Veronica a quick hug. "Oh, V, it's so good to have you back. You always did have a unique way of looking at things."

"I'm not sure how I feel about *being* back," Veronica admitted, "but it's sure good to see you. And I'm in desperate need of your knowledge of the citizens of Fossil." She scrubbed her hands up and down her khaki-clad thighs. "The Tonk's shorthanded and I've been informed I have to lend a hand there until we can get the waitress shortage straightened out."

"Hoo, boy." Marissa gave her a commiserating smile. "I can only imagine how you must have loved hearing that."

"Oh, yeah." She made a face. "From the time we were big enough to wield a mop, Crystal and I must have given up half our Sundays to clean that place." Her antipathy for the Tonk was all tied up with memories of her father — his charm, his lack of ambition, and his innate chauvinism were all inextricably woven in her mind with the family bar. "Of course, I don't have to tell *you* that. God knows I vented to you often enough about Daddy's idea of a woman's mission in life, and Mama's reinforcement of it when she refused to make him lift a finger." She shrugged apologetically for dragging the subject up yet again. "I'll work the Tonk because I have no other choice if I want the place to sell. For Lizzy's sake I'd like to get every penny out of it that I can, so she'll have the freedom to choose what she wants to do with her life. But the instant I find a replacement waitress, I'm outta there."

"Um, I sure don't want to discourage you, sweetie, but the economy's been excellent around here the past couple of years. And that means it's harder to fill the lower-paying jobs, so it might take a while."

"Swell." Veronica's stomach dropped, but she squared her shoulders and shoved the disheartening news aside. "Is that why I came home to find Cooper Blackstock living in Crystal's house?"

"Yeah. The vacancy rate for rentals is almost nil, so I figured why not stick him in that empty house, where he'll be nice and handy to the Tonk."

Because he disturbs me. An image of the way he'd looked this morning popped into Veronica's mind: all smooth-shaven hard jaw, blond hair standing on end, and those dark brows pulled together in a scowl. He'd taken up more than his fair share of the kitchen table as he'd sat across from her, his shoulders blocking her view.

Then she shook the image aside. She'd deal with Blackstock later; right now she had real problems. "God, Mare, I feel like I'm in the middle of a *Twilight Zone* episode. There's a part of me that always worried Crystal would come to a bad end, but it was nebulous stuff, you know? Like her driving drunk and crashing the car, or one of the men she played her eternal games with suddenly flipping out and hitting her. Blackening an eye, maybe, or splitting her lip."

She looked at her friend in baffled horror. "I sure never envisioned anything like *this*. How could Eddie have done it? I always thought he was the nicest, most forbearing guy, because, face it, we both know what Crystal could be like. But this! I mean, I knew they were in the middle of a custody battle for Lizzy, but I never thought . . . I never *dreamed* . . ." Shoving her hair off her forehead, she swallowed hard. "Gawd, I actually encouraged her to let him raise Lizzy, because I thought he was the better parent."

"He *was* the better parent. I guess he just snapped."

"They're positive he's the one who did it, though?" Veronica shook her head impatiently. "Well, of course they are — it had to be him, didn't it? Otherwise he never would have run and left Lizzy to deal with everything all on her own." A bitter taste coated the back of her tongue.

"Eddie and Crystal had a pretty public fight at the Tonk that night, too," Marissa said gently. "He made some threats. And the police found his leather jacket in a Dumpster in the same lot where they found her body. She had trace evidence from it under her fingernails." Then, her face stricken, she reached over and squeezed Veronica's hand. "I'm sorry, V. That was insensitive. Let's talk about something else, what do you say?"

"Yeah." She swallowed hard, wanting desperately to erase the images that had sprung to mind. "Help me figure out someone really good to stay with Lizzy when I have to work."

3

By the time Marissa's kids and Lizzy burst through the kitchen door a few hours later, Veronica had made some decisions concerning her six-year-old niece's welfare. She studied Lizzy for changes as the little girl entered on the tail of lanky, eight-year-old Riley, who was wrangling loudly with his sister Dessa, whose static-charged blond curls seemed to take on the energy of her personality as she argued with pedal-to-the-metal ferocity. Lizzy's golden brown hair was neatly combed as always, her retro pea jacket and jeans spic-and-span, her tennis shoes firmly tied. Her genes were an interesting combination of both parents, and she had Crystal's smaller stature and delicate bone structure. Veronica thought she looked thinner as she trailed quietly in the rambunctious Travitses' wake, her expression solemn. But the moment her gaze settled on Veronica, her entire face lit up.

"Aunt Ronnie?" She stopped dead by the kitchen counter, her backpack dangling from one shoulder where she'd started to take it off. "You're here!"

Riley and Dessa quit arguing and turned to stare at Veronica, who had risen to her feet at their entrance. Backpack thumping to the floor, Lizzy launched herself across the room but stumbled to a halt just inches away from hurling herself into Veronica's arms. Her chin dipped to her chest and her narrow shoulders hunched up around her ears as she stole a hesitant peek at her aunt through the silky curtain of her bangs.

Her uncertainty tore at Veronica's heart. "C'mere, you!" She hauled the child into her arms and held her tightly to her breast. "I've missed you! Do you know how long it's been since we were last together? It's been exactly two months, three weeks, and —"

"Six long *days*," Lizzy said in unison with Veronica, tilting her head back to look up at her aunt as she completed the litany of their time spent apart. She relaxed into Veronica's embrace. "I counted it up on my calendar last night."

Crystal had been in the habit of driving her daughter over the Cascades and dropping her off at Veronica's whenever she had hot plans for the weekend. And since she'd often had hot plans, and an even hotter determination to keep Eddie from having custody of Lizzy one minute longer than their original agreement stipulated, Veronica and Lizzy had grown particularly close this past year. They'd developed the ritual of counting off the days and weeks since their last time together, then regaling each other with the knowledge as soon as they met up again.

"I'm sorry I wasn't here sooner." Veronica

brushed Lizzy's soft hair away from her face. "But I'm here now, and we're family, you and I, so never doubt that I'll take care of you. We'll start by moving you back into your own room this afternoon."

She looked up in time to see Dessa's stricken face and gave the little girl a reassuring smile. "Would you like to come along and help us?" she asked. "Because you do understand, I hope, that you're welcome to visit Lizzy anytime you want. And on the weekends, if your mama agrees, you girls can plan sleepovers." Then she shot a glance at Riley, who was busy making sure everyone knew he was too cool to show an interest in the proceedings. "You're always welcome, too, Riley."

He rolled his eyes, stuffed another cookie from the cookie jar into his mouth, and grunted. Swallowing audibly, he grabbed a plastic jug of milk out of the fridge. "Like I wanna play with a coupla dumb girls." He drank straight from the container, then lowered it and said, "Brad Marshall lives over by you, though. I s'pose I might could do stuff with him while the girls play with their *dollies*."

Marissa got up and plucked the milk bottle from her son's fingers. "Get a glass," she said, then shook her head. "*Might could.* If this is an example of our school system at work, I may have to rethink the way I cast my vote come levy time."

Riley gave his mother a big, unrepentant grin,

and looked so amazingly like a male version of Marissa when she was the same age that Veronica had to bite the inside of her cheek to keep from laughing out loud. Her lips must have twitched, though, because Marissa gave her a stern look.

"Don't encourage him."

"I'm not. I wouldn't." She straightened her face and looked down at Lizzy, still in the circle of her arms. "Do you need any help packing your stuff?"

"Nuh-uh. I did it last night. It's all upstairs; should I go get it now? Don't go away — it won't take me any time at all."

Veronica hated the sudden anxiety in her niece's voice, but she merely smiled and assured her she wasn't going anywhere. Lizzy pulled out of her embrace and turned to her friend. She seemed on surer ground when she said, "You can come help me bring it down, Dessa."

All three kids tramped out of the kitchen and Veronica turned to Marissa. "Oh, man, it's just starting to sink in that my status has been upgraded from aunt to *mom*. It's such a huge responsibility, and Lizzy seems so fragile. What if I screw it up? Oh, God, Rissa — what if I mess *her* up?"

"Take a deep breath," Marissa instructed and rubbed comforting circles between Veronica's shoulder blades. "Now blow it out and listen to me. You're not going to screw anything up."

"How do you *know* that?"

"Because you're good with Lizzy. Because you're crazy about her, and you'll do your best by her."

"I've never been totally responsible for her for more than a week at a time; what if my best's not good enough?"

"It'll be more than enough. Look at what you've already accomplished this afternoon — you managed to settle her insecurities with a hug and that how-long's-it-been thing you two share. And you've arranged for reliable help to take care of her while you're at work. And that, toots, is pretty much the way it goes — you simply take things one day at a time."

So that's what Veronica determined to do for the rest of the day. She'd live in the moment and resolve each matter or problem as it arose. But she was glad that Coop was nowhere to be seen when they arrived back home.

"Man, lookit all this stuff!" Riley said as they passed through the living room. His mouth hung open as he attempted to take in everything at once. "My mom doesn't have *near* as much cool stuff in our house."

Lizzy winced slightly, but didn't say anything. Leaving Riley to explore the downstairs and back yard, Veronica followed the girls upstairs and watched while Dessa emptied Lizzy's suitcase and her niece arranged photographs on her dresser. There were several shots of golden-haired, golden-skinned Eddie, one of Crystal, and even a framed snapshot of Veronica and

43

Lizzy that had been taken at the Woodlawn Park Zoo during one of Lizzy's visits last fall.

She watched her niece delve into the cardboard box and pull out a photo album that she put on the bottom shelf of her nightstand, then a raggedy stuffed pony that she placed carefully on her pillow. Looking around the room, Veronica felt a spark of rancor toward her sister.

It was nice enough, as far as cleanliness and neatness went. But it could have belonged to anyone. There were no special touches that indicated this was a little girl's room, aside from the ones that Lizzy herself had provided. The walls were painted white, the bed sported a plain white chenille spread, and utilitarian blinds covered the window.

Veronica suspected that Crystal had dropped a bundle on that tasteless display that passed for decor down in the living room, and her bedroom similarly bristled with a glittery plethora of objets d'art. Would it have killed her to spare a few bucks to make her daughter's room the tiniest bit special? It ate away at a place deep inside Veronica to admit that her sister probably hadn't possessed much in the way of maternal instincts.

So look on the bright side, she thought with a guilty little lift of her spirits. *You probably can't do a worse job of mothering.*

"It's not surprising Eddie finally flipped out," Coop heard someone down the bar say. "Crystal boasted that she was playing him.'"

From the corner of his eye he saw it was Sandy the waitress who had spoken, and grabbing a cloth, he started wiping down the bar, working closer to where she stood chatting with a woman he'd recently served a gin and tonic.

"Playing him how?" the woman asked skeptically. "Crystal never struck me as the mastermind type."

Sandy laughed. "Funny you should say that, because I think my exact response was, 'Yeah, right — you and who else?' "

"What'd she have to say to that?"

"Nothing, really. She just smiled that smart-ass smile of hers. So I asked her flat out what she meant, and she said —" Sandy's confidential tone of voice suddenly turned brisk. "Can I get you anything else?"

"Huh?" Gin-and-Tonic looked at her as if she'd lost her mind, then sat a little straighter when the waitress tipped her head infinitesimally toward Coop, who was clearly within listening range. "Oh! No, thanks. I'm set."

"Well, I'd better get back to work, then." Sandy hustled off to check the two men playing pool in the corner.

The rational part of Coop understood she was still taking his measure as her temporary boss and didn't want to be caught gossiping, but it took a real act of will not to growl with frustration. This sounded like his first genuine lead. He kept hoping the subject would come up again so he could insert himself into the conversation this time, and kicked himself for not doing so when he'd had the chance. Hell, it would have been perfectly natural to be interested. Crystal's murder was probably the hottest topic in town.

His mood wasn't improved by the fact that it was well past nine o'clock when Veronica finally strolled through the Tonk's front door. He flipped the towel he'd been using to dry glasses over his shoulder and watched as she approached. It was about damn time she'd shown up.

It had been fairly quiet tonight, the way it was most every Wednesday night, and it hadn't actually caused anyone undue stress to handle things without her. But that wasn't the point. He'd told her to be here at eight o'clock, and by God, she should've been here. He'd spent thirteen years as a Marine and wasn't accustomed to having his commands blown off. Especially by some slip of a woman with bones so fragile he could snap her in two without breaking a sweat.

"Good evening, Cooper," she said as she sauntered behind the bar for her apron and tray.

Coop swiveled to watch her tie the white cloth around her hips. She trailed an elusive scent in her wake, and he wasn't sure if it came from her sleek, swingy hair or was embedded in the plush, long-sleeved top she wore over a pair of slim black trousers. Or maybe from that soft white triangle at the base of her throat, where a faint blue vein pulsed.

"You're late," he growled, shaking off the unwelcome image of going over her inch by inch in search of the source. "When I tell you to be here by eight, I *mean* eight o'clock sharp."

She froze with her hands still behind her back, her small breasts thrust against the clingy velvet of her wine-colored shirt. For a few heartbeats, Collin Raye could be heard marveling from the jukebox how quickly a person could go from someone you loved to someone you used to know. Then Veronica's hands came around to curl at her sides as she bridged the distance that separated them. She thrust her chin up at him.

"Let's get something straight," she said as she stopped mere inches away and tilted her head back to level a cool gaze at him. "You're not my daddy — you don't *get* to tell me when to be here. If you have suggestions for improving the service around here, or you want to sit down like rational adults to hammer out a schedule, then I'm more than ready to listen. But you don't order me around, you don't lay down the law, and you sure as hell don't talk to me like I'm some errant lackey who failed to fall in with the party line. You seem to forget that I'm the owner here, not you."

Shit. He *had* sort of forgotten about that. And because she'd managed to piss him off with her little reminder, he'd give a bundle to look her straight in those haughty green eyes and say, *Fine — I quit.*

He savored the fantasy for a few seconds and

47

was warmed by the thought of leaving her to struggle with everything: the waitress shortage, tending bar, the cleanup, staying abreast of the invoices and the supplies to be ordered. It would be interesting to see how uppity she remained then.

But since it would also pretty much defeat his purpose for taking this job in the first place, he let it go. He took a step forward instead, his humor immediately restored when she took a reflexive step backward and bumped up against the lit glass shelves that held an array of liquor bottles. She reached back with both hands to grip the one at hip level, and he felt a feral smile stretch the corners of his mouth. Good. She wasn't as impervious as she'd like to appear.

Leaning over, Coop slapped his much larger hands down on either side of hers, the knuckles of his thumbs brushing her pinkies. "I've got a flash for you, Princess," he murmured. Breathing in the scent of her shampoo, he determined it wasn't the elusive fragrance he'd caught a whiff of earlier, and eyed that soft-skinned hollow at the base of her throat consideringly. Then he snapped his wandering mind back to the business at hand. "You'll be the owner of zip if you don't bother to come in on time to lend a hand. Sandy and I had to cover for you when you didn't show."

"And I'm sure you both did a stellar job."

"Damn right we did. But you're missing the point here, Ronnie."

Her chin did the impossible and angled another degree higher. "I didn't give you permission to call me that. *You* may call me Veronica."

He gritted his teeth. "Fine. You're missing the point, *Veronica*. This bar is too busy for you to make your own hours and blow off your responsibilities. And in the immortal words of Rosetta: You don't pay me enough to do your job and mine, too."

She smacked her hands against his chest, giving him a shove that was surprisingly strong for such a delicately built woman. Caught off balance, he stumbled back a step.

"You're an excellent storyteller, Blackstock. I mean, truly, that was very affecting. It contained all the elements: humor and pathos, the evil villainess, the courageous hero who unflinchingly does his part but is ready to put his big foot down to save the villainess's bar in spite of herself." To Coop's surprise, she flashed him a smile filled with genuine admiration and humor. "There's only one teeny-tiny flaw. I'm not some neophyte who just waltzed in off the street; I grew up in this bar. And Wednesday is bowling league night in Fossil — it doesn't even *start* to get busy around here until well after nine-thirty. So I doubt you had to knock yourself out to handle" — she peered past him at the clientele scattered around the bar — "the seven, eight, *nine* customers in here tonight." Then her smile dropped away and she looked him in the eye. "And even if you had . . . well, I'd be sorry as could be about it, but I still had something more important to do this evening."

"Yeah? You have a hot date with your manicurist or something?"

"No, Cooper, that would have been yesterday's important appointment. Today's was to talk to my niece's teacher and principal, and to bring Lizzy home and settle her back into her own room. She's been kicked around enough lately for an entire battalion of little girls, and I wasn't about to turn right around and leave her the minute we got her squared away. So I spent time with her. And when Mrs. Martelucchi arrived, I spent even more time making sure Lizzy felt comfortable with her, since she's the woman who's going to be taking care of her when I have to work."

"Mrs. Martelucchi? The lady down the street with the *cats?*"

"Yes. She's not incompetent, you know, just because she has a houseful of cats. She's simply lonely. Her son died in Desert Storm and he was her last family member. Marissa suggested her, and she's right. She's kind, reliable as a Swiss clock, and she'll fuss over Lizzy. And frankly, Cooper, Lizzy could stand a bit of fussing. She could also stand to be fattened up a little, and Mrs. Martelucchi just happens to make the best chicken Parmesan in the world." She tucked back a tendril of hair that slid onto her cheek. "All of which brings me to my schedule."

"Hey!" yelled a man at a table by the jukebox.

"Can we get some friggin' service over here?"

Veronica grabbed her cash box, did a rapid count of the money inside, then slid it onto her tray, which she picked up off the counter and braced against one hip. "We'll continue this later." She eased around Coop, then rounded the end of the bar and headed across the room.

He watched the subtle sway of her hips as she threaded her way through mostly empty tables to the impatient man and his cronies. As she leaned over to gather up the empties and exchange the full ashtray in the middle of the table for a clean one from her tray, he admitted he didn't know what the hell to make of her. Just when he thought he had her neatly pigeonholed, she did or said something that upset his perception of her. He kept expecting her to be a replica of her sister, but she seemed to be her own woman instead.

Watching her interact with the guys in the corner reinforced that. From all accounts, Crystal had worked this bar with a sexy sort of come-on-and-get-me-boys attitude. Veronica's demeanor was more lay-a-hand-on-me-buster-and-you'll-be-pulling-back-a-nub.

Coop hoped she wasn't counting on her tips to make the rent.

And he'd sure like to know what the hell her game was. He'd almost believed in her concern for Lizzy. He probably would have bought into it entirely if she'd bothered to show up before yesterday. The woman was no doubt a salesman in her non-Fossil life.

He wasn't aware of the strength of his curiosity, however, until she came back to the bar with the order and he heard himself ask, "So, what is it that you do back in the world?"

She blinked but then said, "I'm a restoration specialist, which is more or less an interior decorator with a history degree." A quick smile came and went. "I just finished a castle in Scotland that'd been modernized to such a degree you could hardly recognize its origins. It had a thirteenth century exterior and a 1950s interior."

"I take it you're not married, then?" Coop took a step back, his backbone snapping militarily erect. Where the hell had *that* come from?

She must have wondered the same thing, for her posture stiffened. "And you assume this because . . . ?"

He shrugged. "It sounds like you have a job that takes you out of the country for long periods at a time."

"And it didn't occur to you that I might have someone who'd understand how important my career is and support me in it?"

"Oh, hell, yeah — that was my first thought. Then I asked myself why Mr. Understanding wasn't here lending you a hand. And I considered the fact that you're not wearing any rings."

She looked down at her bare hands, then back up at him. "Well, aren't you Mr. Observant. But I have to hand it to you — when you're right, you're right. I've yet to meet the man who'll make me exchange my freedom for the opportunity to wash his socks — although I'm sure you can imagine how very tempting the thought is." She gave him a swift once-over. "How about you? Are you married?"

"*Hell,* no."

A smile quirked the corner of her mouth as she picked up the tray he'd assembled. "That sounds definitive enough."

You don't know the half of it, Princess. As far as he could see, marriage was just one big heartache waiting to happen.

He watched Veronica carry her order over to the table. By rights, he shouldn't even care enough about Eddie to be looking for the proof to clear his half-brother's name. Because back when Coop was eight, his mother had divorced his dad to marry Eddie's father.

Mary Cooper Blackstock had been a dyed-in-the-wool snob, which was ironic considering her own beginnings. But perhaps that was the point — she'd dragged herself up from extremely humble roots and was determined to go even higher up the social ladder. Only once in her life had she stumbled on her climb to the prominence she felt she deserved, and that was when she'd married his pop in the heat of the moment. When that heat had burned itself out, she'd turned her efforts into changing a guy who'd been perfectly happy being a mason into her idea of a more suitable mate.

Coop was damned if he'd ever let that happen to him.

He would give his mother this, though: She'd actually stuck it out with them for several years before she'd become upwardly mobile again. But when she'd found Thomas Chapman, a man who'd fit much more precisely into her scheme of the universe, she'd walked away from Coop and his dad without a backward glance. A year after that, she'd given birth to Eddie, a golden child also more in keeping with her vision of perfection.

Coop probably never would have gotten to know his half-brother during his infrequent visits with their mother, except Eddie had been a sunny-natured little dude who'd constantly followed him around and openly worshiped him. What the hell was a guy supposed to do in the face of that?

When Coop's father had died shortly after Coop's fifteenth birthday and he'd had to live with his mom, Eddie had been the *only* bright spot in his life. Aching with grief and belligerent with the knowledge of his failure to live up to his mother's expectations, he'd clashed with her constantly. So when the family moved to Fossil the summer after his high school graduation, he'd cut himself free from Mary's appearance-is-everything style of parenting and hit the road.

Veronica came back to the bar with an order from a new group that'd come in. She climbed onto a barstool while he assembled the order and sat silently for a moment. Chin propped in her hand, she watched him. "So, what about you, then — what did you do before you came to Fossil?"

Coop stiffened, then forced himself to relax. It didn't take a shrink to figure out that early indoctrination at his mother's knee had made him slightly paranoid about allowing people to form an opinion of him based on what he did for a living. So sue him — he had a thing about being accepted for who he was. "I've knocked around from here to there."

"Uh-huh. And what does that mean, exactly? What, for instance, does one who knocks around *do?*"

Finishing the order, he set it aside and leaned across the bar to bracket her in with his forearms. "A little bit of everything, sugar." There was something about her that got to him, and if crowding her struck him as a juvenile sort of retaliation for his unwilling fascination, he nevertheless liked seeing the slight flare of disquiet in her eyes and the way she straightened when she found his face suddenly too close to hers.

She was nobody's pushover, however, for she faced him as coolly as you please. "So what you're saying is that, basically, you're a travel bum who can't keep a job?"

"Hey, I had a job that lasted more than a dozen years."

"And what was that?"

"Drifter." Courtesy of the U.S. Marines.

She looked at him in exasperation. "What qualifies you for *this* job?"

"The fact that I can mix drinks and keep drunks from getting disorderly." He pushed back. "Why? Am I competing with someone else for the position?"

"No, of course not."

"Then what difference does it make where I worked before? The only thing that should matter is if I'm competent at the job you want me to do, when you want me to do it. And, honey, competent doesn't begin to even cover my abilities — I'm damn good at what*ever* I choose to do." He resumed his position draped across the bar and reached out to trace the tip of his forefinger along the curve between her thumb and finger. "You don't have to take my word for it, though — you're welcome to test my proficiency yourself. Anytime. Anywhere." He nuzzled his nose close to her temple and inhaled a whiff of that elusive scent that surrounded her. Then — miffed that it went straight to his head — he tucked her hair behind her ear and crooked his head to whisper suggestively into the exposed orifice. "On any*thing*."

She pushed to her feet. Her face was flushed and her eyes were flustered as she reached for the tray. But she gave him a frosty up-and-down appraisal and said, "Do me a favor. Hold your breath." Then she walked away.

Coop watched her go and thought he oughtta feel a sense of accomplishment at how successfully he'd distracted her. So why did he have that old sick feeling in his gut instead, like the one he used to get when his mother looked at him as if he didn't quite measure up?

And he knew he'd done everything in his power to prove her right?

4

"Aunt Ronnie? Did you know there's a man in our house?"

Veronica pried one eye open. Lizzy knelt at the side of the bed, her freshly scrubbed face so close to Veronica's own that it was slightly out of focus. "Hmm?" She was not a morning person, so it took a moment or two for the whispered words to sort themselves out in her sleep-muddled brain. "A man?" She squinted at her niece.

Lizzy nodded emphatically. "A *big* man. With stick-uppy hair."

Ah. Coop. "That's Mr. Blackstock. I told you about him, remember? He's the man Marissa —" It suddenly hit her that she *hadn't* divulged that information, and she pushed up onto her elbow, biting back the curse that threatened to slip up her throat. "I'm sorry, Lizzy. I meant to tell you about him after we took Dessa and Riley home last night, but then we stopped for groceries, and Mrs. Martelucchi came, and then I had to get ready for work, and . . ." She shook her head at the futility of trying to explain the unexplainable, then shivered as a chill draft seeped under the covers.

At least she *was* covered. Her niece was without a robe, clad only in a lavender-print flannel nightgown, and Veronica lifted the blankets invitingly. "Want to climb in where it's nice and warm, while Aunt Ronnie tries to explain why she's such a forgetful idiot?"

Lizzy scrambled under the covers. "I shouldn't," she said, but scooted deeper into the warmth anyhow. "I hafta get ready for school."

Veronica peered past her at the bedside clock. "School starts at nine-ten, right?" She drew her niece to lie spoon fashion with Lizzy's back against her front and covered them both up, then hooked an arm around the little girl's waist. "Heck, that's more than an hour away. You can spare a couple of minutes for a quick cuddle."

She was rewarded by the feel of her niece snuggling in.

"Now, about Mr. Blackstock," she said. "Marissa hired him to manage the bar, and since you were living with her and there aren't a lot of places in Fossil that are available to rent, she rented him the attic rooms here." Lizzy shifted, and the soles of her feet came into contact with Veronica's shins. Veronica jumped, and the air left her lungs in an explosive *hah!* "My God, your feet are like ice!"

"I'm sorry!" Lizzy scrambled to remove herself from range. "I'm sorry, Aunt Ronnie!"

Veronica tightened her arm around her. "Heyyy. Cold feet aren't anything you have to apologize for."

"But I didn't mean to put them on you!"

Veronica laughed. "You're a female, hon. It's our God-given right to plant our cold feet on the nearest warm surface."

Lizzy glanced over her shoulder, all big eyes. "You're not mad at me, then?"

"Of course I'm not mad at you." *And damn you, Crystal, if you're the one who put this uncertainty in her, this willingness to accept blame for every little mishap.* "I was just startled. Don't you have any slippers, though?"

"I have some at my daddy's house."

Veronica knew that sooner or later she'd have to talk to Lizzy about her parents, but she couldn't quite bring herself to do so now. "So, did you meet Mr. Blackstock?"

"Nuh-uh. When I saw him in the kitchen, I came up here."

"Which is an extremely smart thing to do when you come across a strange man. When in doubt, fade away, I always say. But I'll introduce you, because you'll probably run into him again. The rooms he's renting don't have their own kitchen, so we have to share ours with him." Which didn't thrill her any more than it did Lizzy.

The alarm clock on the nightstand went off, and Veronica reached across her niece to turn it off. "Rats. I suppose we'd better get up. Do you have a robe in your room?"

Lizzy shook her head but gave Veronica a shy smile. "It's warmer downstairs, though."

"Okay. Grab a pair of my socks out of the top drawer for now, and after school we'll go get you some slippers and a robe. I want you to think about what color you'd like to paint your room, too. That white is sort of boring, don't you think?"

Lizzy's big brown eyes showed a spark of interest. "We're gonna paint my room?"

"I think we should. Jazz it up a little, you know?" God knew the entire house needed help if she hoped to sell it so she and Lizzy could get back to civilization anytime soon. And Lizzy's room was the perfect place to start — it would give her niece a lift while they lived here. "Are you ready to make a run for the kitchen?" Lizzy nodded and Veronica said, "Okay, on the count of three, then, here we go. One, two, three!" She tossed back the blankets, and they scrambled off the bed. Lizzy got herself a pair of woolen socks while Veronica gathered together the clothing she'd need for the day. Their teeth chattered.

"Man, oh, man!" Veronica shivered. "I'd forgotten how cold it gets up here. I've got to use the bathroom real quick, but you go ahead downstairs and get warm."

Lizzy shot her an apprehensive look. "What if Mr. Blackstock's still down there?"

"Oh, sweetie, he won't hurt you. He's a nice man." May lightning not strike her dead for such a bald-faced lie, but Cooper Blackstock exuded much too much sexuality for her to seriously believe it was *little* girls he posed a threat to, and she

61

wouldn't have Lizzy scared.

"Couldn't I just stay here and wait for you?"

"Well, sure, if it'll make you feel more comfortable. Put those socks on, though, before you freeze your tootsies off. I'll be as quick as I can."

She didn't bother to dress, just did her business, washed her hands in cold water because she knew it would take forever for hot to make its way up through the old pipes, and brushed her teeth. She was out again in record time. "Okay, kiddo, let's go warm up!"

They raced down the stairs, and Lizzy was actually giggling when they burst into the kitchen. At the sight of Coop reading a paper at the table, however, her laughter died in her throat. She skidded to a halt, drawing back against her aunt.

Veronica curled her hands over her shoulders and looked at Coop over Lizzy's head. He'd looked up at their arrival, and a smile that was surprisingly sweet curved his lips as his gaze settled on Lizzy. His dark eyes softened. "Hey, Little Bit."

Arrested by an expression she never in a gajillion years would've expected to see on that rabble-rouser face, Veronica had to shake herself free of its spell. "Um, Lizzy, this is Mr. Blackstock, the man I was telling you about. Coop, this is my niece, Lizzy Davis."

Something tightened his face for an instant, but the expression came and went before she could analyze it. "Pleased to meet you, Lizzy Davis," was all he said. "Call me Coop."

" 'Kay," Lizzy murmured, but remained firmly pressed against Veronica's midriff.

Veronica's own nerves were doing an inexplicable little swing dance. "I'm surprised to see you up so early," she said to Coop. It had been nearly noon before they'd run into each other in the kitchen yesterday, and she, for one, would still be sleeping if not for her responsibility to Lizzy.

The shoulder he hitched indifferently looked half a yard wide. "I've got things to do." He leaned back in his chair, looking right at home with his paper and his coffee, comfortably clad in an old pair of jeans and a faded black T-shirt, with a camel, burgundy, and black plaid shirt worn open over it.

It bothered her that she found it difficult to look away, and she bent her head to her niece. "You were right, Lizzy; it's much warmer down here. And once we fuel you up, you'll be even warmer yet. What would you like for breakfast?"

"Cereal."

"Is that all? Wouldn't you rather have something warm? A nice, hot bowl of oatmeal, maybe?"

Lizzy made a face and Coop laughed. "I'm with you, Lizzy. That stuff's nasty."

Veronica gave him a look. "It's good for her, though. It'll stick to her ribs until lunchtime."

"Not if she rolfs it up because she can't stand the taste."

Lizzy eased out of Veronica's hold and inched

over to Coop. "I don't like the feel of it in my mouth," she informed him shyly. "It's mooshy." Staring at his hair, she raised a hand as if to touch it, but snatched it back to her side without doing so. Her solemn gaze didn't stop assessing it, though. "How come your hair sticks up like that?"

"I don't know, baby. It just grows that way." He rubbed a big-knuckled hand over his spiky 'do and flashed her a rueful smile. "Maybe it's because I wear it so short. It might lie down better if I grew it out a little, but this length is easy to take care of." He bent his head toward her. "You wanna feel it?"

Lizzy inched even closer and ran her hand back and forth over the thick brush-cut. Her lips curled up at the corners at the feel of his hair beneath her fingers, and Veronica found her own palms itching as she speculated about its texture.

Coop returned Lizzy's smile with a grin of his own. "*Your* hair sure is pretty. It's very shiny."

"Uh-huh." She nodded solemnly. "Like Aunt Ronnie's."

Coop's gaze rested on Veronica for a moment, and she could just imagine what she looked like. Pulling a comb through her hair hadn't been high on her to-do list this morning. "Yeah," he finally agreed lazily, and turned his attention back to Lizzy. "Like Aunt Ronnie's, in a lighter color sorta way."

Veronica poured herself a cup of coffee and

nearly scalded her tongue seeking that first jolt of caffeine. Then she opened a cupboard and grabbed down a bowl and a glass. She turned to her niece. "What time does the bus come, Lizagator? Does it still stop at the end of the block?"

"Yep." Lizzy glanced at the clock on the stove and gave a start. "Oh, no! I hafta get dressed!" She raced up the back stairs.

Coop returned his attention to the newspaper, but paused in the midst of turning a page to spare a glance for Veronica. "You sure know how to clear a room."

Veronica shrugged and said with studied casualness, "I don't have the hang of her schedule yet." But his comment stung, for it forced her to acknowledge the twinge of jealousy his easy way with Lizzy had given her. It was seeing the effortless way he'd won her niece over that had prompted her to ask about the bus, and she cringed inside that she could be so petty. She certainly didn't want Lizzy to fear him, but apparently she didn't want her niece to *like* him, either. What did that say about her?

After setting her dishes on the counter, she pulled a box of cereal off the shelf and reached into the fridge for the milk. She carried everything over to the table, set her load down across from Coop, and went back for her coffee. In an effort to be adult, she plastered a pleasant smile on her face as she took a seat and gestured at the newspaper spread out in front of him. "When did they start delivering the *Fossil Tribune* in the mornings?"

"They don't," he replied. He flipped up the top of the paper so she could see the banner, which read the *New York Times*.

It caught her by surprise, and she merely stared for a moment. Then, collecting herself, she raised an eyebrow at him. "Don't see many of those in this little burg."

Coop shrugged. "I've got a subscription. For this and *USA Today*."

"My, my. How very literate." Then she waved a hand to erase the comment. "Sorry. That sounded as if you're too blond to sound out the big words all by yourself, and I don't usually tend to be so rude." Her gaze got caught up in his pale hair. "Although, if the color fits . . ." She shook her head impatiently. "Gawd, where is this stuff coming from? I mean, it's not like it counts anyway, when Miss Clairol is part of the equation." *For crying out loud, Ronnie. Shut up, shut up, shut up!* She scowled at him. "This is *your* fault, you know."

His black eyebrows rose. "My fault, huh? For what — impaling myself on the sharp point of your little pink tongue?"

A sudden surge of heat spread along her nerve endings, and she gave him the don't-mess-with-me frown she generally reserved for craftsmen who failed to deliver on time. "Why do you have to turn everything into something suggestive?"

"Do I do that?" Amusement tilted up the corner of his mouth.

"You know you do, and somehow you manage to push all my buttons." But telling him as much probably wasn't the brightest thing to admit, for he studied her with that openly sexual speculation that unnerved her so. It was all she could do not to squirm in her seat, and she raised her chin and blatantly changed the subject. "I need a key to the Tonk."

No sooner had the words left her mouth than she regretted them. Damn. *It really isn't necessary to broadcast your every move to this man, you know.* The smart money would've just called Marissa, who no doubt had the spare set.

But it was too late now, for Coop was already nodding. "All right. I'll get one made up for you while I'm out today."

"It will have to be early today," she said ungraciously. "I need it by eleven."

He slowly straightened from his indolent lounge. "Why? What's going on at eleven?"

She had no good reason to keep it from him, and as manager of the bar, he had a perfect right to know. Yet still she heard herself say, "Something I need the key for, okay?"

Then she flinched, for her reply had come out a lot more defensively than the situation merited. She'd used what she privately labeled her "Fossil kneejerk" tone, and that was much too reminiscent of a disposition she'd worked extremely hard to overcome.

A disposition that seemed to rear its ugly head whenever Cooper Blackstock was near.

For as long as she could remember, she'd hankered to see the world beyond Fossil. She'd longed to view beautiful things, to use her mind and make something of herself. But Daddy had teased her mercilessly for her dreams, and since she'd never been particularly good at hiding her feelings, she'd responded, more often than not, with a snappishness it made her wince to remember.

But damned if she was falling back into that pit. She opened her mouth to apologize — which she seemed to be doing way too much of this morning — and to inform him of the reason she needed the key by eleven. Before so much as another "sorry" could pass her lips, however, Coop pushed his chair back from the table with a nerve-twanging screech and stood. On his feet, he took up even more space than he had seated. Or maybe it was his palpable displeasure that seemed to suck all the oxygen out of the room and take up all the available space. The lazy amusement he'd displayed a moment ago had vanished, and it was all Veronica could do to maintain eye contact beneath the hard-eyed, level look he trained on her.

Hands on his hips, he gave her a clipped nod. "Fine," he said. "You'll have your damn key by eleven. But I'll tell you something, Princess: It's a wonder to me that no one's ever wrung that lily-white neck of yours."

And with a final glower, he turned on his heel and strode from the room.

Coop dropped off the newly cut key at ten-thirty and left the house again without exchanging a word with little Miss Veronica. Climbing back into his car, he swore to himself that, come eleven a.m., he wouldn't be anywhere near the Tonk to see what she'd wanted it for. But at five minutes to the hour, he found himself driving by. Whispering curses for giving a damn when he had far more pressing matters to occupy his free time, he nevertheless found himself making a U-turn down the street and parking where he could keep an eye on the bar's front door like some cut-rate private eye from an old B movie.

He scowled as he peered down the block. What was it about this woman, anyway? Aside from that gorgeous baby skin, he supposed she was attractive enough in an uptight, bossy sort of way. She was a far cry from drop-dead gorgeous, though; she verged on skinny and lacked all but a hint of the lush ass and full breasts he usually went for. So why did she seem to be burrowing her way under his skin?

A disgruntled noise rumbled in the back of his throat and Coop reached for the ignition key to turn the car back on. *Ticks* burrowed under a person's skin, too, and he'd simply have to excise Veronica Davis the same way he would any other parasite: with one swift, efficient jerk.

He put the car in gear and glanced over his shoulder at the oncoming traffic. It was time to get the hell out of here. He had things to do.

He had to wait for a step-van to drive past, and before he could pull out into the street in its wake, the vehicle eased to the curb in front of the Tonk. Coop settled back in his seat. He barely had time to read the logo, CASCADE AIR, off the rear panel doors when Veronica came out of the house, hurriedly locked it up behind her, and dodged the light flow of traffic to cross the street to the van.

Storm clouds blocked the sun as she talked with great animation to the driver, an athletically built man in blue overalls who grinned down at her and stood a lot closer than Coop thought necessary for a repairman. A moment later, Veronica let herself and the man into the Tonk.

What's this? Coop climbed out of his car and strode down the street, determined to find out what she was up to. Nothing was wrong with the heating or cooling systems in the bar, so who *was* this guy — some old high school flame? Was she using the Tonk for a nooner? Now, *there* was an appropriate use of the family biz.

And why is it any skin off your dick if she is, Blackstock? It's her bar. He paused with his hand on the Tonk's doorknob, then yanked it open and stepped inside. No, dammit, it was Lizzy's bar. And he was merely looking out for his niece's interests.

He thought about the little girl as he paused to

let his eyes adjust to the bar's dimness. He hadn't expected to melt inside when he met her, but he'd taken one look at those big, grave eyes, and it had been like his experience with her daddy all over again. He never had been able to keep his distance from Eddie, no matter how hard he'd tried, and he had a feeling it was going to be the same with Lizzy.

When he'd decided to keep his identity a secret, he'd thought it would be simple to watch his niece from a distance. Not only would it cover his own butt in case Eddie had shown Lizzy pictures or talked about him, but it would also save her from having to deal with a relative who was virtually a stranger in the midst of all the other shit she had going on in her life.

It seemed naive in retrospect, but he'd actually thought staying detached would be a piece of cake, even when Veronica had finally shown up and he'd discovered they'd be living in the same house. He hadn't factored in the enticement of Lizzy, though. There was just something about her that drew him every bit as strongly as Eddie ever had.

Voices from the back room snapped him out of his reverie, and he pushed away from the door. A moment later Veronica and her repairman walked into the bar, and ignoring the voice that snidely suggested Aunt Ronnie had some enticements of her own, Coop squared his shoulders and sauntered over to meet her.

5

Veronica watched Coop walk across the bar as if he owned the joint and felt her back stiffen. "What are you doing here?"

"I stopped by to see if you needed help with anything." A pleasant smile curved his lips, but the dark eyes inspecting Kody, the installer from Cascade Air, showed a vigilant sort of curiosity.

Her instinctive reaction was to decline his offer in no uncertain terms, and, in truth, there wasn't anything he could do. She bit back the urge to snap out a knee-jerk no, however. As long as he was the Tonk's manager, she didn't have to be, and as holder of that position, he had a right to know what she planned to do with the bar. So, with a sigh, she excused herself to Kody and, grasping Coop's forearm, led him out of earshot.

She immediately regretted touching him. The layer of velvet-soft pinwale corduroy that kept their flesh from touching didn't do a thing to prevent his body heat from radiating through the plaid fabric, and she was highly aware of the corded strength of his arm beneath her hand.

She was highly aware of him, period. *Too* aware. That had been the problem with this guy from the beginning. And she didn't understand it. She'd never gone for the sulky-mouthed, hard-bodied type — her usual kind of man was cultured and favored Brooks Brothers suits with complementing power ties. Coop probably thought culture was pouring a beer into a stein instead of glugging it straight from the can.

The snideness of that thought produced a twinge of shame. Not only was it amazingly snobbish for someone who'd grown up in a bar, she also had a flash of the *New York Times* on the kitchen table this morning.

Then she shrugged the feeling aside. So, big deal; he read newspapers — and more widely than she did, she'd concede. It didn't make him any more likely to pass up a sporting event for a stroll through a museum. And it was the museumgoers, not the jock types, who had always been the kind of man to rev her motor.

She was still grateful when they reached the bar and she could drop her hand without appearing too anxious. "Okay, here's the deal," she said. "I can't stand the smoke in this place, and I'm having an air purification system put in to suck it out of the air."

"And you didn't think that, as manager, I might be interested in knowing this?" His tone was neutral, and his expression gave nothing away. But his body language as he loomed over her with his arms folded across his chest said, *Explain yourself, missy.* "You haven't even gone

73

over the books yet. What makes you assume the bar can afford it?"

She felt her temper rise, but slapped a lid on it. "You're absolutely correct," she said with hard-won mildness. "I should have told you what I planned to do this morning, and I apologize for my failure to do so. But I'm telling you now. And if the bar can't afford it, then I guess I'll just have to pay for it myself." She almost smiled when he blinked warily, then narrowed his gaze as if trying to ferret out the catch. "I should probably tell you, too, that I'm going over to Franklin's Realty today to put the bar on the market, and I frankly hope the new air system will increase its value. But even if it doesn't, I can't stand the way everything from my hair to my underwear stinks to high heaven when I leave here. And I don't like the idea of Lizzy smelling it on me. It seems hypocritical to try to teach her not to smoke herself, then come home every night smelling like the bottom of an ashtray."

Coop examined her statement from every conceivable angle, but couldn't find fault with it. Which was not to say he trusted her any farther than he could lob her. He cocked an eyebrow at her. "Gonna take the money and run, sugarplum?"

"No, *stud-biscuit,* I'm going to take the money and stick it in a trust account for my niece. But you've got the second part right. The instant this place sells, I'm packing up Lizzy and making a break for it. And I'm not looking back until we hit the city limits. Not that *that'll* take more than five minutes."

He wasn't crazy about the idea of her uprooting Lizzy, since his niece would simply have to turn right around and come back once Eddie was exonerated. But since he was hardly in a position to say so, he gave her a clipped nod. "Fair enough. So long as you don't shirk your obligation to the Tonk in the meantime."

"Actually, that brings up another point." She stood ramrod straight in front of him, her shoulders back and the elegant curve of her chin elevated. "It occurs to me that I never got around to setting up a work schedule with you last night. Now, I'm perfectly willing to have you dictate my days off, but don't plan on me starting work any night before nine o'clock."

Christ Almighty. He'd had drill instructors who weren't half the control freak this woman was, and gazing down at her determined little jaw and cool green eyes, he had the strongest urge to muss her up a little, if only to drive that bossy look from her face. She was so friggin' tidy. Her glossy black hair was obviously the product of a pricey cut, for it fell sleekly into place without so much as a strand out of order. He got a quick image of the way it had been this morning, though — all rumpled from sleep and looking as if she'd just rolled out of bed after a hot bout of down-and-dirty sex.

Well, give him twenty minutes and he could make her look like that for real.

That straightened him up in a hurry. Damn, where had *that* come from? It was probably just one of those guy responses to a woman trying to dictate terms. If you can't beat 'em, roll 'em around under the covers until they understand who's boss.

He didn't need to establish his jurisdiction through sex, though, tempting as the notion might be. He was the manager of this joint, and that was all the authority he needed.

"You're a regular little four-star general, aren't you?" Reaching out, he pulled a tendril of her hair out of place and rearranged it against her cheek, his lips curving upward in amusement when she smacked his hand aside and impatiently brushed the strand back in place. Shoving his hands deep into his pockets in an attempt to ignore the way his fingertips seemed to retain the feel of that sleek, satiny texture, he fixed his best don't-screw-with-me expression on his face. "But *I* make the schedule around here, sugar, not you. And if I need you at the Tonk before nine, you'll damn well make yourself available."

"You think so?" Facing off with him, she drew herself up. "Well, I've got news for you, Blackstock. You can beat your hairy chest until the dogs come home —"

"Cows," Coop corrected. When Veronica gave him a blank look, he elucidated, "The expression is 'until the *cows* come home.' "

"Dogs, cows — whatever. Unless it's an emergency, I still don't plan on being there before nine." Then she surprised him by sagging slightly and shoving her fingers through her hair. The action revealed a pucker of worry between her slender black eyebrows. "More than anything else right now," she said, "Lizzy needs stability in her life. With Crystal d-dead and her dad a fugitive, I'm all the family she's got left. Well, except for a stepbrother or half-brother, or some such shirttail relation of Eddie's. But I don't even know the man's name, let alone how to get hold of him, and he's obviously not all that worried about Lizzy's welfare, or he'd have called to see how she's doing."

Coop winced, but Veronica waved the statement aside as if it were of no consequence. "The point is: I admit I don't know beans about parenting, but it seems to me that the most important thing I can do is be there for her as much as possible during her waking hours. I wanted to find a professional to help her deal with the fact that her father's been accused of murdering her mother, but Fossil isn't exactly a hotbed for child psychologists. So I'm not leaving for work until she's tucked in and settled for the night." Her chin racheted up in determination as she gave him a level look. "Work around it, Cooper. The bar rarely gets busy before nine, anyhow."

"All right."

Veronica blinked, then narrowed her eyes. "That was almost too easy. So why does it make me suspicious as all get-out?"

"Beats the hell outta me, sweetpea. But if it

makes you feel better, I agreed because you made a valid argument. As long as it's for the kid, you'll get no argument from me. Start tossing your weight around just because you can, though, and you'll find yourself looking for a new bartender faster than you can say Sex On The Beach."

"Why would I want to say that? Oh! That's a drink, right?"

Coop merely gave her a heavy-lidded look, a smile of satisfaction tugging up the corners of his mouth when he saw her immediately bristle.

Then she brandished a smile so sweet it raised all sorts of warning flags. "And as long as you're being such a reasonable guy, I should probably also inform you that I plan to run a background check on you."

He'd actually been thinking he might have misjudged her, but her little bombshell exploded that fantasy in a hurry. "As in a *police* check?" he demanded. "The hell you say!" He stepped forward, looming over her.

She tilted her head back and looked him straight in the eye. "I'll tell you the truth, Cooper: I don't honestly believe you'd ever harm Lizzy. But you're a strange man living in the same house with a six-year-old girl, and I'll be damned if I'll risk her safety on a gut feeling. My gut's been wrong before. So I'm telling you straight out, I'm going to make certain you don't have an arrest record. And if I find out you do, you're going to find yourself out on the street so fast your head will spin — and the lease be damned."

He couldn't fault her reasoning, but that didn't stop him from feeling insulted right down to the bone. He was an honest man. Hell, he was an ex-Marine — he'd spent thirteen years of his life keeping this country safe for people like her. He didn't take kindly to her thinking he might be some pervert who'd prey on little girls.

With a sound of disgust, he turned on his heel and headed for the door.

Veronica's heart tried to climb into her throat as she watched him go. It was her obligation to protect Lizzy, and running a background check on Coop was just good sense.

"Veronica?"

She turned to see Kody walking up with his clipboard.

"I've got your estimate ready," he said. "You have a minute to sit down with me and go over it?"

She thought of the offended anger she'd seen in Coop's eyes and — more unnerving yet — a glimpse of something that had almost looked like . . . hurt.

Then she shook her head and turned her attention back to Kody. *Don't be an idiot. A Sherman tank couldn't hurt that guy.* "Yes, sure," she said. "Let's grab a seat over here and you can tell me what the damage is going to be."

A red mist hazed Coop's usual cool and logical

reasoning process while he stalked down the street, and he all but ripped the driver's door off its hinges getting into his car. He slammed it shut behind him, started the car, then peeled away from the curb. Heading out of town, he picked up the interstate just beyond the Big K, stomping the accelerator to the floor the instant his car's back wheels cleared the freeway on-ramp. He punched on the CD player, cranked up the volume, and blasted down the highway, speakers wailing and engine screaming.

The car roared through dun-colored, snow-dusted hills and brown flatlands, past apple orchards that hosted row after row of skeletal trees. He blew past nondescript little burgs of cinderblock buildings, and didn't slow down until the skies suddenly opened up about fifteen miles out of town. Then, turning the windshield wipers onto their highest setting and the defroster to full blast to dissipate the rapidly fogging glass, he took the next exit, got back on the freeway heading north, and put the pedal to the metal once again.

The rain poured down in sheets, and a few miles south of Fossil the car hit a patch of standing water and hydroplaned along its surface. The back end fishtailed as Coop fought to gain purchase on the road beneath, and easing up on the gas, he wrested back control of the car and immediately slowed down. No sense killing himself because Veronica Davis had a suspicious mind.

He didn't know why it bugged him so much — in a faraway corner of his mind, he actually applauded her caution. She seemed to be doing whatever she could to protect Lizzy, and who could argue with that? Except . . .

He'd worked damn hard to command a measure of respect in his life. God knew his own mother had never thought he'd amount to anything, and he'd worked his ass off to prove her wrong and become the type of man he could be proud of. He sure as hell didn't appreciate being lumped in with pedophiles and who the hell knew what else.

But there was no sense brooding over it. It was high time, in fact, that he quit thinking about little Miz Davis entirely. During his brief sojourn at the Tonk, he'd gleaned bits and pieces of information on Crystal's murder. He'd also heard some of the popularly believed reasons why Eddie fit the bill as prime suspect. But he hadn't learned nearly as much as he'd hoped to, and he sure hadn't learned anything that would clear Eddie's name. It was time to step up his efforts.

Coop drove to Fossil's small downtown business section and pulled into a neatly paved lot. Then he simply sat for a moment, listening to the rain bounce with a tinny patter against the car roof as he stared up at the cantilevered angles of a fifties-style redwood structure. A discreet sign above the entrance read FOSSIL PROFESSIONAL BUILDING.

Exhaling vigorously to settle the sudden tension that twanged warnings along the nerve endings down his spine, he collected his checkbook from the glove compartment and climbed out of the car. He quickly locked up and dashed through the pounding rain. Damn, it was cold! He should have worn a coat.

A moment later he stopped in front of a door that read NEIL PEAVY, ATTORNEY AT LAW, and shook himself off like a wet dog. He dried his hand against a protected section of the black T-shirt he wore under his plaid shirt, then reached for the handle.

A soft bell pinged overhead when he pushed the door open, and a young woman looked up from behind the counter. She gave him a practiced smile. "Good morning, sir. May I help you?"

Coop crossed plush charcoal carpeting to the curved mauve and gray reception counter. "My name is Cooper Blackstock," he said. "I'd like to see Mr. Peavy."

"Do you have an appointment?"

"No. But if he doesn't have time to see me today, perhaps I could make one."

She picked up a telephone receiver and paused with her finger poised over the intercom button. "May I tell him what this is in regards to, Mr. Blackstock?"

"I'd rather take that up with him, if you don't mind."

Her professional smile didn't falter and, giving him a nod, she depressed the button beneath her finger. "Mr. Peavy," she said a moment later. "There's a Mr. Blackstock here to see you. Yes, sir, Cooper Blackstock." She listened for a moment, then said, "No, sir. He doesn't have an ap— Uh-huh. Uh-huh. Very good, sir."

She reseated the receiver and looked up at Coop. "He has a conference call scheduled with a client in a moment, but if you don't mind waiting, he said he could give you part of his lunch hour."

"Thank you. I appreciate it." Coop flopped down on an uncomfortable gray upholstered Eames-style chair and picked up the first magazine that came to hand. He flipped through its pages without absorbing much more than a vague impression that half its content seem to feature rich recipes while the other half was devoted to dieting tips.

"Mr. Blackstock?"

He looked up to see the receptionist extending a clipboard over the counter.

"I need to get some billing information, please."

He got up and filled out the form. Taking a seat once again, he picked up another periodical.

This one turned out to be an older issue of *Time* magazine, and he found an article that sparked an idea in his mind. It kept him absorbed until a door to the side of the counter opened and the receptionist stuck her head out. "Mr. Peavy will see you now."

Coop made a note of the magazine's date and

issue number and rose to follow her into the heart of the office suite.

She stopped in front of a closed door down the hall a moment later and gave it a quiet tap. They were invited in by a male voice. The receptionist opened the door, then stood back for Coop to enter. She pulled it closed as soon as he'd passed through, and a man who looked to be in his early forties rose from behind an oak desk to greet him.

"Mr. Blackstock, I'm Neil Peavy." His brown hair was receding, but he looked fit beneath his expensively cut suit and had the subtly pampered sheen of a man who takes care of himself. Leaning across the desk, he extended an immaculately manicured hand. They shook, then Peavy waved a hand at the chair that faced his desk. "Please. Sit down." He resumed his own seat. "Tell me what I can do for you."

Coop took the seat indicated and met the lawyer's gaze. "You can give me some information about Eddie Chapman's case."

The man's face closed down. "What are you, a reporter? If so, you should know better than to ask me to divulge privileged communications." He rose to his feet. "Now, if that's all . . ."

Coop stretched his feet out in front of him, casually crossed one ankle over the other, and settled more firmly in his seat. "I'm not a reporter, Mr. Peavy. I'm —" *Nothing I'm about to just blurt out without a few safeguards in place.* He fished his checkbook out of the back pocket of his jeans.

"Look. Let me write you a retainer."

Peavy's eyebrows drew together. "Why would you want to do that?"

"Because I'm looking for the same confidentiality you claim for Chapman. I need the assurance that what we discuss here will be privileged."

Coop could see the lawyer was torn, but as he'd hoped, Peavy's curiosity won out. He gave a clipped nod. "All right."

"Will five hundred cover it?"

When the attorney agreed it would, Coop wrote out the check, ripped it out of the checkbook, and offered it to Peavy.

Neil Peavy set it down on the gleaming desk in front of him, then leaned his weight on his hands and looked at Coop. "Okay, what's this all about?"

"Eddie Chapman is my brother."

Anger sparked in the lawyer's eyes. "I don't know what your game is, Mr. Blackstock, but I think you'd better leave. Eddie Chapman is an only child."

"My half-brother, I should have said." Coop shrugged without apology for the miscommunication. He and Eddie might have had only sporadic contact over the course of their lives, but they'd always considered themselves brothers — and never mind the legal qualifications. "Eddie's the only child of Thomas Chapman, but before Chapman came into her life our mother was married to Dave Blackstock."

Neil slowly resumed his seat. "All right. I'll accept that. But I'm still not certain what it is you want from me. The lawyer-client confidentiality still applies — I can't discuss what he said to me."

"I already know Eddie's innocent," Coop said. "So I have no need to ask if he admitted any wrongdoing to you. I'm merely trying to figure out what caused him to take off."

"I wish I knew." Neil spread his fingers against his desktop and studied his buffed nails. Then he looked up at Coop. "The case against him wasn't all that compelling. He was pursuing custody of his daughter through the legal system and had a very decent shot at attaining it, so in spite of what the DA's office implied, that particular battle was no motive. Eddie and Crystal had a public fight at the Tonk the night of her murder, but they'd had arguments before. The only trace evidence in this case came from his leather jacket, not from him, and he had a habit of forgetting it everywhere he went, so *anyone* could have been wearing it. Hell, he even left it here once. There wasn't a lick of DNA to tie him to the crime, and no one witnessed him with the deceased after they left the bar, let alone saw him wrap his hands around her throat and strangle her." A vein began to thump in Neil's temple and a flush suffused his face, and shooting Coop an apologetic look, he waved a dismissive hand.

"I'm sorry. This gets me hot under the collar every time I think about it. The DA's evidence was circumstantial, and we had a good chance at an acquittal. Eddie was out on bail and doing okay, but when the judge determined there was probable cause for a trial, he ran. Nothing suggests guilt to law enforcement agencies or prospective jurors quite so fast as that does."

"He must have panicked." Coop straightened in his seat. "Can you think of any reason he might have done that?"

The lawyer shook his head. "No, I'm sorry. I don't have a clue. If he'd just sat tight, everything probably would've been over by now."

"Well, one way or the other I plan to find out what's going on," Coop said and climbed to his feet.

Neil rose, too, and offered his hand. "I wish you luck," he said as they shook. "And if you learn anything, I'd appreciate it if you'd let me know."

"I'll do that. And if you think of anything else that might help shed light on this, I'm at the Tonk most nights." Coop smiled crookedly at the attorney's raised eyebrow. "As the bartender and manager, not a patron."

Neil's return smile was avuncular. "That's good to hear. I must make it a point to drop by for a beer some night." He picked Coop's check up off the polished surface of his desk and held it out. "Here. We didn't spend enough time to justify this."

"Bill me for the time I was here and put the rest on account," Coop said. "I'll probably have other questions for you, and I was serious about wanting what we discuss to be privileged. The fewer people who know about my relationship to Eddie, the better chance there is that the real killer will screw up or someone will let something slip."

Neil shrugged as if he had his doubts, but set the check back on the desktop anyway. "All right." He escorted Coop to the door.

The rain was letting up a little when Coop let himself out of the building a few moments later. His visit hadn't turned out to be as informative as he had hoped, but it was a start. He'd just have to keep digging.

Because perseverance counted. And sooner or later, something was bound to shake loose.

6

Veronica finished the last of the sketches she was doing on spec for a prospective client and added them to the letter and estimate she'd put together earlier. She slid everything into an addressed manila envelope, sealed it up, and set it aside to take to the post office the next time she went out.

She stopped in the archway to the living room a moment later and stared at the jumble of gold, gold, and more gold that covered every horizontal surface. It was a good thing the day had turned rainy, she thought wryly, because she'd probably go blind if a stray ray of sunshine ever found its way in here. She shook her head, wondering how on earth two sisters could have such disparate tastes and wondering just where to begin the process of clearing all this stuff out.

She'd already removed Crystal's ticky-tackies from her bedroom, and her reasons for wanting to purge the rest of the house were threefold. First and foremost, her minimalist soul hated the garish clutter, and she was pretty sure if she had to live with it for any length of time she'd end up going postal on everyone. Her politically correct justification, however, and the story she was sticking to should anyone bother to ask, was that it was highly unlikely she'd find a buyer for the house looking the way it did now.

Third, you could barely turn around without knocking something over, so where was Lizzy supposed to play? If the oppressive tastelessness didn't smother the tiny bit of lightheartedness the child had left in her, the sheer number of breakables would surely conspire with little-kid awkwardness to sabotage her ability to navigate the room without coming to grief.

But what if Lizzy *hated* the idea of her aunt making changes to her mother's house? Abruptly overwhelmed by all the responsibilities in her life, Veronica found herself suddenly unable to catch her breath. Panicking, she struggled to draw oxygen into her lungs, but the harder she tried, the more impossible it seemed to become.

Recognizing in a distant corner of her mind that she was hyperventilating, she turned back into the kitchen and grabbed a paper lunch bag out of the bottom drawer. She slid down to sit cross-legged on the floor and shook the bag open; then, bracing her elbows on her knees, she clamped the opening over her mouth and nose as she frantically inhaled and exhaled into the sack.

Oh, God, how on earth had it come to this? She'd forged a good life for herself. She had her career, which was just beginning to enjoy a measure of success, her friends in the city, suave men to escort her to the type of events she liked to attend, and the occasional weekend with her niece, where she got all of the fun of parenting without the commitment.

How had she ended up back in Fossil, working in a bar she'd labored so hard to escape, living in a house whose furnishings made her grind her teeth, and acting as a full-time parent?

Good grief, Davis, you're not the one with the big problems here. When did you turn into such a whiner? Hoping the paper bag had done its job, she lowered it experimentally, then climbed up off the floor.

Enough of the poor-pitiful-me's, appealing as a nice, satisfying wallow might be. It was fruit-less to ask *how* these things had come to pass — the changes were simply a fact of her life and she'd have to adapt to them. There was too much to be done.

She located a cardboard box and faced the living room once again, trying to decide where to start.

She was still vacillating when the back door opened and Cooper strolled in. He walked right up behind her and bent his head until his lips almost touched her ear. "Admiring the glow from all that gold?" His body heat at her back and his warm breath traveling the whorls of her ear sent goose bumps skittering down her right side.

"Absolutely." She turned to face him, forcing herself not to give him the satisfaction of taking the giant step backward she so longed to take. What *was* it about this guy, anyway? Every time he drew near, her skin went all itchy and her hormones started doing the "La Cucaracha."

He glanced past her into the living room. "Your sister sure had interesting taste. Thai cathouses don't use this much glitter."

"You'd know, I'm sure." And she didn't *even* want to contemplate the images that brought to mind. "But don't tell me you don't *like* this." Touching her fingertips to her chest, she gave him a big-eyed look of feigned amazement. "Why, I simply can't imagine. Can you honestly look me in the eye and say you don't find it positively spectacular?"

His gaze zoomed in on her, and for just a second she lost her place. There was a sudden intensity in the depths of his eyes that seemed to make the planes of his cheekbones even sharper than usual.

Then she blinked and gave herself a mental shake. "Did I mention I was an interior decorator? Not that it takes a trained professional to see this room is special, of course." She gave him a vacuous look and heaved a melodramatic sigh. "I just *adore* glitter. It's my life."

His dark-eyed gaze tracked over her from head to foot. "You know, I think I would have guessed that, just from the way you dress."

She looked down at her black sweater, khakis, and black ballerina flats. What was wrong with the way she dressed? Just because it wasn't flashy didn't mean it was dull.

He tapped the box she held against her hip.

"And I suppose your crate here is for . . . ?"

"Why, holding whatever treasures I select for my personal use, of course." Veronica stepped into the room, swept up a particularly atrocious knickknack, and held it up for Coop's perusal. "Isn't this just the *sweetest?*" She dumped it in the cardboard box and selected another, and then another yet. "Gosh, I sure hope I don't clear the entire room. I can be *such* a little greedy guts." She would never in a bazillion years admit this, but his presence actually made the process of packing up much easier.

Within moments, she had a jam-packed box and was beginning to see daylight on the couch, coffee table, and two end tables. She glanced up at Coop, who had propped a wide shoulder against the curved molding of the archway and made himself right at home. "I've reserved the cream of the crop for Lizzy and me, of course, but, please feel free to select something for yourself." She gave him her most innocent look. "You look like the type to enjoy a good bullfight — or to at least sling your fair share of bull — so perhaps the velvet painting of the matador? It has that lovely rococo frame."

He couldn't quite disguise his horror as he looked at the picture in question. But when he looked back at her, a wry smile pulled up one corner of his mouth. "That's mighty kind of you," he said. "But I wouldn't dream of depriving you of such a rare gem." He cocked an eyebrow at her. "And that's no bull."

She actually laughed aloud. Then she glanced down at the photograph she'd picked up to add to the box and went breathless for the second time that afternoon, as a thousand memories slammed through her.

Coop watched the humor that had lit up her face abruptly snuff out and wondered what had happened. He told himself he didn't really want to know. Hell, he hadn't meant to get sucked into her orbit again, but she was like some damn magnet, and whenever he found himself any-where in her vicinity, he ended up drawn in. If he was smart, he'd turn around and walk away right now.

Instead, he tilted his head to see the photo-graph in her hand. "Is that your dad?"

"Yeah." She rubbed her thumb over the like-ness of the dark-haired, laughing man in the pic-ture. "He died two years ago."

"Aw, I'm sorry — it's tough to lose a parent. My dad died when I was fifteen and my mother about four years ago." To drive the sad, defeated look from her face he pointed at a worn-looking woman caught in the act of swabbing down the bar in the background. "Who's this, a former barmaid?"

"Oh, God. Close." She emitted a brittle laugh. "My mother."

"Oh. I'm sorry. It — that is, I just thought —"

"What anyone would have thought, so don't worry about it." Her voice held a cynical sort of dryness, but when she gazed down at the framed

94

photo and her eyebrows gathered over the slender arch of her nose, it looked like she was in pain. "Mama worked herself into an early grave and Daddy let her. No, worse than that — he encouraged it because he thought it was her *job* to make his life easier. His, naturally, was to party with the clients and pour drinks. Mama worked her fingers to the bone trying to keep all the rest of it together." Veronica wedged the framed photo into a tiny space in the corner of the box she'd placed on the couch. Then she simply stood there for a moment, staring at the overflowing container.

Her bent head exposed her nape and Coop had to stuff his hands into his front pockets to keep from reaching out to touch it. "And you resented him for that?" he asked a little testily.

"Some. Mostly I resented *her* for allowing it. Mama could have put her foot down anytime during all those years, but she never did." She shrugged and turned to face him. "All I know is, I'm never going to carry some man on my back, and if I ever do fall in love, it'll be with someone who treats me as an equal partner and carries his own weight."

"I imagine your dad must have been pretty lost when she died, though." Now, where the hell had that come from? He didn't know the first thing about her father or what the man had felt when his wife died. Yet somehow he had the crazy-ass urge to offer Veronica comfort.

Rocking back on his heels, he added cynically,

95

"He had to have missed all the work that was no longer getting done, if nothing else."

Veronica made a skeptical sound. "He missed her cleaning/bartending/waitressing skills, for sure. But he thought Crystal and I would be thrilled to step in and assume Mama's responsibilities at the Tonk."

Coop snorted. "I can just imagine your reaction to that. I bet you told him to stuff it, huh?"

"Not exactly. I worked the Tonk until I graduated from college."

"You're kidding, right?"

"My relationship with Daddy wasn't exactly simple," she said defensively. "I loved him; I resented him. And I guess you're right — he *was* sort of lost after Mama died, and probably for more reasons than the loss of the work she did. I mean, he loved her — I know he did. He just never seemed to notice that she was killing herself in order to keep everything running smooth for him." Veronica picked up a fussy little porcelain shepherdess but paused with her hand suspended over the box to look up at him. "He wasn't a bad man — I don't want you getting the wrong idea. He was the worst sort of chauvinist, but he was also funny and warm . . . and he was my father. He just never understood the first thing about me or what I wanted."

He moved nearer. "Did he understand your sister?"

She garbled a laugh. "Oh, yeah. Those two were peas in a pod. Crystal loved the Tonk, too, and she was a regular chip off the old block."

"How's that?"

"She loved to party as much as Daddy did. And she, too, had a talent for getting away with the least amount of work possible."

"How about you? Did you —"

The back door banged open and his question was swallowed up in the sudden cacophony as Lizzy blew in, trailed by a curly-haired blonde who was about her size and a lanky boy who looked to be a couple of years older. Given their noise level, it took Coop a moment or two to sort out just who was whom in this little party. But once he had, he saw that it was the other two kids who provided all the hullabaloo. Lizzy was her usual quiet self, but she smiled as she listened to her friends and stroked the fluffy kitten she had tucked up under her chin and clutched against her pea-jacket-covered chest.

"Oh, please," Veronica whispered hollowly as she stared at Lizzy and the little cat. "Please, *please*, let this not be what I think it is. That's *all* I need."

Coop had a feeling she was pleading a lost cause, for Lizzy's face lit up the moment she spotted them through the archway. "Aunt Ronnie, Coop! Lookit what Mrs. Martelucchi gave me when I walked by her house from the bus! She said I could keep him if it was okay with you." Hope shone in her eyes. "He's six months old, so he's potty-trained and everything. He goes outside, so we wouldn't have to buy him a litter box."

"Damn," Veronica said under her breath, and Coop marveled that so much vehemence could be so nearly inaudible. Her lips barely moved. "Damn, damn, damn." Then she sighed and, raising her voice, said, "Okay."

"I can *keep* him?"

"Sure, why not? Riley, close the door, honey, so he doesn't get out. He'll need to get used to being here. Have you and Dessa met Mr. Blackstock? Coop, you've met Marissa Travits; these are her children."

"Hey, Mr. Blackstock," Dessa and Riley said almost simultaneously, then grinned at each other and bumped shoulders.

"Call me Coop," Coop said and exchanged pleased-to-meet-yous with both kids.

Veronica crossed the room and plucked the kitten out of Lizzy's arms and held it up until they were nose to nose. The cat had medium-long hair and was solid black except for a white blaze on his chest and one white paw, which he batted at Veronica's cheek. He looked at her through coppery eyes the size of pennies. "What's his name?"

"Boo. For some guy named Boo Radley, Mrs. Martelucchi said." Indifferently, Lizzy shrugged the shoulder that emerged from her jacket as she peeled off the garment. "I don't think he lives in the neighborhood."

A sound of choked laughter rattled in Veronica's throat and Coop grinned.

"If I had a cat," Riley interjected, "I'd name it

98

Booger, or Spike, or something phat like that."

"Fat?" Coop said blankly.

"Spelled with a *ph*," Veronica interpreted. "P-h-a-t. It means cool. Rad." She flashed a sudden smile. "Groovy."

"Ahhh." He found himself grinning back. "Why do I suddenly feel so old?"

Riley shrugged, as if that ought to be obvious. But Lizzy stepped forward and gave Coop's hand a shy pat. "It's just 'cause you don't have any kids of your own," she assured him. Then she blinked. "*Do* you?"

"No," he said and caught Veronica smirking at the haste with which he'd denied it. He narrowed his eyes at her.

Then Lizzy noticed the box of knickknacks and a little frown furrowed her brow. She looked at Veronica. "Are you getting rid of all my mama's pretties?"

"Is that what she called these?" Veronica asked. "Her pretties?"

Lizzy nodded. "Mama says we're not s'posta touch 'em."

"I'm just packing them up safely so you'll have room to play in here without worrying about breaking anything." Veronica squatted down in front of her niece. "Is that okay with you?"

Lizzy hiked her shoulders. "I guess."

"Because I'll put it all back, if it's not."

"No, that's okay."

Veronica brushed back the little girl's bangs. "Would you like to go through the boxes when

I'm done and pick out a few of your favorites for your room?"

Interest sparked in Lizzy's golden brown eyes. "Could I?"

"Yeah. You bet."

"C'mon," Riley said. "Let's go upstairs and play Pirate King."

Dessa jostled her brother. "I getta be king this time!"

"Nuh-uh! You're just a girl. You hafta be a *boy* to be king."

"Then I'll be Pirate *Queen!*"

Riley made a rude noise. "Did I ask you to play Pirate Queen? You can be the stowaway girl who pretends to be the cabin boy." Without awaiting a response, he spun back into the kitchen and led the charge up the back stairway.

Dessa's blond curls seemed to take on the electricity of her indignation. "I don't wanna be the cabin boy again! He always ends up walkin' the plank!" She charged after him and Lizzy paused only long enough to shoot a shy smile at Coop and collect the kitten from Veronica, then pattered up the stairs in her friends' wake.

Coop grinned at Veronica. "You realize, don't you, that you'll have to explain *To Kill a Mockingbird* to her? And somebody ought to teach Riley never to say 'just a girl' to a girl. That's begging for trouble."

She laughed in delighted accord, and he felt confused. He'd been so sure he knew exactly who Veronica Davis was — his image of her had been firmly entrenched in his mind before they'd ever met. Yet every time he saw her with Lizzy, her actions seemed in direct contradiction to the image ingrained in his brain.

Not that he trusted her. Little Miss Ronnie might not wear skin-tight jeans and trowel on the makeup; and she might not go for that sexy, big-hair look, or flirt at the drop of a hat with anyone sporting the equipment to rise to the occasion. But she utilized her sexuality every bit as much as her more obvious sister had done. He didn't know how she did it, but she sure as shit projected *something* that drew a man in. He'd seen it with the air filtration guy this morning. He'd felt it himself.

So no, he didn't trust her; he was no fool. But he might be wrong about her commitment to his niece.

Looking down at her, he demanded, "Why did it take you so long to get here to take care of Lizzy?" Immediately he could have kicked himself. Her reasons had nothing to do with him, so why did he care one way or the other?

He squared his shoulders. He cared because of Lizzy. That was all. But still he squirmed a little, if only mentally, when Veronica stared at him as if he'd lost his mind.

"I'm not sure why you would think that's any of your business," she said slowly. "But Marissa didn't know how to contact me in Scotland, so I didn't learn about Crystal's death until I got back to Seattle late Sunday night. The second I did, I cleared my calendar so I could be here with Lizzy until I can get the Tonk and the house sold and clear up Crystal's estate."

The kids came pounding back down the stairs. "Aunt Ronnie," Lizzy called in her soft little voice, "can we have some cookies?"

Veronica walked into the kitchen to meet them. "Sure. You all know where the cookie jar is. Milk's in the fridge." She tousled Riley's hair as he headed for the table with the now-lidless cookie jar tucked under his arm, stuffing a cookie into his mouth as he went. "Use a glass, bud. We're a family of girls here — we don't like to see washback in our milk."

He grinned at her, showing a mouthful of half-masticated cookie, then plunked down the jar and reached for the cup Lizzy brought over. "Okeydoke. Is it okay if I go see my friend Brad after our snack? He just lives on the other side of the Sooper Save."

"Why don't you call him up and see if he can come here to play, instead?" Veronica picked a cookie out of the jar and took a nibble. "Then we'll find out what your mom has to say about future visits, okay?"

Riley heaved a long-suffering sigh. "Okay."

Coop grabbed a cookie for himself, then excused himself from the little group and headed out. But as he climbed the shallow concrete steps of the Andrew Carnegie–built library a short while later, he couldn't seem to get Veronica's interaction with the kids out of his head.

It was just his bad luck that he was a sucker for a woman with a maternal streak. His own mother hadn't possessed one, so women who were good with kids just did something to him. His heart beat a little too fast and his gut churned uneasily as he pulled open one of the library's big double doors.

You happy now, bud? It's been tough enough keeping your hands off her when you thought she was a selfish bitch and a lousy surrogate parent.

What the hell are you gonna do now?

Moments after Coop disappeared into the library, a man drove past the Tonk. As always when he passed by, he felt compelled to slow down and give the juke joint a quick appraisal. Not that the deed that kept him cruising by had been done anywhere near here, but this was where everything had started that evening, and therefore held a compelling attraction for him. When the car behind him honked impatiently, he resumed a normal speed. And smiled in satisfaction.

For he'd committed the perfect crime, hadn't he? He'd killed Crystal Davis and no one was the wiser, due to his quick thinking when he'd cleverly pinned it on Eddie Chapman. *Hey, hey, hey, Boo Boo.*

He laughed aloud, because the old cartoon phrase was his own private mantra. He'd always been smarter than the average bear.

Not that he'd actually planned to kill Crystal.

But what the hell — plans change. It was her own damn fault she was dead, anyhow. He'd given her every opportunity to cease and desist, but had she listened? Oh, no. She'd just had to keep pushing him.

Well, no Baker Street bimbo threatened to ruin him — he didn't care if she could suck the chrome off a bumper hitch. He'd spent too many years and labored too long building his reputation in this town to allow some avaricious slut with a vendetta get away with pulling that down around his ears.

She'd gotten just what she'd deserved. And hell, it wasn't as if he'd *enjoyed* it or anything. He did appreciate his own adroit thinking, though, and he knew if he could tell anyone, they, too, would have to admit he'd acted brilliantly when he'd arranged the suspicion to fall on Chapman.

So yes, indeed, Boo Boo.

He was definitely smarter than your average-type bear.

7

Coop so seldom used his cell phone that he tended to forget he even had one. So when it rousted him from a deep sleep late Friday morning, he reached over to the nightstand and slapped at the off button on the alarm clock, thinking that was where the sound originated. The phone rang again, and he pushed up onto his elbow. "Oh, for —" He snatched the phone off the nightstand, flipped down the mouthpiece, and punched the talk button. "Yeah!"

"Coop? Steve Parrish here. Did Margery get hold of you?"

"No, why? Has she been trying?"

"For two days now. She called me first thing this morning to find out if I knew where you were. Damn, big guy, isn't the purpose of having a cell phone to make yourself available anytime, anywhere?"

"That's the popular theory, anyhow." Coop tossed his pillow against the headboard and sat up, resting his back against it. Steve was his literary agent and Margery Kellerman his editor. He'd spent thirteen years seeing every hot spot in the world, courtesy of the U.S. Marines, and had kept journals of his experiences as point man in a reconnaissance squad in C Company of the Second Recon Battalion. Somewhere along the way he'd begun to jot down ideas for a book based on his knowledge, and that had led to scribbling chapters in spiral notebooks, which had eventually led to the purchase of a computer and a completed manuscript. He'd then shopped it around to several agents, and felt like he'd hit the jackpot when Steve, who'd been his number one choice, was interested in representing his work. A few months after signing on with the Parrish Agency, his military-techno-thriller had been put up for auction in a bidding war between publishers, and fourteen months after that, his alter ego, James Lee Cooper, had exploded onto the bestseller lists and quickly became a name to be reckoned with.

A cold draft whispered across Coop's bare shoulders and he yanked up the blankets. "What'd Margery want?"

"To report some good news. Two bits of good news, actually. *The Eagle Flies* is going back to press for another ten thousand copies, and it's generating renewed interest in *Cause for Alarm*, so that's going back, too, for another seventy-five hundred. Your wholesalers' book-signing tour obviously paid off. Newsgroup and Levy both put in hefty reorders."

"No kidding? That's great."

"Yeah, I thought you'd like it. Break out a bottle or two of the good beer. It might not be as exciting as the times you've hit the *New York*

Times list, but it's definitely worth celebrating."

Coop thought about that after they'd concluded their call. Between his jarhead training, which had taught him to keep his eyes open and his mouth shut, and an admittedly knee-jerk reaction to his mother's interminable one-is-what-one-does-for-a-living, keeping his own counsel had become such a way of life that he'd carried it over into his new professional existence as well. Although his career was hardly a secret, neither was it something he talked about to every Tom, Dick, and Harry on the street. He believed in keeping a low profile.

But he'd always had Eddie to call at times like these, and until this moment had never fully realized just how much he'd come to rely on that. Eddie was eternally generous in his praise of Coop's accomplishments, and his obvious pride had made Coop feel ten feet tall. More importantly, his little brother made him feel as if he were still part of a family — and frankly, news like this just wasn't the same without someone to share it with.

Coop threw back the covers and climbed out of bed, swearing beneath his breath when his warm feet came into contact with the freezing, uneven oak plank floor. He'd been extremely fortunate: Unlike so many writers who barely eked out enough to keep body and soul together, he was making a very decent living. Part of that could be attributed to good timing — he was lucky enough to have hit upon a period in publishing when the books he burned to write were also those for which the reading public currently had an insatiable hunger. Not to mention that he had a supportive publisher who knew how to take full advantage of the fact and a savvy agent who had the ability to get the best deal for his client. Most likely even Mom would have been impressed.

Yet frustration marred what should have been an exciting time. His brother was in a mess clear up to his eyeballs, and Coop had a load of guilt to live with, knowing that the book-signing tour, which had precipitated his back-to-press good fortune, was the very reason Eddie hadn't been able to contact him when he'd needed his help the most. And hell, perhaps if he'd made more of an effort in recent years to come see Eddie in Fossil instead of waiting until his brother's infrequent business trips had brought him to his part of the country, he'd be in a better position to offer some comfort to Lizzy now. Eddie had been a much better brother to him than he'd been to Eddie.

Hearing a faint scritching at the attic door, Coop silently loped down the stairs and yanked it open. Lizzy's little cat Boo leaped back with a hiss, his black fur standing on end.

Coop squatted down. "Hey, little guy. Did I startle you?"

Boo stalked past him up the stairs and Coop grinned. "Looking for some company, huh? And you've decided I'm better than nothing, I take it.

I get that attitude a lot around here." He grabbed his jeans and pulled them on as Boo explored his room. The cat attacked shadows and showed the shoelaces of Coop's desert boots who was boss, then pounced on the dangling sleeve of his sweater when Coop pulled the garment out of a drawer.

Scooping Boo up in his free hand, Coop extricated the cat's claws from the fine-gauge red wool. Then he gently lobbed the little feline onto the middle of the bed and pulled the sweater on over his head. When he sat down next to the animal to don his shoes and socks a moment later, Boo promptly climbed into his lap, turned in a circle, kneaded what felt like a dozen needle-sharp claws into his jeans, then collapsed in a sprawl along his thigh. A low, gravelly sound like a cement mixer amalgamating its load rumbled in his throat.

The homey sound and comforting warmth reminded Coop that since his arrival in Fossil, he'd neglected one of the few real friendships he could claim. Glancing at his stainless steel watch, he reached for the phone. It was nearly three p.m. North Carolina time, so if Zach was in-country he ought to be off duty by now. Coop punched in a phone number he knew by heart.

It was answered on the second ring. "Yeah!"

"Atten' hut!" Coop barked.

There was the meagerest instant of silence. Then a deep voice demanded, "Blackstock, you sonovabitch, is that you?"

"How's it going, Zachariah?"

"Oh, you know — same old, same old. Just 'bout got my balls blown off in Bali."

Coop rolled his eyes. He and Zach Taylor had been telling each other lies since the first day they met in boot camp as a couple of green, too-macho-to-show-how-scared-they-were teenagers. "You're full of shit, Taylor. There's nothing going on in Bali."

Zach laughed. "I know, but I figured a hotshot writer like James Lee Cooper would appreciate the alliteration."

"That pretentious dumb shit? Hell, I doubt that idiot would recognize an alliteration if it bopped by and bit him on his bodacious butt. How've you been?" Coop demanded and scratched the cat's head. Boo demonstrated his approval by sinking and retracting several of his claws in Coop's thigh. "I've missed you — there's nobody around here to dish me up my daily ration of bull." Except for Veronica, maybe, but since yesterday afternoon he'd been doing his best to pretend she didn't exist.

"I'm fine — I'm being transferred to Pendleton next month." They discussed the impending move for a few minutes, then Zach said, "How about you? How's the search for your baby brother coming along?"

"Not great. I've eavesdropped on conversations in the bar, questioned people with a subtleness that would astound you when the discussions about Eddie and Crystal turned public, and talked to Eddie's lawyer. And so far I haven't turned up a damn thing worthwhile." He stroked his hand down the cat's back from head to tail, and Boo's purr cranked up a few decibels louder.

"What the hell is that?" Zach demanded.

"Huh?"

"That noise? What is that?"

"Nothing." Coop stopped petting. "A cement truck out on the street."

"Christ, what the hell are they using in the mix, rocks the size of ping-pong balls?"

"Sounds like it, doesn't it?" Grinning, he scratched beneath Boo's chin and the volume of the cat's purr immediately cranked up.

"I always had this vision of small towns as peaceful and bucolic."

"Yeah," Coop agreed amiably. "There's another piece of Americana folklore shot to hell."

Zach laughed wryly, then immediately sobered. "So you're not getting anywhere?"

"So far everything I've done has turned out to be a case of too little, too late. I'm here now, but I should have been here *before* Eddie went on the lam. I bought this phone we're talking on too late. If I'd had a cell phone last month, he wouldn't have had to leave increasingly frantic messages on my answering machine. And that's not even mentioning his daughter. I'm keeping an eye on Lizzy as best I can, but how effective can it be when I can't even tell her who I am?"

"Not informing everyone and his uncle that

you're Eddie's brother was a good call, Coop," Zach said flatly. "Whoever actually did the kid's mother would be that much more on guard if they knew your relationship to him. At least this way you've got a fighting chance of someone slipping up and maybe giving you something to work with."

"Yeah, and I even still agree with that plan, in theory. Except Lizzy isn't 'everyone.' She's a sweet little kid who's lost both her mom and her dad in one fell swoop. And that's another worry. I mean, since the day she was born the one thing I could count on in every conversation I had with Eddie was that I'd hear all there was to hear about Lizzy — how much she'd grown, what clever new thing she'd done since the last time we'd talked. He's crazy about her, Zach, and if I don't know anything else in this world, I can be absolutely sure that he'll be back for her, come hell or high water. He's incapable of staying away from her for long."

"And that worries you?"

"It worries me a lot. Because if he grows careless in his need to see her, he could easily find himself cooling his heels in a state pen for so many years that Lizzy will be thirty years old before her daddy ever sees the light of day. And meanwhile, I'm sure as hell no big help, if I can't even tell her who I am."

"Then maybe I'm wrong here. Maybe it's more important for you to come clean, particularly if she doesn't have anyone else."

Coop sunk his fingers in Boo's fur. "Well, she does have her Aunt Ronnie."

"The mother's sister?"

"Yeah."

Zach made a rude noise. "There's a big fucking deal. If Aunt Ronnie's anything like Crystal was reputed to be, that's not saying much."

"No, actually, Veronica's not like Crystal at all. I thought at first that she was, but . . . she's really good with the kid. Lizzy likes her."

"And?"

"What do you mean, *and?* And what?"

"I don't know — your voice changed."

"Like hell."

"No, it did. I can't quite put my finger on it, but . . ." Zach's voice trailed off. Then the sound of snapped fingers came down the line. "Oh, man, I know what it is — you've got the hots!" He chortled. "That's it, isn't it? Damn, this is just too beautiful for words. The Iceman wants to get in Aunt Ronnie's pants!"

Something about hearing his Marine handle linked with his yearning for Veronica of the lily white skin made him say a bit too forcefully, "Bullshit."

"Now, now, Blackstock. You might want to consider very carefully before you go into full-scale denial here. Remember Pinocchio, who wanted to be a real boy, and his lie-detector nose? Well, Geppetto never told him that real boys have a few growing parts of their own, only

113

their woodies *shrink* every time they tell a lie."

It was an automatic reaction to squeeze his thighs together, but Coop countered with a rude noise. "Yeah, right," he scoffed. "If that were the case, we'd have to change your name to Zelda, since a bigger liar never lived."

"Aw, you sweet-talker, you. But see, that's just what I'm talking about. Real boys can lie to their wives, they can lie to the government. But they never ever lie to another jarhead when it comes to matters of the dick. Lie to the guy who's covered your back, and that nasty little reverse Pinocchio factor is just guaranteed to go into effect. Trust me on this."

"Okay, fine," Coop admitted. "So maybe I did wanna get in her pants. But that was yesterday. I'm over it now."

"Careful, boy — you just lost an inch."

"Well, lucky for me I've got it to spare."

"We ain't talking about your *ego* here, Ice. Your dick could be swingin' to your knees — and remember, boy, I've shared barracks with you, so we both know that's a pipe dream — but keep up the lies and you won't have enough left to show the little lady a good time should she ever decide this is going to be your lucky day." Clearly pleased with his allegory, his chuckle rumbled through the line.

"Great, yuk it up," Coop said sourly. "I'm glad you're so amused. I'm trying to function around the fact that I'm one big, raging hard-on these days, and you think it's a real knee-slapper."

Zach roared with laughter.

Coop allowed him a minute to knock himself out before he said, "You got that out of your system, now?"

"Almost." His friend's voice was full of amusement.

"Good, because I'm ensconced in Crystal's house and I've turned the place upside down without finding any clue as to why anyone would want to strangle her. Aside from her parenting or decorating skills, that is."

"What about Eddie's place? Anything worth pursuing there?"

"Damned if I know. I don't have access to Eddie's house."

"So what's your point, Ice? Break in."

Coop laughed. "That's what I like about you, Taylor — you don't let a little nicety like the law stand in your way." He thought a second. "Still . . . I could do that. Or maybe, since Eddie's lawyer is the one person in town who knows who I am, I could check to see if he has a key."

"Yeah, that's a thought, too. Doesn't sound like nearly as much fun, though."

"I'm glad I called, Zach. As usual, your skewed way of looking at the world has helped clarify a few things in my mind."

"Hey, always happy to be of help, bud. Now tell me more about this Aunt Ronnie. I bet she's tall and tan, with a truly sweet set. And probably blond, too — am I right?"

A wry smile tugged the corner of Coop's mouth as he scooped Boo up off his lap and set him on the floor. He climbed to his feet. "Absolutely. It's downright uncanny, the way you can pinpoint these things."

Veronica arrived home to an empty house later that afternoon. She called her answering machine in Seattle; then, in response to a frantic message on it, spent some time tracking down a missing armoire for her Scotland job. She was running low on patience by the time the Portland craftsman who'd been in charge of its restoration returned her call.

"You promised me the work would be completed and delivered before I left Glenkenchie," she said in response to his excuses. "I'm the one who looks bad when you don't come through, Michael, and I give you fair warning right now: If I ever have to field another call from an upset client because you've let me down again, I'll take my business elsewhere. I need craftsmen who honor their promises!"

Needing to work off her frustration, she set to work on the living room and had just finished clearing it of the last of Crystal's kitsch when someone tapped at the front door. Before she could rise to her feet from where she'd been squatting to dust the little Duncan Phyfe–legged end table, the door opened and Marissa stuck her head in.

"Hey," she said and looked around. "Wow. It

sure looks different in here."

Veronica climbed to her feet, dropping the dust rag she'd been using on the end table. "I know. The room looks bigger without all the junk in it, doesn't it?"

"Yeah, it really does. And if you lose that gawd-awful wallpaper and paint the walls a pale color, it'd open it up even more."

"That's next on my agenda, after we paint Lizzy's room. You want a cup of coffee?" She headed for the kitchen without awaiting an answer and said over her shoulder, "So what brings you here in the middle of the day?"

"Did I happen to mention I'm chairwoman of the decorating committee for the Winter Festival this year?"

Veronica stopped dead and slowly swiveled around to stare at her oldest friend. "Sure you are. And I'm Queen of the May." A smile quirked the corners of her lips, and she picked up the pot and filled a couple of mugs with coffee. "You almost had me going there," she said over the fragrant steam. "It would've flown if I hadn't spent half my life listening to your opinions on the women-who-do-good-works crowd."

"It turns out I wasn't a hundred percent right about them."

"Uh-huh."

Marissa didn't laugh or yell *Gotcha!* and Ronnie's smile slowly faded. "Oh, my God, Mare, you're serious, aren't you? You've

117

become a *Junior Leaguer?*"

"I don't know how it happened!" Marissa accepted the mug Veronica handed her and carried it over to the table. She sat and looked at Ronnie morosely. "When Denny was alive, the Bluff matrons didn't even know I existed, or they didn't *want* to know, anyway. I was just some not-so-little upstart from Baker Street who'd married above herself. They tolerated me because Den had too much clout for them to do otherwise, but mostly I was ignored, and that was just dandy with me. But when Den died . . . God, I was lost for the longest time, and I don't know if his clout transferred to me during that period, or if they felt sorry for me, or what, but suddenly I was 'poor, dear Marissa.' And before I knew it, I was going to meetings for this and sitting on committees for that, and the truth is, with a few notable exceptions they're a pretty decent bunch of women. Or at least I thought so until they decided to trust me with the Winter Festival decorations this year. I should have said no thanks. I *meant* to say no thanks, but instead I accepted. Don't ask me why, because I've pretty much been hyperventilating ever since. I don't have a *clue* where to start with something of this scope!"

"Okay, take a deep breath here. Drink your coffee." Veronica watched Marissa follow her instructions, and when her friend seemed to calm down a little, she gave her a gentle smile. "You said you're heading the committee, right?

The nice thing about committees, toots, is that you've got other women who will have plenty of ideas. Why not just sit back and wait for a good one to kick loose?" She reached across the table and gave Marissa a nudge. "Then, of course, as top dog, you get to claim all the credit when it turns out to be a huge success."

Marissa gave her a wan smile. "Much as I admire your deviousness, what I really need is a decorator-type idea. The committee meets on Monday, and you know how I said that with a few notable exceptions this is a nice bunch of women?"

"Uh-oh." Veronica straightened in her seat. "A notable exception is on your committee, I take it."

"Two of them. Angela Tyler-Jones and Diana Wentworth. Otherwise known as the bitch queen of the snobs and her high priestess. It just kills them that I was appointed committee chair."

"Let me guess — could we be talking about women with good haircuts and tight sphincters, who were born and bred on the Bluff, and are firmly entrenched in the belief that those who weren't were put on earth to serve?"

"You got it, sister."

"And I assume *they* assume they're much more deserving of the position since they grew up the princesses of Holly Drive?"

"Ronnie, they undermine me at every turn. They're expecting me to fall flat on my face at

Monday's meeting, and what really kills me is that they're going to be right. I'm way out of my depth here. I don't know what people were *thinking* when they assigned me to chair this."

"Probably that you're a warmhearted, capable woman who is kind to everyone no matter what their station in life. Or *maybe* that you're someone who can do any darn thing she sets her mind to."

"I don't have nearly enough experience to pull this off."

"Ah, but what you've got is even better."

"I do? It is? What?"

"Me."

"Yeah?" Marissa gave her a slow smile. "Ms. Restoration Specialist Designs The Winter Festival? You don't have to go to all that trouble, Ronnie — just point me in the right direction." She shot her a hopeful look. "Unless you truly wouldn't mind? But no. You've got enough on your plate; I can't ask that of you." Pausing for breath, she gave Veronica a sidelong look. "Besides, having you design the decorations would kind of be like using a bazooka to kill a mosquito, wouldn't it?"

Helping Marissa was the *least* that she could do, after all her friend had done for her. And Marissa's faith in her abilities made Veronica feel like some big-deal movie star. So she waved a hand and said airily, "Well, you know us Baker Street girls — overkill is a way of life. The queen snob and her priestess aren't gonna know what hit 'em." She got up to grab a tablet and a pencil out of the junk drawer, then dropped back into her seat. "So tell me. What kind of budget are we talking?"

8

As Veronica had sorted through her sister's clothing, she'd saved bits and pieces in a large ornate box she'd dubbed the dress-up trunk. The first thing she saw Saturday evening, when she came down the front stairs ready for work, was Lizzy and Dessa lying on their stomachs on the living room floor, all decked out like a couple of half-pint hookers. Lizzy wore a stretchy royal blue and black sequined tube dress with a handkerchief hem, and Dessa had donned a slinky black satin nightie over a green and yellow floral one. Hems that most likely had come to midthigh on Crystal fell to the little girls' ankles. They both sported overly rouged cheeks and scarlet lips, and a rainbow of eye shadows had been applied with a heavy hand from lashes to eyebrows.

The toes of Dessa's too-large white pumps pointed in opposite directions to accommodate lying with her legs flat on the floor. Lizzy's ankles were crossed in the air and one pink pump lay on its side on the floor while its mate hung precariously from the toes of her right foot.

Stopping in front of them, Veronica slapped a hand to her breast. "Ladies! You look *mahvelous!*"

They looked up from their coloring book, flashing great big pleased-with-themselves grins. For the merest instant Lizzy's faltered around the edges and her crayon stilled over the page she was coloring. Then, her smile turning shy, she dipped her head to observe Veronica through her bangs. "You sorta look like my mama tonight."

Mrs. Martelucchi took her attention away from *Providence* on the television to glance over. "Why, goodness gracious, everyone's getting dolled up tonight. Ronnie, dear, don't you look festive!"

Veronica reached up a bit self-consciously to finger the silver, bronze, and copper stars that dangled from her lobes and gave her low-cut, cherry-red cashmere sweater set a quick once-over to make sure everything was where it was supposed to be. Dolled up, indeed. She'd even brought out the heavy artillery tonight: her take-no-prisoners water bra, which strove valiantly to provide a modicum of cleavage.

She'd gone whole hog to tart up her entire, ordinary appearance in an attempt to look somewhat less, well . . . *ordinary*. She wore more makeup than usual, and had used a palmful of mousse, her hot rollers, and the judicious application of a rat-tailed comb to add a little oomph to her hair. She'd eat a bug for breakfast before she'd admit it, but Coop's crack yesterday about the way she dressed had prompted the sudden desire for a less proper image, if only for an evening.

Well, that and the way he'd behaved last night, as though she'd suddenly become invisible.

Spreading her arms wide, she consulted the girls. "What do you think? Too much change all at once?"

"Nuh-uh," Lizzy assured her. "You look pretty."

"Real pretty," Dessa agreed.

Veronica's heart squeezed at their solemn praise, and she sat on her heels to give them both a kiss on the forehead. "Thank you, my little pumpkinettes. Coming from two swell lookers like yourselves, that's a real compliment. You sure know how to make a girl feel fine."

On the floor next to her a shopping bag holding additional coloring books began to rattle furiously, and Boo's head popped out. Veronica reached out to scratch the cat between his eyes before turning her attention back to the girls. "Now, I expect you two to be good for Mrs. Martelucchi. Have you got your video?"

"Uh-huh. It's right here." Lizzy pulled it out from beneath a mountain of Barbie clothing and held it up to display the Disney title.

"Okay, good. Mrs. M will make you some popcorn to have with your movie as soon as her program is over. Then, when the movie's done, it's off to bed with you. I don't want to hear about any arguments or wheedling for extra time when I get home. Not that either of you would ever dream of doing such a thing, of course."

Lizzy shook her head in solemn agreement,

but Dessa merely flashed a grin that showcased her half-grown-in new front teeth, and Veronica couldn't help but grin back. "All right, so maybe a pajama party wouldn't be a pajama party without a smidgen of wheedling. Still, be good. Gimme a kiss." After both girls had pursed their glossily made-up lips for her peck, she rose to her feet. "I'll see you in the morning."

She headed for the door and looked back at them while she wrestled into her warm jacket. "Do we have a camera around here, Lizzy?" she asked. "We really should have a picture of you two. It's not every day a girl looks so snazzy."

Lizzy's remaining high heel thunked to the floor, and she hopped up and ran into the kitchen. A second later Veronica saw her push a chair over to the refrigerator and climb up on it. The little girl paused to wrestle her slipping dress back up under her armpits, then teetered precariously on tiptoe as she stretched to reach the top of the fridge.

"Whoa, whoa, whoa a minute there." Veronica crossed to the kitchen. "Is it up here?" She peered at the odds and ends atop the refrigerator.

Lizzy nodded eagerly. "Uh-huh. In the back."

"Okay, I'll find it. You go put your heels back on."

Moments later, Veronica snapped off several frames, grinning with delight when Dessa hammed it up and Lizzy flashed smiles that were far less shy than usual. Then she bade the girls goodnight, let Mrs. Martelucchi know she was putting Boo out when she found him practicing his telekinetic powers in front of the door, and left. She walked briskly across the street and pushed through the Tonk's front door.

It was pleasant not to be hit in the face with a wall of smoke the instant she stepped into the bar, and between that and thoughts of Lizzy and Dessa in their diva apparel, she was smiling as she pulled off her jacket. Her glance drifted past Coop, then snapped back to focus on him. He stood stock-still across the room, staring at her with an intensity that stopped her in her tracks.

It was a masculine look, a *sexual* look, guaranteed to make a woman feel naked and vulnerable. Veronica's heart gave a solid kick against the wall of her chest before taking off like a greyhound after the track rabbit. Hot color moved up her throat and she could only pray the dim lighting would prevent him from noting it across the distance.

Then, as if he hadn't just given her a look laden with enough sizzle to melt her shoes to the floor, he turned on his heel and presented her with his back. Veronica's heart pounded even harder . . . this time with affronted anger.

The chemistry that seemed to set her hormones afire every time she came into contact with him didn't exactly thrill her, but she was dealing with it. She was a grown woman — she knew there was a world of difference between feeling inappropriate sexual attractions and acting on them. But Coop had been working overtime to advance her awareness of him from the moment they'd clapped eyes on each other, and to suddenly be treated as if she'd ceased to exist infuriated her.

He shouldn't be allowed to get away with it.

She strolled up to the bar and lifted the pass-through, letting herself in. "Evening, Cooper," she said to his broad back.

"Veronica." He didn't bother to turn around.

His rudeness made her grit her teeth as she stowed away her coat and purse and grabbed out a clean apron to tie around her hips. Getting to see the girls in their dress-up finery had put her in a wonderful mood, and she wasn't about to let him engage her in a snarling match that would destroy her nice glow. Maybe instead she should take a page out of the Cooper Blackstock book of *I Breathe, Therefore I Promote Sexual Awareness.* Up until last night, he'd been Mr. Touchy-Feely himself, always crowding her, touching her, doing everything he could to heighten her awareness of him, regardless of the fact that they had nothing in common aside from an inexplicable transient attraction. Why not pick up the ball that he'd tossed down and run with it? It seemed only fair.

Her waitressing paraphernalia was on Coop's other side, in the angle where the counter below the bar wrapped around the adjacent wall to make an additional workspace. Glancing around to make sure no one was paying attention, she

127

surreptitiously reached into her low-cut neckline and hiked her cleavage front and center. Then she took a deep breath and brushed her fingers down his arm. "Pass me my tray?"

His sweater sleeves were shoved up, exposing the corded strength of his forearms as he cut up lemons and limes. Long, lean muscle shifted beneath his tanned skin with every twist of his raw-boned wrists. He wasn't a hairy man, and she was highly aware of the smooth warmth of his skin beneath her fingers. She felt the muscles in his arm go rigid, but without a word he set down his knife, grabbed the tray, and passed it to her.

"Thanks." She traced a fingertip down one of the soft veins that snaked prominently along the inner length of his arm. "I'll need my cash box, too."

He slammed it down atop her tray.

"Thank you, Cooper. Looks like the place is filling up, so I'd better get to work. But it's been grand chatting with you."

His head snapped around, and for just a second those dark eyes pinned her in place with an intensity that made her question her sanity. Poking sticks at a tiger would doubtless be less risky than messing with Cooper Blackstock — especially in an arena where she was a rank amateur at best. It took more than a push-up bra, sexy earrings, and red lipstick to pull off the little payback she envisioned — and why she even thought such a thing was a good idea in the first place was anyone's guess. Veronica's nerves pulsed crazily and blood ran hot through her veins. A smart woman would be singing hosannas that Cooper Blackstock had reined in that damnable sexuality of his — not testing to see if the ability to disturb went both ways.

Unable to sustain contact with those fierce brown eyes, she snatched her hand off his arm and glanced around the bar. "Oh, look, there's Kody." Her smile was radiant with relief. Maybe she'd go practice her wiles on him for a while before throwing herself headlong into the big league. Not that Kody struck her as particularly minor league, but at least he didn't have the same effect on her that Coop did.

As she turned to go, Coop reached out a hand to detain her. "Do your job before you go flirt with your boyfriend," he ordered.

"My boyfr . . . ?" Veronica swallowed her initial impulse to jerk her arm free and snarl back at him. Instead, she raised her gaze from his grip on her arm to his narrowed eyes and gave him a little smile she sincerely hoped made her look like the last of the red-hot mamas . . . or at least mysterious. But when Coop abruptly released her arm and stepped back, his face wiped free of all expression, she had a sinking feeling she'd appeared constipated instead. *Not* exactly the look she was shooting for. Snatching up her tray, she stalked away. What the *hell* was she doing playing these asinine games, anyway? She'd had better sense back in junior high school.

She headed straight for Kody's table. They'd

hit it off during the two days he'd spent putting in the air purification system. He was handsome, fit, and easy to talk to, and she felt comfortable with him, a restful change after time spent in Coop's company.

"Hey, there," she said, dropping a coaster on his table. "Have you been served yet?" Sandy, the other barmaid, had staked out the pool table side of the room as her territory and only ventured into what she considered Veronica's if Veronica wasn't yet on duty.

He looked up, and his lean cheeks creased with his smile. "No, but then I just got here."

"Me, too. What can I get you?" When he ordered a domestic draft she made a note of it, then shifted her tray to a more comfortable position. "You know, I was just thinking how nice it is not to be hit with a wall of smoke the instant I walk through the door. Not to mention that I no longer stink to high heaven when I go home at night. That system you put in was worth every penny." Which reminded her, she still had to talk to Coop about being reimbursed for it — but not right this minute. She'd give him a little room first to recover from whatever bug had bit his butt. Shooting Kody another smile, she thanked God for laid-back men. "I've got a few more orders to take, then I'll be back with your beer."

He leaned back in his chair and looked at her from beneath half-mast eyelids. "Looking forward to it."

She didn't know if it was her own good mood or what, but there seemed to be a nicer class of clientele in here tonight. Several people actually went out of their way to tell her how sorry they'd been to hear about Crystal, which she found both kind and friendly. Her memories of the bar during her college years consisted mainly of dealing with the drunks who'd pawed her and given her a bad time, but for all she knew there'd always been a mix of perfectly nice neighborhood people. It was possible they hadn't stuck in her mind because she'd been young, and fielding personal remarks about her lack of curves and dodging wandering hands that grabbed for them anyway had a nasty way of overshadowing all else.

Whatever the reason, it felt as though she smiled and chatted with more patrons in the short time she spent collecting orders than she'd done in all her previous nights combined.

She danced up to the bar. A stool was available and she climbed up on it, having learned to take every opportunity to get off her feet. When Coop came down from the other end where he'd been making change for a patron, she gave him her most dazzling smile. "I need one Bud, a vodka collins and a Cutty on the rocks, a pitcher of Heineken and four glasses, a Manhattan, a diet Pepsi, and a tequila sunrise." "Turn It Loose" was playing on the jukebox, and she joined the Judds with an enthusiastic "mo-woe-woan" in the chorus, tapping her foot in time with the music.

"You're awful damn cheery," Coop said sourly as he assembled the drinks for her order. "You got a hot date later on with the refrigerator man, or something?"

She quit singing to stare at him. "Kody knows about refrigeration, too?"

Coop hitched a shoulder.

"Oh, this is too good." She touched her fingertips to his wrist when he slid the tray across the bar. "Thanks." Hopping off the stool, she reached for her order. "Hey, I just realized something. We're twinsies tonight — our sweaters are nearly the exact same shade of red."

His gaze went straight to her meager cleavage where it rose above the low scoop of her shell, then traveled leisurely up her chest, her throat, her face, to finally meet her eyes. "Oh, yeah. We're a regular Boobsie and Bobsie."

Veronica felt heat rise to her cheeks, but she looked him straight in the eye and raised one eyebrow, a trick that used to infuriate Crystal. "Boobsie and Bobsie, huh? So which one would that make you?" Without awaiting an answer, she picked up the tray and walked away.

Saving Kody's beer for last, she delivered her three other tables. The women in the group at the second table commented favorably on the lack of smoke in the bar, and when she explained about the new purification system, it started a brief, friendly conversation. Excusing herself a few moments later, she tucked a generous tip into her cash box, collected several new orders, then walked over to Kody's table.

Setting his beer down in front of him, she said without preamble, "Coop tells me you know something about refrigeration. Is he right?"

"Yeah."

"Now, this is what I call fortuitous timing." She flashed him a smile. "Do you plan to be here for a while? That is, if I call a friend to come right over, would you talk with her? She's on the decorating committee for the Winter Festival and we've just spent the afternoon wracking our brains trying to figure out a way to keep ice sculptures from melting — or if it's economically feasible to even try to make them last for the entire three days."

Kody leaned back in his seat and looked up at her. "I plan to stick around for a while, but I probably can't give your friend more than a couple of general ideas off the top of my head. I'd have to put some thought into the logistics of such a project."

"Works for me." She pushed upright. "I'll go call her right now."

Marissa nearly didn't answer the phone when it rang. For the first evening in ages, both kids were gone at the same time and she had the house entirely to herself. With a sigh, however, she paused the VCR and picked up the wireless receiver she'd left within reach. It could be about Riley or Dessa, and she'd forgotten to turn on the answering machine to vet her calls. "Hello?"

Veronica's excited voice demanded that she find a sitter for Riley and get her rear down to the Tonk. Marissa was about to decline when her friend added, "I've got a guy down here who knows something about refrigeration, Riss."

"No kidding?" She sat upright. This could be the answer to some of the questions they'd raised during their brainstorming session this afternoon. "Riley's spending the night with Jeremy Witmore. I'll be right down."

She'd grabbed her coat and was headed for the garage when she caught sight of herself in the utility room mirror and stopped cold. She was going out in public, for heaven's sake — she could do better than this. She about-faced and ran upstairs to exchange her comfy sweatsuit for a pair of Levi's and a hand-knit novelty sweater. Then she swiftly unbraided her hair and dragged a brush through it, dashed on some mascara, and rubbed a touch of blush into her cheekbones. She applied her lipstick on her way to the car, and less than ten minutes later was pushing through the Tonk's front door.

She spotted Ronnie at the bar and walked over to join her. Just as she approached, a man got up from the stool next to her friend, tossed a couple of bills on the bar, and walked away, nodding to her as they passed.

"Now, that's what I call excellent timing," she said as she slid onto the seat he'd just vacated.

"Marissa!" Veronica leaned over to give her a one-armed hug. Settling back on her stool, she

134

looked her over. "Wow, you look great. I love your hair."

"You're looking mighty hot yourself. Red lipstick, Ronnie? What's the occasion?"

"Nothing special. I just had a sudden urge for a little change." She raised her voice. "Barkeep! Bring my friend here a drink, will you?" A crooked smile quirking up one corner of her mouth, she dug her elbow into Marissa's side.

Coop sauntered down from the opposite end of the bar. He picked up the cash on the bar, then wiped down the area with a clean towel. "Evening, Marissa." He gave her an appreciative look. "You're looking particularly pretty tonight. How are you?"

"After a compliment like that, I *feel* particularly fine, thank you very much. How about you? Tonight's crowd not working you too hard?"

"Nah, I'm doing all right." He slid a paper coaster onto the bar in front of her. "What can I get you?"

"I'll have a glass of the house white."

"One Chardonnay for the pretty lady, coming right up." He turned and headed for the middle of the bar.

" 'For the pretty lady.' " Marissa grinned at Ronnie. "Isn't he just the sweetest?"

"That's the word I would've chosen to describe him, all right." Veronica's brow developed a tiny pucker as she looked down to where he was selecting a wine glass. "Just sweeter 'n' a lemon drop."

"I suspect you're humoring me, but he is. And would you look at the size of those hands?" Marissa observed him dreamily. "Do you suppose everything's proportionate?" She turned back to Veronica and grinned. "There's a thought, huh? I bet *he* could reach a girl's G spot."

Ronnie squirmed on her stool for an instant, crossing and recrossing her legs. Marissa watched her prop her chin in her hand and silently stare at the hands under discussion, high color blazing in her cheeks as she watched them efficiently assemble three drinks at once. "I don't think I have a G spot," she finally said, turning her head to give Marissa a wry look. "I used to, but it must have atrophied from lack of use."

"Oh, boy, I hear that. In fact, I'll see your hard luck story and raise it with the small town card. At least if an opportunity arises for you, the entire world and its brother doesn't have to know about it. Even if I could find a guy to scratch my itch, everyone up on the Bluff would probably be talking about it before the last moan had faded."

Veronica laughed. "Okay, you win. Your sex life is even more pitiful than mine."

"And isn't *that* depressing."

"Isn't it, though? And since I have no desire to lose the best mood I've been in since I barely *remember* when, I'm going to change the subject. I wish you could've seen the girls tonight, Mare.

136

They did the dress-up thing and, God, they were cute. Do you remember when we used to do that?" Veronica scooped her hair behind her ear and gave Marissa a smile. "You know, I've never felt any particular urge to procreate, but there was something about the continuity of seeing Lizzy and your daughter doing the kind of things you and I once did that really got to me. I took a bunch of pictures, so I'll have some copies made for you when I get them developed."

A glass of wine was placed in front of Marissa, but when she looked up to thank Cooper, his attention was elsewhere. His gaze was all over Ronnie, and Marissa straightened smartly in her seat. Hello! What was this? A smile curled her lips, for the way Ronnie had squirmed at the mention of Coop's hands suddenly took on a whole new meaning.

Well, well, well. With only the slightest twinge, she relinquished her vague fantasy of starting something with him. The moment Coop collected money for her drink and left to answer a summons at the other end of the bar, however, she turned to demand what was going on. But Ronnie slid from the stool and picked up the tray of drinks Coop had delivered along with Marissa's wine. "Come on," she said. "I'll introduce you to Kody before I serve these."

Marissa followed her. She had a dozen questions buzzing in her brain, but before she could form even one, Veronica stopped at a table. "Rissa," she said, "this is Kody. Kody, I'd like you to meet my friend Marissa."

And Marissa took one look at the man lounging back in his chair, with his long legs stretched out under the little table, and every thought in her head vaporized.

9

When Coop came out of the storage room a short while later and saw Sandy standing by the bar rubbing the small of her back, he headed straight for her. "Finally got a minute of down time, huh?" he said as he ducked under the pass-through. He regarded her genially when she started fussing with her cash box. "Take a break, Sandy — I don't expect you to be busy every minute. You want a club soda?"

"Thanks; that'd be great." Looking pleased that he'd noticed her drink of choice, she climbed onto a vacant stool. She sat in a way that emphasized her generous breasts and checked him out from beneath her lashes.

He poured club soda over ice and handed her the glass. "I was just in the back room looking for more vodka," he said conversationally. "Now, I never knew Crystal, obviously, but I gotta tell you, organized she wasn't."

Sandy snorted. "No foolin'. Things have been in a lot better shape since you've taken over."

Coop shrugged. "I'm not really in charge. It's Veronica's place."

"Sure, but she's smart enough to let you run it. Be grateful she's not as big a flake as her sister.

Crystal spent most of her time in here flirting. She was much better at talking up men than taking care of business."

"I heard you talking about her the other night." Coop propped his arms on the bar and leaned toward her, giving her an easy smile. "Not the brightest bulb, I take it?"

"Hardly."

"So, do *you* think somebody was helping her play Eddie?"

"I actually asked her, but she wouldn't say yes or no. She just gave me one a them — whataya call 'ems — coy smiles and said that was for her to know."

It would've all depended on how she'd played it, Coop mused when the waitress returned to work a few minutes later. The only thing Crystal had truly needed in order to get almost anything she wanted from his brother was Lizzy. But if she'd been pulling some elaborate con instead of using her daughter as a bargaining chip — well, from everything he'd ever heard about her, she hadn't been bright enough to do that on her own. So he had to figure out who might have been helping her. If she'd been seeing anyone, Sandy hadn't heard about it. Still, it gave him a direction to pursue, and that made him smile.

But watching Veronica's butt wiggle in time with the Dixie Chicks as she swiped down the last of her tables at closing time a short while later thrust him right back in the same lousy mood he'd been in all evening.

Big surprise. He'd given a great deal of thought to this crazy attraction she held for him, and with the methodical precision he'd been renowned for in Company C he'd decided to take a giant step back from it. Distancing himself was a good, solid decision, and it'd held together just fine, too — until she'd come waltzing in here tonight wearing a pair of sprayed-on jeans and that snug, almost too-thin-to-be-considered-a-sweater-set that molded the most beguiling little tits he'd ever laid eyes on. To add insult to injury, the scoop-necked shell afforded him here-and-gone glimpses of a cleavage so sweet and delicate, the mere thought of it, even now when it was safely out of sight, had him reaching down to discreetly adjust himself.

He dragged his gaze away from the swing of her round little rump and stared blindly at the tally in his hand. Damn. He didn't get it. Usually he went for breasts that were big enough to over-flow his hands. Those little cupcakes of Ronnie's would barely even snuggle into his palms, let alone give his fingers something to hang on to. Yet he wanted to see them, *feel* them, so bad he could practically taste it.

Licking his lips, he scowled. Because tasting her was something else he wanted to do.

"Did I cash my box out wrong or something?" Sandy's anxious voice broke into his thoughts, and Coop realized he'd been looking at but not paying the slightest attention to her reconciled tab.

"No, it's fine," he assured her. For all he knew, she very well could have, but she hadn't turned in an incorrect tally yet. And if by some odd quirk of fate she had this time, he'd cover the difference himself. He just wanted this frigging night to be over.

"You looked mad there for a minute."

"I was thinking about something else." Like how he'd better get his brain the fuck out of his fly. He forced an anemic imitation of his usual easy smile. "Why don't you go ahead and take off?"

He realized his mistake the moment the words were out of his mouth. Sandy's departure would leave him alone with Ronnie, but before he could retract his offer, she'd already flashed him a brilliant smile.

"Thanks!" In a flurry of material, Sandy yanked off her apron and grabbed her coat and purse. The next thing Coop knew, the door was all but smacking her in the butt as it swung closed behind her.

He drew a breath deep into his lungs, then blew it out and stonily kept his attention away from Veronica as she finished setting chairs upside down onto the tables in her section. He could hear her singing along with the jukebox, though, and gritted his teeth. Christ Almighty. It wasn't bad enough she'd gone and dressed all sexy on him, she suddenly had to turn into Miss Personality, too? Where was her usual Princess Standoffish impersonation when a guy could really use it? And what was with the singing? She didn't carry a tune worth jack.

He knew her animation with the customers, and probably the cheerful singing, had something to do with watching Lizzy and Dessa play dress-up before she'd come to work, because he'd overheard part of her conversation with Marissa. He tried not to think about it, though, because something about Veronica's wistfulness when she'd talked about the girls had grabbed him by the gut.

Damn, it was stuffy in here. Coop raked both hands through his hair clear to the back of his neck, where he gouged his fingers into the knotted muscles at the base of his skull in an attempt to work out the kinks that had him all tied up in knots. He wanted out of here, wanted to be out where he could breathe real air. He had to get his head back on straight, and a little cold, crisp air would do the trick. All he had to do was hold on for five more minutes. Hell, he'd once lain patiently behind a sand dune in the desert for seven hours until it was safe to resume a reconnaissance mission — how hard could it be to hang tough for five lousy minutes?

Veronica finished policing her station and, placing her hands in the small of her back, stretched out her tired muscles. It had been a long if fairly fun night, and she felt an abrupt loss of the steam that had powered her all evening.

Her attempt to up Coop's awareness of her tonight had been a total bust, and all she wanted now was to cash out her box and head home to bed. Or maybe, if she could manage to stay awake long enough, she'd indulge herself for fifteen minutes with a nice hot soak in the old clawfoot tub on the second floor.

This burning the candle at both ends by getting up early with Lizzy and then staying up late to close out the Tonk was beginning to take its toll. Every morning she made bargains with herself in order to drag her tired bones out of bed. She held out the lure of taking a catnap during the day to catch up on some of her missed sleep, but somehow never quite got around to it. She kept getting sidetracked by other things.

She collected her tray and cash box, then headed for the bar. Cooper ignored her just as he'd been doing all night, and determined to be equally aloof, she silently reconciled her receipts.

It therefore startled her when, out of the blue, he demanded, "So what's the story with Marissa and your boyfriend?"

"Instant and total chemistry." Looking up, she found herself directing her reply to the back of his tanned neck. Teeth tightening over his refusal to even face her, she added with hard-won equanimity, "And Kody's just a *friend* — I don't know why you'd think otherwise."

Especially after seeing the way he and Marissa had taken one look at each other and all but gone up in flames. They'd sat with their heads together talking in low, intense voices; they'd slow-danced in a wide spot between the jukebox and the crowded tables. Then, about an hour ago, they'd left together, and Marissa couldn't have looked more stunned if she'd taken a direct hit of sheet lightning when she'd come to Veronica to inform her she was leaving and taking Kody home with her — something that wasn't at *all* like her. When Veronica had pointed that out, she'd merely said, "I know," and smiled a carnal little smile.

Veronica didn't mind admitting that knowing what they were most likely doing at this very moment gave her a fair surge of envy. It had been way too long since she'd felt any kind of chemistry with a man, and unconsciously she sighed. "I'm glad someone's getting lucky," she murmured to herself. "God knows it's been forever since I have."

Coop slowly turned. His high cheekbones stood out in sharp relief in the light from the liquor shelves as he took a step toward her, and his voice had an edge that rasped over her nerves as he demanded, "Would you like to?"

Yes. She stared up at Cooper, at those dark eyes that promised all manner of sexual satisfaction, at that pale hair that looked even spikier and more exotic than usual. Oh, yes. She'd like to very much.

But sometimes she felt like driving down the freeway at a hundred miles an hour, too. It didn't mean she'd actually do it. She grabbed on to her resolve with both hands. "No."

Every muscle in his body tensed, and for a minute he looked downright dangerous. He was a full head taller and half again as wide as she, and goose bumps raced up her spine at the knowledge that if he took it into his head to press the issue she'd be utterly outmatched. What truly terrified her, though, was the feminine thrill the image of him doing so gave her.

Then he stepped back. One wide shoulder twitched, and he gave her that heavy-lidded, I-like-my-sex-raw look he did so well. "Your loss, Princess. I could've made you feel real good."

That's exactly what scared her. Her chin went up. "Bully for you. So can BOB."

Coop's black eyebrows snapped together over his nose, and he suddenly seemed even larger yet. "Who the hell is Bob?"

"My battery-operated boyfriend."

The tension left him, and he gave her a head-to-foot appraisal, his gaze pausing on the neckline of her sweater for an instant before raising to meet her eyes. "I'll be damned. So Aunt Ronnie's got herself a little vibrating toy, huh?"

Feeling flushed and cranky, she uttered a rude sound. "There's nothing little about it, bub."

The corner of his mouth twitched, and the tension seemed to dissipate a fraction. But before she could wonder if he might outright smile, he'd turned his back on her again. The cash register opened with a ping, and Coop began emptying its contents into a bank bag. He shot her an expressionless glance over his shoulder. "You got that cash box tallied yet?"

She looked down at the slip in her hand and silently separated out her tips, which she pocketed before passing the box and tally to him.

"Good," he said gruffly. "Get out of here and go home."

Veronica looked between the tray still in her hand and the angle in the counter beneath the bar where she stored it every night when she was through. Cooper was once again blocking her way, and for about two seconds she considered asking him to put the tray away for her. But the edgy set of his shoulders discouraged the idea. She didn't think teasing him was such a hot idea now.

She eased as close as she could get without touching him, then reached around Coop to slide the tray into its usual resting place.

Unfortunately, she'd underestimated the sheer amount of space he took up, and she found herself plastered against his back for a nanosecond as she strained the last couple of inches. She slammed the tray into place and jumped back, highly aware of his heat radiating through her thin sweaters. Aware, too, even in that briefest of contacts, of the sudden rigidity in his muscles as he stilled.

"All right," he growled, "that does it!"

He spun on his heel to face her, and the next thing she knew, his big hands were wrapped around her hips and he was swinging her around and lifting her to sit on the counter. Her head whirled, and she grabbed two fistfuls of his sweater to anchor herself, tilting her chin up to stare at him.

"I was a good soldier," he said in a raspy voice, an unholy fire burning in his eyes as his hands slid from her hips and came up to frame her face. "Even when your eyes, your body language, told me something else, I respected it when you said no. But you sure as hell don't get to tease me, lady. You can't say no in one breath, then rub yourself all over me in the next."

"All over you! I didn't mean to touch you at *all* — I misjudged the stinking distance between you and the —"

He slammed his mouth over hers, cutting off her explanation, and, with a rough sound in the back of his throat, invaded the slick interior of her mouth with one sure stab of his tongue. In contrast, the thumbs beneath her chin keeping her face tilted up, and his long fingers wrapped around the back of her head, were amazingly gentle.

Veronica barely registered the delicacy of his grip, however, for the urgency of his mouth made her feel as if she'd just thrust a finger into an electrical socket, and every cognitive ability she possessed blew its circuit. Stunning sensation shot from her lips to her nipples, then shimmered along nerve endings to her fingertips and toes, leaving a feverish flush in its wake before settling with sweetly insistent pulsations between her thighs. Caught with her eyes wide open, she vaguely noticed the black crescents of Coop's lashes where they fanned against the upper thrust of his cheekbones, and his dark eyebrows as they furrowed above his nose.

Then her eyes fluttered shut. She felt the heat of his body, tasted his flavors with every assured glide of his tongue, and heard her own needy moan as her fingers tightened on his sweater and her tongue came up to tangle with his.

He responded with another rough sound, and the intensity of his kiss shot up several degrees. For a man who was so hard-mouthed all the time, his lips were surprisingly soft as they pressed and pulled at hers, but his tongue was take-no-prisoners aggressive. His thumbs slid up onto her face, where they stroked first the hollows of her cheeks, then her cheekbones from the apples to her temples.

A moment later, he drew his mouth away from hers with a leisurely, soft suction that kept their lips clinging until the very last second. Veronica's lips throbbed and her eyes felt weighted down by the sheer hunger pulsing through her. Slowly prying her eyelids open, she found Cooper staring down at her. His eyes, too, looked heavy-lidded and slumberous, the irises nearly black with an intensity so sexual it curled her toes inside her shoes.

"God, this skin," he said in a low, gravelly voice and, loosening his grip on the back of her neck, dragged his rough-skinned fingertips around to the front. Veronica shivered as he stroked them down her throat, over her collar-bones, and across her chest to the scooped neckline of the thin camisole sweater she wore beneath its matching cardigan. "I thought only babies had skin this soft."

She blinked, trying to summon an ounce of concentration. But his touch set off shock waves of sensation that traveled outward from his fingers to all sorts of interesting places, and her focus fragmented. She rallied enough to murmur, "I'm a long way from being a baby."

"Oh, yeah. I know." He insinuated a fingertip beneath the shell's neckline and trailed it along the satin edge where her breasts rose out of her demi-cup, tracing the bra's outline from shoulder strap to shoulder strap. "A fact for which I'm eternally grateful."

Then he leaned down and bit at her mouth, and Veronica's head fell back in helpless surrender. His hands dropped down to her knees and heat burned through the fabric of her jeans as he pulled them apart and promptly insinuated himself into the space he'd created. Her thighs bracketed his hips, but he didn't close the scant distance that would press his sex between her legs. And suddenly she wanted that more than the air she breathed.

She tilted her hips up to his, but he ignored the invitation and continued to kiss her as if he had all night. Wiggling her bottom against the counter in frustration, she unpeeled her fingers from the front of his sweater and slid her arms up to wrap around his neck. His hands tightened on her legs, his mouth lost its leisurely expertise and ground against hers, and with a needy sound ululating in the back of her throat, Veronica scooted forward to align the heavy denim seam that ran between her legs with the hard, thick ridge threatening the fly of Coop's jeans. Inhaling sharply at the contact, she locked her ankles behind his thighs.

Coop ripped his mouth free and swore. He slid his hands around to grip her butt, and his head fell back. His eyelids slid closed as he rocked his hips against her, and Veronica could only hang on and press back, moving mindlessly.

Abruptly, his eyes opened and he looked down at her. "I want you naked," he growled. "Now."

It never even occurred to her to demur — she unhooked her arms from around his neck and shimmied out of her cardigan. Stepping back, Coop peeled off his sweater and the white T-shirt underneath it with one economical move, and Veronica froze with her hands crossed over her stomach, the hem of the shell held clenched between her fingers momentarily forgotten.

Holy Mary, Mother of — All the moisture abandoned her mouth for parts farther south. His body was beautiful. The stuff from which classical statues were created, except instead of cold white marble, it was golden-skinned with the unseasonable tan she'd noted on his face and hands.

His chest was smooth and hard, with small,

flat, coppery nipples, and his abdomen was a study of rigidly defined sinew. His shoulders were broad with a sharp ridge of bone and lean bands of muscle, and powerful biceps stood out round and hard in his upper arms, while the longer, leaner muscle of his forearms shifted fluidly beneath his skin as he reached for the button on his Levi's.

A tiny trickle of insecurity cut through the hot, pounding haze of her arousal. Her own curves were a far cry from voluptuous. In fact they barely curved at all. Before she could work herself into a state about it, however, his big, raw-boned hands paused, and she looked up to see him watching her. The look of the hunger on his face decimated every doubt.

"You're way behind, Ronnie." He nodded at the shell. "Take that off."

She fumbled its removal, and still had her arms over her head fighting her way out of the camisole when she heard Coop's breath hiss in. In the next second her bra was unhooked and peeled away and hot hands enveloped her breasts. She pulled the sweater away from her face.

Coop handled her breasts as though they were Fabergé eggs, fragile and priceless, and he stared down at them nestled in his hands with riveted absorption. "Damn," he whispered. "These have got to be the tiniest breasts I've ever seen on a grown woman."

"Why, you sweet-talker, you." Veronica battled her way past the befuddling sensations his touch produced and said dryly, "That's *just* what every woman wants to hear — a testimony to the inadequacy of her attributes."

He raised his eyes. "Aw, no, I never said inadequate. Tiny, yes, but mighty. They've sure as hell got the power to bring this boy to his knees." Without relinquishing his hold, he bent his head and kissed her, and she immediately tumbled back into the roiling cosmos of screaming nerve endings he seemed to engender in her without even trying. She felt his thumbs stroking down the slight slopes of her breasts to capture her nipples against his forefingers, and she strained closer. He tugged, and she sucked in a sharp breath.

Raising his head, he gave her a crooked, carnal smile. "Ah, you like that." He glanced down to where the pink tips of her nipples poked through the prison of his fingers and tugged again. A high-pitched moan purled out of her throat and the smile dropped away from his face. He released one breast and grabbed her by the back of the neck, clamping his mouth down on hers. His kiss was almost rough, and moving back between her thighs, he ground his erection against her as though he could work his way inside of her despite the layers of material separating them. Yet he manipulated the breast he still cupped in his hand with incredible tenderness.

He was reaching for the button on her jeans when the phone suddenly rang. To Veronica's overstimulated system, it sounded louder than the alarm bell in the fire station over on Fifth Street, and she jerked in Coop's arms, then pulled back, heart pounding, to blink up at him.

"Let it ring," he growled and reached to draw her back against his chest, but she leaned away from him until the edge of the bar biting into her back prevented her from withdrawing any farther.

"It could be about Lizzy."

Coop swore softly but snatched up the receiver. "The Tonk." He listened a moment and then said, "Yeah, she's right here." With clear reluctance, he extended the receiver to her. "It's Mrs. Martelucchi."

Instant fear clearing the haze of arousal out of her brain, Ronnie snatched it out of his hands. "Mrs. M? Is everything all right?"

"The girls are fine, dear. I didn't mean to worry you — it's just that you're usually here right at two-oh-five and I began to worry when you didn't come home. Sometimes there's a rough element out there when the bars close."

"I, um, got busy here. But I'm sorry, I didn't mean to keep you waiting."

"Oh, that's not a problem, dear, so long as you're all right."

"I am. I'll be right over so you can get home." Avoiding Coop's eyes, she hung up and reached self-consciously for the cups of her bra, bringing them together and fumbling with the catch between her breasts. Cold, hard rationality had returned while she was on the phone, and she froze miserably when Coop's long, tanned fingers came into her line of sight and brushed hers aside to finish hooking her up.

What had she been thinking? She didn't care how hot he made her — and oh, God, she had a feeling that neither a cold shower nor squeezing her thighs together until her knees cramped was going to put out this fire. But having sex on bars — or the closest thing to it — was not her style. She wasn't getting involved with a self-professed drifter with no more ambition than to work the Tonk until the urge hit him to move on. How on earth had it come to this?

She glimpsed the tangle of black hair in Cooper's armpits as he raised both hands and shoveled his fingers through his hair. "I guess this means we go to bed frustrated tonight, huh?" he said and his voice was raspy, barely more than a whisper. "You okay?" He bent his head as if to kiss her.

"Don't!" Veronica jerked her head back.

He stilled, and slowly she raised her head to meet his gaze. His eyes still burned with dark fires, but his face was expressionless as he looked at her. "You've had a change of heart, I take it."

"Yes." Veronica reached for her shell and yanked it on, then snatched up the matching cardigan and slid off the counter onto her feet. "This was a mistake."

"A mistake." The flesh over his cheekbones tightened. Then his eyes went cool as they traveled all the curves and planes of her upper torso. "You just keep telling yourself that, Princess. You keep telling yourself that whenever we get too close. Because, lady, I want you and you want me, and *that's* an imperative that sooner or later you're not going to be able to ignore."

"You think not?" Because she was deathly afraid he might be right, and she would *not* end up like her mother, working her fingers to the bone for an unmotivated, lazy man, Veronica made her voice, her posture, her demeanor, extra confident. She grabbed her coat and purse and sailed, head held high, for the door. "Watch me."

10

Keeping to the shadows, Coop stealthily approached Eddie's house. He wasn't in the best frame of mind for breaking and entering, but he sure as hell was in the right mood. Like an addict, his mind kept sneaking back to the bar and the memory of Veronica half naked on the counter, all smooth white skin, eager mouth, and responsive little tits. God, she was so soft and sweet-tasting, and she'd wanted it every bit as much as he had. No one could tell him she hadn't.

Not even Ronnie herself, he thought fiercely, recalling the cool look on her face when she'd said, *This was a mistake.* He clenched his teeth so hard his jaw ached.

Dammit all, it wasn't as if he didn't know that. Yet the memory of her dismissing what they'd shared as some no-account error only served to infuriate him all over again. God knows why, because she was absolutely right. He'd had no business instigating a session of the hot and heavies with her — not when Eddie was his only reason for being in Fossil. But that sure as hell wasn't something he was about to share with Crystal's sister, and didn't that pretty much say it all? Other than a chemistry that unaccountably kept sparking between them, he and Ronnie had diddily-squat in common.

Go tell it to his hard-on, though. If he hadn't been trained in stealth tactics by the best, he thought sourly, he'd probably be using the damn thing to batter down the door to his brother's house about now.

As he checked out all the doors and windows for a weak spot, he did his best to put himself in the emotionless, single-minded state that had earned him the nickname of Iceman in his recon unit. He concentrated on blocking all thoughts of Ronnie out of his mind and focused instead on what he had to do to get in and out of Eddie's house without detection.

Eventually, he found a basement door that didn't sport the same state-of-the-art deadbolts as the main entries. He jimmied the lock with a credit card in seconds flat and let himself in, hoping to hell Eddie didn't have an alarm system that would bring the cops down on his head.

Aside from a need to burn off this frustration-fueled energy pumping through his veins, he couldn't say for certain what he was doing here. A judge had undoubtedly issued a search warrant and the police were sure to have tossed it thoroughly — with a helluva lot more expertise than he could lay claim to. He'd been trained to get in and get out, to assess the lay of the land or grab the hostage and run, not how to find a needle in the proverbial haystack — so it was unlikely he'd find anything they'd missed.

Yet he had a need tonight to touch base with Eddie, even if it was only through handling things that his brother had handled. Besides, who knew? Maybe something would speak to him. Perhaps something that had meant nothing to the cops would point him down the path he needed to take to clear his brother's name.

Once his eyes had adjusted, he wound through the basement's clutter of odds and ends to a wooden staircase. The door at the top of the stairs was latched, but with the same type of flimsy lock that was on the basement door, and once again Coop used his credit card to good effect. He closed the door behind him and was about to congratulate himself when he heard a low buzzing. Next to the outside door was a security keypad with a blinking red light.

"Shit!" He reached it in two large strides. He probably had thirty seconds, tops, to deactivate the alarm.

Knowing it was bound to be an easy number to remember, Coop punched in Eddie's birthday. The pad kept buzzing. Okay, *too* obvious.

He knew neither his brother's social security number nor the PIN number to his bank account. So what was the most important *date* in Eddie's life? He'd never been married. . . .

If Coop hadn't already been busy running other combinations on the keypad, including his own birthday and that of their mother, he would have smacked himself on the forehead. *Well, duh. The day Lizzy was born, Einstein.*

Then his mind went blank. What *was* Lizzy's birthday? March fourteenth? No, the thirteenth, right?

He punched in three, one, three, but the pad continued buzzing. No, wait, not March — it was in April, because he'd sent her that Fool doll he'd picked up in Vienna. It had made him think of April Fool's Day, which had made him remember her birthday was coming up. Coop tried four, one, three, but the buzz continued. His breath even, his nerves rock-steady, he felt like himself for the first time since Veronica had sashayed into the Tonk dressed to kill. One more try, and then he'd have to get the hell out of here and attempt it again another time. He punched in zero, four, one, three and grinned when the buzzing stopped and the red light blinked out.

Yes! He'd forgotten the adrenaline rush of walking the fine edge of danger. Odd, considering it had once been an everyday occurrence. Amazing how fast one adapted to a different lifestyle. Coop headed for Eddie's home office, figuring either that or his bedroom were the most likely places to pick up an errant clue . . . if any were there to be found.

An hour later, he was ready to concede what he'd known all along: There wasn't a damn thing here that the police hadn't already had their hands all over. Nothing was going to miraculously jump out at him with the key to Eddie's defense.

Yet Coop didn't feel as if he'd wasted his time.

Because all around him were traces of his brother, of the warmth and the joy that made up Eddie. Unlike the furnishings of Crystal's house, which looked like something out of an opium dream, Eddie's home was all soothing earth tones, soft, comfortable furniture, and touches that felt homey and inviting. There were pictures of Lizzy all over the place, as well as photos of father and daughter together, sporting smiles so big you could almost reach out and touch the love. Every room in the house held mementos of Lizzy: little kid drawings framed on the wall of Eddie's office, a disc of clay embedded with a tiny handprint on the nightstand next to his bed. Coop could only shake his head over the injustice of a man who'd only wanted the best for his daughter and had ended up on the run for a murder he didn't commit instead. It was ludicrous.

Coop shook off the frustration that threatened to impinge on his fiercely focused attention and opened the door next to Eddie's bedroom.

It was clearly Lizzy's room, and the first thing Coop saw was the Fool doll he'd sent her on her last birthday. It sat with another doll and a couple of stuffed animals on the pink and white spread on her bed. Something hung from a ribbon around its neck, and crossing the room, Coop saw it was the birthday card he'd enclosed with it. Edging it open with the tip of his finger, he read by the light of the moon his own bold handwriting beneath the printed Italian-language sentiment. *Happy Birthday from Venice, Lizzy*, it read. *Uncle James*.

Not *Love* or *Fond Wishes* — just *Uncle James*. Seeing the place of honor she'd given his gift and card, he felt like the biggest fraud in the world. Some uncle he was. Shame suffused him to know that it was one of the few birthdays he'd even remembered.

He eased open the card again and looked at his signature. *James*. It always took him by surprise to see that name in his own handwriting on personal correspondence. He'd been using it for a couple of years now to sign books, but before he'd become published, he'd never been anything but Cooper or Coop . . . except to his mother. It hadn't really been an issue until she'd left them for Chapman, and even after that it hadn't escalated into open warfare until his dad died and Coop'd had to go live with them full-time.

At first he'd refused to answer to the name, trying to force her to accept him for who he was — just plain Cooper. But his mother had proven to be even more stubborn than he, and "James" he had remained in her household. Whether he was merely there for a weekend visit or under her permanent custodianship, she would brook no blue-collar name for her son. It probably smacked too closely of her own less-than-prestigious roots.

Consequently, it was as James that Eddie had always known him. Because Eddie was Eddie, though, Cooper hadn't minded when his brother called him that. Eddie had said the name with love and admiration. When his mother had said it, it'd simply been a way to make Coop more acceptable in her eyes.

He shook himself free of the reverie, ignoring the gnawing ache low in his gut. All that was water under the bridge. Hell, she'd *died* disapproving of him, but that wasn't important now. What mattered was doing whatever he could to help his remaining family.

Which at the moment seemed to be damn little. He'd take home the folder of Eddie's financial papers he'd liberated. And, taking one last look around Lizzy's room before he eased the door shut, Coop wondered if there was a way to at least get his niece's personal belongings back. It might give her a measure of comfort until she was reunited with her daddy.

As far as being instrumental in clearing Eddie, though, Coop was beginning to harbor a nasty feeling that all he could really do was be in place, ready to take advantage, if a break should ever come his way.

Kody awakened in slow increments the next morning, barely relinquishing unconsciousness enough to acknowledge that he felt exceedingly loose-limbed and stress-free. Honest-to-God contentment hummed through his veins, but it was the physical heat radiating against his chest and across his stomach that aroused his sleep-deprived curiosity. Body heat warmed his entire right side, in fact, and blinking groggily, he raised his head off the pillow to locate the source.

A woman was pressed against his side, her head nestled in the hollow between his collarbone and the beginning swell of his chest. Her face was hidden from view by her sandy brown hair as it spread across his chest and over the arm she'd draped across his stomach, but now that he was more fully awake Kody knew perfectly well who this long, well-rounded body belonged to, and he couldn't have contained the satisfied smile that curled up the corners of his lips to save his life.

When he'd looked up last night to see Marissa standing next to Veronica, he might've been caught in the fallout of a megakilotron bomb, so immediate was the impact she'd had upon his senses. Just thinking about it now made him shake his head. Man. It was as if he and Marissa had been two components of a volatile compound kept on separate shelves — and for good reason, it turned out, because just look at what happened when they'd come together. Mix one part Marissa and one part Kody and — boom! — instant combustion. He'd never felt anything like it in his life.

He wanted to keep on feeling it, though, and he eased his hand beneath the thick fall of her hair to sweep it away from her face. As he shifted to look down at her, his gaze swept across two portraits on the far wall, then snapped back to fix on them.

His stomach sank. One was of a curly-haired little girl with a big smile and gaps where her two front teeth should be. The other was of a slightly older boy who looked to be long and lanky. He had Marissa's eyes. Had her smile, too, minus the dimples.

Kody tried to tell himself that they were probably her niece and nephew, but it wouldn't wash. Not only did the boy look like a male version of Marissa, but there was an inscription in childish handwriting on the little girl's photo. *For Mommy*, it said.

Well, shit.

It wasn't that he didn't *like* kids; he liked them just fine. But he had a bit of a blind spot when it came to them. What man wouldn't who'd watched his sister flit from one man to the next, and had watched the heartache of his nephew getting attached to the men traipsing in and out of his mama's house? Just about the time his nephew Jacob felt safe getting comfortable with the presence of some new guy in his young life, that guy would invariably disappear. And while Kody couldn't do a damn thing to change his sister's behavior, he'd sworn he'd never be responsible for putting the look he'd seen too often on Jacob's face on the face of someone else's kid.

So he tended to date women who came without the baggage. And the few times he had gone out with a woman who had children, he'd been careful to take her out on adult-only dates that didn't include her kids, figuring — rightly, as it turned out — that the attraction might not last. By keeping his interaction with her progeny to a bare minimum, he at least circumvented having to feel responsible for building false hope in a child's mind that this latest male influence to pass through his life would turn out to be something more permanent.

No kid would ever have to watch him waltz out the door with the youngster's heart in his hands.

Kody swept Marissa's hair off her face and tucked in his chin to gaze down at her. Smoothing a finger down her nose, he looked at the faint blue veins in her eyelids, at the crease in her cheek that even in repose any fool could see would turn into one of those knock-you-on-your-butt, killer dimples of hers the minute she smiled.

Hell. He didn't want to give her up. He wanted to explore this amazing chemistry between them to the fullest. Something this combustible was bound to burn itself out in the end, but he sure hated the idea of walking away from it before it did.

But that's exactly what he'd better do. Because no matter how unique this thing between them felt, he wasn't betraying his one true, steadfast principle. He'd already forsaken one of the rules that went along with it — to never sleep in a woman's bed when there were children in the house. His actions last night had been dictated by sheer lust, and for all he knew, Marissa's kids were sawing z's down the hall right now.

He eased her off his chest and slipped out of bed.

He'd stepped into his jeans and pulled them into place but hadn't yet fastened them when he heard her rustling behind him.

"What time is it?" she asked in a croaky voice, and unwillingly, he turned to face her.

Ah, man. Big mistake. She was all flushed from sleep, propped up on one elbow, the top sheet pulled up under her armpits and stretched tightly across those beautiful, full breasts of hers. Her eyes were sleepy and her rumpled hair tumbled over her plump shoulders and down her back — all except for one long wisp dangling over her left eye.

He couldn't help himself: He walked back to the bed and bent down to smooth back the errant tendril. "It's after nine. I've gotta go."

"Already?" Marissa reached out a manicured fingertip and traced the open fly of his jeans, trailing her nail along his skin down one side of the zipper and up the other. She looked up at him with sultry eyes. "Couldn't you spare another, oh, say, twenty minutes? Riley and Dessa aren't due home until noon."

And just like that, Kody found himself shucking off his newly donned jeans and climbing back into bed with her. But as he hauled her into his arms and rolled them over, he promised himself that, no matter how good the sex was, no matter how many things they seemed to have to say to each other, he was taking this slow.

And that meant he only took her out on grown-up, no-kids-allowed dates.

11

Wind buffeted the house that afternoon as Coop sat at the kitchen table with Boo sprawled out asleep on his knee and a tall glass of cold milk within easy reach. On a paper towel next to the glass sat a corned beef sandwich slathered in mustard and mayo and sloppy with overflowing lettuce and tomato. He'd drawn a line down the middle of the yellow legal pad that sat by his right hand, and between alternate bites of his sandwich and quaffs of milk, he jotted notes from a thick tome of *Security Measures of the CIA* on the tablet's left side. Occasionally, he reached for the children's science primer in the middle of the table and clarified to himself the way something worked, then made a note of that on the right side of the pad.

By the time the sound of feet clattering down the back stairs broke his concentration, he'd made decent inroads into his research and wasn't averse to the idea of taking a break. He glanced up and watched Lizzy whirl into the room, only to pull herself up short when she saw him sitting there. Her shiny brown hair had been braided into two neat plaits and she wore a pair of faded rose-pink leggings and an adult-sized white men's-style button-down shirt. Its shirttail hem reached below her knees, and its long sleeves formed a four-inch cuff where they'd been rolled up several times above her narrow little wrists.

"Hi," she said, dipping her head and peeking out at him from beneath her bangs. She gave him one of her shy smiles. "Have you seen my Aunt Ronnie or my kitty?"

"Can't say that I've seen your aunt around," Coop replied honestly while he surreptitiously dumped the cat from his lap and nudged him out from under the table with the side of his foot. Unhappy at being so rudely awakened, Boo made his displeasure known with a disgruntled yowl, and Lizzy's face lit up.

"Oh, look, Boo's right here! He musta been sleeping on one of the chairs." She scooped the kitten up off the floor and held him nose to nose with her, batting her eyelashes at him. Boo watched with interest for a moment before trying to pin down the fluttering movement with a soft paw.

Lizzy peered at Coop out of her unimpeded eye. "Where do you think Aunt Ronnie could be? She's s'posta be here."

"I don't know, Little Bit; she probably just stepped out for a minute. I'm sure she'll be right back; you know how responsible she is that way."

Lizzy looked less than thrilled with his answer. Dissatisfaction wasn't an expression Coop was used to seeing on her face, and watching her soft mouth pull down at the corners caused low-grade panic to spark in his gut. He had to remind himself he was trained to handle all manner of emergencies — so how difficult could it be to divert the attention of one little girl? Focusing his attention on her, he indicated her attire with a jut of his chin. "That's an interesting getup you've got on there."

He succeeded beyond his expectations. Lizzy glanced down at herself, then flashed him a wholehearted grin such as Coop had only seen in her photos with Eddie. He was unprepared for the way his heart seized up with pure, undiluted pleasure at knowing he had caused that smile. *Aw, God, kid, I think I'm in love.*

"This is my *smock*." Lizzy shifted Boo to pinch one of the voluminous folds of her shirt and hold it out as if she were about to make her curtsy to the queen. "Me 'n' Aunt Ronnie are gonna paint my room. Then we're gonna *stencil* stuff."

"That sounds pretty cool."

She nodded vigorously. "*Really* cool."

"What color are you going to paint it?"

"Pink."

"Uh-huh. Would that be Tickled Pink by any chance?" That would be appropriate, he thought, since it was what she so clearly was at the moment.

Lizzy giggled. "No, silly. *Maiden* Pink."

"That was gonna be my next guess. You choose that color yourself, or did your aunt pick it out?"

171

"I picked it all by myself. Aunt Ronnie said we'd divide the, um . . . the . . . I forget the word." Her brow furrowed in concentration. Then, just as quickly, it cleared. "Layber! She said we'd divide the layber — that my part would be picking the color and her part'd be paying for it. And that if she hadda paint, then I hadda paint, too." The look on her face suggested she couldn't think of anything more thrilling. "It's gonna be really pretty — you can come see it when we're done if you wanna."

"I'd like that. So you like pink, huh?" He remembered her room last night with its pink and white bedspread.

"Uh-huh. It's my fave-rit." She gave him another of her bashful smiles. "It's a *girl* color."

"Then that would be the color for you, all right, because you're certainly all girl."

Lizzy's smile was nothing short of dazzling, and she looked at him all bright-eyed, as if he'd just uttered the most brilliant words she'd ever heard. "That's what my *daddy* says!"

Then the back door opened on a whoosh of wind, and Coop didn't have to turn around to know who was there.

Logic dictated only one person would walk into the house without first knocking, but logic wasn't the instinct under which he was operating. Because he could be both stone deaf and blind, and still he'd know. His body seemed to possess an animal instinct that could almost *scent* Veronica the instant she came within range. Call it pheromones, call it musk — label it anything at all, but the reality was downright primal. One whiff and he was all primed to procreate. To go forth and multiply.

To propagate the earth with miniature Ronnies.

Jesus. He sat up in his seat. He had no idea where this shit was coming from, but if that wasn't the spookiest damn notion to ever cross his mind, he didn't know what was. He'd decided a long time ago that marriage wasn't for him and had made it his mission in life *not* to carelessly populate the world with little Blackstocks. He hadn't had unprotected sex since sweating out the consequences after Amy Sue Miller had given him his first taste of heaven on a slightly mildewed lounge pad in her father's pool house when he was fifteen years old.

Lizzy pulled him out of his horror-struck paralysis when she all but danced with impatience and demanded, "Aunt Ronnie, where *were* you? I've been ready forever and *ever.*"

"I'm sorry, sweetie. I realized we only had one paint tray and went over to Mrs. M's to see if she had one that we could borrow so we'd each have our own. That way we won't have to slop paint back and forth."

Coop hadn't seen Veronica since they'd parted on less than cozy terms last night, and he waited to see how she'd handle the meeting. Being ignored entirely wasn't one of the options that had occurred to him. But although she eyed the books on the table in front of him, she acted as if Coop himself were invisible.

Considering she'd merely had to walk into the room to have him sporting a hard-on a cat couldn't scratch, he was in no mood to let that pass. He shoved back his chair, but then thought better of climbing to his feet. Lizzy was way too young for the type of anatomy lesson that would afford her. Tapping his pen in a rapid tattoo against his tablet, he gave Veronica a comprehensive once-over. "I need to talk to you."

Still she refused to look at him. "It'll have to wait," she coolly informed his reference books. "Lizzy and I have a hot date with her bedroom."

"Yeah? I'm good in the bedroom." Visions that were a world removed from painting floated on the peripheries of his mind, and he cleared his throat. Still his voice was rough-edged when he said, "You can use me. Any way you want."

That got her attention, and her eyes snapped up while hot color stained her cheeks. "What?"

"To help paint. I'm handy with a paintbrush, so give me a shirt like you did for Lizzy" — he ran his gaze over the one she had on — "and I'll give you a hand painting Lizzy's bedroom."

Lizzy giggled. "You're too big, silly. Aunt Ronnie's shirts wouldn't fit you."

"I suppose you've got a point." He reached for the unbuttoned plackets of his flannel shirt and began shrugging the garment off his shoulders. "I guess I could just take mine off instead, so it doesn't get paint-splattered."

"How very thoughtful of you, but keep your shirt on, and I do mean that literally." Not a trace of sarcasm colored Veronica's words, but the look in her eyes was anything but polite as she locked gazes with him. "Because, while the words to tell you exactly what I think of your generous offer fail me, Lizzy and I must decline. We planned this as a bonding afternoon for just us girls."

"You can come see it when it's all pretty, though," Lizzy added. She grabbed Veronica's hand, effectively breaking the stare-down her aunt was engaged in with Coop. "Come *on*," she said insistently. "We gotta get started, 'kay?"

Veronica allowed Lizzy to tow her around the corner, and only when they were out of Coop's orbit did she remember to breathe. She felt like knocking her head against the nearest wall. It was bad enough that she was all agog to know why he was reading those books that were on the table. But would this fascination with his body — his big, beautiful body — never cease? *You shouldn't have looked,* she berated herself as she followed her niece up the stairs. *If only you hadn't looked at him.*

But she had. When he'd said he was good in the bedroom and demanded that she *use* him in that insinuating voice, she hadn't been able to resist. Too many images of the ways in which she could do just that had popped into her mind, and, darn it, a woman could only be so strong.

So she'd looked, and it had been every bit the

175

mistake she'd feared it would be. He was so damn male that she invariably got a forbidden sort of thrill out of sneaking peeks at him. It reminded her of when she and Crystal used to sneak out early from their Sunday chores at the Tonk to gorge on candy at Swanson's Sweet Shoppe — she'd known they were gonna get it in the end, but had been unable to resist despite the trouble it would bring down on their heads.

The Coop she was accustomed to seeing, though, was always so spic-and-span. She had never seen him looking anything but smooth-shaven and neatly dressed. And if she'd secretly found *that* devastating, it didn't hold a candle to seeing him barefoot and sort of rumpled-looking in his blue jeans, a brown thermal-knit Henley with its sleeves shoved up his forearms, and an unbuttoned, cuffs-rolled-back, slate-and-tan flannel shirt whose unpressed state wasn't even close to his usual spit-shined standards. Then there was the dot of mustard next to his full lower lip, and the dark stubble that shadowed his jaw.

She'd been so fiercely drawn she could have screamed. And that was *before* he'd offered to take his shirt off. Oh, dirty word — dirty, filthy, *obscene* word! She'd wanted to cup that bristly jaw in her hands, to straddle his lap and . . .

No! She hadn't tossed and turned all night long simply to turn around and cave the first time she saw a pair of big naked feet . . . no matter how much they made Marissa's words come back to haunt her. *Was* Cooper Blackstock proportional all over?

Stop that! Just stop it, Davis, and put him out of your mind right now.

She could do that.

She *would* do it, by God.

She threw herself into the Lizzy Project and, little by little, her enthusiasm became genuine. She and Lizzy painted up a storm, talking about Barbies and best friends and Harry Potter when they weren't singing along with the radio. They finished the walls, then carefully stenciled rosebuds on the plain white dresser and generally had a fine time transforming the room from a starkly impersonal cubicle to a little-girl haven. When it was finished, they both stepped to the doorway to admire their work. "So, what do you think?" she asked, her gaze on a few of the pretties that Lizzy had selected from her mother's collection.

"It's bee-u-tee-ful. It's even prettier than the room at my daddy's house! I never wanna leave."

Veronica's stomach squeezed. Oh, man, what had she done? She had feared she would screw up this new parental role she'd taken on, but never had she dreamed she would do it so swiftly or so utterly.

She'd merely wanted to do something for Lizzy that would make her feel a little bit special. Well, the good news was, she seemed to have accomplished that. The bad news, though — and

177

the thing she hadn't even taken into consideration — was how her niece was going to feel when Veronica slapped the FOR SALE sign on the house. What would it do to Lizzy when her aunt told her to pack her things because they were leaving the house behind, including the room in which Veronica had just helped her become emotionally invested?

Damn. Ah, damn, damn, damn.

What had she been thinking? Had she actually believed that if she didn't bring up the reality of their situation to her niece, it would somehow work itself out or simply go away on its own? She'd been living in a dream world, obviously.

Worse, she was still half immersed in denial, because she was too chickenhearted to tell Lizzy even now. She simply couldn't bear to burst the child's bubble while Lizzy was still all aglow over the day's accomplishments.

So she did the next best thing. She called Marissa and uttered one heartfelt word. *"Help."*

There was a second of silence. Then Marissa asked quietly, "How bad is it?"

"Oh, God." A garbled laugh escaped Veronica. "As bad as it gets. I've really messed up this time."

"I'll be right over. Kids!" Veronica heard her yell. "Help me find my car keys. We're going to —" The connection was severed.

Veronica replaced the receiver and stared out the front window, moodily watching a pop can blow down the center of a deserted Baker

Street. Thank God it was Sunday. The bar was closed, a fact for which Veronica was exceedingly grateful, because she frankly didn't think she could face having to go to the Tonk tonight. Not when she was all torn to pieces over being such a —

"You are *not* a lousy parent!" Marissa said a short while later. "You just didn't give this aspect of it enough thought."

The kids had gone upstairs to admire Lizzy's bedroom, Cooper thankfully had either gone out or was up in his own room, and the two women were ensconced on either end of the living room couch. Veronica hugged her knees to her chest and dug her chin into her kneecap as she gazed at her friend. "Enough thought? I didn't think, period! And I *am* an awful parent. I've never even bothered to sit down with Lizzy and talk to her about Crystal and Eddie." She grasped a handful of her hair and yanked.

"Stop that. You're stretching your eyelid, and it's creeping me out." Marissa leaned forward and pried Veronica's fingers loose. "Jeeze Louise, you're going to rip your hair out by the roots."

"I *should* just rip it out by the roots. I knew she had to be hurting inside with all the awful stuff that's happened in her life, but I took her lack of weeping and wailing at face value and just buried my head in the sand. Out of sight, out of mind, that's my motto. God, Rissa, Lizzy's only six years old, and still she's ten times more mature than I am."

"Not to mention a lot less melodramatic," Marissa agreed dryly. She gave Veronica's foot a poke. "Get *over* yourself! So you put off a difficult conversation longer than you should have — give her a week or so to revel in the room, then sit her down for a heart-to-heart. That's the main rule of parenting, you know. When you screw up, you simply pick your moment, then do your best to rectify the problem. The only way you can completely mess up is if you stop trying."

Veronica felt a spark of hope. "You're right — I know you are. But I still dread telling Lizzy that we'll be moving. She's not going to be happy about leaving Dessa and Riley, never mind the only town she's ever lived in." She stared at her friend as she sorted through her thoughts. "Still, she's eminently reasonable for a six-year-old, and there are definite advantages to the move. At least in Seattle everyone and their brother won't know about her parents, so no one will give her a hard time at school. And she's such a sweetheart I know she'll make friends, but we could always come back here for the weekends until that happens, to make the transition easier. Maybe, too, if I tell her we'll fix her an equally nice room at my place, it will alleviate some of the trauma."

"Exactly. And it's not as if you've sold anything yet, so you're not talking about an immediate change. As far as her room goes, you can promise to duplicate this one exactly, if that's what it takes. There's no law, for instance, that says you can't take that wonderful chest of

180

drawers with you." Marissa smiled gently. "Nice stenciling job, by the way."

Veronica stared at her soberly. "Oh, God, Rissa, *thank* you." They both knew she wasn't talking about complimenting her stenciling abilities.

"You're entirely welcome. Now I'm in need of your expertise. The decorations committee meeting is tomorrow, and Kody said that while we could probably keep the outside ice sculptures frozen long enough for them to remain recognizable the length of the Winter Festival, it would be too costly to attempt it indoors."

"Oh, my God — Kody!" Veronica's back straightened. "I entirely forgot about that — did you two have wild monkey sex after you left the bar last night?" She immediately flapped her hand. "What am I thinking — of course you did. Was he good? Are you seeing him again?"

"Yes; *God,* yes; and yes — although we didn't make concrete plans for the last one."

"I don't suppose you'd consider a few details for that 'God, yes' part, would you?" Veronica cocked an eyebrow, then grinned when Marissa remained closemouthed. "No? Okay, but you gotta know I'm jealous. Have the kids met him yet?"

"No. He left this morning before they got home. It was hard to let him go, but that was the only way it could be handled. Men who sleep over have hardly been a part of my landscape, and I frankly don't intend Kody to be the guy to

181

break that tradition — at least not when my kids sleep at home." The grin she shot Veronica punched her dimples deep into her cheeks. "Which means you're probably going to be seeing a *lot* more of Dessa and Riley come the weekends."

"You know they're always welcome."

"Bless you, my child, I do know that. And if I'm going to start dating again, the kids will obviously have to meet him. But I have to put some thought into how I introduce him into their lives. Maybe a movie or a pizza out — something casual, at any rate, that they won't attach too much importance to if things don't pan out. Until then I appreciate it more than I can say that you're willing to help me have a love life."

"Yeah, well, I'm happy one of us is getting lucky." Veronica opened her mouth to share her own early-morning misadventure, but Marissa's bawdy laugh made her decide not to dilute her friend's pleasure. She'd tell her later.

"You're an excellent friend," Marissa said. "Speaking of which, what am I going to do about the decorations if ice sculptures indoors are out of the question?"

"Well, you know, I've actually been thinking about that, and I think I've got an even better idea."

"Oooh, I like the sound of that. Let's hear it."

"Winter trees. The drama of stark branches and those little white fairy lights is very striking, and between the size of the trees and the shadows the lights cast, they hide a multitude of sins, which is always a consideration in old buildings like the ones on the fairgrounds. Now, I haven't had time to research the costs, and I'm not sure if you can buy artificial trees that aren't all leafed out — they weren't available back when I did this. But depending on the budget, your committee could easily make the trees themselves out of wire and papier mâché, or they could probably hire it done at a fairly reasonable cost. Too bad we're a little pressed for time, or you could sponsor a contest for high school and college students, which would result in them doing most of the work for you." She grinned, then shrugged. "I suppose you could always buy real trees at a nursery and then either donate them for a beautification project after the festival or raffle them off, or both. But that would probably get a little spendy, because you'd have to buy reasonably mature trees. Besides, the beauty of fake ones is that you can use them again and again, and change the look by the way you decorate them. You might even be able to defray the cost by renting them out to other organizations for their affairs — they can be that effective." She discovered her friend staring at her, mouth agape, and felt her spirits take a dip. "You hate the idea."

"Are you kidding? I *love* the idea. I'm just amazed, is all. How on earth do you come *up* with this stuff?"

"Hey, I was an auction coordinator for umpteen years before I started my business." Since Marissa already knew that, Veronica shrugged it off as unimportant, but her friend's praise gave her a warm glow. "That often meant I had a low budget to work with, depending on which organization had hired me at the time, and you know what they say — necessity is the mother of invention. I used the tree idea years ago for a private school's building fund auction, which is why I can't give you an up-to-the minute cost analysis. But I can tell you from experience that it paid for itself in the long run, because the trees got so much attention that the school ended up renting them out to other organizations. Look, let's grab a tablet and make as complete a proposal as we can with what information we have available. We'll include a couple of oversized ice sculptures for outside the exhibition hall doors, because they really are very effective. That should at least give us a starting place for your committee."

"Oh, God, I love this." Marissa jumped up and headed for the kitchen, pausing only long enough to flash Veronica a huge smile. "Thanks, chickie. I'll give you credit at the meeting tomorrow, I promise."

"Are you crazy? That would completely negate the whole point here, which is showing who's-their-faces that you don't have to be born on Holly Drive to do the job."

"You weren't born there, either, so the point would still be made."

"Yeah, but I'm not the one they've been putting down. You deserve to rub their noses in it a little."

Marissa grinned. "I hate to admit it, but I wouldn't mind doing that at all. I'll take full credit, then — and bless your heart. But I'll also do the best damn job that's ever been done, now that you've given me something to work with. And I think it's only fitting that I begin by assigning Tyler-Jones and Wentworth the task of hunting down the various costs, don't you?"

"Oh, yes." Veronica nodded decisively. "Absolutely."

12

Veronica wound her way between the Tonk's tightly packed tables Friday night, dispensing drinks and dodging the hands of a particularly rambunctious young man celebrating his twenty-first birthday with a group of friends. Glimpsing Marissa sitting with Kody toward the back of her section, she headed straight over. She could use a little oasis of sanity tonight.

She saw the moment Marissa spotted her, for her friend's dimples dented her cheeks beneath the verve of her welcoming smile. Marissa's lips formed words, but Veronica shook her head and shrugged helplessly. Attempting to make out normal conversational tones over the din in here tonight was like trying to communicate without raising one's voice across the tin-can telephones they used to fashion with a length of string stretched between their bedrooms back when they were kids — it simply wasn't possible. Reaching the table, she balanced her tray on her right hip and leaned down. "Am I glad to see you! But I'm afraid I didn't catch a word you said."

Marissa raised her voice. "It wasn't anything earth-shattering. I was merely stating the obvious — helluva crowd here tonight."

"No fooling! It's been a madhouse since I came on duty — I think this past week must have given everyone a severe case of cabin fever."

A cold snap had blown down from the mountains and turned Fossil's on-again-off-again rain squalls into a genuine winter storm. First it had snowed several inches. Then freezing rain had blown in on a fierce wind, and by the time the weather system had blown itself out, trees had been left sheeted in ice and the streets had turned to rinks. When it started to snow again, it had actually been a relief. At least with a layer of snow cushioning the ice, walking and driving weren't quite as hazardous.

Today offered the first sign of improvement. Shortly after noon the sun had finally come out again, and while temperatures still hovered around the freezing mark, the threat of additional snow or freezing rain seemed to have passed.

"Hasn't it been *nuts?*" Marissa yelled. "I was getting pretty squirrelly myself by the time things finally settled down. I was too chicken to drive down the bluff roads, but I'm telling you, I was just about ready to brave it, ice or no ice. Dessa hasn't given me a moment's peace since it started snowing Monday night, worrying that tonight's sleepover at the VFW hall would be canceled."

Veronica nodded. "I know what you mean. Lizzy was anxious, too, and it didn't help to tell

her that tonight's shindig was sure to be resched-
uled if the weather caused it to be canceled. It's a
good thing it cleared up when it did or we'd have
some unhappy kids on our hands." She smacked
the tabletop with the flat of her hand. "Hey!
That reminds me: How did the Winter Festival
meeting go?"

Marissa's smile was dazzling. "Oh, Ronnie, it
was great! They thought I was a genius! And my
absolute favorite part was watching Tyler-Jones
and Wentworth struggle to say something gracious, when they were clearly prepared to pa-
tronize the poor, clueless upstart."

Veronica laughed. "Chalk one up for the girls
from the flats."

"Exactly. It was *so* sweet."

A man two tables over signaled impatiently
and Veronica straightened. "The natives are getting restless — I'd better get back to work. What
can I get you two?"

For the next hour and a half she was run
ragged trying to keep up with all her orders, and
the grabby birthday boy didn't help. She used an
old trick and started taking his order from the far
side of the table.

Around eleven-thirty, things finally began to
settle down as the crowd thinned out, and Veronica's ringing ears were grateful when the
decibel level dropped to normal.

Being able to communicate without shouting
didn't do much to address her aching feet, however, and, ignoring a gesture from the birthday

boy that may or may not have been a summons for another drink, she took advantage of the momentary lull to join Marissa and Kody at their table.

She collapsed onto a chair and toed off her shoes. Resting her left ankle on her right knee, she rubbed her foot and groaned. "Oh, that feels good. Thank God someone finally responded to our ad, because I don't know how much longer I can keep this up."

Marissa studied her with interest. "You've hired someone, then?"

"Not yet, but a woman's coming in for an interview tomorrow, and unless she's a serial killer, she's got herself a job as far as I'm concerned." She smiled wryly. "Maybe even then. I'm feeling that desperate."

Involuntarily, she found herself searching for Coop. The moment she spotted him, though, she knew she was courting trouble. For even knowing full well she should look away, she ate up the sight of him. It wasn't until he suddenly glanced up from the drink he was mixing and looked straight at her that she wrenched her attention back to Marissa and Kody.

Desperate was the word, and it wasn't simply because she didn't like working at the Tonk or because she needed to start paying attention to her own business if she wanted a business to return to once she'd settled her family affairs. It wasn't even because she was burning her candle at both ends and sooner or later something had to give. The real problem was the attraction between her and Cooper. It just kept growing stronger and stronger, while her will to fight it grew weaker and weaker. She had to put some distance between them.

Before she ended up doing something downright foolish.

"Um, about the job candidate," she said, sternly focusing her attention back on her self-derailed conversation. "Would you pick Lizzy up from the VFW hall tomorrow when you collect Riley and Dess, and keep her for me until I finish interviewing the woman?"

"Sure," Marissa said. "Maybe, if the roads aren't too big a mess, I'll take the kids down to King's Theater to see the new Disney." She turned to Kody, stroking a proprietary hand down his arm. "You up for a cartoon with three kids? Only two of them are hyper." She smiled crookedly. "Of course, those would be mine."

For just a second Veronica thought she glimpsed discomfort in Kody's expression, but then he grinned.

"Appealing as an invitation to sit in a theater full of screaming kids sounds," he said easily, "I told my dad I'd come over and give him a hand shoring up the basement stairs."

"Well, okay," Marissa said. "But I'm telling you, you don't know what you're missing."

Their gazes met then and held, and Veronica could practically see the electricity that sizzled between them. She would've fanned herself if

190

both her hands weren't already occupied massaging her aching feet, and she tried not to be jealous when they abruptly pushed back from the table and rose to their feet.

Marissa's voice was throatier than usual when she looked down and said, "Um, Ronnie, we've gotta —"

"Say goodnight," Kody finished for her when her sentence trailed into a vague little hum. He grabbed her hand and gave Veronica a sheepish smile. "So, uh, goodnight, then." He hustled Marissa out the door.

"Hey, don't mind me," Veronica murmured. She dropped her foot to the floor and felt around for her shoe. "I've got to get back to work, anyway."

She made a quick detour to the ladies' room to wash her hands and apply a dash of lipstick, then headed back to the floor. A woman was just taking a seat in Sandy's section and Veronica promptly changed directions to give her a wide berth. The last person she wanted to hook up with tonight was Darlene Starkey.

Darlene was an average-looking woman of around fifty, with the lean musculature and worn hands of a farmworker, and the immaculate beige pageboy of a society doyenne. She lived halfway up the Bluff, which was considered a part of the pricey neighborhood but not of its upper echelon. Though she was originally from somewhere other than Fossil, it was popularly believed that she'd grown up in an area like their own flats and had married up when she'd hooked up with David Starkey. Nobody knew for sure, though, because Darlene wasn't talking.

Which was pretty ironic when you stopped to think about it, considering she was the biggest gossip in Fossil. Darlene was well-known for her unapologetic nosiness and acerbic tongue, and Ronnie thanked heaven for small favors that the woman was in Sandy's section tonight rather than her own. Things were hectic enough around here already without having to deal with carrion wanting to pick over her sister's bones.

Perhaps because her attention was divided, Veronica failed to maintain the guard she'd kept up most of the evening around the birthday boy. As she bent to clear a table, she entirely forgot that he was at the table behind her — until a hand reached between her legs and grabbed her where no man had the right to get grabby without her express invitation.

Veronica yelped in shock and straightened. She saw Coop drop the glass he'd been building a drink in and vault the bar, sending two patrons scrambling to get out of his way. His expression said someone was going to bleed, and like a paused film suddenly set back in motion, she jerked out of her paralysis. Without conscious thought, she swung the empty beer mug that she'd been clearing behind her, chopping it sideways as hard as she could. A yip of pain ripped the air and the hand cupping her crotch dropped away.

She whipped around, but before she could go for the birthday boy's throat, a man in a beautifully cut suit who'd been seated two tables over stepped between them. He leaned down in the young man's face. "Do you have any idea what kind of legal trouble you just bought yourself, junior?"

The drunken celebrant hugged his arm to his chest. "I think she broke my elbow," he moaned.

Coop skidded to a halt next to Veronica. His dark brows were gathered ominously, but the murder in his eyes gentled as he grasped her by the shoulders and peered down into her face. "Are you okay?"

No. Did you see where he touched me? God, I feel so dirty. "Yeah, I think so."

"Good." He set her aside. "Because I'm going to kill him."

"Oh, no, you don't." She stepped into his path, her breasts flattening against his diaphragm when he didn't stop fast enough to avoid her block. "That privilege is mine."

Coop had to smile at that, albeit a bit grimly. Veronica Davis was nobody's victim. But something shadowy and violated lurked beneath the fury in her eyes, and the urge to shelter her was a living thing in his chest. Instead of wrapping her up in his arms as he was tempted to do, however, he followed her lead and turned his attention to the birthday boy.

The depth of his rage unnerved him. He'd

learned years ago that powerful feelings tended to get in the way, and he'd taught himself to relegate negative ones to a locked-down area of his mind until he could safely deal with them. At the moment, however, he'd gladly tear the little deviant apart limb by limb — starting with the hand that had dared touch her that way.

Luckily, Eddie's lawyer stood squarely between him and the impulse. Wrestling his temper into submission, Coop heard Neil Peavy say pleasantly, "I hope you got a lot of enjoyment out of turning twenty-one tonight, son, because this might be the last party you attend for quite some time."

"Wha'chu babblin' about?" Even looking as if he realized he'd gone too far, the kid apparently felt the need to posture for his friends.

"I'm babbling," the lawyer said in an avuncular tone, "about your eligibility to be tried as an adult for sexual assault."

The young man quit fussing with his elbow and sat up straight. "Hey, man, I was just having a little fun!"

"Is that a fact?" Neil turned to Veronica. "Did you have fun as well, Ms. Davis?"

"No," Veronica replied in no uncertain terms. "It was bad enough when he grabbed my rear a couple of times earlier. But for him to touch me . . . where he did . . . as if he had any right —" A shudder wracked her frame.

Neil turned back to the young man, who didn't look nearly as cocky as he had a moment ago. "You hear that, boy? She didn't have fun." He shook his head. "That's not good for you. Because the legal system has no sense of humor, and if a woman isn't laughing, then they aren't likely to, either. There's a whole raft of charges that can be brought against a guy who touches a woman without her consent. A couple of those charges could get you a good, long term in Monroe penitentiary, should you be found guilty. And trust me, junior, given the public nature of your display and your lack of contrition, you've just seen to it that you'll be found guilty as hell if Ms. Davis here decides to press charges."

Coop had a feeling Peavy might be exaggerating the consequences a bit, but it worked like a charm. The birthday boy suddenly seemed cold-stone sober. Face bleached of color, he turned to Ronnie and said, "Ah, jeez, lady, please. I shouldn't have touched you like that, and if you'll just not press charges I will never do anything like it again." He scrubbed a trembling hand over his mouth. "Honest. I *am* sorry."

Veronica gave him a long, slow perusal. Then she turned to Neil. "If I don't press charges and it turns out he's a big liar —"

"No, ma'am, I ain't! I'll never touch another woman without her permission as long as I live!"

"If he turns out to be a big, fat liar," she reiterated, giving the young man a hard look, "and he does something like this to another woman . . ."

"Then you can still press charges. Or if the

statute of limitations has expired, you can come forward as a witness for his next victim."

"There ain't gonna *be* a next victim," the young man said earnestly, and swiped a film of sweat from his forehead with the back of his hand. "I'm not even the kinda guy who *has* victims. Swear to God."

Veronica turned to him. "Excuse me," she said coldly. "But you sure as hell were that kind of guy two minutes ago."

"I was a full-of-myself *fool* two minutes ago!"

"That's a given," she agreed. "But why should I believe you've suddenly turned over a new leaf? What are you *now* that's so all-fired different?"

"Scared shitless."

"Good," she snapped. "You should be scared."

"And sorry. Real, *real* sorry."

"Yeah? For how long? How do I know you won't revert to a grabby little pervert a week or two down the road, when your fear isn't quite so immediate?"

"Because," said the young man, and he met her gaze with sober intensity, "if I'm *ever* tempted to do anything like this again, I'll just think about an inmate named Bubba ordering me to pick up his dropped soap in the group shower. And I swear on my mother's soul I'll remember how you shuddered when you talked about how I touched you."

Veronica studied him a moment. "Let me see your driver's license." When he complied, she copied its information onto her order pad, tossed the license back to him, then jerked her head toward the door. "Go on, then. Get out of here."

Chairs scraped as the birthday boy and his subdued group of buddies scrambled to get away before she could change her mind. Barely pausing long enough to toss a pile of bills on the table, they raced for the door.

Ignoring the money, Veronica turned to Peavy. "Thank you, Mr. . . . I'm sorry, I don't even know your name."

"This is Neil Peavy, Ronnie." Coop reached past her to offer Peavy his hand. "That was well done. You threw the fear of God into him without bloodshed." He smiled wryly. "I'd love to say I could've done the same, but the truth is I don't think I could."

"I agree, Mr. Peavy," Veronica said. "As confrontational as I felt, I would've only made him defensive. Your way was much more effective. Thank you again."

"It was my pleasure," Peavy said pleasantly. "I'm pretty sure it was your own reaction that had the most impact, but I'm glad to have been of help." He gave her a concerned look. "That must have been a nasty shock. Are you all right?"

"Yes. I believe I am." But she suddenly realized Shania Twain, singing from the jukebox, was the only voice she heard, and she glanced around to see she'd attracted the attention of the entire bar. Cheeks flaming, she tipped her chin in the air.

"What?" Coop demanded, then he, too, looked around. He'd been so tuned in on Veronica he hadn't noticed everyone watching the contretemps as though it were a nighttime soap.

"Show's over, folks." He reached over to give the nape of Veronica's neck a gentle squeeze, then headed back to the bar. Locating Sandy on the way, he called, "Let's get those orders up."

Veronica visited with Neil Peavy a few moments longer, then cleared the birthday boy's table and collected more orders. When she'd worked her way back to the bar and noticed the man sitting there, she stopped short, blowing out a disgusted breath. "Oh, perfect. This is *just* what I need to top off my night."

Troy Jacobson flashed her a brilliant white smile, and his expensively barbered hair gleamed with the patina of antique gold beneath the dim lighting as he leaned forward on his stool. "Is that any way to greet an old school chum?"

"High school jocks who had sex with my sister while going steady with the head cheerleader didn't make my chum list," she said brusquely. She knew her antagonism was all out of proportion, but she couldn't seem to help herself. It was turning out to be that kind of night. And didn't it just figure the man would be even better-looking than he'd been back when? If there were any justice in the world, he would've lost his hair or had a potbelly under that navy blue sweater with its discreet designer logo. She looked around pointedly. "Where *is* Miss Perky Pom-Poms, anyway? I heard you two got married."

A shadow seemed to scud across his eyes, but it passed so quickly Veronica was left wondering if she'd seen it at all. "She's at our condo in Maui."

"And you're here *alone* while the wife's away? My. You must be slowing down."

"Jesus, Veronica, I was an eighteen-year-old football star then — which is pretty much synonymous with young, arrogant, and stupid. People change, you know?" He studied her a moment. "Besides, if Crystal never had a problem with our arrangement, why the hell does it bug you so much?"

She shrugged. "I actually believe loyalty is important. But hey, that's just me, and you're absolutely right," she agreed coolly. "Crystal didn't have a problem, so I guess it's none of my business. Wasn't then, isn't now. What can I get you to drink?"

"I've got it," Coop said, and he clunked a drink down on the bar in front of Troy with enough force to slop a little over the edge. "That'll be four twenty-five, pal."

Veronica looked up to see the protective man of a short while ago no longer in evidence. In his place stood a scowling giant, and his displeasure seemed to be directed straight at her.

Swell. What was *his* problem? Before she

could decide whether to demand an explanation or shrug it off, however, Darlene Starkey came up and slid onto the vacant barstool next to her. Tonight just kept on getting better and better.

"Hello, dear," Darlene said.

Ronnie gave the woman a brief nod. "Mrs. Starkey."

"Darlene, please. Mrs. Starkey makes me want to look around for my mother-in-law."

Veronica smiled tightly but didn't reply. Instead, she gave Coop her order and cleared her tray of empties.

As soon as she finished, Darlene touched her on the arm to reclaim her attention. "I was dismayed to hear about Crystal, dear. I'm so sorry."

I'll just bet. Other Tonk patrons had told Veronica virtually the same thing, and she'd taken comfort from their condolences. Yet the words from Darlene made her teeth clench. The older woman's eyes were too avaricious, and Veronica had a feeling that what Starkey really meant was, *Do spill all the juicy details.*

"Thank you," she said coolly. "You're too kind."

Darlene studied her a moment with a small smile on her face. She took a sip of her drink, then set the glass down on the bar in front of her and slid a cigarette out of her purse. Placing it between her lips, she struck a match and inhaled deeply. She shook out the match, exhaled a stream of smoke, then looked past Veronica to where Troy Jacobson sat two stools down.

"People rarely change as much as you claim," she remarked as soon as she'd caught his eye. "Rumor has it you were seeing someone on the side again a few months back."

Troy's knuckles turned white where his hand tightened around his glass. "Yeah, my wife heard that same rumor," he agreed. "Which is why she's in Hawaii and I'm home." Tossing back his drink, he climbed to his feet. He pulled a roll of cash from his pocket, peeled off a bill, and dropped it on the bar. Then he drilled Darlene with the full measure of his displeasure before giving Veronica a sober look. "Rumor has it wrong," he said flatly. He turned on his heel and strode for the door.

Coop picked up Troy's glass and set it in the sink. Wiping down the bar, he looked at Darlene. "Try not to drive away any more of my customers, will you?"

She shrugged and took a drag off her cigarette.

"Just out of curiosity," he continued, "are you implying that Mr. Scotch-and-Water there" — he indicated Troy with a jerk of his chin as the man exited the bar — "picked up where he'd left off his high school fling with Ronnie's sister?"

"I'm not implying a thing." Darlene snubbed out her cigarette. "I simply said a story's going around that Troy's stepping out on his pretty little wife."

"Darlene deals in rumor and innuendo," Veronica informed Coop. "It's her job."

"No, dear. It's my hobby." Sipping her drink,

she slowly twirled around on her barstool to face Veronica. "And my, aren't *you* the dark horse. For instance, rumor had it you couldn't wait to shake the dust of this town from your heels. Yet here you are, right back where you started."

Veronica flinched. That was one of her darkest fears — that she'd end her days at the Tonk, playing waitress to a bunch of drunks.

"And not only serving drinks again," Darlene murmured, "but cozy as can be, to boot, with your sister's murderer's lawyer."

"My what?" Wondering if she looked as clueless as she felt, Veronica stared blankly at the town gossip. She didn't have the first idea what the woman was talking about.

Darlene looked content as a cat with fresh kill. "Don't tell me you don't know. How delicious." She lit another cigarette. "The knight in shining Armani who snatched the young knave's hand from your snatch? He's none other than Neil Peavy."

"Yes, I know. Cooper told me."

"Ah, yes, the enigmatic Cooper. Yet another dark horse — only this one's a stallion." She coolly inspected him before turning her attention back to Veronica. "Though I doubt I have to tell *you* that." As heat scalded Veronica's cheeks, Darlene said, "Did Cooper also tell you that the inestimable Mr. Peavy is Eddie Chapman's attorney of record?"

Shock was a fist in Veronica's gut. No, that was a small detail he'd kept to himself. And how the hell did he know him, anyway?

But she maintained a composed expression as she met the older woman's gaze. "I'm pretty sure you know the answer to that already. This certainly appears to be your lucky day, Mrs. Starkey. You should be able to dine out on my motley little drama for a month."

Darlene exhaled a stream of smoke. "At the very least."

For the rest of the night Veronica adopted a serene, I-am-the-queen attitude that effectively kept the curious off of her back. But anger percolated beneath the surface, and the minute Sandy left at the end of their shift, Ronnie smacked her tray and cash box onto the shelf below the bar and turned to Coop.

"You didn't think I might want to know?"

He didn't pretend confusion over her reference to a comment made two and a half hours ago. "When was I supposed to tell you? While the attention of the entire bar was on you? Before you thanked Peavy for defusing the situation with your young mauler? Or, hey, I know: maybe when you were having that old-home-week-reunion moment with Mr. Scotch-and-Water."

"His name is Troy Jacobson, and don't change the subject. I'd like to know —"

"Troy." Coop shook his head in disgust. "Christ. That figures."

Momentarily distracted, she tilted her head way back to stare up at him, and never even thought it odd to find they stood mere centimeters apart. "*What* figures?"

"Ol' Troy's name. I should have known — he had that smooth, I'm-just-an-ol'-country-club-boy look. He's one of the Bluff honchos, I take it."

"His family owns one of the region's largest packing plants," she agreed, then shrugged impatiently. "But getting back to —"

"So, tell me, Princess, why *were* you so bent out of shape that ol' Troy was doing the down-and-dirty with your sister back in high school? Did you want him for yourself or something?"

"*What?*"

"Watching you with ol' Troy, I couldn't quite figure out which bothered you the most — that your sis slept with him, or that the cheerleader married him."

Veronica smacked both hands onto Cooper's chest and shoved him back a step, then followed right along in his wake, stretching to her fullest height to thrust her nose up under his. "You want to know what bothered me the most? It wasn't that Troy Jacobson was screwing the girl from Baker Street while keeping the Bluff princess pristine, although I did think that stunk. It was the fact that my sister let him get away with it! She willingly played the cheap bimbo from the wrong side of the tracks, and didn't even give a damn that she was a freaking cliché!" Suddenly aware of the heat of him beneath her fingers, Veronica dropped her hands to her sides and stepped back. " 'Want him for myself,' my butt.

Try not to be more of a jackass than you can help, Blackstock. The day I pine for a guy with the morals of an alleycat is the day I give you permission to just shoot me."

"Okay, so maybe I was a little off the mar—"

"Here." She tugged her apron free and tossed it at him. It had been a long night and she was in no mood. "Finish closing up yourself. I'm outta here." She grabbed her coat from under the counter, dodged beneath the pass-through, and headed for the exit, pulling on her jacket as she crossed the floor.

"Hey, get back here," Coop growled. "We're not through."

Veronica paused with the door half open to look back at him. Faint color stained his high cheekbones and his dark eyes burned with emotions she could only guess at as he glared at her. Her own face felt hot and her heart beat so fast and laboriously, she was surprised it didn't drown out the sound of Patsy Cline lamenting to the empty room about her sweet dreams.

"Maybe you aren't, buddy," she said, "but I sure as hell am."

13

The man locked the mahogany double doors behind him and tossed his keys on the entryway table, then listened to the echo of his footsteps as he crossed the slate-floored foyer. His home had that hollow feel that only an empty house can produce, and he walked into the den, clicked on the brass-trimmed banker's light on his desk, and stared down for a moment at the framed photograph that sat on the polished cherrywood. Then he reached for the decanter and splashed a couple fingers of scotch into a cut-crystal tumbler. Collapsing with his drink onto his big leather chair, he picked up the remote control and keyed up a jazz music station. Very carefully, he replaced the remote where he'd found it.

Which was pretty damn restrained of him, if he did say so himself — considering what he'd really like to do was wing it through the huge window overlooking the few lights still on down in the flats. *Damn* that Starkey bitch.

The woman was a troublemaker. She always had been, but he would not tolerate her stirring up interest in the Crystal Davis affair.

One side of his mouth curled up as he gazed down into the amber swirl of single malt in the bottom of his glass. Interesting word choice; one that undoubtedly qualified as a bona fide Freudian slip. His affair with Crystal was something he'd gone to great lengths to cover up, and there was no way in hell he'd allow some bigmouthed gossip to churn up waters he'd managed to smooth over with such masterful originality.

Not that she'd said anything of real import. But he hadn't become smarter than the average bear by leaving things to chance. No, siree. The moment he perceived a problem, he jumped into action. He studied everything that could possibly go wrong and strategized ways to minimize the potential risk.

He saw no reason to treat the Davis matter any differently. It was a dead issue — no pun intended — and he intended to see it remained that way. The entire town believed Eddie Chapman had killed her. They were happy with that conclusion, and the last thing anyone needed was a bored rumormonger reviving interest in whom Crystal may or may not have been sleeping with. That kind of gossip did no one any good, so Darlene Starkey had better watch her mouth.

Because if she persisted in shaking the tree just to see what she could get to drop out at her feet, he might be forced to do something about it. And she wouldn't like the result.

By the time Coop completed his final military

leg lift and rolled to his feet, sweat was pouring freely off his torso. He'd done a hundred push-ups, another hundred crunches, and an equal number of lifts, but the aggravation that pulsed through his veins hadn't abated one damn bit, and after taking an impatient swipe at his chest with a towel, he picked up a barbell, hoisted it up on his shoulders, and plunged into a set of squats.

The woman was driving him nuts.

"Maybe *you're* not through," he mimicked in a falsetto as he sank into yet another crouch, "but I sure as hell am." He uttered a succinct opinion of her parting shot.

He'd been trying to apologize, hadn't he? He admitted he'd jumped to a hasty conclusion about Mr. Scotch-and-Water, but had she even waited around to hear him say he was sorry? *Hell, no.* If he was willing to extend an apology, the least she could do was stick around long enough to listen to it.

On the other hand, maybe it was just as well she hadn't, because what would he have said if she'd demanded an explanation? Coop's face burned, and he didn't attempt to convince himself it was strictly from exertion.

He could hardly credit it, but he'd been jealous. *Jealous,* for crissake! He'd like to deny it, but the truth was he'd taken one look at the strong reaction Ronnie'd had to ol' Troy, and the man's clear desire for her good opinion, and that old green-eyed monster had twisted through his guts like a python at feeding time.

He finished his first set of reps and stood breathing heavily. The barbell shifted on his shoulders and he automatically adjusted his stance, moving his feet a little farther apart and sliding his grip nearer the weights at the end of the bar. Man, what was it about her, anyway, that invariably threw him so out of whack? Maybe he couldn't cop to an impressive array of relationships with women, but having relations with a willing female had always come fairly easily to him. Generally he was reasonably suave with the fairer sex.

But not with her. For some reason, being around Ronnie made all his usual moves mutate in ways he didn't expect. She'd rejected him more than once, but had that caused him to shrug and look elsewhere for satisfaction? No, sir. He kept wanting her, and only her.

Impatiently, Coop shifted his weight. Hell, he thrived on competition, that was all. Attributing anything else to this thing he had for the fair-skinned Ms. Davis was a waste of time. *Think about something else, Ice.*

That produced a snort. *Like what? How that handle actually used to apply, maybe?*

Swearing steadily beneath his breath, he threw himself into another set of squats.

Veronica pulled the plug in the old clawfoot tub and climbed to her feet as the water swirled down the drain. The hot bubble bath had felt marvelous, but it certainly hadn't left her in the relaxed state she'd envisioned. Reaching for a towel, she ruefully acknowledged that the eighty-mile-an-hour spin her mind was engaged in might have something to do with that. A spin caused mostly by Cooper.

A laugh escaped her. *Mostly, my sweet fan-danny.* It was caused entirely by Cooper.

She'd love to blame this restless edginess on the Tonk — God knows it had been a crazy night from start to finish. But although the evening had definitely added to her stress level, it was Coop — or, more specifically, her inappropriate reaction to him — that had her engine all revved up. Physically, she was worn to a nub, but mentally, she was so wired the prospect of sleep felt like a long shot.

Stepping from the tub, she quickly finished drying off, then rubbed a circle in the mirror above the sink. Maybe if she heated up some milk . . .

She grimaced as she draped her towel to dry. Yeah, right — like warm milk would relieve her of anything except the contents of her stomach. The steam began to dissipate in the underheated bathroom about the same time she completed rubbing apricot baby oil into her skin, and teeth chattering, she snatched up a clean set of pajamas and pulled them on. Then she hurriedly washed her face and patted on a little moisturizer. Warm milk was definitely out, but perhaps a glass of wine —

Eww. Toothpaste and wine — there was a combination she'd just as soon not contemplate. Who was she trying to kid anyway? The only sleep aid she needed was ridding her thoughts of Cooper Blackstock. She couldn't *believe* she was so hot and bothered over this guy. Aside from wanting to jump his bones, what did she have in common with him?

Absolutely nothing, that's what. And probably the only reason she wanted his body so much anyway was because she'd imposed that edict that said she couldn't have it. Sort of like her old college roommate, who'd never seemed to want a cigarette as badly as those times when she couldn't locate a match.

Suspecting that was a load of manure, she decided to lay the blame squarely at Marissa's door. Yes, sir, *that's* whose fault it was. Seeing her friend act like one big pulsating hormone around Kody was putting thoughts into her head.

Cursing the cold floorboards in the hallway, Veronica made a dash for her bedroom. She barreled through the door and dove for the bed. *Damn,* it was cold up here!

It seemed to take forever, but eventually her heart slowed to a steady rhythm and her body heat warmed the bed to the point where she could actually stretch out without immediately jerking back at the shock of encountering an icy patch of sheet. Little by little she began to relax, and when her racing brain also grew calm, she finally dozed off.

Only to be rudely jerked from sleep moments later by a horrendous crash overhead.

Veronica jackknifed straight up in bed, her heart pounding as if it were trying to beat its way out of her chest. Throwing back the covers, she raced out into the hallway, where she promptly stubbed her toe against she-didn't-know-what. Cursing, she half limped, half hopped to the end of the hall and opened the doorway up to the attic. Immediately her ears were assaulted by a barrage of truly inspired cursing. "Are you okay?" she called as she hobbled up the stairs.

"Only if your definition of *okay*," Coop snarled, "is a dumb-ass, clumsy mother-fu—" Sounding as if the necessity of censoring himself were choking him, he cut himself off mid-obscenity just as she reached the top of the stairs. "Dammit, I can't *believe* I let that drop."

Oh, God. Veronica stopped dead and stared at Coop. He stood in front of his bed, and it was like the night in the bar when he'd taken his shirt off all over again. Only this time sweat sheened his golden skin from his forehead to the low-slung sweats clinging to his hips. Man, oh, man, the guy had a body — she'd guess in part courtesy of all those weights stacked not far from where he stood.

She smoothed a finger along the satin-edged neckline of her thermal pajamas. By rights, she ought to be freezing, since the attic got even less heat than the second floor. Ice etched a blue-white pattern on the panes of the small sash window to the left of the bed, yet she felt like she could've been on a tropical island. Heat pulsed through her veins and spread its warmth clear out to the tips of her fingers and toes. She looked at Cooper and wanted nothing more than to yank open her top and press her breasts against that hard, tan chest. And if that didn't warn her to make tracks just as fast as she could hustle her arousal-stunned body, she didn't know what would.

She tore her gaze away from Coop's torso and glanced at the barbell that was plainly the object of his wrath. Then she cleared her throat. "So, if I've got this straight, you're a dumb-ass, but basically an uninjured one?"

His mouth looked so sulky she wanted to just eat it up. But then it quirked in a self-deprecating smile. "Yeah. That about covers it."

The smile was truly her undoing. He was so clearly cranky, yet he didn't allow his bad temper to keep him from seeing a glimmer of humor in the situation. "Good," she said firmly. "Then I won't hurt anything if I do this."

She launched herself at him.

Coop caught her midfly. He'd barely scooped one arm under her round little butt and clamped the other across her back before he toppled over. They hit the bed kissing.

He ended up with Ronnie sprawled on top of him, and he tightened his arm beneath the swell of her bottom to anchor her there. Sliding his free hand up to cup the back of her head, he held her in place while he slaked a hunger that felt as if it'd been building forever. God. Her mouth felt so soft . . . tasted so sweet. He'd begun to think he'd never get to kiss her again.

He'd lost track of the passing minutes by the time she raised her head and blinked down at him. Tangling his fingers in her hair to prevent her from moving too far away, he smiled up at the swollen, bee-stung look of her lips. He raised his head to trace them with his tongue.

She moaned softly and lowered her mouth to give him freer access, and everything that was male in Coop rose up to stake a claim. He tightened his fingers and raised his head up off the mattress to deepen the kiss, but it wasn't enough, and he rolled them until he was propped over her. The sudden move ripped their mouths apart and Coop grinned at the bemused look on Veronica's face as she blinked up at him.

"Wasn't I just on top?"

"Yeah." He made an adjustment that settled his weight more firmly atop her. "But now I've gotcha in your rightful place — in the subservient position."

Her eyes narrowed to little crescents. "With that attitude, I'm guessing you don't get lucky real often."

He attempted to look innocent. "What? You think my technique could stand a little work?"

"Your technique could stand a stick of dynamite."

Coop brushed his fingertips along her hairline. He dipped his head and kissed her, all soft suction and demanding tongue, then pulled back to look down at her. "I feel like I've been wanting you, waiting for you, forever."

"Oh." Veronica swallowed with difficulty. "Your technique just improved by leaps and bounds." She lay beneath the warm press of his body and looked up at him. His dark eyes smoldered with desire — desire *she* had caused — and it made her feel incredibly powerful. She could get addicted to causing such a strong reaction in a man like Cooper Blackstock.

"Yeah, well, it's about to deteriorate again," he growled. "Because when you look at me like that —"

She licked her lips. "Like what?"

He whispered a swear word and lowered his head to kiss her. It was rough, fast, and on the edge of control, and when he pulled back and stared down at her, he was breathing hard. "Like that. When you look at me like you don't even require foreplay, like you wouldn't stop me if I spread your legs and —"

Sensation speared deep between her thighs and a soft little moan escaped her.

As if the sound were the final straw and his patience for talk had just disintegrated, Coop clamped his mouth down on hers. He kissed her with such strength and authority, it pushed Veronica's head deep into the mattress. Cupping her face between his hands, he pumped his tongue against hers in a rhythm as old as time and as carnal as original sin.

She wrapped her arms around the strong column of his neck and clung, pressing herself as close as she could get while returning his kiss for all she was worth. Long before she'd had her fill, though, his mouth was gone. But she didn't have time to protest its loss before she felt it hot against the angle of her jaw, just behind her earlobe. Then, without giving her a moment to acclimate to that, he eased down the column of her throat. He kissed her softly in one spot, fiercely sucked her flesh against his teeth in the next, then immediately soothed the place with the flat of his tongue before moving on. Sounds of satisfaction rumbled deep in his throat as he made his leisurely way down to the triangular hollow at the base of hers. As he laved it with his tongue, he slid a hand between them. His fingers traced the edging on Veronica's pajama top to its uppermost satin button. Slipping it free, he moved on to the next.

And the next. And then to the one after that. Until the front halves of her top slid apart, and Coop pushed up on one elbow to better view his handiwork. His vigilance caused a tight ache to form deep between Veronica's legs. Seeing his sudden stillness as her breasts emerged from the concealing cloth was like having that tightness stroked. Her nipples went taut.

"Here they are," he whispered and touched a gentle fingertip to the tip of one beaded nipple.

"I've spent way too much time thinking about these babies when I should've been concentrating on other things. I kept remembering how they looked, though. How they felt." He pinched her nipple between his thumb and forefinger and tugged. A smile crooked the corner of his mouth at the little yearning sound that purled out of her throat, but he didn't take his attention away from her soft curves. "How much you liked it when I did this."

Looking at the top of his down-bent head, she demanded, "Rub against me."

"What?" He glanced up, his dark brows gathered in perplexity.

"I want to feel this." She reached out and stroked her hand down his chest and along the solid ridges of his abdomen. "When I walked in and saw you without your shirt, I wanted to rip my top open and rub up against you."

She didn't have to ask him twice. He fell over her, catching himself on his palms before bending his elbows to lower his chest against her breasts. He slowly stropped himself against her. Up. Down. Side to side. And his dark eyes took in her every reaction. "Like this?"

Veronica's breath hissed in and her eyelids drifted closed. "Yessss. Exactly like that." She arched her back to maintain contact, then slowly opened her eyes and looked up at him. He continued to stroke his chest against her, staring down at her. She anchored herself by clutching his waist and did her best to move in counterpoint. The rub of smooth skin against smooth skin created drag and friction, making her nipples feel on fire. The ache deep inside intensified, and feeling restless and in need, she arched her pelvis and struggled against his weight to separate her legs. "Oh, God, Cooper. Please."

He whispered a curse and surged between her thighs, grinding the hard thrust of his sex against the soft notch of hers. Lowering his head, he kissed her roughly.

A moment later, he ripped his mouth free. "I want you naked." He levered himself off her and shoved to his feet next to the bed. Staring down at her breasts, at the curve of her abdomen where it dipped in at the waist before flowing into hip, he shucked free of his sweats.

Veronica froze in the midst of raising her hips off the mattress to push down her pajama bottoms. "Oh, my." Her gaze didn't bother to follow the sweatpants' progress once they'd cleared his hips. *Oh, my, oh, my.* Not wanting to appear to be gawking — even if that's exactly what she was doing — she murmured, "You really are a blonde."

That startled a laugh from him. "Of course I am. What'd you think — ?"

"That you dyed your hair." But she didn't want to talk about that; she simply wanted to gaze, entranced, at his penis.

Forget that it was long and thick — or even that it had been a while since she'd seen such an aggressive piece of male anatomy in the flesh.

Coop's erection rose out of a thatch of sandy blond curls and jutted straight up. Except it *wasn't* straight. You could probably fit an inverted soup bowl between root and tip. "It . . . curves," she said faintly.

"The better to reach your G-sp—"

"I mean it really *curves*." It reminded her of a scimitar — all boldness and flash. Sort of like Coop himself. She stared at his penis so long that it began to bob and weave, bouncing its smooth head off his navel.

He reached down and wrapped his hand around the base to hold it still, eyeing her warily. "I can't figure out if that look on your face is pure admiration — or if you're ready to run for the nearest hammer to pound this into your basic, everyday hard-on."

"You know, all of a sudden 'straight' strikes me as kinda boring." She licked her lips. "Gimme."

He laughed and dove on top of her. They rolled and wrestled, but the deeper their kisses and the more body moved against body, the less playful their manner became. When Coop's fingertips brushed the hot, wet folds between her thighs, they both stilled. For a moment, the only movement in the room was the minute, circular stroke of his fore and index fingers as they separated the plump furrow and slipped and slid along its length.

When his fingers suddenly scissored around her sweet spot and clamped closed, Veronica's hips arched up off the bed. She groped between them, wanting to touch him in return, but he kept himself just out of reach. "Please," she panted. "I want . . . oh, God, Coop, I want —"

He eased his fingers down until just the tips slid inside her. "What do you want?" he demanded, gently massaging the ring of muscle there.

"To touch you. To feel you inside me."

"Ah, man." Leaning back, he fumbled in the drawer of the nightstand for a condom. "I planned to show you a little more style than this, to maybe explore that multiple orgasm thing you gals've got going for you, but I don't think I can hold out." He ripped open the foil packet and rolled the protection on.

"I don't need you to hold out. I don't *want* you to." The idea that he felt a vestige of performance anxiety and wasn't simply the indefatigable sex machine she'd first taken him to be did something to her. Something she immediately repudiated. This was about sex. That was *all* it was about. "C'mere. You can still show me your style — just make it the short version."

"You got it." But when he rolled on top of her, he didn't instantly enter her. Instead he teased. He kissed her. He fondled her breasts. He stroked his erection up and down the slippery folds between her thighs. He even pressed the head of his penis against her opening.

But he didn't enter her.

Veronica's hips instigated an age-old rhythm,

and her hands slid down to grasp the hard cheeks of his buttocks. The next time he flirted with penetration, she dug her fingers in, trying to anchor him in place. She burned to feel him inside her, and spread her legs farther apart. Finally she just flat out drew her knees back so he wouldn't miss the target on his next pass. He growled in appreciation. But still he didn't give her what she wanted.

Coop had no idea why he was teasing her this way. His balls felt as if they were turning blue and he wanted nothing so much as to bury himself in her. Yet something held him back. Some crazy need for . . . he didn't know what.

The next time he thumbed his dick down to tease her opening, though, he feared he'd have to cave. He eased just the head inside her, and knew right away it wasn't one of his brighter moves. She was so hot and wet and — oh, God — *tight*, that he didn't know why the hell he was holding back. He retracted his hips in preparation for the drive home and felt all ten of Ronnie's nails sink into his butt, staying him. Boo had nothing on this woman when it came to the claw department.

"You pull out and tease me one more time and you're a dead man." Her cheeks were flushed, her shiny hair mussed, and her eyes flashed fire. "I want it deep, and I want it *now!*"

Laughing, he planted his palms flat on the mattress, tensed his buttocks, and thrust his hips forward, sinking into her.

She started coming before he bottomed out, and Coop's laughter stopped up in his throat. "Ah, man." He felt her contracting around him, heard her breathy moans spiraling several octaves higher, and pure satisfaction exploded through him. Holding himself deep, he ground against her as he felt her climax go on and on. Maybe *this* was what he'd been waiting for. All he knew for certain was the feel of her coming apart beneath him was the biggest rush he'd felt since leaving Company C.

When her orgasm tapered off he began to move, pumping steadily in smooth, hard strokes. Ronnie wrapped her legs around his hips and moved in concert with him, and he sucked in a breath. He picked up his tempo, digging his toes into the mattress for leverage. He was close — God, so close.

Then Veronica's breath began to hitch, and realizing she was building again, he gritted his teeth and forced himself to alter his pace to keep from going over the edge. "You really took that multiple-orgasm crack to heart, didn't you?"

"Oh, God, Cooper." She stared up at him with glazed eyes. "I can't . . . believe . . . I'm so close . . . again," she panted, unwittingly echoing his thoughts. Clearly reading the strain on his face, she added politely, "You needn't wait for me, though."

The temptation to take her at her word was sweeter than honey, but he resisted it. He slid a hand between their bodies and delved into the wet, slick heat between her legs. Locating his primary target near the top of her cleft, he feathered the little pearl of nerve endings with a light touch. "Ladies first," he insisted. He just hoped to hell his eyes didn't look as crossed as they felt.

But all his good intentions went up in smoke as his orgasm began to build just beneath the point where she sheathed him so tightly. Involuntarily, his thrusts picked up speed. "I'm sorry, Ronnie," he panted. "I don't think I can hold back."

It didn't matter, because a low whine began to unfurl in her throat and he felt her contract around him once again. Her climax unleashed the tight rein he'd been holding on himself, and he pounded into her with mindless ferocity. He could feel paradise beckoning, and with a roar he slammed deep one last time and came.

And came.

In blinding, white-hot pulsation after white-hot pulsation.

Moments later, shuddering with satisfaction, he eased down on top of her. He scooped his arms beneath Veronica to hold her to him and rolled to his side, careful to stay connected. He felt the little aftershocks of her orgasm pulse around him, and was suddenly filled with a ferocious possessiveness.

It made him uneasy, for that wasn't an emotion he'd expected to feel. Since she had virtually assured him it would be a cold day in hell before she'd have sex with him, he'd automatically assumed that a big part of his wanting her stemmed from that. He'd also assumed that once he had her, one time would be enough.

But as he stroked a hand down her hair and cuddled her to him, he had a sinking feeling he'd been wrong on both counts.

14

It was almost noon when Veronica awoke in a tangle of limbs with Cooper. Whispering a curse, she eased his long fingers off her hip, unwrapped his arm from around her, and after extracting her thigh from between his, silently rolled out of bed. Oh, man. What had she done?

Shivering, she searched for her pajamas. A relationship with Coop had about zero chance of progressing, and she never should have allowed it to get this far. Things might start out all hunky-dory, but she had too many issues with unambitious men to believe great sex could suddenly make those problems no longer matter.

But, oh. Boy. She paused with her pajama top half on and looked over at Coop sprawled out in the middle of the bed. *Great* didn't even begin to cover it. He'd joked about multiple orgasms, but she'd never dreamed she was actually capable of having them. Last night she'd lost count of how many he'd helped her to. Twice during the early morning hours Coop had pulled her out of sleep for slow, lazy bouts of curl-your-toes sex, and she was so relaxed now it was a wonder she could move at all. If she didn't know better, she'd suspect a thief had snuck in and stolen all her bones.

She straightened guiltily. But that was hardly the point. Never mind that he kept drawing her like a compass needle to magnetic north; she had to walk away before Cooper Blackstock started to matter too much.

She'd just as soon not do it bare-assed, though. Where the heck were her pajama bottoms?

She eyed the bed consideringly. They were no doubt at the bottom of it, between the sheets where she'd kicked them off. Did she leave them where they were and steal down to her room wearing only her jammie top, or did she try to retrieve them? The former would be the prudent thing to do if she wanted to avoid talking to Coop this morning.

But that was too chickenhearted. She knelt at the side of the bed and lifted the covers enough to slide her arm under, sweeping the sheets for the lost article. When her fingertips suddenly brushed Coop's warm calf and the side of his knee, she stilled for a moment. Then, drawing a calming breath, she determinedly swept another quadrant.

"That's flattering, Princess." Coop's morning voice was a hoarse rumble. "But as well endowed as I am, you're still several inches south of the good stuff."

Freezing with her arm buried to the shoulder beneath the blankets, she slowly turned her head to look at him. Stubble shadowed his jaw and his hair was smashed flat on one side while sticking up like a rooster comb on the other. Even with those Godiva-dark eyes of his looking all sleepy and satisfied, he wasn't exactly Mr. Allure first thing in the morning. So how come she had to steel herself against his appeal? "Are we talking about your ego, Blackstock? That seems to be the most sizable organ around here."

"Ouch." His teeth shone white in the pale winter sunshine that filtered through the window. "Not nice, sweetheart. But I forgive you, 'cause I know you're not a morning person."

Before she had a chance to reply, he tossed aside the covers and sat up, leaning forward to slide his hands beneath her armpits. As if she weighed next to nothing, he plucked her up and laid back down with her. "Come cuddle with me for a few minutes."

"I don't have time. The interview —"

"Isn't until one." He settled her to his satisfaction and pulled up the covers. Rolling onto his side, he propped his head on his palm, reached out to gently smooth her hair behind her ear, and gave her a slow, killer smile. "Good morning."

It was pointless to struggle, she assured herself, pretending that her decision had nothing to do with the fact that being with him felt so wonderful. So . . . right. "Mornin', yourself."

"You look mighty fine first thing in the morning." A skeptical sound escaped her, but he blithely ignored it. "I especially like that bottomless thing you've got going there. In fact —"

He slithered beneath the covers, and the warm brush of his body against hers as he snaked his way toward the bottom of the bed brought Veronica up onto her elbows. A moment later, Coop's hands eased her legs apart and she felt the press of his mouth high against her inner thigh.

"I really like this bottomless thing a lot," his muffled voice said. Then he proceeded to show her how much.

"Oh . . . my . . . gaaw—" Why not take what was offered and simply enjoy it? Obviously she'd grown fond of Coop, but it wasn't as if she were in danger of falling in *love* with him or anything. So really. Why not just appreciate this for what it was?

He did something devastating with his tongue and her elbows melted out from under her.

It was, after all, just a tiny moment out of time.

An hour and a half later, when Veronica let herself back into the house after the waitress interview, she found Cooper sitting at the kitchen table. Except for a lack of shoes, he was his usual spit-shined self again, his hair damp and spiky, his cheeks and jaw gleaming with that special sheen only babies' bottoms and the freshly shaven seem to achieve.

Looking up, he gave her an intimate smile and shut down a laptop computer she hadn't known he owned. Before she finished closing the door behind her, he'd risen to his feet. "How'd the interview go?"

"Wonderful — her name is Barbara, and she's starting tonight." Veronica executed a little dance step. "Which means I don't have to work."

"Sandy could probably use a day off, too."

"I know. She told me once that she wanted the hours, but I don't think ten-hour shifts, five days a week, were exactly what she had in mind. When you've got a free minute, we'll have to sit down and look at the Tonk's profits. She's been so great about putting in the overtime without complaint that we oughtta be able to manage a small bonus for her next paycheck. I also plan to be there tonight to work out a schedule for the three of us. I'd like to reduce my role to fill-in waitress if it's agreeable with Sandy and Barbara. I need to get back to my own career."

Hands in his jeans pockets, Coop rocked back on his wool-stocking-clad heels and studied her. The look in his eyes made Veronica's heart pick up its beat. Disconcerted, she glanced over at the coffee brewing on the stove, glad for the excuse to look away.

She didn't hear Coop cross the floor, but as she reached for a mug on the second shelf, his arms wrapped around her and she felt him, solid and warm, against her back.

"Ever made love on a kitchen counter before?" he murmured.

Veronica felt her body begin to prepare itself

for him, but she managed to sound reasonably cool when she replied, "No, and I don't intend this to be the afternoon that changes." His hands came up to cup her breasts and she sucked in a breath. "Lizzy's probably going to come barreling through that door at any minute." Even so, she leaned back against him.

Coop raised his left hand from her breast long enough to turn his wrist and peer at the face of his watch. "Damn. You're right. Marissa called to say the timing was off for the matinee at the King and she'd be dropping Lizzy off between one-thirty and two." He bent his knees and rubbed his pelvis against her bottom. "Wanna see what I can do in ten minutes?"

She really did, and that scared her. "Tempting as the prospect sounds, I think I'll pass."

He pressed a kiss against the side of her neck. "Are you sure? Speedy doesn't necessarily have to mean we sacrifice quality. It can still be fun —"

The front door banged open and the house was suddenly filled with the sound of children's voices.

"Then again, it could be tough trying to explain what my pants are doing down around my ankles," he said dryly and stepped back.

Veronica laughed. "Not to mention what Aunt Ronnie's doing with juice can rings on her butt. Obviously you didn't check out the state of the countertop before you made your proposition."

"Yeah, right." He gave her a get-real look. "A

white-glove inspection was not real high on my list of priorities." He stepped over to the table and fit his laptop in its leather case, then zipped it up. Plucking it off the table, he came back and brushed his thumb over her cheekbone. "Just so you know, I'm not packing up my marbles because I was denied the opportunity for sex."

"But you're taking them home anyhow?" She ought to be relieved, but part of her mourned seeing him go.

"It's either that or give an anatomy lesson that Marissa might object to her kiddies learning. Not to mention what my bro—"

He cut himself off, and the odd look that crossed his face piqued Veronica's curiosity. She didn't have an opportunity to satisfy it, however, for Lizzy, Dessa, and Riley clattered into the kitchen with Marissa not far behind, and when she turned back from greeting them Coop was disappearing up the back stairs.

Chaos reigned for a while after that, but eventually all the news concerning the children's sleepover had been rehashed and reenacted, and Marissa packed up her brood and left for home. Lizzy went upstairs, and a short while later, Veronica girded her loins and set out after her. She'd put off discussing Lizzy's situation far too long already, and in good conscience she could procrastinate no longer.

But she sure didn't look forward to it. How did one talk to a little girl about the death of her mother, when the entire town was saying her

231

father was the one responsible for it?

Pausing outside Lizzy's door, Veronica drew a deep breath, blew it out, then tapped for admittance. She half hoped Lizzy had dozed off after her big night out, knowing from experience that sleep wasn't exactly the order of the evening at the annual VFW overnighter.

Her cowardice got exactly what it deserved when Lizzy promptly threw open the door. Exhaustion flew scarlet flags in her cheeks and her eyes looked overbright, but she danced in place with almost manic alertness. "Hi, Aunt Ronnie! I'm playing with my Barbies. You wanna play with me?"

"Sure." Berating herself for cravenly grabbing the excuse to put off the dreaded talk a few moments longer, Veronica took her time perusing the selection of dolls. "Point me to the Drill Sergeant Barbie. I'm in the mood to make Ken clean a few latrines."

"I don't got one of those," Lizzy said. "But you can play with this one." She extended a doll that was decked out head to foot in pink. "She's my fave-rit."

"Aw, Lizzy. Have I told you lately what a sweetheart you are?" Accepting the proffered doll, Veronica sat cross-legged on the bed and spent a few minutes divesting Barbie of her pink apparel, then dressing her in a gossamer dress and searching for the proper accessories to trick her out. Eventually, though, she'd fluffed the doll's skirt and settled her in her pink Barbie-mobile. Drawing a calming breath, she looked at her niece.

"I owe you an apology."

The little girl looked up with bright interest. "You do? What for?"

"For putting off talking to you about your mama and daddy for so long."

Lizzy stilled and the brightness left her eyes. "I don't wanna talk about Mama."

Veronica didn't blame her. But she had to wonder if her niece had talked to anyone about Crystal's murder. "Losing a mother is terrible for anyone," she said, slowly feeling her way. "But I imagine it must've been doubly tough for you because you lost your daddy at the same time, and I'd like to talk a little about how you're doing."

Lizzy looked away. "Doin' fine." Her tone was patently unencouraging.

"I'm glad to hear that. It must make you sad, though."

"Uh-huh. But not alla time. Sometimes Mama . . ." Lizzy's voice trailed off, and her narrow little shoulder hitched with faux indifference. The look she shot Veronica seemed to be equal parts unhappiness, defiance, and apprehension.

"Sometimes your mama could be really hard to live with," Veronica supplied gently.

Lizzy nodded.

"Yet she was still your mama, and you loved her and didn't want anything bad to happen to her."

"*Yes.*" Nodding harder, Lizzy inched closer.

Veronica reached out and hugged Lizzy to her side. "It's okay to miss her one minute and be almost glad she's gone the next. There are no right or wrong emotions in a situation like this. I grew up with your mama, and I have those mixed up feelings myself." She held her niece tightly and rubbed her cheek against the top of Lizzy's head. "I bet some of the kids at school say mean things to you about it."

Lizzy raised her head. "They say my daddy killed my mama," she said indignantly. "Daddy didn't do that! He'd *never* do sumpin' like that."

"The police think he did, Lizagator."

"They're wrong! My daddy *told* me he didn't do it. He swored on the *Bible.*"

Veronica didn't know what to say to such conviction, so she simply snuggled Lizzy closer. A single conversation wasn't going to change or improve Lizzy's situation, but she was glad they were having it. All in all, it was going better than she'd dared hope. The hardest part — broaching the subject of Crystal's death with her niece — was done. Now she and Lizzy merely had to discuss the future, and that was a cakewalk in comparison. "You realize we're eventually going to have to leave Fossil, don't you?"

"*No!*" Lizzy ripped herself free and turned wild eyes on Veronica. "We can't leave — we have to be here!"

Veronica blinked at the panic-edged vehemence in her niece's voice, then pulled herself together in order to assemble an explanation Lizzy'd understand. "I'm not talking about immediately," she said soothingly. "But sooner or later we'll have to move to Seattle. My work—"

Lizzy leaped to her feet and faced Veronica with her little hands fisted at her sides. "You can do your work *here*. We can't leave."

"Honey, I realize starting a new school can be difficult, but the upside is no one will know about your parents, so you won't have to worry about kids saying mean things to you. We'll fix you a room at my house that's every bit as nice as this one, and although I know no one can replace Dessa, I promise you'll make other friends."

"I don't *care* about that stuff!" Tears poured down Lizzy's cheeks and she trembled from head to foot as she faced off with her aunt. "We have to be here so my daddy can find me when he comes back!"

"Oh, baby." She reached for Lizzy, but Lizzy sidestepped, and Veronica's hands dropped to her sides. "I don't think your daddy is coming back."

"He is so! He *told* me. He said he hadda go because the au-tor— the auth-or—"

"The authorities?"

Lizzy nodded vigorously. "Uh-huh. *Those* people had made a mistake and wanted to put him in jail for what happened to Mama. But he promised he'd be back for me! He *promised*."

It went a long way toward explaining Lizzy's calmness during the series of upheavals in her

235

life. She was anything but calm now, however. Unable to bear seeing her shake and cry so hard, Veronica reached out and hauled her into her arms. "Shh-shh," she crooned, rocking her and stroking her hair. "Don't cry. We'll straighten it out. Somehow or another, we'll straighten it all out."

Just how they'd do that, though, she hadn't a clue.

Coop's concentration was shot to hell, and finally giving up the attempt to write, he shut his computer down and put it away. He couldn't believe how close he'd come this afternoon to giving the game away.

He rocked his wooden chair back on two legs and stared up at his bedroom ceiling. Man, what *was* it about Veronica that made him so careless? Caution used to be his middle name, but he'd been screwing up right and left ever since he'd met her. When it'd occurred to him down in the kitchen that Eddie might not appreciate him exposing Lizzy to the earthier facts of life, he hadn't thought twice about nearly saying so.

Coop whispered a curse. That was his problem right there, of course — he hadn't thought. He felt comfortable with Ronnie, and that wasn't good. Not if it meant shooting his mouth off without first thinking things through. He had to quit letting his dick do all his brainwork for him and start behaving like the trained professional he once was.

The door at the base of the attic stairs suddenly banged open and soft footsteps sounded on the wooden steps. On immediate alert, Coop automatically cataloged the weapon potential in the ordinary items around him as he silently eased the chair back on all four legs and rose to his feet. An instant later he recognized Ronnie's black hair as her head crested the balustrade. Against all reason, and contrary to everything he'd just been telling himself, he relaxed his vigilance, happy to see her.

Veronica, on the other hand, looked anything but relaxed when she reached the top of the stairs. "I've got big trouble."

Bridging the distance between them, he reached out to guide her to the chair he'd just abandoned. "Sit down," he invited and pressed on her shoulders until she collapsed onto the seat. He circled the narrow table that doubled as his desk and swung around a mismatched chair. Straddling it, he crossed his arms over the top rail and propped his chin atop them. "Tell papa all about it."

"Well, see, that seems to be my problem," she said, scowling at him. "Parenting. If we were in school and this were a pop quiz, I'd get a big fat D-minus at it." She related her conversation with Lizzy, then jumped up to pace the narrow confines of Coop's room. He turned in his chair and watched color fluctuate in her cheeks as she stalked from table, to bed, to the top of the stairs, and back again.

"I thought I was starting to get a handle on it." She laughed harshly. "What a joke — I didn't even see what direction the problem was coming from. But what am I supposed to tell her?" she demanded hotly. "That her father, who's wanted for the murder of her mother, will indeed be back for her? That he's a smart man, so don't worry about it, darling, because he'll find us at my place in Seattle?" She thrust her fingers through her hair, scraping it off her forehead. "I certainly can't tell her that it'll be a cold day in hell before I allow him to take her away."

Indignation on his brother's behalf straightened Coop from his indolent slouch, but he kept his tone even. "You think he'd hurt her?"

"Not physically. Eddie was an excellent parent who probably loved Lizzy more than anything in the world. But he ceased to be a blue-ribbon dad the day he became a fugitive. What does he plan to do, dye her hair to change her appearance? Teach her to answer to a new name every few months? She'll learn to lie and be constantly moved from place to place to stay one step ahead of the law. What kind of life is that for a kid?"

Coop hated to admit it, but she had a point. *Still.* "Are you one hundred percent convinced her father is the killer?"

"Of course not. But the fact that he ran is certainly damning. You have to admit that's a tough detail to work around."

"Maybe he panicked when he found himself taking the rap for someone else's deed."

"Like who?" she demanded skeptically. "The One-Armed Man?"

"From what I hear, he's far from the only guy your sister had something going with. I don't mean to speak ill of the dead, but folks say she got around."

Veronica flopped back down in her chair. "Yeah, she was no angel. But as far as I know, the only person she had a genuine beef with was Eddie." She blew out a breath, fluttering a glossy strand of hair that had flopped over her eyebrow. "Which brings us full circle." Then an arrested expression crossed her face.

He straightened in his seat. "What?"

"Huh?"

"You just had a look in your eye."

"Did I?" She shrugged. "It's called frustration."

"No, it was something else." And he wanted to know what.

But Veronica's expression had smoothed out and become unreadable. "You're imagining things."

No, he wasn't. She knew something, or suspected something, or had thought of something — he'd swear to it.

But much as he longed to pursue it, he'd let it go. For now. Otherwise, he was pretty sure she'd just turn stubborn on him.

Sooner or later, though — and he intended it to be sooner — he planned to find out if whatever caused that brief look on her face might help to clear Eddie.

15

An icy wind cut through Veronica's jacket as she hurried across the street to the Tonk. When she finally reached the tavern door, however, she hesitated. Aside from Tuesday, when she'd filled in for Sandy, she'd actually managed to get to bed at a reasonable hour each night this past week. She ought to feel well rested. The only problem was . . . she hadn't gotten any more sleep.

She'd awakened in the wee hours every morning to find Cooper either climbing into bed with her or already there — and herself divested of her jammies and in a high state of arousal before she was even fully awake. And Coop hadn't been satisfied to simply make love to her once and then wander back to his own bed. She'd generally lost count of her orgasms long before he'd climbed out of bed again and gone up to his attic room.

And oh, my, just thinking about it took the windchill factor right out of the air.

Spine stiffening, she reached for the knob. *That* wasn't what brought her to the Tonk. She liked to think things through, so it hadn't been from any burning desire to keep Coop in the dark last Saturday that she'd failed to share with

240

him her sudden recollection of a telephone conversation she'd had with Crystal shortly before she left for Scotland. The sudden flash of her sister's excitement over the champagne treatment she'd received from some guy she'd been seeing had popped unbidden into Ronnie's mind out of the blue and reminded her that Crystal was no longer around to enjoy the sort of uptown treatment she'd adored. In that moment, Veronica had desired nothing more than an opportunity to mull the memory over in private.

But that was five days ago, and she'd done all the mulling she could stand, so the time had come to talk to Coop. Supposing, of course, he was even still interested. It was just as likely he wouldn't be, since what she had to report was pretty inconsequential — just a chance remark, hardly earth-shattering news.

And certainly not worth making a special trip to the Tonk for. Stepping inside, Veronica paused for a moment to appreciate the irony while she soaked up a little of the Tonk's warmth. This place had always represented her worst nightmare, yet lately she found herself inventing feeble excuses to drop by.

She located Coop behind the bar, listening to something a patron said while he assembled a drink. As she watched, he threw back his head and laughed, and all the moisture in her mouth dried up.

Oh, boy. She was in big trouble. She kept thinking this attraction between them would lessen, but so far it'd only grown worse.

Not that she planned to let it get out of control or anything. She was an adult — she could handle it. Squaring her shoulders, Veronica strode over to the bar.

"Hey, there," she said as she climbed up on a recently abandoned stool.

"Hey, yourself." Coop smiled at her and leaned across the bar as if he meant to kiss her. When Veronica jerked back, his face went blank. Too blank, and she had the distinct impression he was displeased with her.

It bothered her that she cared. It was his problem, not hers, so it shouldn't matter. It wasn't as if she would change her actions even if she could. She barely knew how *she* felt about this relationship; she certainly wasn't about to put it on display for the Tonk's clientele. Particularly not when she'd noticed that Darlene Starkey was here again. One public kiss, and the entire town would have an opinion on her relationship with Cooper before she'd managed to form one herself.

"Get you something to drink?" Coop's voice, cutting into her thoughts, was clipped and aloof.

Veronica shifted on her stool, wishing she could redo the last few minutes, handle it differently so Coop wouldn't be angry with her.

That she desired to placate his male ego at all made her feel defensive. "No," she replied stiffly. "Thanks. I just dropped by to talk to you for a few minutes, but obviously it wasn't one of my brighter ideas." She slid off the stool. "We can talk another time." It was a safe bet that wouldn't be later tonight. Somehow she doubted Coop would be sneaking into her bed after this.

"Wait." He reached across the bar and stayed her with one large hand, gently pinning her much smaller one to the bar. "Don't go."

Veronica gave an experimental tug and discovered that she was unlikely to be released without a struggle. She leaned closer to him over the bar. "I can't do the public affection thing," she said in a low voice. "I'm sorry if that angers you, but I won't have the entire town speculating about what's going on between us."

"I know. I thought for a minute you were ashamed of me, or at least ashamed of what we —"

"No! But you have to understand how it would look. You work in the family tavern and you live in my house —"

"And kissing you over the bar could start up a whole slew of rumors. I get it." He gave her hand a gentle shake. "So have a glass of wine or something, and just keep me company for a while." His fingertips stroked down the back of her hand to the ends of her fingers as he released her. He met her gaze levelly. "Please."

She didn't think he was a guy who put himself in the position of supplicant easily, and she climbed back up on the stool. "I'd love a glass of the house white."

The momentum that had sent her across the street was broken, however, so she didn't plunge right in about the conversation with Crystal. She divided her attention between watching Cooper and visiting with the various customers who stopped by to say hello to her.

It was amazing to discover she'd actually begun to make friends with a few of the Tonk regulars. As it turned out, though, her bad memories weren't the whole story. She'd taken the actions of a few and blown them up in her mind until they'd come to represent the entire clientele. She was beginning to believe that there were actually more nice, everyday people who came in here than waitress-groping drunks.

And watching Cooper was just plain impossible to resist. He was too appealing, too compelling, with that big body and fluid grace, with his exotic coloring, and those dark eyes that looked at her as though she held the secrets to his hottest fantasies. It gave her the uneasiest suspicion he was coming to mean more to her than she'd like to admit.

And yet . . . would that truly be so awful? She didn't plan to get serious about him or anything. Heck, she hadn't harbored any burning desire to get serious about any of the other men she'd dated, either, but she'd certainly never had a problem admitting she felt something for them. Was that due to the fact that her usual type was a suit-and-tie-wearing professional, and Coop was anything but? And if so, did he therefore merit less consideration, or respect, or whatever it was she feared she was denying him, simply because he was a different breed of cat? She wasn't generally such a snob.

Veronica sat a little straighter on her stool. She *wasn't* a snob, but she'd been behaving perilously close to one. Well, that attitude stopped now. Overcome by a sudden feeling of freedom, she gave Coop such a brilliant smile that he blinked.

"Wow." Bracing his forearms on the bar, he leaned into her and returned fire with a killer smile of his own. "What was that for?"

"Hmm?" If she didn't have so many reservations about public displays of affection, she'd lean forward and take a big, juicy bite out of his luscious lower lip. Instead, she drew back with self-conscious primness and said, "What was what for?"

"That billion-kilowatt smile you just gave me. Tell me what I did to earn it, so I can do it some more."

Smiling anew, she marveled at the pure happiness that suffused her. "Perhaps," she said softly, "it was simply for you . . . being you."

"Hot damn," he breathed. "You know, it's freakin' slow in here for a Thursday. I wonder if Barbara knows anything about bartending."

Veronica was actually giving the notion some serious consideration when a man cleared his throat and Coop straightened. It jerked her out of her dream world and back to the realm of good sense. Good grief. It was bad enough that she was probably fooling herself that the Tonk's patrons hadn't begun to speculate about her relationship with Cooper. If by some miracle it had escaped their notice, having the two of them race out of here in a red-hot lather would certainly guarantee everyone's attention. Resisting the urge to touch her arm with her fingertips to see if the heat Coop generated in her every time he came within touching distance would make an audible sizzle, she picked up her wine glass and emptied it in one long gulp.

Ruddy color stained Coop's cheekbones, but he gave the man who'd interrupted them a level-eyed look. "What can I get you?" he inquired as he cleared the bar of empties and used a dish towel to wipe up the condensation that had puddled beneath a highball glass.

"Bourbon and seven," the man said and took the vacant stool next to Veronica's. He gave her a friendly nod, then immediately turned his attention back to Coop. "Do you remember me?"

Coop paused with the can of 7UP suspended over the drink and studied the younger man. His mouth tipped up in a small, crooked smile. "Sorry — can't say that I do. Did you recently change your drink? I'm much better at matching liquor with its owner than I am with names."

"You've never made me a drink."

Coop raised his eyebrows, and the man shook his head impatiently. "I'm sorry — I'm going about this all backwards. I'm David Pessein."

246

He thrust his hand out and Coop wiped his hand on his towel, then shook it.

"I didn't really expect that you'd remember me," David said, "since I was just a kid when we met. But I've heard of your exploits for so many years, I feel as if I know you, and when I heard you were working here I just had to stop in to say hello. I moved to Spokane a few years ago, but I'm back visiting my family — so I wanted to come by to tell you how sorry I am about Eddie."

Veronica blinked. She'd assumed it must be a case of mistaken identity, but Coop abruptly went very, very still, and she shot him a glance. At the look on his face, the warmth that their flirting had wrapped around her heart turned to ice. She knew that blank face. It was the one he wore when he didn't want his thoughts read.

She swiveled around to face the man at her side. "Eddie Chapman, you mean? Did you know him?"

"Sure. He was probably my closest friend, growing up. And personally, I can't envision him doing what everyone's saying he did. Which is another reason I felt so bad about not contacting James here."

"James?"

"Cooper, I mean." He turned back to Coop with a laugh. "Sorry about that. Eddie always said it was a losing battle trying to remember to call you that, so what chance do I have to keep your name straight?" He shrugged good-naturedly. "He idolizes you, you know."

Oh, man. I so *don't want to know the reason behind this*. Veronica's stomach roiled, and her heart tried to pound its way out of her chest. But still she couldn't prevent herself from asking. "Why?"

He apparently didn't find it odd that she was the one asking questions, while Cooper merely stood on the other side of the bar regarding them both with a complete lack of expression. "Jeez, where to begin? The Marines was a biggie, of course — that's a majorly macho deal when you're a kid. But let's face it: I think James — I mean Coop — could have been an accountant and still Eddie would have thought he was the biggest, baddest thing to swagger down the pike. That's just the way little brothers tend to be."

Brother? Veronica's gaze swung back to Coop. An icy fist seemed to close around her heart as she waited for his denial — that this man was mistaken, that Coop wasn't the person Eddie's friend thought he was.

Instead, Coop looked at her for just a moment before essaying the merest shrug. Then he turned back to Eddie's friend. "I do vaguely remember you," he said imperturbably. "It's good to see you again, David."

Betrayal screaming through every nerve ending in her body, Veronica got down off her stool and silently walked away.

The minute Coop finished closing down the Tonk for the night, he strode across the street, let himself into the house, and headed straight up the stairs to Veronica's bedroom. He tried the doorknob and eased out the breath he'd been holding when it turned beneath his hand. But he didn't have time to give thanks, because the door only opened half an inch before bumping up against an immovable object. She'd braced a chair under the knob.

He rattled the door lightly. "Let me in, Ronnie. We have to talk."

She didn't answer, but he knew she was awake. He could feel her on the other side of the door, her hurt and fury nearly a palpable entity.

She hadn't been alone in her shock over Pessein's announcement. It had caught *him* flat-footed, and he wasn't exactly proud that his first thought had been for his own dilemma now that his anonymity was blown. But then he'd had to watch the blood drain from Veronica's face before she'd taken off without a word. After her departure, news of his connection to Eddie had taken less than five minutes to make the rounds. It had set the bar abuzz, and considering that the Starkey woman had been present, the odds were good that the entire town would be buzzing about it by morning.

At the moment, though, he didn't give a damn about any of that. Let them say whatever the hell they wanted. The only person whose opinion really mattered to him was Ronnie.

And apparently she wasn't talking.

"Let me in." Stroking his hand down the

door's old wooden panels, he pressed his eye to the crack, but he couldn't see anything. "I can explain." Somehow.

He heard her get up and pad toward the door, and his heart gave a thump of relief. He caught only the meagerest glimpse of her tousled hair, then a slice of her face when she reached out for the chair. Even in the dim light, her eye appeared swollen, as if she'd been crying. His gut clenched. He'd never meant to make her cry, but he'd fix it. Somehow, he'd fix it. Catching her eye, he attempted a gentle smile.

She stopped and stared at him for a moment. Then slowly she reached out.

And firmly shut the door in his face.

16

"I don't think you're gonna like this, sweetie," Marissa said the next day in her kitchen as she handed Veronica a cup of tea and took the stool next to her at the breakfast bar. "But if Coop is Eddie's brother, I can almost see why he kept it to himself."

"How can you say that?" Veronica had come to her friend for comfort, but instead felt betrayed all over again. "You think it's *okay* that he made love with me and didn't bother to tell —"

"Hello!" Marissa snapped erect. "You two had *sex?* When the hell did this happen?"

"Last Saturday." Veronica rubbed her hands over her cheeks, looking at Marissa over her fingers. "Well, the first time, anyhow."

"The *first* time. How many times are we talking about?"

"Oh, God, Rissa, he screwed my brains out." And admitting that gave Veronica the same conflicted feeling she'd been battling since last night: a hot-and-cold rush of arousal, balanced against chilled skin and a stomach that pitched queasily. "For five nights, several *times* a night," she added, and gave Marissa a very brief rundown of Coop's middle-of-the-night appearances. "We had sex so many times I lost count. And not once did he say a word about his relationship to Eddie."

"That *pig*."

A small knot in Veronica's stomach unraveled. "Thank you. That's more like it."

"Yes, well, don't go getting too comfortable," Marissa advised, giving her a look, "because you're not off the hook yet yourself."

"Me? What did *I* do?" Veronica demanded. "I'm the victim here. I should be getting tea and chocolate."

"You've got your tea and chocolate." Pushing the plate of Oreos closer, Marissa gave her a stern look. "But you've got some explaining to do, girl. I can't believe you did the wild thing with Cooper Blackstock several times a day for five days straight and never said a word about it to your very best friend!"

"I was going to tell you." Veronica shifted uncomfortably on her stool. "Only I wanted to get it straight in my own head before I even attempted to explain it out loud."

"What's to get straight? Correct me if I'm wrong, but the guy looks like about two hundred pounds of raw sex on the hoof."

Veronica would have loved to laugh it off, to pooh-pooh the very idea or say indifferently that he was "okay." But she could feel her eyes glazing over at the mere memory of what Coop could do with that big body of his. She slapped her hand down on the granite countertop.

"That's not the point."

"Great sex is always the point," Marissa said. "Or at least it makes a valid point all its own. And it *was* great sex, wasn't it?"

"Oh, yeah," she agreed without thinking. Then she ruthlessly shoved aside the memory of exactly how great and firmed up her backbone. "But the truth is, until last night I was still denying to myself that we even *had* a relationship. And as it turns out, my instincts were pretty damn good, weren't they? Cooper Blackstock and I have nothing. Nada."

"Because he didn't tell you he was Eddie's brother?"

"That, definitely. I know now that he tried to worm information out of me without identifying himself. I feel duped, Rissa, and it hurts. But you know what's even worse? I have this awful feeling that Cooper is far too much like my father."

"Oh, sweetie." Marissa reached over and rubbed her arm. "Surely not. The word around town is that he was a Marine."

Veronica nodded. "David — the guy who blew his cover — mentioned something about that last night, so I suppose it's true."

"Then he can't be all *that* lacking in ambition."

"Except he's, what — thirty-four, thirty-five years old? Hardly old enough to have retired from the service. So, what's he doing with his life?"

"It's possible he's self-employed like you," Marissa said neutrally. "Maybe he, too, has a career he temporarily put on hold."

"Why, though? Mine's in limbo because both the Tonk and the house need to be sold, and I'm the only one left to handle it. Not to mention that Lizzy needs —" She gave her friend a stricken look. "*Lizzy*. Oh, my God, Rissa, I've been so self-absorbed I entirely forgot this makes him Lizzy's uncle." She sat militantly tall on her stool. "That son of a bitch! He's been living in the same house with her, and he never said a word. Not a single, solitary word to let her know she has someone else she can depend on." Then she laughed sharply. "Of course, that may actually have been a favor, considering she can't. Depend on him," she clarified when Marissa raised an eyebrow at her. Then she scowled. "You know what I mean."

"Yeah, I suppose I do. Are you going to tell her?"

"Why do I get all the fun jobs?" Veronica knuckled the headache brewing in her temples. "Still, as much as I'd love to avoid being the one to drop that little bomb on her head, I certainly don't want her hearing it from someone at school." She stared glumly at the brightly colored magnets that pinned childish artwork to Marissa's refrigerator. "Isn't this just great?" she demanded sarcastically. "Like she needs another shock."

"This might actually be welcome news,

254

though," Marissa said quietly. "I would think, at this point, that Lizzy could use all the family she can get."

They sat silently for a moment, drinking their tea and decimating the plate of Oreos. Then Marissa looked over at Veronica. She pushed her teacup back, drew invisible doodles on the countertop with her fingertip for a moment, then cleared her throat. "Speaking of men, I might have a not-so-dependable guy problem on my own hands."

Veronica, who had been watching her friend's uncharacteristic avoidance tactics with puzzlement, frowned as if Marissa's words had been delivered in a language other than English. Then it sank in that there was only one man to whom she could be referring. *"Kody?"*

"I'm starting to think he doesn't want anything to do with my kids."

Veronica laughed. "You're kidding." She immediately saw by the look on Marissa's face that she wasn't. "You're not kidding. I'm sorry — I didn't mean to make light of the situation, it just caught me by surprise. Kody seems like the kind of guy who'd be great with kids."

"Yeah, that's what I assumed, too. But our dates have all been either for nights when Dess and Riley are spending the evening away from home, or for things like stopping by the Tonk — late-night dates that he always picks me up for after the kids are in bed."

"Yeah, but that could easily be coincidental,

couldn't it? I mean, that's usually when you're available, and when he's avail—"

"Anything's possible, Ronnie," Marissa interrupted. "But I don't think this is a coincidence."

"Why not?"

"I've just got one of those gut feelings," Marissa said. "It's been nibbling away at the edges of my consciousness for a while now, but I guess I haven't wanted to examine it too closely, you know?"

"Oh, yes," Veronica agreed fervently. "I understand all too well." She studied Marissa's melancholy expression. "Aside from the obvious — that anyone who fails to recognize how great your kids are is pond scum — what's your bottom-line feeling about this? About him? I've never seen anything as immediate as the way you two hit it off. Was that merely really good chemistry — or are you in love with him?"

"The smart money would probably say chemistry, since I haven't known him all that long. But I'm really afraid it might be love. I haven't felt like this about a guy since Denny."

Veronica reached over to squeeze her arm. "Then hadn't you better come right out and ask him what the deal is? Not to argue with your gut or anything, but you could be reading this all wrong."

"I suppose it's possible," Marissa said slowly. Then she sat taller in her seat and looked at Ronnie with sudden resolve. "No. You're right. This is too important to try to solve with guesswork. I'll give him a call tonight and arrange to get together. I need to find out what's what."

Veronica thought about it as she drove home. She hoped with all her heart that Marissa was wrong. But as she parked the car in front of the house several moments later, she suddenly remembered the night of the VFW overnighter and the look that flashed across Kody's face when Marissa had invited him to go to the movies the following day with her and the kids. And she wondered if maybe her friend wasn't on to something. There had been something in that fleeting expression.

Which *she* could just as easily have read all wrong. If she hadn't, though — well, what a damn shame that would be. She truly wanted a happily-ever-after ending for her friend; no one deserved one more.

The last person she expected to find in the living room was Coop, and she stopped dead at the sight of him sprawled out on the gold and green brocade sofa.

He rose to his feet. "I'm glad you're back. I've been waiting for you."

Her heart began to pound and she could feel the flush that surged up her throat and onto her face. "Have you? What a waste of time. Because I have nothing to say to you . . . James."

His face went hard. "My name is Cooper! Only my mother called me James — and she only did so because it held more upscale connotations for her than Coop. She was real big on that kind of thing."

" 'Connotations.' My. What a big word for a bartender/Marine." She didn't flicker so much as an eyelash as they engaged in a heated stare-down.

"Isn't it, though," he agreed flatly. "You'd be amazed at what words I know."

Although his face wore that aggravatingly cool lack of expression she'd come to detest, Veronica instinctively knew she'd hit a nerve. She ought to be happy about it, since God knew discovering he was Eddie's half-brother had scraped all *her* nerve endings bare. Instead, she felt . . . dishonorable.

And wasn't that the shits? How had he managed that? A smart woman would just turn right around and walk away. But, interested in spite of herself, Veronica couldn't quite prevent herself from inquiring, "So James isn't actually your name?"

"It's mine, all right. My legal name is James Cooper Blackstock. But I've been known from birth by my middle name. Only my mother used the James part of it, and even she didn't get insistent about it until after she married Chapman."

"She was hardly the only one," Veronica felt compelled to point out. "According to your new best friend David, Eddie called you that, too."

"Jesus, Ronnie, it was the name he heard from birth. Mom refused to call me anything else."

"Fine. Thanks for setting me straight. But you can call yourself whatever you want — I still have nothing to say to you." She started to turn away, then suddenly remembered Lizzy and swung back. "No, that's not true. You'd damn well better be down here to do more than talk to me. You'd better be waiting for Lizzy to get home, so you can explain to her why her uncle has been living in this house but hasn't seen fit to share the truth of his relationship with her."

He froze. "Aw, man," he said, clearly miserable. "She's gonna hate my guts."

Veronica was surprised to see that Mr. Poker Face was quite visibly distressed at the notion. "I guess that's just the chance you'll have to take. You weren't the least bit shy last night about letting people find out you're Eddie's brother. You think it won't be all over her school by tomorrow morning?" She stepped up close and thrust her nose up under his. "It's bad enough that some little bully-brat's gonna get his jollies finding a way to rub her nose in it. I'll be damned if I'll let her be caught flat-footed by the knowledge, to boot."

A muscle flexed in his jaw, but he gave her a curt nod. "I'll talk to her as soon as she gets home."

"Good." She stepped back. "Then I guess we have nothing left to say."

"The hell we don't!" He grasped her arm. When she stared pointedly at his tanned fingers, he promptly set her loose. But he crowded close, his dark brows gathered over the thrust of his nose as he scowled down at her. "What the hell should I have done, Ronnie? That first night, if

259

I'd walked into your kitchen and announced I was Eddie's brother and I was here to clear him of your sister's murder, you would have tossed me out on my ear."

"Quite possibly I would have. But we'll never know for certain now, will we? You didn't give me the chance to make a decision one way or the other. And do I really have to remind you that you've had plenty of opportunities since then? Night after night you could have told me. But you know what, Blackstock? I don't recall hearing a single word come out of your mouth that would've clued me in to the identity of the man I was sleeping with!"

Hell, no, he hadn't told her. He hadn't wanted to give her up, and had feared that admitting he was Eddie's brother would force him to do exactly that. Coop straightened defensively. No, that wasn't it. That made her sound too . . . important in his life. Not that she wasn't important, of course, just not *that* important, and — well, that wasn't the reason, was all. Yet he heard himself mutter, "I didn't want to give you up, okay?"

"Uh-huh." Her voice was flat, disbelieving, and she didn't look as though he'd just handed her a powerful weapon. She looked pissed. "So basically what you're saying is that you'd found yourself a handy-dandy little lay and didn't want to screw it up — you'll pardon the pun — with anything so messy as the truth."

"That's not what I said at all! Jeez-us!"

Ramming his fingers through his hair, he stared at her in frustration. "This is why men hate talking things over with women. We tell you one thing, and you hear something entirely different!"

Watching her open her mouth to no doubt blast him anew, his control snapped. He wrapped his hands around her upper arms, pulled her to him, and clamped his mouth over hers in a fiery kiss that was chock-full of aggravated heat. For several heartbeats he lost himself in her unique taste. Then he ripped his mouth free, set her back on her heels, and took a step back, licking his lips to retain her flavor.

"You and me together?" he said. "Man, Ronnie, if that didn't turn out to be more wicked potent than I ever expected. But once I'd got a taste, I wanted to keep *on* tasting it, which I figured would never happen if I told you about my relationship with Eddie. So, yeah, I kept it to myself. I probably shouldn't have, but I didn't want to find myself suddenly locked out of your life." He gave her a hard look. "Which is exactly what happened the minute you found out."

"Proving that once again women are inherently unfair. Yes, indeed, we simply revel in making men pay for itty-bitty transgressions like *making time with us under false pretenses.*" Her laugh was harsh, unamused. "Leave it to a guy to turn this all around so it's *my* fault you had to lie to me." Shooting him a final furious look, she turned on her heel and stalked from the room.

Coop's first impulse was to chase after her and make her listen to reason. Instead, with a frustrated growl, he threw himself down on the couch. Boo appeared out of nowhere and launched himself onto his lap, promptly sinking needle-sharp claws into Coop's thigh when his precarious landing caused him to slide.

Grimacing, Coop reached down to unhook the kitten from his leg. Settling him on his lap, he stroked Boo's plush black fur from the top of his head to the tip of his tail, and smiled crookedly when the cat's gravel-truck purr kicked into gear. "So, did you catch any of that?" he asked, scratching him under the chin. Boo craned his neck and gazed through slitted eyes into the distance, his motor rumbling like an overloaded cement mixer. "Looks like I'm in the doghouse."

The cat slanted him a look, then closed his eyes and jacked up the volume on his purr.

"Yeah, I don't get women, either. They're so friggin' emotional, not cool and logical like us guys." Coop stared thoughtfully at the empty doorway where he'd watched Ronnie storm out. "Still. Maybe — now, don't go quoting me here — but just *maybe* she has a point. I didn't want to get involved with her in the first place because of our blood ties to my brother and her sister. But you know what, little buddy? Somehow we got involved, anyway. And I'm telling you right now, Boo, if you don't learn anything else during your nine lives, you can take this to the cat food bank." He pinned the supremely indifferent kitten with an intense look. "Problematic siblings or not, I am not ready to give her up."

He and the cat were still sitting in the same spot a short while later when Lizzy got home from school. At the sound of the back door opening, Boo leaped from his lap and raced into the kitchen to greet his mistress. Coop, however, remained where he was for a moment, listening to the kitchen door close and the sounds of the fridge opening and closing and the clink of the cookie jar. He couldn't believe how nervous he was. He'd reconnoitered an Iraqi hostage stronghold guarded by men with automatic weapons and felt less trepidation than he did at the prospect of facing his six-year-old niece.

But sitting here acting like a chickenshit would get him absolutely nowhere, and the clock was ticking. As long as his cover was blown anyway, he planned to get some answers he hadn't been able to get by pretending to be someone other than Eddie's brother. Climbing to his feet, he rubbed his hands down the thighs of his jeans.

He found Lizzy sitting at the kitchen table, swinging her legs while she dunked cookies in a glass of milk. Boo prowled the floor, alternately leaping at her swaying foot and staring hopefully at the hand carrying food from glass to mouth. "Hi."

She looked up and gave him a big, milky smile. "Hi, Coop! I'm having a Lassie dinner."

"A what?"

"That's what Aunt Ronnie calls milk and cookies: a Lassie dinner. She said some kid named Timmy always got milk and cookies after Lassie rescued him." She shrugged. "It was some show about a dog that she watched when she was jus' a little kid."

Coop sat at the table across from her. "How was school today?"

Her narrow little shoulders hitched. "Okay, I guess. It was gym day, and Mr. Pelby made us do squat thrusts before we got to use the balance beam."

"Squat thrusts'll make you strong."

"I s'pose." She shrugged again. "I think they're dumb."

Okay, so much for chitchat. He leaned forward in his seat. "Listen, Little Bit . . . I'd like to tell you something."

She finished draining her glass and replaced it carefully on the table, then looked over at Coop and gave him her solemn, milk-mustachioed attention. " 'Kay."

"I don't know how to pussyfoot around this, so I'm just gonna say it straight out: I'm your uncle."

"Nuh-uh!" Her leg abruptly stopped swinging and she gave him an indignant stare. "My uncle's name is *James*."

"Actually, baby, my whole name is James Cooper Blackstock, but I've always gone by Cooper. Only your daddy's mother, who was my mother, too, and your daddy called me James."

264

She stared at him, then, abruptly, pushed away from the table and ran from the room.

Coop remained where he was. "Well, that went just fucking swell," he muttered to Boo, who was chasing down the crumbs that had landed on the floor at Lizzy's abrupt departure from the table. His niece hadn't reviled him for a lying, scum-sucking dog, but she'd probably never speak to him again, either. The prospect bothered him more than he liked to think about, and he didn't have the first idea what he could do to make it right.

When he heard footsteps suddenly clatter back down the stairs, he straightened in his seat. The tread faltered at the bottom of the stairs for a moment, then Lizzy poked her head around the wall, tucked her chin, and shot him a glance from beneath her bangs. A second later, she eased into the room, a bulky album clutched to her chest.

Coop sat very still while she crossed the room, afraid to make any sudden moves that might scare her off. Pushing her abandoned milk glass aside, she set the album on the table, then climbed onto the chair across the table. Silently she flipped through the pages, then turned the book so he could see. Her soft little finger landed squarely on a photograph. "That's you."

It was a full-body snapshot of him in his dress blues, the visor of his hat shadowing his face. He remembered the day Zach Taylor had taken it. "Yeah. I was a bit younger then." Like ten years.

"You sent me a doll from Bennice. That's in Italy."

His throat went tight, and he nodded. "Venice," he corrected her softly. "A Fool doll that I got at Carnival. Did you like it?"

"Uh-huh." She nodded solemnly. "Next to Celebration Barbie, it's my fave-rit, but I don't have it right now, 'cuz it's at my daddy's house." She climbed down from her chair and circled the table to stand in front of him.

She studied him for a couple of moments, then nodded as if making up her mind, and clambered up onto his lap. "So. You gonna bring my daddy home?"

17

"So, 'Uncle Coop,' also known as Uncle James, is Lizzy's new best friend," Veronica glumly informed Marissa over the clatter of crockery in the Dinosaur Café the following Monday. "While *I'm* the Unbeliever — which I'm pretty sure is second cousin to the Antichrist."

Marissa skooched her chair in to let a burdened waitress squeeze between the tables in the steamy, crowded restaurant. As she returned Veronica's look across the table, her mouth curled up in a lopsided smile. "You don't think you're being just the teeniest bit melodramatic?"

"No. That would be claiming my kinship as first cousin." The café door opened, letting in a blast of cold air, and Veronica hunched her shoulders against it, cupping her hands around the heat of her cup of soup. "You should've seen the look on her face when she walked in on a phone conversation I was having with a prospective client. You would've thought I was going to roust her out of bed in the dead of night and drag her from hearth and home."

"You've got a new job lined up?"

"Not yet. But yesterday I had a message from a woman named Georgia Levinstein. Do you remember the eighteenth century farmhouse I redid in Maryland?"

"Of course. It was your first solo job, and you sent me pictures."

"Apparently Mrs. Levinstein saw my work on it. She has a Greek Revival house in Boston she wants me to take a look at. It's not like I even agreed to it," she said defensively, then took a savage bite of her turkey sandwich and chewed furiously. Swallowing, she faced her friend a bit indignantly. "I told Mrs. Levinstein I was engaged elsewhere at the moment and that it might be several months before I'd be free to even submit a proper proposal for a new project. But she agreed to wait, and Lizzy walked in during the part where I was telling her that meanwhile if she wanted to send me photos, I'd be happy to do a little research and put together a pre-proposal, in which I state my understanding of the client's goals. I do this because it gives the client a rough estimate of what it would take to accomplish those goals — both in time and money — and it ensures us, if both parties are still interested later, that we weren't talking apples and oranges during our original conversation."

"So Lizzy walked in on this and . . . ?"

"Completely misconstrued it and went running to the solace of Coop's big ole protective arms." She laughed without humor. "It's ironic, isn't it? He was worried she'd hate his guts, but instead she just loves him to pieces. *I* seem to be the villain in this little melodrama, because Coop believes her daddy is innocent, while I . . . well, I don't know what the hell I believe anymore." Then she shrugged and looked around, taking in their surroundings. "But enough about me. Believe it or not, I didn't ask you to lunch to whine. This place is nice. And dinosaurs is a catchy theme, given the name of the town. Who are the proprietors? Anyone I'd know?"

"Nope. It's a couple who moved into the area a few years ago."

"Well, it's a great place, and the food is excellent. In fact, I noticed this entire part of town seems to be enjoying a resurgence."

Marissa suddenly laughed. "That reminds me. Guess what the city planners have started calling it?"

"You've got me — give me a hint."

"Okay, what would you call something that's been designated the *old*est part of town?"

Ronnie considered the emphasis her friend put on the word. "I don't know, historic Fossil? There are a couple of pretty buildings down in this area, but they're not of any real historical value. Come to think of it, there's not a lot of history in this town, period. We're an agriculture region whose hub sprawled out piecemeal every time it grew." She set her spoon alongside her soup bowl. "I give. What do they call this part of town?"

"Old Fossil."

"Excuse me?"

"Old Fossil."

Veronica laughed. "Get outta here. They couldn't possibly have missed the redundancy."

"Swear to God." Marissa crossed her heart with her index and fore fingers, then held up her hand as if taking a Girl Scout oath. "Even after it was pointed out to them in a veritable flood of letters to the editor in the *Tribune* that fossils by definition are antiquated or from another geological age, they still insisted it gave the area a certain panache."

Veronica laughed. "Who's on this committee — your friends Wentworth and Tyler-Jones from the Junior League?"

Marissa grinned. "Nah, but thanks for the I'm-your-bud-therefore-I-hate-who-you-hate moment. You truly are a best friend."

"Oh, my gosh, that reminds me. If I were such a good friend, I would've asked you right away what Kody had to say for himself when you talked to him about the kids. *Has* he been avoiding meeting them?"

"I don't know yet. We haven't been able to get together. It seems like whenever I have the time, he can't get away. And when he has the time, I'm tied up." Marissa shrugged, but a tightness around her eyes gave lie to her apparent indifference. "We've made plans to get together Wednesday evening, though. Could the kids stay the night with you? I thought it might be less disruptive than rousting them out of bed in the middle of a school night."

"Sure. They can come straight from school, if you'd like."

"No, I'll bring them down after dinner. We won't burden you longer than necessary."

Veronica made a rude noise. "Big burden. If they get too noisy, I'll give Mrs. M a call and take a walk around the block. Heck, maybe I'll call her to come over and watch TV with me, anyway. I think she misses the kids since I've stopped spending so much time at the Tonk."

Another eddy of cold air blew across her shoulders as the door behind her once again opened and closed, and Veronica shifted slightly in her seat. "Next time we come here, we're grabbing a table out of the path of that doorway. Either that, or coming on a warmer day."

"It's sure been colder'n a witch's leftie lately," Marissa agreed.

"Which is probably not a bad thing for the Winter Festival. I seem to recall bigger, rowdier crowds whenever it snowed or we had a cold snap. Speaking of which, how are the decorations coming along?"

"Great. I've got a crew working over at the fairgrounds as we speak. We took your advice and made papier-mâché trees, and they turned out so well that several of the committee decided to make more for the ice rink. I plan to stop by after we leave here."

A couple sauntered into Veronica's line of vision and took a table a few yards away. Even from the back, they drew attention as the man assisted the woman in removing an expensive-looking overcoat and ushered her into a seat. Both were blond: The man's hair gleamed as gold as an antique doubloon, while the woman's was a pale honey tousled bob that looked casual and thrown together but had probably cost the earth to attain. He was tall, and she was tiny, but both looked fit in wool sweaters and jeans that Veronica would be willing to bet sported a designer brand on the hip pocket.

She only knew one man that pulled together, so she wasn't exactly knocked for a loop when, having rounded the table and taken a chair that faced her own, turned out to be Troy Jacobson. "Which must make that his wife, whatzername," she murmured.

"Have you taken up talking to yourself now?" Marissa inquired. "Who must be whose wife?"

"The pom-pom queen. Golden Boy Jacobson's wife."

Marissa glanced over her shoulder. "Oh, Nancy, you mean. I didn't know she was back in town." She gave Veronica a look across the table. "She's actually quite nice."

"If you say so." Ronnie shrugged. "I suppose it isn't her fault he was such a jackass back in high school. I'm just having a knee-jerk moment. Give me a second — it'll pass."

As if realizing he was the subject of their discussion, Troy suddenly glanced up from the menu he'd been perusing and looked straight at Veronica. Without so much as a flicker of recognition, he immediately turned his attention back to his menu.

She opened her mouth to say something scathing about it to Marissa, but then kept the comment to herself. She recalled Darlene Starkey's reference to an affair Troy was supposedly having and his less-than-happy retort that his wife had heard the same rumor — which was the reason she'd still been out of town. If appearances were anything to go by, the couple had resolved their differences, and Veronica had to admit that in his place, she probably wouldn't point out the sister of his onetime lover, either.

A little devil nevertheless nudged her to go over and introduce herself, but she reined in the impulse and concentrated on her visit with Marissa. And after they paid their check a short while later and rose to go their separate ways, she managed to pass within greeting range of the Jacobsons' table without uttering a word.

The minute he heard sounds coming from downstairs, Coop saved the file of his current chapter and shut down his computer. It was too soon for Lizzy to be out of school, which meant Ronnie had to be home. For the past several days, she'd managed to avoid him or had given him the bum's rush when she couldn't avoid him, so this was too golden an opportunity to let pass. Coop pushed back from the little table he used as a desk and headed for the stairs.

He found her putting her coat in the living

room closet. Stopping in the doorway, he propped his shoulder against the jamb to observe her for a moment. She moved with economical grace, and watching her as she reached out to hook the hanger over the rod, he couldn't believe how much he'd missed her these past several days.

The really scary part was that it wasn't only the sex that he missed. He missed her conversation and her way of looking at things. He missed the warmth of her laugh.

He hadn't thought he'd been particularly quiet when he entered the room, but when Veronica turned and saw him standing there, she jumped. "Hey," he said softly, pushing away from the jamb. "I didn't mean to startle you."

"Then stop prowling around like a damn cat!" she snapped.

With an inward sigh, he approached her. "Are you going to stay mad at me forever, Ronnie?" He looked down at her clear skin, flushed with ire, and at her soft mouth set in such hard lines against him, and stuffed his hands in his pockets to keep from reaching out to touch. "I'm *sorry* I didn't tell you who I was, okay? I didn't set out to hide my relationship with my brother, but when Marissa assumed I was answering the bartender ad, it occurred to me that I'd probably have better luck clearing Eddie's name if no one knew who I was."

Her mouth twisted, and he expected her to lambast him again for the opportunities he'd had to tell her the truth once they'd made love. She surprised him, however, when she merely said, "I understand what makes Lizzy believe in Eddie's innocence. She's a child and he's her father. But what about you? What makes you so all-fired sure, against every bit of evidence, that Eddie didn't do what the entire judicial system is sure he's done?"

"I don't believe the entire system does believe in his guilt. His lawyer couldn't understand why he ran — he claims the case against Eddie wasn't all that strong. But I don't need a lawyer to tell me my brother's innocent. I know Eddie. And you must have spent enough time talking to him and seeing him with Lizzy to have formed an opinion of the kind of man he is. Can you honestly say you don't have a single doubt he's guilty?"

"I don't know," she finally admitted. "I want to say yes, because the evidence all seems to point that way, and why else would he run, if he weren't guilty?"

"But?"

"But . . . my first reaction, when I heard that Crystal was dead, was sheer disbelief. Not only because she'd been *murdered*, but because Eddie stood accused of it."

"He didn't do it, Ronnie."

She studied him in silence for a moment, then finally said, "I can see you honestly believe that."

"I more than believe it — I know it in my gut."

"And your gut's never wrong?"

"Rarely."

Again she considered him, before saying slowly, "That man David said you were in the Marines."

"Yes. For thirteen years. My friend Zach and I were point men for a recon unit."

She walked over to the couch and sat. Coop felt encouraged, even though she was perched on the edge as if she might get up and leave at any moment. He took a seat at the opposite end.

"So when you told me you'd been a travel bum for thirteen years," she said, "that was —"

"Courtesy of Uncle Sam."

"I was going to say a lie, but since we really didn't know each other then, I suppose it was none of my business. So, what's a recon unit?"

"Reconnaissance — a unit of soldiers who survey a region to obtain information. Usually about an enemy."

"And the point men . . . ?"

"Scope out potential enemy territory ahead of the rest of the unit."

She gazed at him for a moment, then blinked and said, "Sounds dangerous."

Coop shrugged.

"Lizzy seems to think Eddie will come back for her. Is that what you believe, too?"

"Knowing the way Eddie feels about her? Yes."

She stiffened. "I won't let him take her, Cooper. Unless he gets his life straightened out,

I'll fight you, I'll fight him — I'll even fight Lizzy herself before I'll allow Eddie to ruin her life by taking her on the run."

She leaned forward to study him intently. "I admit, though, that you seem to have a decent grasp on people's characters. So, if I agree to have an open mind about Eddie's guilt in my sister's death, will you agree to keep him away from Lizzy if he shows up?"

Suppressing the sudden surge of warmth that wanted to wrap around him like a blanket simply because she'd expressed faith in his ability to assess character, Coop merely said, "He'd have to be able to see her." Before she could protest, he qualified, "I could arrange for it to be while she's sleeping, though. I'll agree not to let him speak to her, but he needs to be able to see for himself that she's all right."

"All right. Thank you."

"Don't thank me, Ronnie. As much as I'd like to get back in your good graces, I'm not doing this for you. While I see your point concerning the quality of Lizzy's life if she were constantly on the run, I also don't see where it would be appreciably richer or fuller without her father. I agree to keep them separated for Eddie's protection. I doubt Lizzy's ability to keep it to herself if she saw him, so until we get to the bottom of this mess, I agree to your terms."

"Fair enough."

She rose to her feet and so did Coop. Gazing down at her, he thought how earnest and solemn she looked as she stared up at him. For the first time in days she didn't appear angry with him, and he was so pleased about it, he instinctively reached out for her.

She smoothly sidestepped him.

"Ronn—"

"Several nights ago you said I had 'a look' in my eye. Would you like to know what put it there?"

He'd rather kiss her. No, that wasn't the correct response. Coop squared his shoulders. Of course he wanted to know. Clearing Eddie's name was the ultimate goal here. Taking a step back to keep from doing something stupid, he gave her a clipped nod.

"I remembered a conversation with Crystal, which I needed to think about before I discussed it out loud. Then, the other night, I was going to thrash it out with you, but . . ." Her voice trailed off.

"You discovered I was Eddie's brother."

"Yes." She hesitated, then gave him a look that was surprisingly prim. "It might not mean anything, but I feel you have the right to know that Crystal was involved with a man before her death."

Coop snapped to full attention. "Who?"

"I don't know. I'm assuming he was married, though, because she didn't want to talk about it — and the only time Crystal *ever* avoided giving me way more information than I wanted to know was when she was pretty sure I wouldn't keep my disapproval to myself. She detested being lectured."

"Did she give you *any* clue who he might be? A first name, anything?"

"No. She called him her 'honey,' but that was it. I'm pretty sure he was wealthy, though. I had Lizzy for a long weekend early last fall when Crystal went to Hawaii with the guy. She came back raving over the luxury hotel he took her to."

"What hotel? That might be a place to start."

"The Royal Hawaiian. She showed me pictures of it — it's this great, turreted pink hotel that was built in the 1920s. Crystal was absolutely blown away over the accommodations. They stayed in a pricey suite overlooking the ocean, which apparently is considered *the* premier location, and she loved the fact that the hotel served pink champagne."

"Do you have any guesses to the guy's identity?"

"No." But something flickered in the depths of her moss-green eyes.

"Darlene Starkey intimated Troy Jacobson was having an affair," he said neutrally. The man had rubbed him the wrong way the one and only time they'd met, so he felt he had to bend over backward not to let that color his attitude now.

"Darlene deals in rumors."

Hell, he didn't like her defense of Jacobson any better today than he had that night in the bar. "Your sister had an affair with him once."

"But we have no real reason to suppose she'd

279

taken up with him again."

Coop was trying not to feel low-grade pissed when she slowly added, "Still, I suppose it was seeing Troy with his wife at the café a while ago that made me think of Crystal's mystery man again. He's certainly rich enough to qualify. Except . . . didn't he say something that night at the Tonk about his wife being at their place in Maui? It doesn't seem like he'd mess around in his own back yard."

That took a little steam out of his awakened hunting instincts. "The Royal Hawaiian is on Maui?"

"No, it's on Waikiki Beach on Oahu. But still —"

"Then we're not really talking his back yard," he interrupted. "But I'll tell you what. You have the dates Crystal took her jaunt with her rich lover?"

"Not off the top of my head. But they're in my appointment book upstairs."

"Good. You get the dates, and I'll call an ex-Marine buddy of mine who's become a private detective. Seems to me the place to start would be to determine whether or not Jacobson was even out of town during that period."

She went upstairs, and was back again shortly. "Here you go," she said and read off the dates to him. She also handed him a photograph. "I don't know how this could possibly help, but I thought you might be interested in seeing the photo she sent me when she got back."

"Is this the Royal Hawaiian?"

"Yes. Gorgeous, isn't it?"

The snapshot showed a distinctive building of Spanish-Moorish architectural style, replete with arches and a dome-shaped turret. In the foreground was a coconut grove and the photo could easily have passed for a postcard . . . if not for a little brown and white spotted dog lifting its leg against one of the palms.

Coop grinned, and not just at the incongruous picture. He didn't know how the snapshot would specifically help, either, but, feeling exultant to be doing something constructive for the first time in what felt like forever, he reached for Ronnie again.

She wasn't fast enough to dodge him this time, but she slapped a staying hand on his chest. "Don't," she said and jerked her head out of the range of his descending mouth. "Don't mistake my willingness to look beyond your brother for my sister's murderer for anything else. I'm still angry with you, Cooper."

So he set her loose. But silently, he vowed to see what he could do about that.

18

The next morning, Veronica nearly stepped on a cellophane-wrapped bouquet of scarlet tulips that tumbled into her bedroom when she opened the door to go downstairs. For a moment she stared down at the bundle of blossoms as if it were a snake poised to strike. Then, with a shake of her head, she slowly bent down to pick it up.

There were at least a dozen flowers, and she worked her fingers to the center of the bunch to retrieve a small card. It was unsigned, but she didn't need to see Coop's name to know who had sent these. The bold black handwriting that took up every centimeter of space was a signature all its own. *I Miss You*, it declared with Cooper's typical let's-just-forgo-the-bull-shit straightforwardness. *And not just for the reason you might suspect.*

Veronica hugged the offering to her breast. Oh, man. She was in big, big trouble. It had been hard enough to force herself to step back from his proffered kisses yesterday. How was she supposed to hold firm in the face of this?

Especially when she, too, missed the pleasure of his company — and, like him, not simply for the reasons one might suspect. Savoring the vision of Cooper buying her flowers, then stealing down the hallway to prop them against her door, Veronica set off for his room, the tulips still cradled in her arms.

She'd nearly reached the door at the base of the attic stairs when she came to her senses and stopped.

What was she doing? And what on earth was she *thinking?* Well, she obviously wasn't thinking at all, and if she was honest with herself, she'd have to acknowledge that fabulous sex was *all* she and Cooper had between them. And even if the potential for a deeper, more emotional commitment existed, was that what she really wanted? The *last* thing she intended was to end up like her mother. She absolutely refused to be enthralled by a man with no discernible aspirations.

Ronnie turned away, thinking she ought to just find the nearest trash can and toss the flowers. She certainly didn't need any reminders around to tempt her into changing her mind. She nodded incisively. Yes, indeed. An intelligent woman would unload these babies faster than you could say, *Heartache waiting to happen.*

Unfortunately — except for her father's repeated warnings about her being too damn smart for her own good — nobody had ever accused her of being overly brainy. And probably never would.

She headed for the kitchen to put the tulips in water.

★ ★ ★

Marissa couldn't remember the last time she'd felt this nervous. As she paced the first floor of her house Wednesday night, she tried very hard to assure herself she was blowing this whole Kody-and-the-kids thing out of proportion. But deep down inside, she feared that wasn't the case.

She'd left Riley and Dessa at Ronnie's house forty-five minutes ago, and the only thing she could do now was wait for Kody to arrive. To get her mind off her roiling stomach, she tried to come up with creative reasons to explain why Veronica had seemed restless as a caged bear when she'd dropped off the kids. But her heart wasn't really in it. Her attention kept drifting back to the kitchen window, searching for a glimpse of Kody's truck.

A short while later, headlights swept the kitchen walls as he drove into the circular drive behind the house. Despite her intentions to remain cool and unaffected, Marissa found herself at the back door before he'd even cleared the cab of his van.

"Hi," she said softly as he crossed the brick patio. She stepped back to hold the door open for him.

"Hi, yourself, sweet stuff." Kody leaned down to give her a thorough kiss. Raising his head, he studied her for a moment. "It feels like it's been a millennium since I saw you last." He rubbed his thumb over her lower lip, then entered the kitchen.

Marissa closed the door and joined him. She'd rehearsed this moment several times, but now that she had him here, she didn't know quite where to start. "Would you like a cup of coffee?"

"No, thanks," he said and reached for her. "I wouldn't say no to a little sugar, though." Pulling her close, he lowered his head to kiss her again.

Heat spread out from his hands at her waist, and she wanted nothing so much as to melt into him and let the embrace just take her away. God knows she'd earned it — she'd pretty much been living on nerves alone for the past week. Yet when the intensity of his kiss cranked up several degrees and she found herself allowing the lean strength of Kody's body to support more and more of her weight, she pulled back.

He blinked down at her.

"I was thinking," Marissa said, then had to clear her throat when her voice emerged sounding like Minnie Mouse. "We've been dating for a while now, and you've never even met my kids. How would you like to come over and join us for hamburgers tomorrow night?"

"Tomorrow? I, uh, can't. I've got something going with my dad."

Her heart sank right down to her toes. She hadn't been imagining boogie men where no boogie men existed. Dammit — just once she'd like her gut to be wrong, but everything she'd feared was right in front of her eyes. It was in the slight fidget in Kody's posture; it was in the strained smile on his face, and the way he couldn't quite hold her gaze. "So, bring him along," she said levelly. "He's more than welcome, too."

"Sorry. That won't work."

"Friday, then," she said flatly.

"I've got, uh —"

"Something else terribly important to do," she supplied when he faltered. She walked over to the back door and held it open. "I think you'd better leave now."

"What?"

"I may be slow, but I'm not an idiot," she said and rattled the door. "Get out."

"Rissa, this is not what it must seem like —"

"Isn't it? Because what it *seems* like is that I'm good enough to bounce around a mattress when the mood strikes you, but when it comes to me meeting your family or for you to meet mine, I'm not suitable."

"No!" He reached out to touch her, but she jerked back and his hand dropped to his side. He leaned into her with determined intensity, however, and said, "Listen, it's just . . . my sister dates a lot of guys, and I've seen my nephew Jacob disappointed again and again, when her men disappear from his life just about the time he's starting to depend on them. So I have this little quirk about staying away from the kids of the women I date."

Anger rose like a red tide in Marissa's veins. It came from so many levels at once she could hardly keep them all straight, let alone under control, but she held on to her temper with furious determination. "Uh-huh," she said with curt equanimity. "Well, it's certainly nice to know where I stand in your life. I'm one of the women you date."

"You're the *only* woman I've dated in quite some time." But Kody felt as if the ground beneath his feet had suddenly turned into a dangerous bog. One wrong step and he'd be sucked into the quicksand, never to be seen from again.

"I see." Her tone was neutral, but her eyes were lit with fury. "So rather than being one of many, I'm *the* woman you deign to sleep with but very carefully do not allow into any other part of your life."

She made it sound so contemptible, but it wasn't like that. "I don't want to be responsible for putting the look I've seen in Jacob's eye in any other kids' eyes, is all. It's been my experience that —"

"All women are whores?"

"*No.*"

"I think that's exactly what you think. That all women are whores who care more about getting sexual satisfaction for themselves than they do about the welfare of their children."

Even knowing he shouldn't go there, he heard himself blurting, "The first night we met —"

"I fell right into bed with you," she interrupted in a clipped, concise tone. "Therefore it's only reasonable to assume I must do the same with every man I meet."

He raked a frustrated hand through his hair. "Will you let me finish a goddamn sentence? Or at least not put words in my mouth?"

"Oh, I beg your pardon. You don't think you were just one of many, then?"

He hesitated a moment too long because that *was* what he'd thought . . . at first. But then he'd gotten to know her better.

Before he could tell her he no longer believed she slept around, however, she gave a sharp little nod. "That's what I thought. Well, I have news for you, hotshot. I don't fall into bed with every man I meet. I thought you were special." She laughed without humor. "Hell. I thought I was falling in *love* with you."

Kody's heart thumped against the wall of his chest, then began to pound in earnest. He took an involuntary, eager step toward her, but she slapped a restraining hand to his chest. Then, her eyes electric with rage and her soft mouth mulish with resolve, she backed him up, step by determined step.

"The truth, however," she said flatly, "is that I don't really know you. And you sure as hell don't know the first thing about me if you think I'd expose my kids to the kind of meet-your-new-uncle scenario you described. I just thought it might be nice if they could get to know the first man I've dated since their father died. But clearly I was wrong."

She reached around him, and a corner of his mind registered the miniblinds on the back door rattling as the door opened. But he didn't pay the sound any heed, because his attention had fixed on the words "love" and "first." They ricocheted around his brain like bullets shot into a rock talus.

"I must have been dreaming," she said. "But you know what? I'm wide awake now. And I don't want my kids anywhere near a man who thinks their mother is a selfish slut." Then she gave him a firm nudge.

And the next thing Kody knew, freezing wind was whistling through his parka as he found himself outside on Marissa's patio, staring at the swaying miniblinds as the kitchen door closed with a thump in his face.

Cooper placed his newest offering — a framed snapshot of Lizzy and Dessa wearing garish dress-up garb and too much makeup — against Veronica's bedroom door, then slowly straightened. This wooing business was hard work, and he didn't have the first idea how today's gift would be received. Hell, he didn't even know if it could be considered a gift. The photograph was Ronnie's to begin with, but he'd taken it to a little frame shop over on Third and had it matted and framed for her. He ought to get points for that, but when it came right down to it, who knew if he would? Women were unpredictable.

It was a quarter to three in the morning, and standing in the hallway like a supplicant, he was sorely tempted to let himself into her room the way he used to do. It would be easy to have her aroused and willing before she was even fully awake.

His hand reached out for the doorknob.

Then he let it drop to his side. He didn't think he could stand to discover she still slept with a chair propped under the doorknob to keep him out. And if she had quit doing that, could he repay her renewed trust by promptly betraying it? She was actually beginning to speak to him again, and she'd made a huge concession when she'd agreed to help him look beyond Eddie as a suspect in her sister's murder.

Leaving her door untouched, he turned and headed for his room. He wasn't sure if it meant he was mature, or the world's biggest chump.

But he had a bad feeling that, either way, he wasn't going to sleep worth a damn tonight.

Veronica waited until Coop's soft footsteps faded completely before she threw back the covers and slid out of bed. Shivering when her warm feet hit the cold floorboards, she crossed the room and silently opened her door. Looking down the hallway, she ascertained that the coast was clear, then snatched the flat package off the floor and used her hip to ease the door closed again. A second later she climbed back into bed, turned on the bedside lamp, and pulled the covers up to her chest, tucking them beneath her armpits.

For a moment she simply sat and savored the endless possibilities that a wrapped present constitutes. She scooped one of the double-dipped chocolate-covered macadamia nuts that had been yesterday's gift out of a dish on her nightstand and popped it in her mouth while she studied the plain brown wrapping of tonight's present. Its militarily sharp corners elicited a small smile. They were so . . . Coop. Then she carefully flipped the package over, slid a finger beneath the paper's edge, and unpeeled the three pieces of tape that held it together. She pulled the paper off and turned the gift right side up.

"*Oh.*" It was one of the photos she'd taken the night Lizzy and Dessa had played dress-up in Crystal's finery. Coop had mounted the snapshot in royal blue matting the same color as Lizzy's dress. And where Veronica would've expected him to select a plain, no-nonsense frame, he'd chosen a pewter one that was wondrously, femininely ornate. He'd obviously picked it out with her in mind.

And that made the gift extra special.

Damn. She was so tired of fighting her need for him, and her desire to go up to his room was almost beyond bearing. The strength of her craving caused her to look at her mother's motives in a brand-new light.

Had Mama felt anything close to this burning

neediness for Daddy? It was difficult to think of one's parents as sexual beings, but maybe the reason her mother had put up with her father's shiftlessness for all those years was because he'd made it worth her while . . . in other areas.

She pushed the thought aside; she didn't even want to go there. But a small smile tickled the corners of her mouth. "You go, Mama," she murmured. It was kind of nice to think that maybe her mother had gotten *something* in return for all her years of sacrifice.

Veronica set the photo on her nightstand and turned off the lamp. Then she lay in the dark and attempted to woo sleep by imagining her life back in the real world once everything here was all settled. No matter how many tricks she used to relax her mind, however, she couldn't seem to find a comfortable spot to settle her restless body. She turned repeatedly from side to side, then finally kicked off the covers and climbed to her feet.

She couldn't take it any longer. There was only one way she'd get any sleep tonight.

A moment later she paused outside the attic door, wondering if she'd lost her mind entirely. Then she straightened her shoulders. She'd get Cooper Blackstock out of her system once and for all. Maybe *then* she could put some real thought into getting her life back under control.

She was going to be smarter than Mama, though. She'd go about this the way a man would. They'd use each other to slake this need that vibrated between them, but she was keeping her heart inviolate.

She quietly opened the door and tiptoed up the stairs.

Dim, diffused moonlight filtered through the frosty window, and she could see the outline of Coop's big body beneath the blankets and quilt heaped on the bed. Swiftly, she crossed the room and lifted the covers to slide in beside him.

His still body radiated heat like an energy-efficient furnace, so she nestled up to him and thought of the way he used to seduce her while she was still asleep so she'd awaken fully aroused. And she grinned in the dark.

She could do that.

Snuggling closer, she kissed his chest, then smoothed her hand down the ridges of his abdomen to the hard plane where his pelvis narrowed between his hipbones. Licking her lips, she reached out to wrap her fingers around his penis.

And found it solid as a rock, standing fully erect.

Wait a minute. She raised her head up off his chest and strained to see his face. "You're not asleep."

"It's hard to discard thirteen years of training, sweetpea." His voice was a low rasp in the dark. "Soldiers learn to sleep light, and never allow anyone to sneak up on them." His hand, broad-palmed and warm, wrapped around hers and demonstrated a rhythm that pleased him. He sucked in a sharp breath when her fingers tightened around him. "Aw, man," he whispered. "You can sneak up on me anytime you wanna." Then his hand slid away to cradle the back of Veronica's head, and he twisted around to kiss her.

It was as if her denials of missing him — of missing *this* — were a combustible vapor, and his kiss the spark that blew them to kingdom come. A greedy murmur climbing up the back of her throat, Veronica released her grip on Coop's sex, wrapped both arms around his neck, and kissed him back with everything she had.

For several long moments the only noise in the room was the damp, suctioning sound of long, slow, deep soul kisses. Finally, Coop raised his head fractionally and stared down at her. "God, I've missed you, Ronnie. Nobody tastes the way you do. No one else has a mouth so sweet."

His words thrilled her, and a tiny frisson of unease threatened to introduce an icy trickle of reality into the hot passion that encased her. For just a second, she surfaced long enough to remember her vow to protect her heart. But then he brushed a strand of hair away from her cheek and rained kisses all over her face. His other hand slid down the front of her pajamas, leaving unfastened buttons and erect nipples in its wake before sliding beneath the elastic waistband on her bottoms.

His fingers delved between her legs, slipping and sliding, plucking and probing. "Oh, yeah," he growled when she moaned, and then touched her in ways that finessed escalating sensations out of her. "*More.* I love to hear you having a good time."

Her breath came in increasingly ragged pants, and she couldn't have prevented the needy sounds that escaped her throat to save her life. She stared up at him, at the flush that was discernible across his sharp cheekbones even in the dark and at the concentration that gathered his eyebrows above his nose as he watched her orgasm build.

And at the very moment he finally drove her over the edge of sanity, when she heard herself whisper, "I love you, Cooper, I love you," she couldn't for the life of her figure out which was the stronger emotion she felt.

Relief? Or horror?

 —   **19**

Lizzy, Riley, and Dessa tumbled out of the car the second Coop brought it to a full stop in the fairground parking lot. They pelted toward the main gate, and Coop grinned at Veronica's and Marissa's rapid-fire warnings about the perils of getting separated, which they shouted at the kids' retreating backs. Filled with the same jazzed feeling of expectancy he used to get just before a mission, he climbed out of the car and locked up.

He couldn't believe he felt this much anticipation at the prospect of attending a small-town winter festival — with two women and three kids, no less. For the space of about ten seconds, he tried to tell himself that his response was simply the pleasure of having his first Saturday night off since rolling into town.

Then he gave it up as a lost cause. Watching Veronica's neat little butt as she hustled in the wake of the kids, he admitted what he'd been trying to deny for the past few days. His contentment, this feeling of anticipation — everything revolved around Ronnie. He didn't give a rat's ass about the festival. It was attending it with her that stoked his anticipation.

He had it bad, and it was long past time he quit

dancing around the fact. He'd had sex with a number of women in his life, but they'd simply come and gone — no pun intended — without making so much as a ripple in his routine. And that had been fine with him. A few laughs, some mutually satisfying sex, that's the most he'd ever wanted. Then either the woman had headed down the road or he had.

He'd never burned to know what made a woman tick, much less cared what she thought about . . . until now. And as for intimacy, until recently he'd never actually believed there was a difference between having sex and making love.

He'd been wrong. And the past few nights, he'd pulled out all the stops. He'd used every trick he'd ever learned and a few he'd invented on the spot when he'd made love to her . . . all of which had been geared toward getting her to say, "I love you, Cooper," again.

It was pitiful.

Not to mention unsuccessful. The words hadn't passed her lips since she'd let them slip Thursday morning. He hated admitting the possibility it might have been merely sex talk.

Especially when he had a feeling it was turning out to be the real deal for him. And what was worse, he didn't even have the good sense to feel uneasy about it. Hell of a note for a guy whose survival instincts were generally honed to a razor-fine edge.

She turned back suddenly and caught him looking at her butt. Giving it a subtle wiggle, she flashed him a grin. "Get a move on, Blackstock! You don't wanna get separated." She did a Groucho Marx wag of her eyebrows. "Dire things can happen to you."

"Yeah, the word is out." Letting go of everything but the prospect of spending an evening with her, he caught up. The crowd began to thicken as it funneled toward the main gate, and Coop used the concealment of the sudden press of bodies to hook his arm around Ronnie's waist and pull her back against him. Lowering his head, he growled in her ear, "I hear tell I'll have to pay my own admittance fee out of my 'fun' money if I don't stay with the group."

She shivered, but gave him the elbow to gain her release. She fussed for a moment with the fuzzy green scarf wound around her neck, then turned around to walk backward in front of him. Her cute little fleece hat had a brim that was turned back and pinned in place with a cocky little brooch. With mock gravity she said, "That's right. We moms, whether natural-made or newly elected, gotta impose order."

"Or what? Chaos will reign?"

She gave him the million-dollar smile again and added a friendly little tap on his chest. "Exactly."

"Aunt Ronnie, Uncle Coop, will you guys *come on?*"

Coop laughed and picked up his pace. Beating Veronica to the ticket booth, he pulled out his wallet and bought tickets for everyone, then shepherded his little group through the turnstile.

The kids took off like a shot and raced right past the closest exhibition hall. Amused at their single-minded drive to reach their destination, Coop said dryly, "Something's clearly got a bigger draw than whatever's in that building."

"The ice rink," Marissa agreed. "Hall A is mostly craft stuff, which the kids don't have heaps of interest in. Although Riley will want to participate in the Cake Walk later on. He never misses an opportunity to score dessert." She displayed a wan imitation of her usual smile, her dimples nowhere in sight.

He'd heard through the Tonk grapevine last night that she and Kody had broken up, and he saw Ronnie give her a concerned once-over. Marissa was clearly attempting to put a good face on things, but it wasn't difficult to see she was desperately unhappy.

He reached over to touch the sleeve of her royal purple boiled wool jacket. "Kody's an idiot, if you ask me."

Agony flashed across her face for a moment, and he wished to hell he'd kept his big mouth shut. She was clearly taking the breakup hard, and cluing her to the fact that everyone was discussing it wasn't the brightest thing he'd done today.

But then her chin rose to a regal angle. "Fossil being Fossil, and the Tonk being the Tonk, I guess I shouldn't be surprised the news has already made the rounds." Resolution fired her eyes and squared her shoulders. "But I appreciate the sentiment, Coop. Kody's idiocy is exactly the reason I had to send him packing."

Well, hell, Veronica thought. Wanting to smack herself in the forehead, she sighed in resignation instead. Please — it wasn't temptation enough that Cooper had a razor-sharp mind and was a treat in bed? How was she supposed to keep her heart from melting into a great big puddle at his feet when he turned out to be sensitive to her best friend's pain, too?

She'd all but ground her molars into dust the past couple of nights, trying to keep from blurting *I love you* over and over again while they'd made love. During the day, she could almost talk herself into thinking that what she felt for him was merely lust. But inevitably night came, Cooper crawled into her bed, and all her defenses began to crumble. It was during the quiet aftermath, when all the heat had died down and *still* she harbored this aching need to simply lie quietly with him, that she began to seriously suspect she was fooling herself. Sex wasn't the only draw. Clearly her heart was very much engaged.

Not that she hadn't continued to fight the good fight. She'd managed to keep the words clamoring for release under lock and key. Now, however, watching the effect of Coop's championing on Marissa, she would've said them out loud without a second's hesitation. Luckily for her, the three of them emerged from the path between Hall A and Hall B just then and came upon Wonderland.

"Oh, my God, Rissa," she breathed. "This turned out *spectacular*."

"I simply stole your idea." Marissa's shrug lacked so much as a vestige of her earlier enthusiasm for the project, and it broke Veronica's heart. Her friend had been so upset Thursday morning that she'd hardly been able to talk. All she would say about her breakup was that Kody didn't want to be involved with a woman with children.

It made Veronica see red. How *dare* he go out with Marissa in the first place if that was his attitude? She'd really, really like to get her hands on that man. It would be a pleasure to wring his neck.

But she merely said, "I disagree. What I gave you was the bare bones of an idea. You expanded it into *this*." She waved a hand to encompass Marissa's handiwork. "This is like a fairy world."

Fairground personnel had constructed the annual skating rink in the field where the carnival midway was set up every summer, between the exhibitions halls and the rodeo arena. Benches sat around it, and the decorations committee had ringed everything with a score of realistic-looking papier-mâché trees. Hundreds of tiny white lights shimmered from the bare branches to glitter off the ice, dancing across rosy-cheeked skaters as they circled the rink.

Steam rose from two vendors' carts and scented the crisp, cold air with hot dogs, cocoa, and hot cinnamon-laced cider.

The ice rink was a popular attraction, and the degree of skill ran the gamut from a young woman in the center who spun like a seasoned member of the Ice Capades, to a child barely past toddler age whose every wobbly step seemed to land her on her well-padded little bottom. But the level of ability didn't appear to have any bearing on anyone's enjoyment. Veronica recognized the mayor ice-waltzing with his wife. And Eddie's lawyer Neil Peavy sat on the same bench as Darlene Starkey — although they were probably not together. An old schoolmate of Veronica's laughed with her children as they untied their rental skates just one bench over from where Lizzy, Dess, and Riley were donning theirs.

Coop bought her a cup of hot chocolate topped with whipped cream and garnished with a candy cane, and she divided her time between smiling at the tortoiselike caution with which Lizzy circled the rink and watching the rowdy teams over by the arena as they worked to convert huge blocks of ice set on nests of hay into recognizable shapes for the ice-sculpting contest. From the raucous laughter that drifted across the field, she suspected their cardboard cups contained something other than hot cider.

"Veronica?"

She turned at the questioning voice and saw

the classmate she'd noticed standing next to her. *"Deb?"*

"Yes." The woman laughed. "Oh, good, I was afraid I'd get one of those blank, who-the-heck-are-you looks, since we didn't know each other particularly well in high school. I just wanted to stop by to say welcome back."

Veronica smiled. "Why, thank you."

"These are my daughters, Megan and Rachel." After greetings were exchanged, Deb said, "Megan's in Lizzy's class. We'll probably be running into each other at school events, and I wondered if you'd like to get together to have a cup of coffee some afternoon. If you're not too busy."

"I'd like that very much. Thanks." They traded phone numbers and warmth stole through Ronnie as she watched the other woman walk away with her daughters. She turned her attention back to the rink, but couldn't help but smile at the unexpected feeling of acceptance Deb's gesture gave her.

She jumped when Coop suddenly murmured in her ear, "That Lizzy, she's a speed demon." A cold breeze blew up her back as her jacket and the hem of the sweater beneath it were suddenly displaced. Then the draft was plugged, and warmth radiated out from the point where Coop's hand spread against the bare skin of her back. "Good thing it'll be years before anyone has to worry about her getting behind the wheel of a car."

He stood behind her and a little to one side, and Veronica knew he probably wore that neutral expression he so often assumed. She tilted her chin up to catch a glimpse of him from the corner of her eye and discovered that, to the contrary, he was smiling fondly at Lizzy as she skated at a snail's pace around the periphery of the rink.

Veronica looked front and center again in time to see Riley zoom past like Harry Potter after the Golden Snitch, and assured herself that the casual observer would never guess Coop's long fingers were stroking heat down the shallow groove of her spine.

Left up to him, he'd no doubt touch her openly and not care who saw them. He certainly wouldn't give a flying flick about the gossip. But because it mattered to her, he remained the soul of discretion.

And suddenly, she was filled to the brim with a love so fierce and all-consuming it should have frightened her straight into an early grave.

He was so much more than a man with a way about him in bed. Though he looked like the kind of guy who could break a person's neck with a single wrench of his strong hands, he'd been unfailingly gentle with her and Lizzy. He had a good heart. She cranked her head around fully this time and smiled up at him. "I love you," she murmured when she caught his eye, and smiled when his body stilled and his eyes went hot. She marvelled that saying the words aloud didn't frighten her a bit. The futility of a lasting relationship would probably hit her all over again tomorrow, but for tonight she'd go with the flow.

Because emotions like this didn't come along every day of the week. And for this one evening, at least, she was going to simply luxuriate in feeling so wonderful.

Except for that black period right after Denny died, Marissa couldn't recall a time in her life when she'd felt so awful. She was trying hard to act normal — for the kids' sake and for Ronnie and Coop — but it was tough.

God, it was tough. All she really wanted to do was beat her breast and howl.

She'd been looking forward to this night ever since Ronnie had pointed her in the right direction and the decorations had finally begun to take shape. She'd daydreamed about it, anticipated the triumph of seeing all her hard work pay off. Now she wanted only to go home, crawl into bed, and pull the covers up over her head.

For the children's sake, she was determined to get through the evening without falling apart. She could do that later, once they were in bed and she was alone.

Again.

That thought straightened her backbone faster than ten strong, self-issued lectures ever would. The man who could turn Marissa Travits into a self-pitying whiner had yet to be born. She firmed up her chin and turned to Coop and Veronica. "Are you two getting as cold as I am just standing around here?"

"Colder," Ronnie said. "I quit feeling my feet about five minutes ago."

As they called the kids off the ice, Marissa noticed a hint of movement from the corner of her eye and caught Cooper sliding his hand out the back of Veronica's coat. Well, well. When had *this* recommenced? And here she'd thought Ronnie was being civil to him tonight strictly for Lizzy's sake.

There was no opportunity to get the true scoop, however. The kids had no sooner tumbled off the ice, changed out of their skates, and bolted into Hall A than they immediately fell to wrangling. Or at least hers did.

"Mom, me 'n' Lizzy wanna go see the Rebecca Circle booth," Dessa said, her cheeks flushed scarlet from the sudden warmth. Her blond curls floated around her head in a static-charged nimbus as she danced anxiously in place. "They're s'posta have doll clothes — Susie Posser said so, and her mama's in the circle, so she oughtta know. Let's go find it, 'kay?"

"No way!" Riley said. "Doll clothes are for sucks."

"Are not!"

"Are so! Let's go see the pie-eating contest. How come you didn't enter me in that, Mom? I bet I coulda won that easy." When his sister stuck out her tongue, he gave her a shove, and

306

being her mother's daughter she immediately shoved back. Marissa's head began to pound. She gazed at Lizzy, standing just beyond the battling Travitses, making no demands, and wondered why *she* couldn't have had at least one nice, quiet kid.

Then Coop stepped in. "Tell you what," he said, easily extracting Riley out of reach of his sister. "Why don't Riley and I go check out the pie eaters, and you ladies go do the doll clothes thing? Then we'll all meet back where they're raffling those quilts over there in — what? — half an hour?"

Marissa agreed with unseemly speed and watched as Coop slung an arm around Riley's shoulders.

"Come on, sport," he said. "Let's go see who eats the most pies."

"Bet I could," Riley said as they walked away. The last thing Marissa saw before the crowd swallowed them up was Riley beaming up at Cooper as if the man walked on water. It killed her to know that could just as easily have been Kody — except he'd sooner gnaw off his own arm than get to know her kids.

"You okay?" Veronica asked in a low voice a few moments later while the girls poured over the handmade creations at the Rebecca Circle booth. "You're looking pretty pale."

"Love isn't supposed to hurt like this, Ronnie. I sure don't remember hitting lows like this with Denny."

"You knew Denny all your life, and he was the original Mr. Mellow. It was probably a quieter love. But were the highs as high?"

"No." And the sex hadn't been as hot, either. But acknowledging that filled her with guilt, and she promptly changed the subject. "So you and Blackstock are an item again?"

Veronica gave a sheepish nod. "I can't seem to make up my mind if it's a match made in heaven — or Ma and Pa Davis revisited."

"I like him, Ronnie. He strikes me as a good man."

"Yeah. I was just thinking the same thing."

"But when did this all happen? Last I knew, you were refusing to give him the time of day. And why on earth didn't you tell me?"

"He's been . . . courting me since I found out about Eddie." She gave a brief rundown of the middle-of-the-night gifts outside her door. "It paid off Wednesday night . . . or I guess I should say early Thursday morning, if you want to be literal."

"Oh." Marissa felt her heart squeeze — that was the same night she and Kody had been breaking up. "I guess that answers my second question, then."

"You were pretty upset when we talked," Veronica agreed. "I wasn't about to say, *Well, sure, but enough about your night — let me tell you about the great sex I had.*"

Marissa would have sworn laughter was impossible, but that managed to surprise a genuine belly laugh out of her. Bless the irreverent humor of a best friend. Hooking her arm around Ronnie's shoulders, she reeled her in for a hug. "Thanks, pal. I love you."

"I love you, too. And I promise you're gonna get through this."

"Yes. I am." *Eventually,* she thought, but decided that was okay. It might take a while, but wonder of wonders, she actually did believe that in due time, she would come through it okay.

Or at least she did until she glanced a few booths down the row, and looked straight into Kody's eyes.

She was laughing. How the hell could she *laugh?* Kody felt as if his heart had been chopped right out of his chest — he'd been walking around without it since Wednesday night. He stared at Marissa across the few crowd-packed yards that separated them and didn't see past his own pain to the paleness of her complexion or the unhappiness in her eyes. He saw only the sweet line of her lips curving up.

The moment she spotted him, however, the smile dropped away from her face. Worse, she deliberately lifted her chin and turned away. But not before her eyes went blank, as if she didn't even know him.

Kody couldn't believe it. Ever since she'd slammed the door in his face, he'd been worried sick about her state of mind. Haunted by the hurt in her eyes, he'd played and replayed their last conversation in his mind a hundred times, held imaginary chats in which he'd made her understand his point of view.

Hell, he'd even wondered if he was *wrong*.

And she acted like they were strangers? They needed to talk.

Before he could move, though, a group of high school boys sauntered between them and blocked Kody's line of sight. He shifted to keep Marissa in view, but adolescent boys were built along larger lines these days, and he lost sight of her. When he tried to move around them, he got trapped between a group of boisterous gray-haired ladies and a towering display of calico-topped canning jars full of homemade preserves. He tried to ease around the group of women, murmuring excuse me's and hanging on to his patience by a thread when they merely chatted on about the unwed status of somebody's grand-daughter, oblivious to his urgent need to get by them. Finally, just when he'd reached the point of snarling and bodily moving a few of them out of his way, they moved on and he squeezed past the boys. He headed purposefully toward where he'd last seen Marissa.

But she was nowhere in sight.

"You shoulda seen it, Mom," Riley said around the huge bite of hot dog in his mouth. "There was pie all *over* the place! I bet their moms give 'em what-for when they see the laundry basket. Those bibs they wore were useless — there was berry juice and apple filling all over those guys. It was totally phat."

"I'd be totally fat, too, if I tried to put away three and a half pies," Coop said and managed not to grin when Riley rolled his eyes in disgust.

"*Phat,* not *fa-at.* With a *ph.* Jeez. Don't you know *nuthin'?*" Then he suddenly got it that he was being teased and flashed a great big openmouthed grin.

"Riley, do you mind?" Marissa said. "We'd just as soon not look at your half-masticated hot dog."

"Sorry, Mom." Swallowing audibly, he immediately turned to Coop where they sat side by side on a bench in the food arena, a roped-off area at the back of the exhibition hall that an unimaginative man might merely see as an accumulation of picnic tables. "You're pullin' my leg, aren'tcha?" He butted his shoulder into Coop's biceps. "Did you see the size of that one guy? He was *fat!* I thought he'd win for sure, 'stead of that skinny guy."

"Ah, but it's those wiry ones with the hundred-mile-an-hour metabolisms you have to watch out for," Coop said. Then Lizzy claimed his attention, and he tucked into his soup while he listened to her recite a litany of all the wonderful doll clothes she'd left unpurchased, and duly admired the one outfit she'd bought for her Celebration Barbie.

All the while, he was conscious of Ronnie on his other side and kept hearing her voice saying *I love you* over and over again in his head. Holy shit. You didn't just drop that kind of bomb on a man and just sashay away. Pressing his left thigh against her right leg beneath the table, he wished he didn't have to be so damn circumspect. He wanted to swagger around with her tucked under his arm. He wanted to flex his muscles and win her cheesy prizes from the booths in the game alley. But mostly, he wanted to maneuver her behind the Washington Apple Commission's twenty-foot plywood Delicious apple over in the corner, steal a few kisses, and demand to hear it again.

He saw Troy Jacobson and a good-looking blonde he assumed was his wife over by the Junior Achievement stand. Coop had heard from his ex-Marine buddy this afternoon, and Jacobson had definitely been out of town during the dates Ronnie had given him. Though that nailed him as a contender for Crystal's secret lover, right now Coop didn't give a damn.

Bracing the heel of his hand against the bench on the far side of Ronnie's hip, he turned and looked out over the crowd. To the casual eye he wouldn't appear to be paying the least bit of attention to the woman at his side. "I love you, too," he murmured for her ears only, before turning back to the table and tucking into his piece of apple pie.

Beside him, he felt her stiffen to attention, and smiled between bites. Good. Turn-about was only fair play.

The man ushered his companion through the exhibition hall toward the main door. "I hope you don't mind that we're leaving early."

"No, of course not," she said. "I know you've had a busy week."

"Yes, I'm worn out." It wasn't easy sometimes, being smarter than the average bear. People could be such fools, and mostly that worked in his favor. But occasionally it would be nice to have someone with whom to carry on a sharp-witted conversation. Someone at least within *range* of his intelligence, who'd be capable of appreciating his brilliance. He got tired of having to reel it in all the time for fear of making those less fortunate nervous.

He'd had a few bad moments when Cooper Blackstock had been outed as Eddie's brother. But the guy turned out to be all flash and no substance. For all that Blackstock was rumored to read tomes the size of a child's booster seat during his downtime at the Tonk, he was, after all, merely a onetime soldier turned bartender.

Hardly in *his* league. He'd seen Blackstock this evening and laughed out loud, then had to come up with an explanation to divert the woman at his side. But, shee-it. Some big-deal Marine he'd turned out to be, ushering around a bunch of children.

As usual, he had absolutely nothing to worry about.

20

"Good morning, gorgeous."

Veronica pried one eye open and peered blearily at the owner of the warm, intimate voice murmuring in her ear. Coop's face swam into focus, his lean cheeks freshly shaved, his pale hair sticking up in wet spikes. Dressed only in a pair of worn sweats that rode low on his hips, he was all hard bone and muscle and smooth, bare skin that smelled deliciously of milled soap.

Flashing her a crooked smile, he waved a coffee mug beneath her nose — then demonstrated a distinct mean streak by whipping it away as soon as she reached for it. "Give me a kiss," he said, "and I'll let you have it."

She promptly puckered up.

Coop laughed. "Makes me wonder what else I could get you to do for your morning coffee." He kissed her thoroughly, waited for her to sit up, then handed her the mug and watched with patent amusement as she eagerly gulped several scalding sips.

She gave him a look of disapproval over the rim of her cup. "I bet you're one of those disgusting people who pop out of bed whistling a happy tune."

He delivered a few bars of "Whistle While You Work," and then had the nerve to grin when she swung a pillow at him. He dodged it effortlessly. "You've got lousy aim."

"Maybe, but I've got great multitasking skills. Not just anyone can pillow fight without spilling a drop of coffee, you know." She took another swing. "You oughtta see me simultaneously pat my head and rub my stomach."

He plucked the pillow out of her fist and tucked it beneath his armpit as he flopped down on the mattress next to her. Then, rolling to his side, he propped his head on his hand and gave her a soft-eyed smile.

"You seem marginally more awake, so let's start over. Mornin', gorgeous."

She knocked back the remainder of her coffee, set the mug aside, then launched herself at him, laughing as they rolled. She ended up on top and, shaking her hair out of her eyes, pushed away from his chest to grin down at him. "Mornin' yourself, handsome." Hardness nudged her stomach and she raised an eyebrow. "Again?" She wiggled against his erection and watched with delight as his dark eyes lost focus. "You had me up half the night. Doesn't this thing ever get tired?"

"Huh-uh." He worked his sweats down, then locked his long fingers onto her bare bottom and moved her to the position he desired. "Let me in, Princess."

"Well, I don't know." She felt her eyes cross

when his penis slid up and down the slick folds between her legs to hit and then retreat from her sweet spot. But she managed to say in a creditably bored tone, "There's only so much time before Marissa brings Lizzy home, and I'd planned on painting my toenails."

He raised his head to suck one of her nipples into his mouth. Not until she moaned aloud did he release it. "Let me in," he said persuasively, "and *I'll* paint your toenails."

"Deal." As if there'd ever been any doubt. Raising her hips, Veronica reached between them to grasp the hard shaft of his sex and held it steady while she sank down on him with one sure, smooth slide.

Half an hour later, she emerged from the shower, pulled on clean undies, khakis, and a sweater, then followed the scent of freshly brewed coffee down to the kitchen. The room was deserted and she called out Cooper's name as she refilled her mug.

"In here."

Carrying her coffee, she walked into the living room and saw him sitting at the end of the couch, sorting through an array of nail-polish bottles lined up on the end table. She stopped in her tracks. "Get out! Are you really planning on painting my toenails?"

"Hey, a deal's a deal. Never let it be said that one of the few, the proud, would go back on his word."

She studied him skeptically. "Have you ever done this before?"

"Nope. But it ain't brain surgery, sweetpea — how hard can it be? I happen to have excellent small motor skills." He crooked a peremptory finger. "Gimme a foot and I'll show you."

Delighted, she sat at the opposite end of the couch and stretched out her leg.

Coop picked up her right foot, cradled it in his lap, and rubbed his thumbs into the arch, making her groan in sheer, unadulterated pleasure. "What color do you want?" he asked. "I'm sort of leaning toward the Siren Red, myself."

"Oh, by all means — Siren Red it is." She watched his big hands engulf the bottle as he went to untwist the cap. "You need to shake it first."

"Sure. I knew that. Like spray paint." He shook it vigorously, then twisted the cap off. Cupping the arch of her foot in his hand, he raised it and painstakingly applied the first stripe of color to her big toe. He applied another stripe, then a third, blending each into the one before. When the nail was covered, he pulled his head back to study the result. "Looking good." He dipped the brush back into the bottle, before moving on to the next toe.

A moment later, as he was about to start on her left foot, he glanced up. "I heard from Rocket yesterday."

"Who?"

"John 'The Rocket' Miglionni. My private detective buddy."

Veronica stiffened slightly. "What did he say?"

"Jacobson was definitely out of town during the dates you gave me. Rocket's digging into his movements during that period. He's trying to get a copy of the hotel records, but says that even if he can obtain one, it's probable Crystal and her boyfriend checked in under an assumed name. So the most likely trail to follow is Jacobson's. Rocket's going to trace it from Fossil to see where it leads."

Veronica watched Coop finish painting the last two toenails before she said carefully, "I know you very much want it to be Troy, but . . . have you seen him with his wife? He seems genuinely crazy about her."

The absurd jealousy Coop experienced whenever he heard Ronnie defend Jacobson swamped him. Forcing cool, rational logic, he took a deep breath, raised her foot, and blew on the wet polish. Then he looked at her over her toes.

"I don't deny that," he said levelly. "But that doesn't necessarily rule him out. Guys don't always equate love with fidelity. They figure the sex they have on the side doesn't count as long as their emotions aren't involved. So if he slipped up with Crystal just that one time and she threatened to tell the little woman when he wanted to break it off — well, that would give him about as strong a motive as you can get."

Ronnie tugged her foot out of his hand. "Is that the rationale you'd use? That sex with an-

318

other woman wouldn't count as long as you didn't love her?"

"Hell, no." He was a little pissed that she had to ask — she sure didn't seem to have any trouble believing *Jacobson* wouldn't cheat. "But I lived in a man's world for a long time, sweetpea, and not all guys are as virtuous as me." He waited a beat, hoping for a smile. When it didn't come, he decided to change the subject, since the last thing he was looking for this morning was a fight. "I heard Marissa tell you last night that she saw Kody at the exhibition hall. Is she all right?"

"Yes. No." She shook her head impatiently. "She will be — or at least I hope so." Then she blurted out furiously, "That bastard! I could just smack him for what he's doing to her."

"Yeah, it's a shame. They always struck me as very happy together, and he seemed like a nice guy."

"A *nice guy?*" She sat a bit straighter on her end of the couch. "Your nice guy just dumped my best friend because she has kids."

"That's rough, but maybe in the long run he's doing her a favor, Ronnie."

She looked at him as if he'd just suggested they sell Lizzy to a white slaver. "*Excuse* me?"

"Well, come on. Not everyone is equipped for fatherhood or willing to take on the responsibility of raising another man's kids. Maybe getting out before even more people got hurt was the kindest thing he could do."

"Then he should have made his excuses the day after they met," she said hotly. "Because that's when he would've learned about them. Marissa's kids are her life and her heart, and he knew darn good and well going in that she was a package deal. *Damn*." She smacked her thigh with the flat of her hand. "How can a man make a woman love him, then turn around and do something so awful? How can he mess with her emotions like that?" She shook her head. "You know, she'd be crazy to take him back, even if he came crawling on his knees begging for forgiveness."

"Oh, there's an attitude. What, are you afraid she might turn into your mother?"

Veronica stilled. *"What?"*

Okay, that was probably a tactical error. But still. "I don't get you, Ronnie. No one gets to make a mistake? Forgiving and moving on doesn't mean you have to subjugate your will to another person, like you seem to think your mother did with your dad. It just means you've forgiven and moved on."

"You don't get me? I can't believe *you'd* bring my mother into this. And why the big defense, anyway? Is this one of those boys-will-be-boys-so-let's-all-stick-together male code things?"

The question brought him up short. Why *was* he defending Kody? It wasn't like he had some big vested interest in the outcome. The more he'd gotten to know Marissa, in fact, the more he'd come to admire and respect her, and Ronnie was right — Kody's breakup with her could've been handled a lot more intelligently than it had been.

Shit. Coop rolled his shoulders. He must still be smarting more than he realized over Ronnie's defense of Jacobson.

"Yeah, I guess it is." He looked her in the eye. "What can I tell you, it's a knee-jerk reaction." He tried out a smile on her. "And a pretty dumb one, when I don't even disagree with you. I sure don't want to spend our time together fighting about Kody. I'll concede he's a jerk, okay?" He reached for her foot and tugged it toward him to inspect her pretty, red-tipped toes. "How about this paint job, hey? Have you ever seen such fine workmanship?"

For a minute he thought she was going to stay irritated with him. But then she smiled, too. "I think I can honestly say it's the grandest I've ever had." Then she tilted her head to one side to inspect his face. "So. About your friend Rocket. How on earth did he ever come by a nickname like that?"

"Well, every Marine has a handle. And Rocket, he always swore that that was what he had in his pants for the ladies."

"Because he was so fast?"

Coop snorted. "No, you little witch. Because of his size — and what he fancied he could do with it."

"Ah. How very . . . boastful of him."

"Not without reason, as it turns out. Spending a lot of time on ships and in barracks, you see a lot of naked guys. Now, Rocket's one of those lean, spare types. But his . . . missile was anything but. We're talking a sixty-millimeter mortar, at the very least." Coop shrugged. "He had the goods. So a handle was born."

The Travitses' doorbell rang, and Marissa heard, "I'll get it," shouted from two separate quarters. Footsteps reverberated like a herd of spooked buffalo as Dessa raced down the staircase and Riley pounded toward the front entrance from the great room. Marissa shook her head and went back to folding the whites in the living room, feeling sorry for the poor slob on the other side of the door. The only people who came to the front entry were generally there to sell something or collect donations. In either event, her kids were better than a junkyard dog for discouraging unwanted solicitations — it was a rare day, indeed, that a salesman didn't remove the Travitses' name from his list.

She heard the grunts and cut-off exclamations that meant her babies were jockeying for possession of the door handle. A second later, Riley shouted in triumph and the flames in the living room fireplace flared higher from a sudden influx of oxygen as the front door was yanked open.

A man's voice rumbled pleasantly for a few moments, then the kids yammered ninety miles an hour. He spoke again, only to have Dessa and Riley immediately pipe back up. Marissa had intimate knowledge of their ability to talk a person right into the numb zone, so she listened with only half an ear as she finished rolling the last pair of socks, expecting at any moment to hear the door slam.

Instead, Riley's voice called, "Ma-awm! Some guy wants to talk to ya!"

She set aside the pile of whites in her lap and rose to her feet. This should be good; not many salesmen got past the Dynamic Duo. She was smiling as she walked into the foyer, but the smile congealed on her lips at the sight of the man standing in the open doorway. She stopped dead. "Kody."

"You know him, Mom?" Dessa demanded. "He said you did, but we've never met him, so I didn't believe him. I guess you can come in, then," she informed Kody and stepped back to allow him entrance. When she closed the door behind him, the foyer immediately warmed several degrees. Dessa skipped back to stare up at Kody, who hadn't taken his eyes off Marissa. "Mom always says don't invite strangers into the house, but if she knows you, I guess you aren't a stranger. How come *we* don't know you? We know *all* of Mom's friends. Her best friend is Veronica Davis. Veronica's niece Lizzy is *my* best friend. Maybe you know them? They're —"

"That's enough, Dess. You and Riley grab your stacks of clothes and go put them away."

"But I was gonna have a cookie."

Forcing herself to focus on her daughter,

Marissa recalled the chore she'd set the children earlier this evening. "Have you finished cleaning your room?"

"Nooo."

"Then you can have a cookie when you finish the job you were given. How about you, Riley?"

"I finished mine ten minutes ago," Riley said virtuously.

"Lamebrain," Dessa snapped.

"Girly-girl."

Dessa flew at him. "Am *not!*"

"Are s—"

"That's enough, both of you." Maybe Kody had a point about not wanting to get involved with her children. "Go upstairs." She turned to her son. "Riley, I heard you in the kitchen earlier, so you've had your cookie. Put away your clothes, then go entertain yourself for a while, or *I'll* find something for you to do. And believe me when I tell you it won't be Nintendo."

The kids left grumbling, and Marissa waited until they'd collected their clean clothing and disappeared up the stairs before she turned to Kody. Her heart was pounding so hard she actually looked down to see if it was visible, half expecting to see it thumping in and out of her chest like some Saturday morning cartoon character's. It wasn't, of course, and she forced coolness into her voice when she looked back up. "What are you doing here?"

"I've missed you." He took a step closer. "God, Marissa, I never knew it was possible *to* miss someone as much as I've missed you," he said in a low, rough voice.

Oh, yeah, baby, declared her body, but she took a step back. "I appreciate that. I've missed you, too. But if that's all, I'll say goodnight. I've got another load of laundry to put in the dryer." She edged for the door.

"No! Please. That's only part of what I wanted to say. I came to invite you and your kids to my father's house for pizza Friday night."

She stopped, turning back to stare at him. "What?"

"I've thought about everything you said." Kody stepped up close. "Hell, Riss, that's all I've *been* able to think about. And maybe you were right." He raked a hand through his hair, then gestured toward the living room. "Do you think we could talk for a minute?"

Marissa studied him a moment, then nodded and led the way.

She watched him look around at the furnishings, which were more formal than those in the great room, and at the fire burning in the fireplace. Then he looked back at her and smiled. "This is nice. I don't think I've ever been in here before."

That's because we spent most of our time in my bedroom. Marissa took a seat at the end of the couch.

Kody sat on the opposite end. "My sister Janice sleeps around with too many men," he said.

She must have made a face, because he said,

"That didn't come out right. It's not that I think her sex life is any of my business. But she's got Jacob. I love that kid — he's the brightest little boy in the world. But Janice brings men home, Rissa, and Jacob gets attached. Then just about the time he begins to think the current boyfriend might be daddy material, the guy's gone, only to be replaced by someone else. Dad and I are the only constant male influences he has in his life."

He looked Marissa straight in the eye. "So I guess when you brought me home the first night we met, I did sort of assume you made a habit of it. And when I discovered you had kids, I was determined to stay the hell out of their lives so I'd never have to see the look on their faces I've seen too many times on Jacob's."

Not that she couldn't sympathize, but hadn't they already covered this ground? Marissa was tempted to show him the door again, but remembering the look on his face when he talked about his nephew, she reined in her impatience.

And was glad she had a moment later.

"But that was before I got to know you, Marissa," he said in a low, intense voice. "Not just your moves in bed, but your sense of humor, your quick mind, your loyalty to your friends. And probably more than anything else, your dedication to your kids. I knew by about day two that you were nothing like Janice, and I started to fall in love with you." Moving closer, he reached out and touched her hand. "But I guess the habit of keeping my distance was ingrained by then, and I didn't know how to change gears. But I want to try. I want that more than I can say."

It was pretty much everything she'd longed to hear from him, so why did she suddenly feel so scared? "My kids can be a handful," she warned him.

His eyes crinkled at the corners. "So I guessed. They're a couple of pistols, aren't they?"

"They're a couple of semiautomatics."

He grinned. "Like their mama. I look forward to getting to know them — though I gotta tell you, it scares me a little. What if they don't like me?"

"Why are you saying all the right things all of a sudden?" she demanded. "They'll like you a lot — I know they will. But what if you and I try, the way you want, and it still doesn't work out? At least when things went sour between us before, I had the comfort of knowing it was your fault."

He eased his arm along the back of the couch behind her shoulders. "I don't ever wanna have to miss you again the way I did this past week," he said. "So I guess we'll both just have to work extra hard to see that things do work out." He slid his hand onto her shoulder.

"And you think having pizza with my kids and your father is the way to go about it?"

"It's a start." He bent his head to hers and bestowed a soft kiss on her lips. Pulling back, he looked her in the eye. "Don't you think?"

Warmth suffused her clear out to the tips of her fingers. "Yes. It's a very good start."

21

"You look very pleased about this," Veronica said after Marissa told her the news. She slapped her gloved hands together to keep the circulation going. "It's good to see you so happy again."

Presidents' Day was cold, clear, and the final day of the Winter Festival. She and Marissa had claimed one of the benches that ringed the rink to watch the kids get in one final skate. The papier-mâché trees with their hundreds of tiny white lights didn't look as fairylike as they had in the dark, but they were still wonderfully effective, and brilliant sunlight glinted off the giant ice sculptures that flanked the arena across the field. Fair food scented the air, and the sound of laughter rode the crystalline air all around them.

"The downside, of course, is this means Coop was right," Veronica said, looking at her friend's radiant face. "I hate to admit it, but he was. Which makes me quite the bitch, I guess."

Marissa gave her an amused smile. "Care to share why?"

"I went off on him yesterday about Kody. I said you'd be an idiot to take him back even if he came crawling — at which point Coop warned me not to confuse you with my mother."

"*What?*"

"He said I seemed to think forgiving and moving on meant subjugating one's will to another, the way Mama always did with Dad."

"What utter rot."

"Yeah, that's what I thought, too. I was positive he was full of it. But maybe not, Riss. It stuck in my mind, and I thought about it quite a lot yesterday and last night." She tucked her cold hands into her armpits and looked at her friend. "What if he's right? I mean, I was certainly willing enough to have you remain miserable if that meant not letting Kody get away with hurting you in the first place. That's not exactly rational thinking." Pulling a hand free of its warm nest, she reached out and touched Marissa's sleeve. "I'm sorry. Sometimes I'm not a very good friend."

"Oh, please. You have got to rein in this dramatic streak. Go with your first impulse — Cooper's theory is full of holes."

"But I'm not so sure that it is. I was pretty rabid about this — and I really did think for a while that forgiving Kody gave him carte blanche to forever mess with your emotions."

"Hell, Ronnie, you grew up with a mom who waited on your dad hand and foot and never once made him pull his share of the weight, simply because he had the ability to charm her socks off and wasn't above using that talent. So you slipped me into her slot for a minute. Big deal — it was a brain fart. But you're happy for me now, right?"

"Absolutely."

"And you're not secretly thinking, *Rissa, you stupid slut, what* are *you doing taking this cretin back after he failed to instantly recognize your many sterling qualities?*"

A muffled laugh escaped her. "No."

"Then get over it. Coop's a cutie, and clearly he's crazy about you. But he's just plain wrong about this."

Veronica suddenly felt light as a helium balloon, and she flashed her friend a crooked, self-deprecating smile. "Or he was right when he said it, but I glommed onto a momentary truth and turned it into a big, fat obsession."

"There's always that possibility, too."

"Why do I keep letting the things that bugged me so in childhood continue to affect me today?"

"Beats me. Family dynamics just seem to have a way of doing that to a person."

Thinking that they certainly had affected her relationship with Cooper even though she'd worked overtime not to allow them to, Veronica said with heartfelt sincerity, "Well, I wish they would knock it the hell off."

But that wasn't likely to happen as long as she and Cooper kept dancing around the things that drove little wedges into their ability to fully trust each other. So she vowed then and there to tackle him about it at the first opportunity.

Later that evening, after he'd slipped into her room and made love to her, Veronica thought about that pledge as she snuggled against him in postcoital bliss. Resting her head in the hollow of his shoulder, she drew patterns on the smooth skin of his chest with her fingertip, and for several long moments, while their heartbeats slowly regained their normal rhythms, the temptation to simply keep her worries to herself kept her silent. She had a feeling asking questions would only open up a new can of worms, and she didn't want to ruin the peaceful feeling of perfection she got from lying in his arms, all logy and replete from his lovemaking.

But her conscience kept clucking bad chicken imitations over her procrastination, and eventually she murmured, "Coop? Can I ask you something?"

He held her to him with one strong arm while his free hand lightly stroked her from armpit to hip beneath the blankets. "Sure."

"How do you plan on earning your living once the Tonk is sold? Are you going to ask the new owner to keep you on?"

His hand stilled midstroke. "No. I only took the job in the first place because it seemed like a good place to gather information to help clear Eddie."

"So what will you do, then?"

"This or that."

Her heart sank. "I . . . see."

"Do you?" He stiffened and rolled away until

331

they were no longer touching, and the sudden chill in Veronica's bones was the result of more than lost body heat. "Then why do I get the feeling you don't approve?"

"It's just — isn't that pretty much the same thing you said the first time I asked about your work history before coming to Fossil? I thought we'd progressed beyond that."

"Funny, and *I* thought we'd progressed beyond the let's-judge-Coop-by-what-he-does-for-a-living stage. But apparently not." He climbed out of bed and stood facing her, unself-conscious in his nudity. "You claim you love me."

"I *do* love you."

"If you care for me so damn much, then what difference does it make what I do for a living?"

"Well, I'll tell you what — it probably shouldn't make a darn bit of difference, and it wouldn't . . . if we lived in Utopia." She sat up, pulling the covers with her, and tucked them under her arms. "But we have to live in the real world, and aren't you the guy who accused me of confusing Marissa's situation with my mama's? I know I sometimes have a tendency to say black when you say white, but I gave your accusation a lot of consideration. And I had to admit that you had a point. So, as much as I'd love to tell you that I've seen the light and outgrown it, the sorry truth is, I haven't. I won't be like her, Cooper. I can't."

"Shit." Coop grabbed his jeans off the little

slipper chair where he'd tossed them earlier, stepped into them, and began working them up his long legs. Veronica's heart pounded over how fast everything had gone to hell as she watched him tug the denim over his hard butt.

He glanced over at her as he reached inside his fly and rearranged everything safely out of reach of the zipper. The abrupt laugh that exploded out of his throat was sharp-edged and humorless. "I guess you gotta appreciate the irony." But the hint of bitterness in his eyes negated the wry self-deprecation of his voice. "Here I came to town braced to meet another Crystal — but it turns out you're my mother instead."

"What?"

"Nothing I ever did was good enough for her, either." The bitterness grew more pronounced. "Is it too damn much to ask that just once in my life someone want me for who I am rather than what I do?"

His cool, expressionless "military" look was gone. He looked at her with dark eyes that burned with anger and stark, raw pain.

The anger she could have lived with, but she couldn't bear seeing such wounded vulnerability on the face of a man normally so contained, and she climbed out of bed to wrap her arms around his waist and press herself against him. "No," she said and rose onto her toes to kiss him with almost motherlike gentleness. Then she pulled back and looked into his dark eyes. "It's not that much to ask at all. We'll just go along the way we have been for the time being, okay? I'll be honest with you — eventually, I'm going to need some answers. But for now —"

"I love you," he said fiercely as his own arms clamped around her so tightly she could barely breathe. "God, Ronnie, I never knew it was possible *to* love someone the way I love you. All I ask is that you love me for *me* for a while. Just for a little while."

It wasn't an unreasonable request, given what he'd just divulged, and Veronica readily agreed. A tiny niggle of unease still hummed along the lining of her stomach, but she firmly shoved it away. She didn't begrudge him some time in which to come to believe in the strength of her feelings for him. Time was probably a very good thing — she could use a little of it herself.

The issues would sort themselves out eventually. So, really, there was no burning hurry to settle every single difference between them tonight.

It wasn't as if the two of them were rushing off to get married, or anything.

22

"I think we oughtta get married."

Unable to believe the words had come out of his own mouth, Coop simply stood by the stove for a moment, staring at Veronica. Finally, he blinked, turned the heat down under the chicken stock, and wondered if he looked half as shocked as she did. Considering the proposal had leaped fully formed from his subconscious to his lips, it wouldn't surprise him.

Yet it felt so right.

"*What?*" Her voice cracked, and she cleared her throat. Setting down the paring knife she'd been using to chop vegetables for the soup pot, she stared at him as if he'd just spoken in tongues, her slender eyebrows gathered above her nose. The day was cloudy, but a ray of sunlight found its way through the kitchen window to pick out blue highlights in her hair. Her pale complexion held the faintest hint of a flush along the high arc of her cheekbones.

He stepped forward, discovering an unprecedented need to persuade her. "It's a good idea, Princ—"

"It's a *crazy* idea!"

"Well, yeah, that, too — but only if you insist

on being absolutely literal-minded."

"Coop, we've known each other, what, a month?"

True. And it hadn't even been a full three days since he'd asked her to love him on personal merit alone.

Remembering *that* mindless little piece of neediness made him take a large step back, both literally and from the subject under discussion. He shoved his hands in his pockets. "I talked to Rocket while you were at that parent/teacher thing," he said stiffly. "And I'm sure you'll be delighted to know that Jacobson is officially off the hook. He's been cleared."

Personally, he found the news depressing as hell. He'd been so certain Troy Jacobson was the man who'd killed Crystal, so sure that finally they'd caught a break in clearing Eddie's name.

But Rocket said no. And since Coop respected Rocket's thoroughness as an investigator, he now found himself in the position of not only having to search from scratch for another likely candidate for Crystal's murderer, but also of having to admit — if only to himself — that Ronnie's precious Troy was blameless as a nun.

That pinched.

And it was no doubt what had led to his rash proposal, or whatever it was he'd just done. He'd been discouraged by Rocket's findings, but then Ronnie had waltzed into the house, pumped up from the conference with Lizzy's teacher, and had roped him into helping her cook dinner.

Making soup together in a warm, steamy kitchen on a cold afternoon, while the little girl they were responsible for played up in her room, had taken a lot of the sting out of his disappointment. Somehow he would help his brother. It might not happen today, or even tomorrow, but one way or the other he *was* going to get to the bottom of it and see that justice was done.

Meanwhile, it didn't hurt that he had this. This warm and fuzzy, familylike sense of belonging that wrapped around his heart like a fleece blanket. Aside from his relationship with Eddie, it wasn't something with which he'd had much experience. He could sure get used to it, though.

He watched Veronica blink at his abrupt change of subject, but she didn't give him the load of grief that she could have over it. Instead, she walked over and touched gentle fingertips to his forearm. "I'm sorry," she said, all earnest green eyes as she looked up at him. "I know you must be terribly disappointed Troy's innocent. And it's not so much that I was rooting for it *not* to be him, I just had a tough time reconciling the rendezvous at the Royal Hawaiian with the way he appears to feel about his wife. He treats her so deferentially, so *carefully,* which seem to me the traits of a man trying very hard to get back into a woman's good graces. It simply didn't seem compatible with sneaking off for a quickie with my sister."

"Yeah, he's a goddamn prince."

Her understanding smile and consoling little there-there pat on the arm made him want to snarl.

"Just out of curiosity," she said, "how did Rocket eliminate him?"

"He tracked Jacobson's movement from Fossil on the day Crystal left for Hawaii. It turns out," he admitted glumly, "he was in Spokane talking to the people in charge of designing new labels for the apple juice and applesauce divisions of his enterprise."

Her smile was so empathetic and on his side that Coop suddenly found himself back on the previous topic. "You know, it *isn't* such a crazy idea."

She blinked in confusion. "Troy getting new labels?"

"No. Us getting married." Her fingers fell away from his arm, and he reached for her hand. "It's not all *that* off the wall," he insisted. "People who've known each other a damn sight shorter than you and I have get hitched all the time and make it work. And building a relationship slowly is sure as hell no guarantee. I once knew a Marine who was engaged to a woman for seven years — and they ended up in divorce court eight months after they finally got married."

"Coop —"

He squeezed her fingers. "Do you love me, Ronnie?"

"You know I do."

"And God knows I love you. We've lived together, more or less, for over a month now."

"We've lived in the same *house* for over a month. We've been lovers for five minutes, cosmically speaking. It's a small distinction, I know — but telling."

"Whatever. I'm trying to make a case here."

"Oh, well, then, excuse me." She gave an imperious wave. "Continue."

"Thank you." He took heart from the fact that her gaze was full of bright-eyed attention. "Although I know Eddie's name will ultimately be cleared and he'll reclaim Lizzy, I don't know when that will happen. If we got married, we could provide a stable home for her until that time comes." *Okay, that's weak.* He waited for her to point out that they could do that without marriage — that they were, in fact, doing it now.

But she didn't. She simply laid her fingertips directly over his heart on his thermal-T-shirt-clad chest, looked up at him with those gray-green eyes, and said, "Tell me what you want to do with the rest of your life."

"Live with you."

"You know what I'm asking."

Yeah, he did. He also knew this was the time to tell her about his writing. He could put her mind to rest once and for all, and if the soft expression on her face was any indication, his marriage proposal was in the bag.

But dammit, he needed his *own* mind put to

rest, and well she knew it. "What difference does it make, Ronnie? If you care for me the way you say you do —"

Her hand dropped to her side. "Can you possibly *be* any more unfair?" she demanded hotly. "You want me to agree to marriage, which is a huge step, but I'm supposed to do it blind?"

"Why not? It seems to me that none of this would even be an issue if you loved me as much as you say you do." He thrust his hands in his pockets to keep from touching her. "So, what will it take to make me acceptable in your eyes? What if I told you I make six figures? Would you marry me then?"

"My reservations have nothing to do with money!"

"No?" he demanded cynically. "That's sure as hell what it sounds like to me."

"Damn you, Coop, it's about a lot of things — your insecurities, my insecurities, the way we were raised, and the knee-jerk manner with which we both still seem to react to that. It's about my need not to be my mother, and your need for me not to be *your* mother. God!" she shoved her hair back off her face, drew a deep breath, and blew it out. "Money is *not* the issue. I can support myself. But I need to know you possess some kind of ambition. I *need* that." Staring at him, she pressed the heel of her hand against her forehead as if to contain a headache trying to pound its way out. "More than that, though, I need you to trust me."

"Funny. That's what I need, too."

Her gaze went abruptly shuttered. "No, what you want is complete compliance. I'm supposed to take a blind leap of faith, while you keep your fistful of secrets clutched to your chest. God forbid you should make any sacrifices of your own."

She had a valid point, and all he needed to do was meet her halfway. A good marriage, he imagined, was based largely on compromise. He opened his mouth to tell her how he'd made his living the past five years.

And heard himself say instead, "So. Do you wanna get married, or what?"

Betrayal flashed in her eyes, but was gone almost before the pain of causing it registered in his gut. "Or what," she said with flat distaste and took a huge step back as if to distance herself. "I can't do this anymore," she said. "To hell with the sale of the Tonk and the house — I don't have to actually, physically be here for either of them. And I refuse to keep going around in circles with you about this."

Her chin rose, and the look in her eyes caused Coop's stomach to do a slow, greasy slide. "I give up," she said. "I'm packing up Lizzy and going back to Seattle."

Veronica closed the bedroom door behind her a few moments later and stumbled over to her bed. Sinking down to sit on its edge, she wrapped her arms around her stomach and bent at the waist, rocking mindlessly. Oh, God, oh, God, she hurt. She hadn't known such pain existed.

How was it possible to have fallen so fast and so utterly for a man she barely knew? She'd always thought that if she fell in love, it would be with a career man — someone smooth and diplomatic who shared her interests. A tough-as-nails ex-Marine lacking all capacity to trust never once entered into the picture. And a big, physical man who made her feel all hot and jittery and out of control sexually had sure never been part of the plan, either.

A light knock sounded at her door, and Veronica straightened, hating herself for the hope that sprang to life in her breast. "Yes?"

"Aunt Ronnie? Can I come in?"

She slumped. "Yes, of course." Then, not wanting her niece to suspect the adult in charge of her was an emotional wreck, she pulled herself together and plastered a smile on her lips.

The door opened and Lizzy poked her head into the room. "Can I watch TV until dinner? My homework is done."

Veronica nodded. "Sure. But come in for a minute first."

Her niece stepped into the room, but gave her a wary look. "Are you okay? You look kinda . . . funny."

She nodded, unable to give actual voice to the lie, then patted the bed and waited until Lizzy settled herself next to her. "Honey, listen. I know you don't want to leave here, but we're going to have to."

"No!" Lizzy stiffened and made a move to climb to her feet, but Veronica reached out and grasped her hand. She stroked her free hand down the smooth fall of Lizzy's shiny brown hair, taking comfort in its warm, silky texture.

"I know you're worried that your daddy won't be able to find you, but your Uncle, um . . . James" — pain splintered through her — "will still be right here in town to let him know where you are. And even if he weren't," she said more strongly, "your father knows where I live." Lizzy didn't need to know that Eddie had better not show his face at her door without a full pardon in his hand.

"But —"

"I'm sorry, honey, I know it's difficult to start a new school midterm, but I have a business that's going to fall apart if I don't give it some attention."

" 'Gotta put food on the table for my little daisy blossom,' " Lizzy said glumly.

"What?"

"That's what my daddy useta say when I didn't want him to go away on a business trip." Her childish voice deepened. " 'I have to, sweetheart. I gotta put food on the table for my little daisy blossom.' " Then her expression lightened. "Maybe Uncle Coop can come with us."

Veronica's dry swallow felt as if she'd swallowed ground glass. "No, he needs to stay here

343

to take care of the Tonk until it sells. But you can come back and stay with him on some of the weekends, if you want." She forced her lips into another smile that she could only hope didn't look as false as it felt. "Wouldn't that be nice?"

It broke her heart all over again when Lizzy's shoulders sagged in defeat.

"I guess," her niece said morosely.

"Déjà vu," Coop muttered cynically when, having closed down the Tonk for the night, he found himself outside Veronica's bedroom door. "Haven't you played out this scene before, bubba?"

Yet still he stood there in the dark hallway, one hand pressed against the panels as if he could feel Ronnie's warm heart beating on the other side of the cold wood. Half of him wanted to ease open the door, let himself in, and find a way to resolve this awful distance between them.

The other half was pissed as hell to once again be in a position where he had to beg for the scraps of someone's affection.

The soup that he and Ronnie'd had so much fun making together this afternoon might as well have been fish paste. It had taken everything he had to sit there at the kitchen table with her and Lizzy and act as if nothing were wrong. Swallowing had been beyond him, and he had the feeling Veronica hadn't fared much better.

And come to think of it, Little Bit hadn't appeared all that perky herself. She'd pushed her spoon around her bowl with about as much enthusiasm as the adults had shown. Not one of them had managed to swallow more than a bite or two.

He reached for the doorknob. Dammit, this was crazy. He was going in there and waking Ronnie up to hash this out once and for all.

And say what, exactly? His hand dropped to his side. Because the plain truth was, he wasn't willing to budge from his position and neither was Veronica. So what the fuck was there left to talk about? Coop turned away from the door.

It was simply too soon, he told himself. So he'd do the smart thing and let it go for tonight. Once the two of them had had a chance to sleep on it, they'd talk.

Things were bound to look much brighter in the morning.

The only thing that looked brighter was the weather. Sunshine poured through the windows when Coop came downstairs the next morning, and the cold that had lately permeated the exterior walls no longer emanated its pervasive chill. The temperature was definitely on the rise. As he poured himself a cup of coffee from the half-full pot on the coffeemaker's hot plate, he heard Veronica's voice in the living room. Taking his cup, he made a beeline for the doorway.

"I realize it's late notice, but I really do need to see Mr. Peavy as soon as possible," Veronica was saying as he walked into the room. She looked at him, then turned her back. "Lizzy Davis and I are moving to Seattle, but I thought I'd better first discuss the legalities of taking her with Mr. Peavy."

Coop went cold. She was leaving? Without so much as attempting to work anything out, she planned to just pack up her toys and go home?

"Yes, I'll hold."

He set his mug on a little gilt table and took the giant stride that brought him within an inch of her back. He wanted to reach out and spin her around to face him, but didn't quite trust himself to touch her.

"Go away, Cooper," she said in a gritty little voice without turning to face him.

"The hell I will. Why are you running?"

That spun her around and her eyes sparked with temper. "*Why am I running?* Why do you *think?* You're an intelligent man — put your mind to it, and I'm sure you'll come up with a reason or ten." She yanked the telephone receiver, which had slipped beneath her chin, back up to her mouth. "He'll give up his lunch hour for me?" she said to the person on the other end of the line. "Thank you — I'll be there at noon on Monday, then. I truly appreciate this."

Coop hadn't moved when she turned from recradling the headpiece, and she brushed against his body. The touch reverberating right down to his toes, he stared down at her. "I can't believe you're going to cut and run for the city."

"Believe it," she said flatly. "In fact, I'm

346

driving over this morning so I can talk to someone about transferring Lizzy to a new school. Tomorrow I'll clear out a room for her at my place."

No. He felt hammered by all the emotions crowding in on him, clamoring for attention. She couldn't just leave. She couldn't simply turn her back and waltz away. "You're taking Lizzy out of school today?"

"No, Marissa will take her for the weekend. I'll be back on Monday for my appointment with Neil Peavy, then I'm making arrangements for a permanent move."

"And you're going to just walk away from what you and I have without the least discussion?"

"What's left to say, Coop? I need something from you that you're not willing to give me, and you seem to need the same thing from me. This hurts too much. We need to put some distance between us before we end up tearing each other apart."

Oh, that was good. Hands jammed deep into his pockets, he stared down at her. "Too late," he said.

Then he turned and walked away.

23

Rain misted the windows of Veronica's Seattle condo as she let herself in shortly after three that afternoon. With a dejected sigh, she set her purse on the antique Jenny Lind chest in the tiny foyer, walked into the living room, and looked around.

She'd always been inordinately proud of her place. She'd worked hard to earn the down payment to purchase it and had patiently searched the past few years for just the right pieces to furnish it. Yet today, instead of providing her with a sense of homecoming, her pride and joy left her empty.

But then, there'd been no shine to any aspect of her day. The drive from Fossil, which ordinarily she'd swear she could do in her sleep, had seemed to take forever. Seattle traffic had been a bollixed-up mess, the Puget Sound weather was its usual unrelentingly gray drizzle, and life in general just sucked.

Oh, perfect. A one-woman pity fest to round out my day. That certainly demonstrates admirable strength of character. What truly sucked, she admonished herself, was her attitude. Neither the traffic nor the weather were any worse than usual — she'd simply gotten spoiled living in eastern Washington, where the sun shone much more frequently and there were fewer idiot drivers per capita.

She laughed shortly, the sound harsh in the empty apartment. Having Fossil emerge favorably in a comparison to Seattle was certainly a wild twist. If she were in a better frame of mind, she'd no doubt appreciate the irony.

Then the bravado that she'd been shoring herself up with disappeared, and she sank into the leather love seat in front of the condo's gas fireplace. Twisting her fingers together in her lap, she gazed blindly at the framed Frye Museum reproduction of a Pre-Raphaelite painting that hung above the mantel.

Who was she trying to kid, anyway? The truth was, having strength of character simply wasn't all that high on her list of priorities today. She'd stopped at the neighborhood elementary school to discuss Lizzy's transfer before coming home, and the women who worked there had been friendly and helpful. Other than that, her day had been one long blur of pain.

How could a man she'd met barely a month ago have assumed so much importance in her life? And how on earth could breaking up with him, when they'd barely had time to form a relationship in the first place, hurt and hurt and then hurt some more? Try as she might, she couldn't foresee any relief from this agony.

Wanting answers was pointless, as well. There just weren't any answers she could live with. The knowledge made her feel leaden and old. She

349

didn't want to move, and she didn't want to talk to anyone. She just wanted to remain right here in front of the cold fireplace until the pain became more bearable.

Instead, she had to be a grown-up. She'd been thrust in the role of parent, which meant she wasn't allowed to indulge her desire for a cathartic beating of the breast. Worse, she had to be honest. So try as she might to convince herself that this was her real life, and that her brief, magical sojourn with Coop in the garishly decorated house in Fossil had been the aberration, her heart knew the truth. And it was killing her. The only way she could see to possibly change anything was to move her and Lizzy back here as soon as possible, so they could start re-creating yet another new life together.

Until then, she didn't have a prayer of mending this awful ache in her heart.

"Freakin' females," Coop muttered for what felt like the umpteenth time the following Sunday morning. "Nothing but trouble, you ask me. It's *good* to have the house all to myself."

He'd long ago finished the research he needed to start his new book, and he should've begun the first draft by now. And he would have, if life with creatures bearing the double X chromosome hadn't gotten in his way. But now he had all the time in the world and as much privacy as a man could use to get some pages under his belt. So what if yesterday he'd pissed away the opportunity? One minute he'd had the entire day stretched out in front of him and the next thing he'd known, it was time to go tend the Tonk and he hadn't accomplished a damn thing. Big deal. Today was gonna be different. He was planting his butt in the chair and not moving until he had five or six pages written.

Eight hours later, he shoved back from his computer, swore at the cursor blinking relentlessly on the blank page beneath *Chapter One,* and stomped downstairs. He needed fuel; that was his problem. He'd get something to eat, then this logjam in his head would clear up.

Twenty minutes later, he was back. He blew out a frustrated breath, glaring at that mocking cursor. Fuel apparently wasn't the magic bullet, either. Shitfuckhell. He needed to *concentrate,* but he couldn't seem to keep his mind from wandering. It was just too frigging quiet around here.

Lizzy was hardly the noisiest kid in town, but there were certain sounds he'd grown accustomed to hearing, and he found himself listening for them in the quiet house. Worse, he paused every few minutes to listen for Ronnie.

Dammit, he'd promised himself he wouldn't do this. She didn't want him — not without a host of qualifications to test his worthiness, at any rate — and that was that. He wasn't going to beg for her love. Face stony, he once again tried to focus on getting some work done. At this point he'd settle for one usable page.

He finally gave up around ten o'clock and picked up a book to read. Fifteen minutes later, he threw it aside. For this, they were paying the author the big bucks? What tripe. He didn't know why the hell it had seemed so intriguing the other day.

He went downstairs and turned on the television, but there wasn't a damn thing worth viewing. How was it the cable company could charge their customers through the nose, offer a hundred and fifty stations, and *still* not manage to put out one single program worth watching?

Well, the hell with it. He dumped Boo, who had climbed up onto his thigh, and climbed to his feet. He might as well go to bed. He could stand to catch up on his sleep, anyhow.

But that apparently wasn't in the game plan, either. Instead, he tore the bed apart tossing and turning. Finally, around five in the morning, he got up and went into the bathroom in search of some aspirin. He knocked back a couple and considered tromping across the street to the Tonk to get himself a bottle of bourbon. But damned if he'd let any woman reduce him to that. He was an ex-Marine, dammit. One of the few, the fuckin' proud.

He returned to the bedroom and hung a towel over the window in hopes that if he ever *did* get to sleep, the morning sun wouldn't wake him up again an hour or so later. Then he climbed back into bed, punched his pillow into submission, and concentrated on breathing in and out very slowly. When last he looked at the alarm clock on the bedside table, it read a quarter to six. Some time after that, he finally dozed off.

The sound of the door snicking open at the bottom of the attic stairs awakened him what seemed mere minutes later. But when he looked at the clock, he saw it was nearly eleven in the morning. Quiet footsteps started up the stairs, and Coop's mood took a huge upward swing for the first time since Thursday night. Ronnie was back, and she must have had a change of heart. Otherwise, he was pretty sure she would never come within fifty feet of his bedroom. He pushed up on one elbow.

But it was golden hair, not shining black, that crested the balustrade, and a male voice that said so low as to be almost inaudible, "James? You up here?"

Shock, welcome, and a crushing disappointment all coursed through Cooper's system. *"Eddie?"* He threw back the covers and climbed to his feet, reaching for a pair of khakis. He was pulling them up his bare flanks when his half-brother reached the top of the stairs. Hastily fastening his pants, he took an eager step forward, then hesitated. He wanted to hug his brother, but he'd lived so long in a world of men discouraging of such actions that self-consciousness froze him in place.

Eddie took the step that bridged the gap between them and threw his arms around Coop. They clasped each other fiercely, then, with mutual slaps on the back, stepped back.

Coop looked at his half-brother, who was several inches shorter than he. Where Coop had taken after his father, their mother's genes dominated Eddie's makeup. He was built along slighter lines, lean and graceful, and even in exile managed to look like a *GQ* cover model. His golden hair shone in the weak light that filtered around the edges of Coop's towel-covered window, and his cheeks sported the gleam of the freshly shaven.

It had been months since Coop had seen his brother, and Eddie's situation was about as serious as it could get. So he meant to say something profound — or at least pertinent. Instead, he heard himself say, "Jesus, your shoes are even shined. Pretty damn spiff for a guy on the run."

"Hey, one can't let a little thing like being accused of murder lower one's standards." Eddie's self-deprecating smile came and went, a brief showing of white, even teeth. Then he sobered. "It's really good to see you, James."

"It's good to see you, too, little brother. But you're taking a helluva chance, coming here."

"I had to see Lizzy, to make sure she was okay. I've been watching the house off and on since yesterday, but while I was surprised as hell to see you living here, I never caught so much as a glimpse of her. Where is she? Does Veronica have her? Did she take her to Seattle or something?"

Ronnie's name coming out of the blue made

Coop flinch, and he set his shoulders against the flick of pain abrading his raw nerves. "Not yet, but she's getting ready to." Keeping his voice level, he explained how she'd been taking care of Lizzy and was across the mountains making arrangements to move them both to her home. "Lizzy spent the weekend at Marissa's. She'll be home after school, and Ronnie even sooner, so we'd better make use of this opportunity. You hungry?"

"Yeah, I guess."

"Come on down to the kitchen. We can talk while I throw together some breakfast."

He retrieved the towel he'd hung over the window and carried it with him downstairs. He tossed it to Eddie, with instructions to pin it over the door window to block the view should anyone come calling. While his brother did that, Coop pulled out frying pans, fired up a couple of burners, and gathered provisions from the fridge.

Then he wrestled with his conscience. Feeling torn between the concerns Veronica had put in his head and the old familiar need to take care of his baby brother, he finally said, "You do realize you can't actually speak to Lizzy, don't you?" He looked up from cracking eggs into a hot pan to gauge his brother's reaction.

Eddie clearly wasn't thrilled, but he nodded. "Yeah. I'd give my left nut to hug her for a minute and find out for myself how she's holding up, but I know it'd be too painful for her if I turned right around and disappeared again."

"Not to mention dangerous for you. You can't expect a six-year-old to keep that sort of secret."

"I get it, James, all right?" Eddie paced to the living room doorway and back. "I can't believe I'm in this house." He disappeared into the front room on his next circuit and returned with a framed snapshot of Lizzy in his hand. When he caught Coop watching him rub his thumb over the two-dimensional image of his daughter's face, he jerked his head in the direction of the living room and said with studied carelessness, "What happened to all the Happy Hooker shit?"

"Veronica packed most of Crystal's stuff away." He scooped the eggs onto plates, fished bacon out of the pan on the back burner, and carried everything over to the table. "Grab some juice or milk outta the fridge, will you?" The toast popped, and he went back to get it.

Passing a piece to his brother a moment later, he took his seat and looked across at Eddie as his brother stared moodily at the photo he'd propped in front of him on the table.

"I'm sorry about the Lizzy thing," he said. "Veronica's been carping at me about you — she's worried sick about the quality of Lizzy's life if you were to snatch her and take her on the run with you."

Eddie shrugged, pushing his food around his plate. "Her concerns are legitimate. I did intend to grab Lizzy and run, but with all the time I've had to think things through, I've seen that'd be dumb." He touched his fingers to the photograph again. "She'd be miserable. She looks pretty happy here. Veronica's good for her, isn't she?"

"Yeah. She cares about her, Eddie. A lot." He pointed his fork tines at Eddie's plate. "Quit playing with your eggs and eat the damn things. You're gonna need your strength if we're going to figure out how the hell to get you out of this mess."

Eddie took one bite, then another. Moments later, he was using the last of his toast to mop up the egg yolk on his plate. He looked across the table at Coop.

"I didn't do it," he said in a low, fierce voice. "I mean, sure, Crystal and I fought that night — she'd been milking me for years, using Lizzy as a bargaining chip to get more and more money out of me, and I was fed up and pissed off when I came by the Tonk to tell her she'd never see another penny once I got custody. But I sure as hell didn't kill her over it. And I can explain about my jacket —"

"Jeez-us," Coop said, insulted. "I know damn well you didn't do it."

"I left it somewhere," Eddie went on, oblivious. "You know how I'm always doing that. What was it Mom used to say, that if my head wasn't screwed on, I'd manage to leave that behind, too? I've wracked my brains trying to recall where I left the coat, but I just can't remember. You can bet the bank, though, that whoever killed —" He stopped, blinked once, and then stared at Coop. "You believe me?"

"Hell, yes — I *know* you, Eddie. It never even occurred to me you might have done it. I haven't had a lot of luck discovering who did, but I found out from Veronica that Crystal had some secret honey she went to Hawaii with last fall. Someone 'influential' is how Ronnie said she described the guy. Find him and we'll probably have found the killer. For a while there I was pretty sure it was Troy Jacobson, but he's been cleared."

"Why Troy? Because of those rumors that were going around last fall that he was seeing someone on the side? I never believed that."

"Holy shit. What is it about this guy that inspires all this fucking loyalty?"

Eddie shrugged. "He's pretty decent. Besides, you'd have to be blind to miss the fact that he's carrying an Olympic-sized torch for his wife."

"So I've been told." Coop shrugged aside his rancor. "You have any ideas who it *could* be?"

"Not a one. But at least it's a place to start — that's more than I've had up until now." He gave Coop a sober look. "I really fucked things up, didn't I? Not the least of which was telling Lizzy I'd be back for her. I never should have made a promise I had no idea if I could keep. She deserves better."

"I imagine you were flying blind, and it didn't help that I wasn't around for you when you needed me. I'm sorry about that, Eddie."

His brother shrugged. "It was my problem. I'm a grown man, and you're not expected to sit by your phone on the off chance your little brother might need to be bailed out of jail."

"Still. I wish I'd been there for you. Maybe if I'd been around, we could have figured a way out of this mess that didn't entail running. That was your worst mistake, I think — people took it as a sure sign of guilt. What the hell possessed you to do it?"

"I don't know; I just panicked. My lawyer —"

"Neil Peavy," Coop said.

Eddie gave him a curious look. "You know Neil?"

" 'Know him' might be stretching it a bit, but I've talked to him about your case."

"Then you must understand why I panicked. When he told me at my bail hearing that things were about as bleak as they could be, but that maybe he could plead me down to a lesser charge, I freaked. All I could think of was that they were going to take me away from Lizzy for *years*. I didn't expect to get bail at all, so when I did, I took it as a sign that I'd better get the hell outta Dod—"

"Wait a minute." Coop sat forward. "What do you mean, Peavy told you your case was bleak?"

"Just that. He said the evidence was stacked so high against me he could barely see over the top."

"That can't be right; he told me he didn't know why you'd run because your case was

359

wholly circumstantial and very weak. And the fact they gave you bail seems to support that." Coop rubbed his fingers over his forehead while he stared across the table at his half-brother. "Are you sure you didn't misunderstand?"

"Hell, no, I didn't misunderstand! He said I'd most likely be sent away for years. That Lizzy would be graduating college by the time I got out again." Eddie rubbed his own forehead. "Why the hell would he tell us two different stories?"

Coop's hand dropped down to the tabletop. "There is no good reason. Unless he had a vested interest in seeing you take the fall."

Eddie stared. "Neil . . . and Crystal?"

"You know the players a helluva lot better than I do. Is it possible?"

"Jesus. I can hardly wrap my mind around the idea. But . . . sure. Anything's possible." He sat straighter. "In fact, that would explain how Crystal always seemed to know just how far she could go to squeeze an extra dime out of me." He pushed his chair back from the table. "That son of a bitch! Wait until I get my hands on him. If I'm going to jail for murder anyway, it might as well be for one I've actually committed."

Coop reached out to touch Eddie's arm. It was rigid as steel beneath his soft sweater, and the younger man all but shook with fury. "This is no time to fly off the handle, little brother. You gotta keep your cool and help me think this through."

Little by little the tension drained out of

Eddie, and he resumed his seat. "That Hawaiian trip with Crystal must have left some sort of trail," he said in a hard voice. "Maybe we can nail his ass by following that."

"I've got a private detective on it now; it should take him no time at all to find some definitive proof. I'll give him a call."

He was halfway to the phone when a thought suddenly struck him and he froze. "Oh, shit, Eddie! Veronica!"

His brother twisted around to look at him. "What about her?"

"She has a noon appointment with Peavy to talk about the legality of taking Lizzy out of town." He checked his watch. "That means she's with him right now."

There was no reason the knowledge should make cold dread swim in his gut. Logic said she'd be okay — Veronica had no reason to suspect Peavy of any wrongdoing, and the chances of her tumbling to his involvement in her sister's death were nil. Yet Coop's Marine instincts had the short hairs on the back of his neck standing on end, and he grabbed his keys.

He didn't care how safe it ought to be. He didn't want Ronnie within ten miles of that guy.

24

"I'm so sorry to be late," Veronica said breathlessly as she followed Neil Peavy into his office. "A tanker truck jackknifed up on Snoqualmie Pass, and traffic was at an absolute standstill. But I should have allowed more time — I know you're giving up your lunch hour for me." She set her purse on his desk and began pulling off her good wool coat.

"Don't worry about it," the lawyer said easily. "I eat lunch at my desk half the time, anyway, and I let my girls go out for theirs, so you're not disrupting a thing. Have a seat and catch your breath. Can I get you anything?"

"A glass of water would be great." She still felt frazzled as she sat down in the mauve upholstered chair that faced the gleaming oak desk. She hated being late for anything.

She looked around for a place to put her coat and purse, and finally piled them in her lap. Then, while Neil went down the hallway to the water cooler, she checked out the office with irrepressible professional interest.

A narrow, fenced rock garden outside the wall of low windows to her right provided privacy and light. And while she saw room for improvement in the office's professional appointments, she shrugged that aside. What interested her more were the personal touches that said something about the owner.

Neil Peavy's personal effects said he was very neat, had a strong interest in the importance of his position in Fossil, and played tennis to win. Two trophies from the Fossil country club stood in a place of honor on the credenza behind the desk, and several photographs shared space with the requisite framed diplomas and awards that graced the walls. Neil was featured in most of them with people whom Veronica assumed to be captains of industry or other prominent notables, since she recognized Troy Jacobson in one and Fossil's mayor in another. She reached out to nudge the small oak frame on the desk around in order to get a peek at what it displayed, only to pull back as the lawyer came back into the room.

He handed her a cup, and Veronica sat back in her chair and sipped her water as he rounded the desk and took his seat. He waited politely for her to swallow, then smiled. "What can I do for you?"

She lowered the cup and gave a rueful shrug. "I don't actually know if you can help me. But I figured that since you're Eddie Chapman's lawyer and you know the history between him and Crystal, you'd at least be the person to ask." When Peavy regarded her with attentive interest, she explained, "I'm moving back to Seattle at the end of the week and plan on taking their daughter Elizabeth with me. So I need to know about the legality of simply packing her up and taking her out of town. Also, I know Eddie paid child support, which of course Lizzy hasn't received since he skipped bail. I'd like to know if his estate, or whatever you'd call it, can reinstate that. I can afford to take care of her without it, but it would be nice if the money she's due could be put in a trust fund for college or something."

Neil reached for a navy folder. "I reviewed Eddie's file when Margaret told me you'd made an appointment." He set the folder on the pristine desk before him, but didn't open it. Instead, he rested his fingertips on its cover, regarded the file's clearly marked name tab for a moment, then looked up at her. "Your questions touch on two separate areas of the law, so let's take it one step at a time. The short-term answer to your first inquiry is, yes, you may take your niece to Seattle. That's one advantage of a town this size — no Child Protective Services to impose restrictions on your guardianship. Not that CPS would likely stand in your way, since everyone knows you're devoted to the child's welfare. As for the long term . . . did your sister leave a will?"

Ronnie nearly laughed. The man clearly hadn't known Crystal if he assumed for even one minute she would've taken the time to do anything so responsible. That sort of long-term planning had never been her sister's strong suit. "I'm afraid not."

"Then my suggestion is that you go see an attorney when you get back to Seattle and have him or her petition the court on your behalf for custody of your niece. As it stands now, you have no legal status, since Ms. Davis died intestate and left no provision for her daughter's care. Gaining guardianship would also address the question of child support. Eddie had a legal agreement with your sister to pay a generous monthly stipend for Elizabeth's support. But he also had the wherewithal to flee to a life of luxury in a country that holds no extradition treaty with the United States, so his assets were frozen when he failed to appear for trial. In order for a portion of those assets to be released for the child's support, you'll need to be appointed her legal guardian. It would be a conflict of interest for me to represent you, but I'd be happy to recommend someone in your area. I know several competent Seattle attorneys."

"I'd truly appreciate that, Mr. Peavy."

"Please. Call me Neil."

"Neil, then. Thank you." Finished with her water, she started to set the cup on the desk, but its shining surface, looking far too capable of being marred by a water ring, made her hesitate. Securing her purse and coat on her lap with her free hand to keep everything from spilling, she set the cup on the floor. When she straightened she saw the lawyer observing her with a look that, for just an instant, made her feel like a classless bimbo.

But she must have imagined the hint of scorn,

for he simply gave her a mellow smile and said, "Not a problem. I'll just write down a couple of names here, along with their respective phone numbers."

"I probably should've done something about this already," she admitted. "But everything has happened so fast that I've simply taken it one day at a time. I can see the wisdom in establishing a legal claim, though, so please don't undervalue the importance of your advice. You've shown me my goal, and given me a starting place to reach it. For that alone, both Lizzy and I thank you."

"Then you're both very welcome." He finished writing down the promised information on the back of a business card and leaned forward to pass it to her.

Veronica set her bag on the desk to keep it from dumping onto the floor and reached for the proffered card. As she leaned forward to accept it, however, her coat started to slip. Her quick attempt to anchor it sent Neal farther across the desk as if to lend her a hand. His elbow caught a corner of the oak photo frame, sending it skittering toward the edge of the desk. Veronica made a grab for it, but all that accomplished was to knock her purse into her lap and her coat to the floor.

She laughed at her own clumsiness as her hand closed over the frame. "Well, that'll teach me to use more care folding my coat," she said as she looked down at the photograph in the frame. "The slippery stuff's supposed to go on the *inside.*" Then shock froze the laughter in her throat.

Rather than the photo of a loved one she'd expected to see, it was a disturbingly familiar snapshot of a coconut grove and a beautiful coral-pink building of soaring arches and minaret-topped turrets . . . with a small brown and white dog lifting its leg against one of the trees in the foreground.

Dear God. It was the exact same photo taken during Crystal's getaway with her "influential" man. Although influential wasn't quite the word Ronnie would use to describe a lawyer who slept with one party in a custody battle while representing the other.

She took a deep breath and held it. She'd have to be a fool not to connect the dots, but her sudden suspicion that she was alone with her sister's killer was unbelievably horrendous. She had to keep her cool until she could get to Coop. It was the only thought she could seem to hang on to.

She had to tell Cooper.

It seemed like a millennium since she'd glanced at the photograph, but in reality only seconds had passed. Carefully replacing it on the desk, she shoved down the awful fear and gave Peavy a strained smile. "You know what they say," she said with the equanimity perfected dodging drunken hands at the Tonk. "You can take the girl out of the small town, but you just can't take the small town out of the girl." She shrugged, gathered her coat, and rose to her feet. "I won't take any more of your time." She slipped into her coat and made a production of checking the floor for lost articles from her purse. When she felt she could meet the lawyer's gaze without giving herself away, she straightened and offered her hand. "You've been very helpful, and I plan to take your advice." *Just two more minutes and you're out of here,* she told herself as Peavy rounded his desk to accompany her to the door. *All you have to do is keep it together for two minutes more.*

She managed to do precisely that, chatting lightly as they walked down the hall. When they reached the front door she was sure she was home free. But just as she began to pull it open, Peavy's hand came over her shoulder and pushed the door closed again. Her heart climbing to her throat, she gave him a coolly questioning look over her shoulder. "Is there a problem?"

"Yes," he said softly. "This really is quite unfortunate, but I'm afraid I can't let you go."

"I beg your pardon?"

Hands on her shoulders, he turned her to face him, and the easy smile on his face, so at odds with the cold flatness of his eyes, chilled her. "I admire your efforts, and your ability to think on your feet, Ms. Davis, but you don't have a very good poker face. The photo apparently gave me away — I assume that slut Crystal kept a copy for herself?"

"I don't have the foggiest idea what you're talking about," she said with chilly dignity, "but I do take exception to your language regarding my sister." She tried to shrug out of his grasp. "Now kindly remove your hands and allow me to leave. Lizzy will be getting home from school soon, and I still have a dozen things —"

The sharp shake he gave her shocked her into silence. "Don't play the innocent with me, missy. I didn't get to be smarter than the average bear by being taken for a fool."

She blinked. "The average what?"

Ignoring her question, he said dreamily, "I love that picture. It gives me a tingle every time I look at it, remembering what I got away with." Then he gave her that awful charming smile again. "Let's you and I take a little ride."

"Let's not." Getting in a car with this man sounded like a dangerous plan. Veronica intended to stay right where she was until his office staff returned from lunch. Which, God willing, would be any minute now.

"Are you laboring under the delusion I'm asking you?" he inquired gently. Releasing her, he stepped back. "This is not a request. Get your keys, because we *are* going for a ride."

She grabbed for the door handle and jerked it open. But as she drew breath to scream, she was yanked back and spun around so fast her head swam. Neil's hands clamped around her throat, cutting off her breath.

"You Davis women have a real knack for

making me angry," he said with that appalling pleasantness, then eased up on the pressure constricting her windpipe. But his hands remained in place around her neck, his thumbs an implicit threat as they pressed lightly against the hollow of her throat. "You keep pushing me," he said mildly, "and I'll squeeze the life out of you where you stand."

Her heart felt as if it were trying to pound its way out of her chest, but she met his gaze as coolly as she could. "And how will you explain my corpse littering your lobby?"

"No explanation will be necessary." The chilling affability never left his face as he looked her in the eye. "I'll dump your cold, stiff remains in my closet until I can do something a little more permanent about them after the office closes for the night."

That chilled her right to the bone, but damned if she'd let him see. She raised her chin. "You'd never get away with it. People know about my appointment with you."

" 'People' being Coop Blackstock, I presume?" He laughed in her face. "Big deal. The man's an itinerant *bartender,* for God's sake. Let him ask any question he wants. I'll simply act properly puzzled." He gave her a look of baffled concern that appeared all too genuine to her horrified eyes and said with warm sincerity, "Ms. Davis is *missing,* you say? I don't understand this — I just saw her this afternoon, and she was fine when she left my office."

"Why are you doing this?" she whispered. "Why did you kill my sister?"

"Because she was a greedy little bitch who didn't know when to leave well enough alone. We had a mutually satisfying relationship — and since I knew to the penny what Chapman was worth — I even helped her squeeze a few extra dollars out of the man to support her little glitter habit. It should have been enough for her. But she always wanted more, and when Eddie got fed up with paying her extortion and instructed me to file for custody of the child, everything spiraled out of control."

"So you *killed* her?"

"I didn't set out to, no. But Crystal never knew when to call it a day. She kept demanding I get Eddie off her back, and it wasn't for any sentimental attachment to her little girl, I can tell you. She was afraid if she lost custody, she'd also lose the cash cow Chapman had been up until then."

Veronica cringed, fearing he was right.

"She refused to listen when I explained I couldn't simply *command* Eddie's compliance," Neil continued. "She became more and more insistent that I do something, which was annoying enough. But then she went too far." He looked at Veronica, and for the first time his fraudulent geniality was nowhere in evidence. "She threatened to expose our affair if I didn't do something."

Oh, Crystal, Veronica thought in despair. *Why*

371

did you never think things through?

Then the awful smile was back. "Killing her probably wasn't what she had in mind," he said in an amused voice. "But that's what little girls get when they push their luck. I have a position to maintain in this town. There was certainly no way I was about to allow some Baker Street trollop to ruin me."

Low social status made one a perfectly acceptable candidate for *murder?* Veronica hit her flash point. She gave Neil a hard shove that caught him off guard and sent him staggering back. Once again she tore open the door, then kicked back at the man reaching for her, and plunged for freedom.

She made it through the doorway before her hair was gripped from behind, jerking her to a halt. The gleamingly sharp-edged blade of a Swiss army knife twitched into view and waved menacingly back and forth before her eyes.

"Don't be fooled by its length," Neil murmured in her ear. "Because it will do the job quite handily if you give me any more grief." The blade disappeared, but a second later she felt its tip scratch against the nape of her neck as Neil pulled the law office door closed behind them. "Make one peep and I'll show you exactly how much damage a blade this size can do."

"Figures you'd be one of those guys who insist it's not the size that counts, but what you can do with it," she muttered as he directed her to her car. "It's always the ones who don't *have* the size."

The tip of the blade pressed a little harder against her nape. "You Davis girls just don't know when to zip your pretty little lips, do you? Keep it up, and I'll be forced to zip them for you. Permanently."

Like you don't plan to do that anyway. Veronica had no illusions on that score; she knew too much now.

But damned if she'd go without a fight.

He stopped at the passenger side of her car. "Unlock it and climb in slowly," he ordered.

Not having any choice, she fumbled her keys out of her purse and did as she was told. She contemplated diving for the driver's door, figuring that while her lower body might be in danger of getting slashed, the small blade wouldn't do anywhere near the damage it was capable of inflicting on her vulnerable neck.

But Peavy gripped her arm and climbed in right alongside her, not giving her even an inch to maneuver. He closed the door behind him, and gave her that damn smile again.

"Buckle up," he advised. "We wouldn't want you getting hurt."

25

"I'm probably making a big deal out of nothing," Coop said as he gunned the car up Commercial Street toward the city center.

"But you don't think so, do you?" asked Eddie at his side.

"No." He glanced over at his brother. "Ronnie never hesitates to tell me I'm full of shit when she thinks I am. It ties my gut up in knots just to think what she might say if she tumbles to the truth about Peavy."

"The chances of that happening are pretty slim, don't you think?"

"All but nonexistent." But his nerves kept sparking a warning to get there *now*, all the same.

Suddenly he was jolted out of his preoccupation. "Jesus!" he said. "*You* shouldn't be here. It's broad-freakin'-daylight — if anyone sees you, they'll haul your ass off to jail so fast we won't see you for dust. And that's only if the cops don't shoot first and ask questions second."

"I don't think we have to worry too much about the cops," Eddie said wryly. "Fossil's police department is hardly what anyone would classify as SWAT central. But if we do get stopped, we'll tell them the truth: that I was on my way to the station to turn myself in."

Coop stared at him for a second. "Are you serious?"

"Yes. I shouldn't have run in the first place — it was a chickenshit, knee-jerk reaction. And despite all those nights I spent rabidly planning different ways for taking Lizzy on the lam, I know it's out of the question. So it's time I faced the music. Once we've made sure Veronica is okay, we'll go to the station and see if we can't straighten out this mess."

"You really aren't the kid whose image I've been packing around in my mind all these years, are you?" Coop asked slowly. It shouldn't have come as any big revelation, since on an intellectual level he'd realized for a long time now that his half-brother had grown up.

Emotionally, though, and despite his brother's earlier willingness to take responsibility for his actions, a revelation was exactly what it felt like.

"I'm sure it comes as a shock, considering my recent behavior," Eddie replied wryly. "But the truth is, I quit being a kid the day mine was born."

Coop was suffused with a sudden sense of all the years that had been lost. "I haven't been much of a brother to you," he said slowly. "I'm sorry."

"What?" Eddie turned to stare at him. "Where the hell did that come from?"

"I haven't been there for you — haven't been

around nearly enough. Not when I should have been."

"Hey." Eddie shrugged. "We've covered this ground. Besides, we've seen each other."

"Yeah, when you made the effort during your business trips to my side of the country." He thought about it a moment. "It's kind of ironic, really. Here I've been locked into thinking of you as this perpetual kid . . . when the truth is I'm the one who needs to grow up and get on with it. I've spent too damn many years letting Mom's opinion of me dictate my actions, and it's kept me from coming back to see you — if that meant having to return to this part of the world. Never mind the way my feelings for her years after her death, for crissake, have kept me from . . ." Ruthlessly, he chopped off that conversational tack. Thinking of the way he'd screwed up with Veronica as well wasn't something he could afford to contemplate right now. Not and hang on to the last vestige of focus he had left.

So he concentrated on the things he could control. "I'll tell you something that being in Fossil has taught me, though. It's my loss that I missed out on so much of your life." Pulling up to a red light, he looked over and met Eddie's gaze. "But I give you my word that those days are over. From now on, I plan to be around a lot more for you and Lizzy." Then he grinned. "Whom, incidentally, I've enjoyed the hell outta getting to know. She is one sugarcoated little heartbreaker."

Eddie's face creased in a tender smile. "Yeah, she's a peach, isn't she? And I'll tell *you* something, James. Maybe my taking a powder wasn't a totally bad thing, if it got you out here where you could get to know my baby. Not to mention that if you hadn't come to Fossil, no one ever would've tumbled to Neil being the one responsible for Crystal's death. So let's go collect Veronica. Then we can concentrate on —"

"Holy shit!" Coop craned around to stare as a familiar blue Volvo passed him, going in the opposite direction. "Hey! That was her!"

"Who?" Eddie twisted around to look also.

"Ronnie." An icy fist of apprehension clenched his gut as he looked for a place to hang a U. "She's not alone," he said grimly. "I couldn't see exactly who was with her through those tinted windows, but I can tell you this much. There's a man in her car."

Never let them transport you. The words kept repeating in Veronica's head until she felt ready to scream. What on earth had she been thinking? *Aren't you the woman who said, "Well, duh," when the experts on that Oprah episode about learning how to defend yourself said never let your assailant transport you?*

No one had mentioned, though, how good sense and rational thought flew out the window when one was terrified. Too late, she realized she should have taken her chances back there in the parking lot. How likely was it that Peavy would've killed her right outside his own law offices?

Not very, genius. Stupid appeared to be the word all right. Stupid, stupid, stupid!

"Did you say something?" Peavy's voice was patently amused.

Eat shit and die, you rat-faced bugger. Conscious of the knife point that rested against the side of her neck, she pressed her lips together and kept the suggestion to herself.

"Not to me, apparently." Peavy shrugged. "Ah, well. Intelligent conversation would be a bonus, but I don't actually require it. Turn left at the next light."

That would put them on Orchard Road, which for one short block housed Fossil's answer to Rodeo Drive: a row of upscale, expensive shops that catered to the Bluff crowd. Veronica had the feeling Peavy wasn't going to suggest they go shopping.

More likely he'd direct her beyond town to either the Hawthorn or Bagley orchards, both of which were on this road. *The very-isolated-this-time-of-year Hawthorn or Bagley orchards,* she thought, and shivered. She'd better make her move fast if she planned on saving her ass anytime soon.

It would help, though, if she had some inkling of what that move might be.

Her senses felt heightened as she made the turn, and she was extraordinarily aware of the elegant gold lettering that spelled out TOUCH OF

CLASS (FINE ACCESSORIES FOR THE DIS-
CERNING HOMEOWNER) on one of the store-
fronts, and of the bare-branched birches
reflected off the black-tinted picture window of
the Natural Touch Day Spa next door. She recognized Darlene Starkey, who was loaded down
with packages bearing distinctive logos from
specialized shops, her pageboy hairdo looking
freshly done as she strode briskly toward her
prized Mercedes-Benz parked in front of Tout
Suite's Fine Apparel.

And suddenly Ronnie's brain started to function once again.

Oh man, oh man. The only way Peavy had any
chance of pulling this off was if his anonymity remained intact. He'd appeared so confident
lounging in the seat next to her that the fear
hazing her ability to reason had equated it with
invulnerability. But her car had tinted windows
— otherwise, he'd undoubtedly be slouched
down to avoid detection. *Well, it's time to burst
your balloon, you murderous bastard.*

Adrenaline suddenly roaring in her veins, she
changed lanes. She had the satisfaction of seeing
Peavy jerk upright from his indolent pose as his
side of the car drew nearer and nearer to the row
of cars parked along the curb. With a horrendous
screech of metal on metal, she sideswiped
Darlene Starkey's much-loved pearl-gray
Mercedes-Benz, jammed on the brakes, and
threw the gearshift into park. In the next instant
she was out of the car, leaving Neil Peavy

trapped in the passenger seat.

"Hey, Darlene," she called to the horrified woman who'd stopped dead in the middle of the sidewalk with her packages in a heap at her feet as she gaped at the wreckage. "Have I got a scoop for you!"

"Yes!" The awful headache-producing tension loosened its grip on the muscles in Coop's neck the moment he drove around the corner and saw Veronica standing safely on the sidewalk, contemplating her car squeezed up against a badly creased Benz. When he saw who stood next to her, he put two and two together and laughed out loud in relief. "That's my *girl*."

"She is?" Eddie gave him a startled look. "Get out! You and Veronica?"

Coop merely gave him a huge grin. He drove up the avenue, intending to pull alongside Veronica's car to block the driver's door. Before he could do so, however, Peavy suddenly slid from her car on that side and hit the street running.

Eddie swore. "The son of a bitch is getting away!"

Coop rocked to a halt at the curb. "Don't go after him," he commanded as they tumbled out of the car. He headed straight for Veronica but said over his shoulder, "Cops see you running down the street with bloodlust in your eyes, and they really will shoot first and ask questions later." Then he shrugged. "Besides, where's he gonna go? The guy's miles from home, and be-

380

tween Ronnie and us, we should have enough to convince the police to keep an eye on his bank account so he can't lay hands on any ready cash." But that could come later.

He strode up to Veronica and hauled her into his arms, satisfied when she immediately wrapped her own around his neck and clung. Feeling the tremors that pulsed through her body, he tucked his chin to get a good look at her, but she was firmly burrowed into his chest. "Are you all right?"

"Is *she* all right?" Darlene Starkey, puffed up like an outraged cat, threw down the cigarette she'd been dragging on furiously and glared at them. "She's a goddamn crazy woman, is what she is! Did you see what she did to my car?" Then she caught sight of Eddie and gave such a high-pitched shriek that Cooper half expected dogs to start barking. "Ohmigawd! It's her sister's killer! Call the police!" She started fumbling her own cell phone from her purse.

"Yes, do call the police," Veronica said firmly. Coop felt her turn her cheek against his chest to look at the other woman. "But tell them to arrest Neil Peavy. He's the one who killed Crystal, and he planned to kill me, too. He admitted as much."

Avid interest replaced Darlene's fury.

Coop wrapped his hands around Veronica's shoulders and stepped back to hold her at arm's length, where he could get a good look at her. He blew out a breath when he saw for himself that she truly was all right. "It scared the hell out of me when I saw you with that murderin' son of a bitch," he told her. "Eddie and I had just figured out he was responsible for Crystal's death when I remembered you had an appointment with him. Then, when I saw he was in the damn *car* with you, my heart about stopped." Taking a deep breath, he loosened the stranglehold he'd had on his pride these past several days and admitted, "I've been an idiot, Ronnie. I should never have withheld what I do for a living from you."

"I don't *care* what you do," she replied. "I can't believe I thought it was so important in the first place."

"Yeah, nothing like a little brush with death to drive home what's really —" He suddenly became aware of blood trickling down the side of her neck, and it chopped his thought right in two. Reaching out, he wiped the rivulet off her skin with a fingertip, and red-hot anger rose in a scalding tide as another trickle immediately took its place. He swore viciously. "What did he do to you?"

She reached up and touched the spot herself, then pulled back her bloody fingertip to inspect it. "He was holding a pocketknife to my neck," she said slowly. "It must have nicked me when I hit Darlene's car. That's funny, I didn't feel a thing."

"I'll stomp that son of a bitch into paste!"

"No, Coop, wait —"

Setting her loose, he pivoted on his heel and

ran flat out in the direction he'd seen Peavy go. Rage was a red mist obscuring all else — a total departure from his normal cool-headedness. He was marginally aware that Eddie was hot on his heels, but he couldn't get past the fury pumping through his veins long enough to caution his brother to stay put.

He had more than a dozen years of reconnaissance missions under his belt, and he knew acting the hothead was not the way to run one's quarry to ground. But hard as he tried he couldn't seem to access his customary clear-headed logic.

"I saw him turn at the next corner," Eddie said, catching up, and when they reached the corner themselves the two brothers skidded around it with barely a reduction in speed. Coop glanced down the alley in the middle of the block as he ran past. But he was halfway to the next corner before it registered that he'd seen something under the far side of the alley's Dumpster that hadn't belonged. He skidded to a halt.

Eddie slid to one alongside him. "What?" he panted.

His rage draining away as suddenly as it had come upon him, Coop signaled his half-brother to be quiet. "Italian loafers," he explained softly, in cool command once again as he eased back toward the mouth of the alley. "I saw them under the Dumpster." He lowered his head to speak directly into Eddie's ear. "You've got the most at stake here, so how do you want to go in?

Fast and silent, by the book, or do we scare the bejesus out of the guy?"

Eddie tipped his head back and gave Coop a crooked smile. "Oh, scare the hell out of him, definitely."

"Yeah, I'd say we've earned that much. On the count of three, then." Mouthing *One,* he held up a finger. Then he held up a second. On the third he let out a Rebel yell and charged down the alley, Eddie shouting at the top of his lungs behind him.

They cornered Neil Peavy, who had shrunk back against the wall and was waving his pocketknife at them on the far side of the Dumpster.

"Look, he's armed and dangerous," Coop said. "Dangerous, that is, if you happen to be a hundred-and-twenty-pound woman." His hand whipped out and knocked aside Peavy's knife hand, then located a pressure point in the man's neck. He squeezed it, and the knife dropped from Peavy's fingers.

"You wanna get that, Eddie? Pick it up by the tip, or better yet with a handkerchief if you've got one. We wouldn't want to smudge those nice, clear fingerprints." Then he looked into the face of the man who had set up his brother for a murder charge, and who'd threatened and terrorized Veronica — not to mention made her bleed — and felt the anger start to creep back in.

Something of what he felt must have shown in his eyes, because Peavy suddenly babbled,

"You'd better call the police! Then I'm talking to my lawyer."

"Or I could just dispense my own brand of justice, right here, right now, and save everyone a lot of time and trouble," Coop said conversationally, applying more pressure yet. Peavy sagged to his knees. "It wouldn't be following the judicial process, exactly, but do you imagine anyone would really care? After all, for all the politicians who spout family values and hearth and home, Uncle Sam doesn't always practice what he preaches, does he? Take the selective services, for example. I can't speak for all of them, of course, but I do know the Marines like to snatch young boys from their mamas' apron strings — then turn them into trained killers. That's what they did for me." He smiled coldly. "What do you say I demonstrate what they taught me? We'll save the taxpayers the hassle of prosecuting you."

Eddie tapped him on the arm and jerked his chin toward the mouth of the alley. The sheriff and his deputy were entering it with their guns drawn.

Releasing Peavy, Coop raised both hands where the cops could see them, and catching their eye, made a subtle gesture to indicate that they give him a moment. Nodding, they moved slowly in his direction, and he looked down at the man on his knees at his feet. "Or," he offered, "you can buy yourself some time by telling me how you framed my brother. You once mentioned that Eddie left his leather jacket in your office."

Peavy's lip curled. "It's like he *wanted* to be framed. Crystal got a real charge out of me wearing it while I banged her brains out, I can tell you. She liked the irony of seeing it on the man the fool assumed was representing his interests."

"So you were wearing it when you killed her?"

Peavy shrugged. "Like I'm going to incriminate myself," he said, then regarded Coop with cold arrogance. "On the other hand . . . what the hell. Yeah, I had it on when I killed her — fat lot of good that will do you. You can tell the authorities whatever you damn well please, but once I assure them I would have admitted to anything when you threatened to kill me, who do you think they'll believe? The itinerant bartender brother of an accused murderer, or a respected attorney?"

"Well, I don't know. Let's ask the sheriff. Do you see me threatening to kill this man, sir?" Coop had the satisfaction of seeing horror dawn in Peavy's eyes when the sheriff stepped around the corner of the Dumpster.

"Can't say that I do," the sheriff said and reached past Coop to haul the lawyer to his feet. "Neil Peavy," he intoned, "you're under arrest for the murder of Crystal Davis." He read the rest of the Miranda warning, then turned to Eddie, who was being handcuffed by his deputy. "Under the circumstances, I'm sorry as can be

386

about this, son. But there's a process we still need to follow before you can be released."

Eddie merely smiled. "Hey, by all means, let's all go to jail." He looked Peavy squarely in the eye. "The difference is that this time *I'll* be the one who'll walk out again."

Several hours later, when all the red tape had finally been cut through and the charges against Eddie had been dropped, it was decided that Veronica should go into Marissa's first to prepare Lizzy for her father's return into her life. Marissa looked up with a huge grin when Ronnie opened the kitchen door, but the kids, who sat at the breakfast bar eating dinner, barely glanced up. Dessa and Riley were in the midst of a spirited argument, and Lizzy watched them without much interest as she pushed her turkey noodle soup around her bowl with her spoon and drummed her heels disconsolately against the rung of her stool.

"Lizzy?" Veronica said. "I've got good news and better news, sweetie. Which would you like first?"

Her niece looked up without enthusiasm and shrugged. "I dunno. The good news, I s'pose."

"We won't be moving you to Seattle after all."

Lizzy's face lit up. "For real?"

"Absolutely. You'll be staying right here."

The child's attention was clearly engaged now. "So, what's the better news, then?"

"There's someone here to see you." Ronnie

stepped aside, and tears filled her eyes at the undiluted joy that suffused Lizzy's face when Eddie
walked through the doorway.

"*Daddy!*" She launched herself from her chair.

"Hello, baby." Eddie swooped her up in his
arms, and Lizzy clung like velcro, her narrow
little arms wrapped with frantic tightness about
his neck. He pressed his cheek to the top of her
head and closed his eyes as he inhaled a deep
breath of his daughter's little-girl scent.

A warm hand cupped Veronica's nape. "How
'bout you and I slip away?" Coop suggested hus-
kily in her ear. Without waiting for her response,
he raised his voice and said, "Eddie, we're
leaving you my car. We'll see you at the house tomorrow — or this evening, if you wanna stop by
to pick up anything of Lizzy's. Marissa, thanks
for watching her."

Then he turned Veronica around and guided
her out the door.

She was so glad simply to be with Coop and so
busy trying to get all of today's events straight in
her mind that she didn't pay attention to where
he was driving them until the car rolled to a stop
in a deserted copse of birch trees alongside the
river. "Oh, my gawd," she breathed, looking
around. "This is where everyone used to come to
neck, back in high school."

"So I've heard," he agreed, reaching for her.
"Seems appropriate."

And hauling her in, he kissed the living day-
lights out of her.

Veronica wrapped her arms around his strong neck and kissed him back with everything she had. "God, Cooper," she said when they came up for air. "I thought I'd never see you again — thought I'd never get to tell you how much I love you." She cupped his lean jaw in her hands. "And I do, you know. I love you so much."

"Yeah? Enough to marry me?" He held his breath.

"Absolutely," she said. "Anytime, anyplace. Like I said earlier, I don't care what you do with the rest of your life . . . as long as you do it with me. In fact, bartending is a nice, portable skill. It might come in handy when my work moves me around." Her smile faltered. "I'm sorry I made such a fuss about it before. You and I are not our parents, and if being threatened by Neil Peavy was good for nothing else, it drove that fact home and showed me what's really important in life."

"Uh, about that." Coop eyed her a bit warily as she sat back to give him her bright-eyed attention. He reached out and tucked her hair behind her ear. "About my employment situation — I, uh, actually do have a vocation."

"You do? Other than bartending, you mean?"

"Yeah. I'm a writer."

She blinked. "A what?"

"A writer, an author. I write novels under the name of James Lee Cooper."

She was silent a moment as if digesting his news. Then her eyes widened. "*The Eagle Flies*

389

James Lee Cooper? *Cause for Alarm* James Lee Cooper?"

"Yeah. You've read me?"

"For God's sake," she said, her spine suddenly ruler-straight. "You're a famous author. Steven Spielberg made a *movie* from one of your books. And you let me think you were a ne'er-do-well without an ounce of ambition?"

He felt a silly grin stretch his mouth. "Ne'er-do-well. There's an expression you don't hear every day."

She smacked him on the arm, not amused. "You must have laughed yourself silly over my pitiful insecurities!"

That wiped the smile from his face. "Believe me, sweetpea, I didn't find a damn thing amusing about either of our insecurities."

"I could kill you, Cooper Blackstock."

"No, you couldn't." He reached for her again. "You love me to pieces, and you're probably so relieved I have an honest-to-God job you could sing." He bent his head to kiss the angle of her jaw. "And admit it," he murmured. "You've read me."

She turned up her nose. "Maybe."

"Maybe, hell. You've read me. And what's more, I bet you thought my stuff was great."

She shrugged, but tipped her head back to allow his lips to roam down her throat. "You were okay."

He laughed. "You don't give an inch, do you? I always liked that about you." When she grinned at him in return, he cupped her elegant little chin in his hand and raised his head to stare down into her eyes.

"Veronica Davis," he said, "I love you to pieces. And I'm telling you right now, my bossy little darlin': You and I are going to have ourselves one hell of a fun marriage."

"Yeah," she agreed as she snuggled in. "I do believe we will."

Epilogue

"I can't believe another good man's about to bite the dust."

Coop grinned at Zach Taylor and rocked his kitchen chair back on two legs. His friend had come out from North Carolina to be his best man the day after tomorrow, and this was the first free minute they'd had to kick back since his arrival. Coop saluted him with his beer bottle. "Well, hey, now, let me think about this. A lot of laughs, intelligent conversation, regular lovin'. That's not biting the dust, Midnight; that's the good life. You oughtta try it yourself sometime — I can highly recommend it."

"No, thanks. I've got Glynnis. That's about as close to having responsibility for someone of the female persuasion as I care to get."

"How is your baby sister?"

"Same old, same old. Still falling for the wrong guys and spending all my money."

Coop gave the ceiling a crooked smile. "Could be worse. At least you've got the money for her to spend."

"I sure wish she'd learn to handle her own, though. Jesus, Ice, she's gonna come into her trust soon. I break out in a cold sweat just thinking about it. If she's not overdrawing her bank account, she's handing her money out to every fast talker with a sad story to tell. And that's just with the interest she's given to live on. I don't even wanna think about the damage one of those jokers she dates could do to the principal." Zach took a sip of his beer, then shrugged and gave Coop a look over the long-necked bottle. "But enough of my problems. It sure looks like you got yourself a winner."

"Yeah." Coop felt a silly grin stretch his lips and didn't even care. "I never knew it was possible to feel this way about a woman. She makes me —"

The back door opened with a bang as it bounced off the wall, and the woman under discussion blew in on the wind that had grabbed it out of her hand. Veronica laughed and kicked the door closed behind her.

"Sorry about that. I should have made two trips from the car instead of trying to carry all this stuff in one. No, don't get up," she said as the men started to lower their chairs back on all four legs. "I'm just going to dump everything right here."

"Lizzy and Dess had their final fitting for their flower girl dresses today," Veronica said as she pulled steaks for tonight's dinner from a sack. "Wait until you see them. Talk about cuter than cute."

She listened to the men talk as she put away the groceries and smiled to herself, feeling the weight of Coop's gaze on her more than once. The thrill of being the recipient of all his love and attention just kept growing stronger.

Finishing up a few moments later, she grabbed herself a beer out of the fridge and carried it over to the table where the men sat.

Zach wasn't quite as tall as Coop, but he had the same look of honed muscularity and tough competency about him. Physically, they were a study in contrasts, and Ronnie imagined that seeing the two of them walk into a joint side by side must have set more than one woman's heart to pitty-patting. "You two remind me of Snow White and Rose Red."

They stared at her with identical looks of outraged masculinity, and she threw back her head and laughed. "That's not a slam on your manliness, fellas — God knows there's enough testosterone in here to drown a cat. I meant your coloring. It's a cool contrast — Zach's hair is as dark as your eyebrows, Coop." She met the other man's pale gray eyes. "Is that how you got the handle Midnight?"

"No. I'm good in the dark."

Even crazy in love with Coop, she wasn't one hundred percent immune to that deep voice or the sight of the little scar that bisected his upper lip, and her own lips quirked in amusement. "Somehow I don't doubt that for a minute."

He grinned at her, a flash of white teeth in a face as tanned as Coop's had been when they'd first met. "I can see why Ice is so crazy about you, lady. But what I meant was, I have exceptional night vision."

"Oh." This time Ronnie's amusement was directed at herself.

"Coop tells me the two of you are going to make your home here."

"Yeah, isn't that a kick in the pants? Fossil was the last place I wanted to be — and here we discover we both really like it. Not to mention the bonus of staying close to Eddie and Lizzy." And to Marissa and the kids, too. "Oh, God, that reminds me." She turned to Coop. "I got a nibble on the Tonk today, and you'll never in a million years guess who it's from."

He cocked an eyebrow at her.

"Darlene Starkey!"

Slowly he lowered his chair. "You're kidding. I can't quite see her tending bar."

"She doesn't plan to. But apparently she's convinced the Tonk is a hotbed of information. And you know how she adores being the first to know anything." She inspected the nice buff job on her nails for a moment before shooting him a satisfied little three-corner smile. "So who was I to dissuade her from the notion?"

Coop grinned. "Come here and give me a kiss. You're just too damn cute." His voice was teasing, but as he looked at her, his smile slowly faded and his eyes went hot.

Zach set his bottle on the table and climbed to his feet. "I don't mean to drink and run, but there's a James Lee Cooper story upstairs calling my name."

Veronica blinked, and gave Zach a brilliant smile. "Don't you just love that guy's books? By all means, don't let us keep you. We'll see you at dinner."

The moment he cleared the door, though, she grimaced. "We've gotta get a grip on these hormones, Cooper. I think we drove him away."

"Get a grip, hell." Coop half rose from his seat to reach out and grasp her wrist. He tugged, and she rounded the table to sit in his lap. He immediately wrapped her in his arms and buried his face in her neck, inhaling deeply. He raised his face and gave her a sleepy smile. "Everyone can just get used to it," he said. "Because, Princess, this boy's head over heels. And if they think a demand for a kiss in my own kitchen is too much . . ." He shrugged. "All I've got to say is, there's going to be a lot of offended folks in town. Because, sweetpea, they ain't seen nothing yet."